BOSTON BOLTS HOCKEY: SNOW

BRITTANÉE NICOLE

This is a work of fiction. Names, characters, places, and incidents either are the product of the author's imagination or are used fictitiously. Any resemblance to actual persons, living or dead, events, or locales is entirely coincidental.

Boston Bolts Hockey: Snow © 2026 by Brittanée Nicole

First Edition January 2026

Cover Art: elenbushe_art

Cover Photo : Michelle Lancaster

Formatting by Sara of Sara PA's Services

Editing by Beth at VB Edits

❀ Formatted with Vellum

DEDICATION

To new beginnings.

"It was official. A new season had begun.
After all, seasons change, so do cities; people come into your life and people go.
But it's comforting to know that the ones you love are always in your heart.
And if you're very lucky, a plane ride (or a book) away."

– Carrie Bradshaw
Sex and the City

CONTENT WARNING

Alzheimer's
Death of a Parent
Abuse, Abandonment and Neglect by a Parent
Trauma

FOREWORD

Dear Reader,

With each book I write, the world I build becomes more connected and complex. This book, like all the books in this series, can be read as a standalone. However, you will see some character overlap and since I know many of you enjoy the easter eggs I hide and prefer to read in order, here is a suggested reading order as it comes to this world:

Revenge Era: Ford Hall and Lake Paige

Mother Faker: Beckett Langfield and Olivia Maxwell

Pucking Revenge: Brooks Langfield and Sara Case

A Major Puck Up: Gavin Langfield and Millie Hall

Hockey Boy: Aiden Langfield and Lennox Kennedy

Trouble: Cade Fitzgerald, Declan Everhart and Melina Rodriguez

War: Tyler Warren and Ava Erickson

Playboy: Daniel Hall and Hannah Prescott

Beauty: Noah Harrison and Sienna Langfield

This is simply a suggestion. You can start with any book and work your way through the series in any order you prefer.

Want more of the Langfields? Check out the 8 chapter epilogue, _Seasons of Love_ in the Langfield Brothers Boxset.

All of these books take place in the Boston Billionaire World so you will see or hear about those characters as well.

I hope you enjoy this world as much as I enjoy writing it.

XO,
Brittanée

PLAYLIST

MAN I NEED - OLIVIA DEAN
DIET PEPSI - ADDISON RAE
DADDY ISSUES - THE NEIGHBOURHOOD
LINGER - ROYAL OTIS
SO EASY (TO FALL IN LOVE) - OLIVIA DEAN
ELIZABETH TAYLOR - TAYLOR SWIFT
WHERE IS MY HUSBAND! - RAYE
I MISS YOU, IM SORRY - GRACIE ABRAMS
BABY STEPS - OLIVIA DEAN
THINKING 'BOUT LOVE - WILD RIVERS
EVERYTHING IS ROMANTIC - CHARLIE XCX
RIPTIDE - VANCE JOY

True or False:
every good book has a
playlist you put on repeat

CONTENTS

Chapter 1
Savannah

"GET off your knees and stop showing off," I holler.

I wobble, then go down ass-first. Flopping back on the cold ice, I sigh up at the gray sky. Then I close my eyes and give up completely.

"Just tap my shoulder when you're done," I tell Addie. "Hopefully I won't have frozen over by then. If I have, it's been fun."

The sound of skates slicing across ice gets louder, and when I force my eyes open, I find my friend looming over me, blocking out the gloomy sky. "Stop being so dramatic."

The gorgeous brunette smirks down at me, batting her honey brown eyes.

"I didn't complain when you made us do that pole dancing class last week."

I huff out a breath. On top of being annoyingly pretty, Adeline Langfield is good at everything. During her first attempt, she contorted herself until she was upside down on the pole, legs spread like a literal pinup girl.

Gliding backward with the grace of a professional figure skater, she waggles her fingers. Then she dips down and launches herself into the air, her body spinning in a way even Olympians would envy. Bitch.

With a laugh, Josie does the same. While she doesn't nail the spin the way Addie did, she does a little twirl that my ass would never even attempt.

The final girl to complete our quartet, Sutton, skates up to me with an ease I don't have. "Need help?" She holds out a hand.

I clutch her wrist, but instead of accepting her help, I pull her down with me.

Giggling, my blond friend lands on top of me, then wiggles to the ice beside me.

I sit, shaking off the cold sensation creeping up my spine, and watch Josie mimic every one of Addie's movements.

The two aren't anywhere near the same caliber, yet Josie is a hell of a lot better than Sutton and I are. Makes sense, considering Josie's dad is Tyler Warren, one of the best wingers the Boston Bolts has ever seen. And because the rink we're on is located in the backyard of her childhood home. She grew up skating, so following Addie is no hard feat.

Okay, maybe it is, since Adeline Langfield is as good on skates as Tyler Warren himself. At twenty-six, she is one of the PWHL's best female goalies. Though she's giving up that career at the end of this season to join the Boston Bolts as their first ever female goalie coach.

Josie's no slouch, but even she seems to be regretting her suggestion that we have our girls' night at her parents' place. "I think our moms were spot-on when it came to girl time. Brunch and mimosas would be so much more relaxing."

Addie grins. "My mom and her best friends had book club nights. And wine. I assure you, our plans are better."

Sutton spreads her legs and extends an arm, stretching to one side, then the other. "Mine had brewery nights. And jumping off the pier after a few too many drinks."

Pretty sure I'd dampen the mood if I mentioned how my mom didn't have any friends because she was a narcissist, so instead I say, "All of them included alcohol. We're definitely missing out."

Addie rolls her eyes. "Fine. How does spiked hot chocolate by the fire sound?"

My smile is automatic. "Delicious."

Twenty minutes later, we're curled up on the oversized couches in the Warren home. Josie's parents and her younger brother are at a hockey tournament, so we have the house to ourselves for the evening. It's one of those perfect winter homes, set deep in the woods in the suburbs of Boston, with its own little pond and huge windows that look out over the sprawling property. Tonight, every inch is covered in snow, making it a white winter's dream.

Inside a fire burns in the oversized stone hearth, creating a cozy glow. While Josie and Addie move around the kitchen, getting snacks and drinks together, I shove my still stiff toes between the couch cushions and take in the beautiful view.

I can't imagine being comfortable in a house of this size, but I'm the only one here who's even slightly fazed by all the signs of wealth surrounding us. While Josie's life was hard before being adopted by Tyler Warren and his wife, Ava, this has been her home since she was eight.

Addie's family money puts the Warrens to shame. The Langfields are Boston royalty, owning both the city's hockey and baseball teams, as well as a tremendous amount of property.

I'm actually interviewing her aunt tomorrow. She's just taken over as creative director of the magazine I work for, *Jolie*. The owner, Catherine Bouvier, has been trying for over a decade to get her to come on board, and she's finally done it.

Sutton's family is wealthy as well. Despite hailing from a tiny island off the coast of Maine, Sutton's mom is *the* Elizabeth Sweet. America's sweetheart turned four-time Tony Award–winning actress and now director. Sutton followed in her mother's footsteps and is starring in her first lead on Broadway this spring.

And then there's me, the girl from Las Vegas whose only family consists of a narcissistic mother, an absent father, and the Italians who live on the second floor of my three-story walk-up in Southie.

How the hell did I end up in a room with these three impressive women? I have my job to thank for that. Josie and I met when we were hired by *Jolie* at about the same time. When she discovered that I was all alone in Boston, she invited me over for dinner with her family. I tried to object, but according to her, the Warrens are known for collecting strays, and I'd always have a place with them.

True to her word, she's included me in holidays, family game nights, and girls' nights like this for the last four years.

Josie's and Addie's families are close, so they've known one another most of their lives. Josie is two years older than Addie, but because she spent a good part of her childhood fighting a serious illness, she was a few years behind in school and went to college with Addie. Then there's Sutton, who's also been close with Addie since they were little girls. While getting close to people with that type of history would normally scare me—as any type of commitment does—as Josie promised, they brought this stray in and haven't let me go since.

"How are things going with—" I snap my fingers, racking my brain for the name of Sutton's latest boy wonder. When it doesn't come to me, I shake my head. "Hot bartender with the lip ring?"

Sutton snorts. My ability to remember the name of just about any man is nearly nonexistent, and my friends know it. Men serve their purpose, sure, but considering that no man has ever not disappointed me, I don't go out of my way to befriend them. Especially not the ones Sutton dates, since there always seems to be someone new. Despite the revolving door, Sutton isn't a player. Not in the slightest. That'd be me. Sutton Jones is a serial monogamist who believes every man she meets will be the love of her life.

Okay, maybe that's a bit of a stretch, but with the way she waxes poetic about every one of them, it sometimes feels like it. She's in love with the idea of falling in love, not with the men themselves.

"Oh, you didn't hear." Addie shuffles into the room with two mugs in each hand. Her caramel balayage looks darker, her hair still damp from outside. Her cheeks are rosy, and her deceptively innocent big brown eyes dance with the promise of secrets. "He ghosted her after she asked him to spend the holidays with her."

"You what now?" I carefully take two of the drinks from Addie as Sutton takes a third.

"Obviously he wasn't the one for me." Sutton takes a sip and sighs. Despite her annoying desire to fall in love, I adore the way she doesn't let these setbacks dampen her sparkle. She says that every Mr. Wrong brings her one step closer to Mr. Right.

"Or," Josie says as she sets a platter of brownies on the table, "and don't take my word for it because I know jack shit about relationships, but maybe asking a man you've been out with twice to spend the holidays with your family is a step too far?"

I point at her, lips pressed together. "That one's onto something."

Sutton huffs. "Whatever. Can we talk about something else?"

"Ah, yes." Josie zeroes in on me. "Let's talk about the interview you have scheduled this week."

I survey Addie. "Only if you're comfortable with it."

She shrugs. "My aunt is one of my favorite people. Couldn't tell you if any of the tabloid gossip over the years is true, though. To me, she's always been the only woman other than my mother who can put my father in his place. It's fun to watch."

I snort. "My kind of woman."

"And her closet is incredible," she adds. "She invited us to come over and pick out anything we want for Camden's party."

Eyeing my ample chest, I shake my head. "I don't think these things will fit into anything your aunt owns." I'm curvy, with wide hips and thighs. And these double Ds have a life of their own half the time.

I also have an addiction to chocolate and cake. Any kind of dessert, really. So my stomach is soft. I'm essentially the complete opposite of dainty Sienna Harrison, with her petite features and B cup.

"Yeah, I'm not fitting these boobs into any of your aunt's dresses either," Sutton says, chin tucked and eyeing her own rack. While her breasts aren't as large as mine, she's waif thin, so they look enormous on her body.

Addie waves a hand. "She could alter just about anything in her sleep. Plus, she's now got the contents of the *Jolie* closet at her fingertips. There are a ton of options in every size."

My heart stutters. *Jolie*'s closet is what legends are made of. My figure is more in line with Catherine Bouvier, the head of the magazine and the fashion icon of our generation. If I find anything she's worn in that closet, I will cry.

Literal tears.

"See? Now you're excited," Addie says, chin lifted and smug smile in place. "So outside of the piece you're doing about my aunt, what else is going on with work?"

Josie's eyes cut to mine. She knows as well as I do that I need to knock it out of the park with this article since the other column I work on hasn't been getting the numbers we need. Still, I'm not a quitter. I can turn it around. I just need a fresh idea to get readers interested again.

Hoping my friends can help me brainstorm, I dive right in. "Honestly, I need a really good hook for the next edition of Calliope's Column. All I talk about is sex and orgasms. Don't get me wrong, I love sex and orgasms—"

"Who doesn't?" Josie crows.

Addie rolls her eyes and Sutton falls back against the couch with a dramatic sigh. She thinks love is required for sex, but since she falls in love just about weekly, I don't think she's missing out too much.

I huff. "It feels like all I do is mimic the original Calliope." I shrug. Honestly, I don't even know who that was. *Jolie* purchased the column years ago, when the original Calliope was ready to retire. Since then, women at the magazine have taken turns acting as the dating and sex guru. I've been the author for almost a year, and it already feels tired. "I want to do something smart and edgy and..." I groan and slump back. "I don't know. More helpful than just telling women the best position for a G-spot O."

"I thought that was super helpful." Addie arches a brow. "I mean who knew that it was impossible to reach in missionary?"

"When was the last time you even had sex?" Josie asks, eyes narrowed on our friend.

Addie's jaw practically unhinges. "I have sex."

Another huff escapes me, this one full of skepticism. "When?"

"I have sex." As the words leave her mouth, her eyes dart to one side. "I'm just going through a bit of a dry spell."

"Well you better un-dry that spell, because you're about to be working with a bunch of really hot men," Sutton says. "If you think you're horny now, just imagine how horny you'll be having to spend all that time with JJ"

If possible, Addie's jaw drops farther. "Take it back."

Sutton grins, eyes dancing. "Why? We all know it's true. You as his coach? There's gonna be all kinds of delicious gossip flying. Bet you could write a year's worth of Calliope columns using Addie's life experience alone. The first headline: How Not to Fuck Your Enemy."

"JJ is not my enemy." Addie lifts her chin, keeping her expression even in a pathetic effort to look nonchalant.

"Oh no, just your archnemesis," Josie teases.

Addie huffs. "He's a player. And a dad. And married."

"Ugh, I hate his wife." Josie scowls.

"Doesn't matter. He's still married, and I'm not interested." Addie scrutinizes me. "So you'll have to come up with something else ridiculous to write about."

I sink against the couch, nerves swirling in my stomach. Yes, I will. The question is, what?

Chapter 2
Savannah

"THANK YOU!" I call to the Uber driver as I step onto the broken sidewalk. The door to my building is decorated with a glowing wreath and the banister is wrapped in a string of Christmas lights, thanks to the first-floor residents. They're a family of six in a two-bedroom apartment. I don't know how they do it, but I rarely hear the eighteen-month-old twins even cry. Even now, just after nine, the only sound echoing in the tiny foyer area is laughter. The building has seen better days, but I love every inch of it. Especially the people inside.

The Donovans live on the first floor. John is a firefighter. When he's not on shift, he's busy with the kids. His wife Erin is a pediatric nurse. They work opposite shifts to save on childcare, yet every time I see them together, they're smiling.

I pause outside their door, letting the happiness that spills out into the hallway soak into my bones. The television is on, but I can still make out the voices of both parents. If I had to guess, Erin is headed to work in an hour or so. She probably just woke up and is spending a little time with the kids before she leaves.

"Come on, Pip," John says. Piper recently turned four. "It's time for bed."

"Can we fly there?" she asks, her high-pitched voice so sweet.

I watch her and her siblings on occasion. Once in a while, when one parent is running late and the other has to leave for work, they call me and I'll pop down to help out. That little girl in particular has a ton of energy and a lot to say.

My kind of girl, obviously.

"A jet or a bird tonight?" he replies.

He never says no. God, what that must be like. When I was growing up, my house was either extremely loud or extremely quiet. Loud because my father was yelling or quiet because I was home alone.

My father believed children should be seen, not heard. Maybe not even seen, honestly. He left when I was eleven.

My mother? She fought. Fought with him. Fought to keep him. Berated me for being the reason she was stuck with him.

"If only you hadn't been his." She said it often. As if it was my fault that she cheated on her boyfriend and got knocked up by the man she didn't want.

With a breath out, I step back from the Donovans' door and trudge up the stairs. Thinking about my parents always puts a damper on my mood, so I try not to do it often. Twice in one night is well beyond my usual limit. I typically try not to think of them more than twice in a month.

The smell of garlic and tomato sauce hits me as I round the steps onto the second floor. The nightly news blares from inside the apartment, but Rosalie is louder.

"That boy was always bad news," she says in that thick Italian Boston accent that always makes me smile.

"Huh?" her husband Nick says.

I try not to laugh as they bicker. It's the same argument they always have. She tells him that he needs hearing aids. He tells her he can hear her just fine.

"You can't hear me at all."

"Exactly. Just like I like it."

She curses at him in Italian, and then the sound of the TV cuts out.

Shit. Now that the building is silent, I have to tiptoe by their door.

I've almost made it to the next set of stairs, the floorboards barely creaking, when the door swings open and I'm yanked inside their cozy apartment.

"Have you eaten?" Rosalie asks. "You don't look like you've eaten. Nick, doesn't Savannah look hungry? Go get her a drink while I make her a plate."

Her hair is so blond it's nearly white, but her eyebrows are thick and dark. As she surveys me, they rise in excitement. She's always excited. Sometimes it's from anger, sometimes because she's been given the opportunity to feed another person. Either way, her energy is always high. I absolutely love it. Even the anger. This woman's ire is rarely mean-spirited. Or maybe I just like the sound of her voice when she rants in Italian.

Nick grumbles from the couch. Then he heaves himself forward. It takes him three tries to stand up, but when he does, he breaks into a face-splitting smile. His hair is black with streaks of silver. His mustache too. He wears suspenders, a button-down shirt, and pressed pants every day. He also reeks of cheap cologne and garlic. Always.

"Chianti?" He shuffles to the bar where he's always got a jug of red wine.

"I'm really not hungry or thirsty," I tell them. All I want is to climb into my bed and prepare for tomorrow's meeting with Sienna.

But turning them down is pointless. I've never made it out of their apartment without indulging. Not that it's a hardship. No one makes a meatball like Rosalie. Or a zeppole. Zeppole are my ultimate indulgence. The powdered sugar. The fried dough. The ricotta custard filling.

Just thinking about them makes my mouth water. I search her kitchen, looking for evidence of a fresh batch. I have to do it covertly, though, because if she catches me and she doesn't have any on hand, she'll insist on making a batch, and I'll be here all night.

"None of that." She waves a hand and scurries to the stove, where a pot of red sauce is still simmering. She doesn't microwave food. Hell, she doesn't even own a microwave. While I live on frozen food.

Within seconds of entering the apartment, I've been shooed into a kitchen chair that's covered in plastic that scrunches as I settle, and a heaping plate of pasta, meatballs, and ricotta, along with a piece of bread is placed in front of me.

Nick slides a glass of wine across the table and settles opposite me. Then the two of them watch me, eagerly waiting for me to take my first bite.

I know the drill. I pick up my silverware and cut into a meatball, savoring the flavor. When I plaster on a smile, telling them how delicious it is—it really is, despite my lack of excitement—they launch into their usual line of questioning, talking over one another.

"How was your day, amore?" Rosalie asks as Nick says, "Did you take that car service again?"

That car service is Uber, and even though it's been around for decades and every driver is vetted and tracked by their app, he still swears taxis are safer.

"Yes, I took an Uber home—"

Nick tsks at that.

"And my day was good. I spent it with the girls."

Rosalie nods, her nearly white curls held in place by a ridiculous amount of hairspray. "What about that boy you went out with last week?" She looks at Nick. "The mechanic you set her up with. What's his name?"

"Alfonso." Nick angles forward, scrutinizing me. "He says you canceled."

"I'm not dating." I shovel another bite of food into my mouth, cursing myself for hesitating at their door. I should have rushed up to my apartment before they figured out I was home.

By "not dating," what I mean is I'm not dating Rosalie's cousin's nephew or their godson's grandson or Nick's barber's best friend's son. The Donadios mean well, but none of those men are my type.

I'm sure there are good men out there. Men like John Donovan on the first floor. Some might even be related to the Donadios or one of their acquaintances. But I'm not meant for that kind of relationship. I wouldn't know what to do with it if I found it.

I like my quiet life upstairs. My girls' nights. My vibrators.

I'm far less likely to be disappointed by others if I stick to relying only on myself.

"She's not dating," Rosalie parrots, shaking her head.

"She just hasn't met him," Nick says to her, like I'm not even here.

"No, she hasn't met her Nico." With a warm smile, she brushes her hand against his cheek.

They've been married for sixty-two years, and still, he looks at her with pure affection and she touches him like she can't help it.

That doesn't seem like the worst thing in the world.

With a shake of my head, I focus on my food. Unlike Sutton, I don't believe that a love like that is bound to find me.

Chapter 3
Savannah

Calliope's Column
Why sex doesn't have to involve love...

"DELETE." I jab the backspace over and over until the page is blank again. "Why I suck at writing sex columns." I type the words into the headline with a roll of my eyes and delete that too. Stating the obvious won't save this column.

When I arrived this morning, I found a calendar invite from Cat, my boss, in my inbox. The subject of the meeting she scheduled for Monday? The Calliope column. The writing is on the wall. If I don't come up with something brilliant before then, she's gonna can it.

Josie showed me the ad revenue from the last quarter, and my low numbers mean it's more difficult to attract ads. If the numbers don't change, there's no softening the blow. I'll be out of a job.

"Fuck." With a red painted nail between my teeth, I bite down. I can't lose this job. Unlike my friends, I don't have family around to help while I'm in flux. I left home at eighteen and never returned. My mother calls me for money after she spends all her earnings at the casino or the bar.

One would think a woman who's worked in a casino for twenty-five years would know that the house always wins. She swears the money she spends is an investment because eventually one of the big spenders at the tables will fall for her, and then she'll be set for life.

Maybe if she had even one redeemable quality outside her still slim figure and oversized breasts, someone would be interested in more than a weekend.

I certainly couldn't spend more than a couple of days in her presence. Fortunately, she doesn't guilt me into coming home for the holidays or anything like that. Oh no. She's always got plans, and in the four years I've been in Boston, she hasn't made the trip to see me once.

My apartment might be small, but rent is high in this city. Without this job, I'd be lucky to hold on to it for three months.

Unease swirls in my stomach.

Nope. We're not going there. I cannot return to Vegas.

"What am I going to write about?" I say aloud.

"What a great question." Josie pops up on the other side of the half wall of my cubicle, a bright smile on her face. "And I happen to have an answer."

One thing I love about Josie is that even though she grew up around immense wealth, her style doesn't scream traditional *Jolie* like every other girl in this office. Most of the women here are the definition of a pick-me girl. They wear the most expensive designers and go broke doing it. Josie, on the other hand, loves thrifting. She couldn't care less who made a piece, as long as she likes it. Right now she's wearing tight purple leather pants few people could pull off with a cream fringe vest over a black leotard. Her strawberry-blond hair is pulled to the side in a loose French braid, and the pretty freckles dotting her cheeks and the bridge of her nose act as a better blush than any I've seen on the market.

I wave her into my cubicle. "Don't just stand there, talk."

Every bit of wall space around my desk is covered. One wall has an oversized calendar where I keep track of every plan Addie makes for us. And her games. Since it's her last season in the PWHL, we're even more dedicated to going to as many as we can.

The opposite wall is adorned with Post-its in a variety of colors, each with a random idea written on it.

I glared at them when I sat down this morning, frustrated that not a single one sparked any kind of motivation to write. The other wall is plastered with pictures of me with the girls over the last few years.

The newest addition is a photo of the four of us jumping off the pier in Monhegan, Maine. It's from this summer, when we stayed at Sutton's parents' cottage for a long weekend.

It's taken from behind, and my ass is ginormous in comparison to the other girls, but still, I love the image. The water is ice cold even in August, but Sutton acted like it was warm.

Josie hops up on the edge of my desk, tugging her oversized turquoise bag onto her lap, and pulls out a photo album. "Last night after you girls left, I was searching for a book in my dad's library, and I came across this." She holds up the green leather album and wiggles it.

I roll back a couple of inches. "Listen, I know they aren't biologically your parents, but if that is like a couple's boudoir photo shoot or something, then I'm gonna side-eye the shit out of you."

She scowls. "Ew. That's—" She shakes her head, closes her eyes, and blows out a breath. "You know what? I'm not even going to dignify that with an answer, pervert."

I shrug. "Listen, I don't believe in yucking anyone's yum, but that would be—"

"Gross."

I snort. I love riling her up. "Plenty of women our age would kill for a shot with Daddy War."

Seriously, the man is a Bolts legend. Not only was he the best captain the team's ever had, he's got his wife's name and their wedding date inked onto his hand. I've heard rumors he has ink in honor of her elsewhere too, but I would never tease Josie about that. Besides, I'm sure it's just urban legend. Who in god's name would tattoo their damn balls?

Josie pushes the album back into her bag and stands. "You know what? You don't deserve my help."

I lurch from my chair and clutch her arm before she can leave. "No, I'm sorry. You know I have diarrhea of the mouth. I can't help it. It's a disease."

With a roll of her eyes, she plops back down. "If you weren't so pretty, I'd ditch you."

I bat my lashes. "So my boobs and pretty eyes make me good eye candy? Is that why you put up with me?"

She barks out a laugh. "Something like that." Setting the now open album on my desk between us, she points to the first picture. "This is my parents' wedding album, creeper."

As I take in the image, my heart lifts. "Aw, they look so young." I spin the album and study the picture of Ava in a white winter jacket in front of city hall. Daddy War is in a simple black suit. The sleeves of his Oxford are rolled, exposing his tatted arms as he cups her face and kisses her in front of a burgundy Rolls-Royce SUV with a license plate that reads Mrs. War.

I snort. "Fancy."

Josie smiles softly at the picture, eyes glassy, and brushes her fingers against the page. "That was the day we became a family," she says, voice filled with emotion.

I have to look away from her. I love her story. The miracle of how her parents chose her. But sometimes it's hard to think about. Because no one in my life has ever chosen me.

With a forced smile, I lift my chin. I don't need anyone to choose me. I'm choosing myself. "So why are we taking a trip down memory lane?"

Sniffing, she turns the page. "Because of this." She taps a piece of paper that's been glued into the album. It's yellowed a little with age and is crinkled like it was balled up at some point but then smoothed back out.

"The Good Wife's Guide," I read aloud. I skim the article quickly, noting the illustration of a woman wearing a dress and apron, circa 1955, according to the date at the top. She's holding a plate of pancakes and wearing a blinding smile.

The "guide" makes me twitch. It's absurd. "Prepare yourself. Take fifteen minutes to rest so you'll be refreshed when he arrives."

My eyes practically bulge out of my head.

"Put a ribbon in your hair."

Josie's lips are twitching.

"Wait." I stab the page with one finger. "Why is your mother's signature at the bottom of this?"

Ava Warren. The words almost bleed into the page, the strokes wild.

Josie giggles. "I have no fucking clue, and honestly, I almost don't want to know—" She shakes her head. "Listen, things were volatile between the two of them back then. They did a good job of hiding it from us, but we all knew how much my mom couldn't stand my dad."

"But she's so kind." I shake my head and flip through more pictures.

There are years of memories documented here. It's clear in every image that Tyler Warren has always been head over heels in love with his wife.

I glance back up at my friend. "What does this have to do with my column?"

She bites her lip, her eyes flashing with excitement. "I was waiting for you to ask. I think you should write an article like this—about dating."

"I do write about dating." Confusion washes over me. I love Josie, but I don't have time for riddles or brainstorming ideas that already aren't working.

"No, you write about sex. You don't date."

I tilt my head back and forth. "Okay, I'll give you that."

"But you'd be good at it."

My stomach flips, but I ignore the reaction. "Oh, would I? And why is that?"

She scoffs. "Because you don't care."

It's a bit harsh, but I guess the truth can be sometimes. And once again, she isn't wrong, so I go with it. "You want me to write a column about how I don't care about the dates I go on or the outcome?" I frown. "I don't see how that's going to bring in ad revenue."

"People our age are bucking traditional marriage and dating. They're choosing to have kids with friends and live in mom communes instead of putting themselves out there."

"Smart." Smiling, I lean back and cross my arms.

"Not for someone like Sutton." She flips back to the article and taps it. "There are no longer columns out there that focus on falling in love.

No tips for how to spot the jackasses and how to make relationships work."

With a sigh, I throw out my hands. "Okay, but I don't know how to do any of those things."

She sits up like I've made her point.

I'm so confused.

"Right," she says. "But because of Sutton, you know what not to do."

Slowly, I straighten, my mind whirling.

Josie points at me, her smile painfully bright. "See? It's brilliant. We've watched our best friend try and fail at finding a relationship over and over. But what if you showed her that she isn't the problem? It's what she's doing."

"A column on how not to date," I say slowly, my wheels already turning.

She purses her lips. "Or a how-to in reverse." She hums, trying that idea on for size. "You do everything wrong, and in turn help your readers avoid common mistakes."

"And Sutton," I say, letting the idea really percolate.

Josie snaps the album closed. "And Sutton."

"So I date a bunch of guys, do what she does, and get dumped, repeatedly." I shrug. "Works for me."

"Yes. An 'it's not him, it's you.'" She tilts her head and scrunches her nose. "Kind of."

I giggle, amusement washing over me, and pick up my pen. "That's the title." Quickly, I scribble it on a hot-pink Post-it.

It's not him. It's you. (Kind of.)

I nibble on my lip. "But I need a list of things she's done wrong over the last few months."

"Give me a bottle of wine, a pad of paper, and a couple of hours, and I'll fill a notebook for you."

I cough out a laugh. "What if she gets mad?"

"Sutton?" She scoffs. "The girl doesn't know how to hold a grudge. That's another one of her faults. She forgives too easily."

I shake my head. "That's her personality, not a fault. And it's admirable. We're just tougher on people. And I can't fake who I am." I tap my pen against the sticky note. "This will be good. I'll do some of the things that people regularly do wrong, like inviting someone they just met to spend the holidays with them."

Josie laughs. "Right. Or talking baby names the morning after you first sleep together."

Without my permission, a gasp escapes me. "No one does that!"

Josie's green eyes go comically wide. "Tell that to Kyra."

"Who's Kyra?"

She lets out a long breath. "The girl I was sleeping with a few weeks ago."

I shake my head, smiling. "What names did she like?"

Head dropped back, she groans. "Brighton. And Binx."

There's no stopping the cackle that leaves me. "Binx sounds like a cat name."

She waves her hand. "Whatever. The point is, I liked Kyra until she jumped the gun."

I wince. "Maybe she just liked you."

She only shrugs. I may not date, but Josie does. In fact, she dates enough for the both of us. Sometimes men, but mostly women.

"Then there's the constant texting," she says, jotting down notes as she goes. "The insecurity, jealousy, possessiveness—"

I throw up a hand. "Possessiveness can be hot."

She puts a question mark next to it. "Fine, not hot possessiveness. Like when you want to go out with your friends and he or she freaks out or guilts you into staying home instead. Yeah, my friends are hot, but the insecurity isn't."

Giggling, I pull my shoulders back. "Was Kyra jealous of my boobs?"

She eyes my tits and scoffs. "Everyone's jealous of your boobs."

I glance down at them and grin. "They are fabulous."

"You think you'll really do this?" she asks, steering the conversation away from my fabulous rack.

I survey the title on the Post-it, then the blank document on my screen. It's not much, but it's a hell of a lot more than I had before she came in here. Besides, helping Sutton learn how to date could be considered a public service at this point. I can't listen to her crying over another loser. Next time she meets a guy, I want her to know precisely what to do and what not to do so a guy will stick around long enough for her to decide whether he's worth it.

Also, it kind of sounds fun. More fun than having dinner with the retirees in the apartment below me. And much more fun than reminding them over and over that I'm not interested in dating their second cousin's great-nephew.

"Yeah, I think I am."

Josie claps and bounces in place. "Yay." She hops to her feet. "You better get ready for your interview with Sienna, but don't forget we have the holiday party at Camden Snow's this weekend."

"Right, how could I forget?" I tease. It's probably the most exciting event I've ever been invited to.

Josie picks up her parents' wedding album and slips it into her bag, then sashays away. At the entrance to my cubicle, she peers back at me. "You never know, maybe you'll find your first victim—I mean date— there."

CHAPTER 4
CAMDEN

WITH A SHAKE OF MY HEAD, I pocket my phone. It shouldn't bother me. I won't let it bother me. Three deep breaths, then I step into the restaurant. Moving on.

"There he is," Daniel says, waving an arm to catch my attention.

Shit. How he and Hannah beat me here is a mystery. Figured they'd be getting freaky in their hotel room and I'd have at least fifteen minutes to improve my mood before dinner.

But since I don't, I force one of my cavalier smiles. "Met a woman in the bar." I pat my pocket. "Got her number."

The lie comes easily. I'm sure my sister would have a lot to say about that.

Hannah rolls her eyes and pats the seat next to her. "Well, then we better eat quick, huh?"

Chuckling, I bend and kiss her cheek. Then I slide into the seat. "As if the two of you aren't itching to get back to your room."

Daniel drops a hand to his wife's bare thigh and squeezes.

She turns to him and smiles. It's one of those soft ones. Sometimes Hannah is a ball buster. Most of the time she is. But when it comes to Daniel and her two children, Maverick and Monroe, there's only love.

"Mav said if he catches us naked one more time," she laughs, "he'll start a TikTok channel about it, so we're being good on this trip."

I slap my chest and suck in an exaggerated breath. "Fuck, Han, don't scar the boy."

Daniel presses a kiss to his wife's cheek, smiling like he's the happiest guy in the world. And he has every right to be. A beautiful family. A hall of fame career. Though we both hung up our skates nearly a decade ago.

After he retired from the game, he went to work with his father. It surprised the hell out of all of us. He's now an executive with Hall Records, and he's damn successful, using that charming personality to win over prospects and sign new talent. Most importantly, he rarely travels for work. That was important to him. It always killed him to miss out on anything his kids were up to. Since the moment Hannah first told him she was pregnant eighteen years ago, he's been a wonderful, dedicated father. And he's so ridiculously in love with his wife. If there was a picture to go along with the word *whipped* in the dictionary, it'd be a headshot of him.

Though with Maverick following in his footsteps, Daniel still chases the game plenty.

Like today. We're all in New Hampshire for Mav's game. He and Beckham, War's son, play together these days.

And because I'm Mav's godfather, I hit as many games as my schedule allows. Though this one was actually worked into my schedule as the head of scouting for the Boston Bolts. I'm here trying like hell to draft the number one high school center in the whole country—Maverick Hall.

After the server takes our drink order, Hannah turns to me. "So I take it things are over with the woman from last month?"

I stare at her, my mind going blank.

"The one you brought to the game in Foxboro."

Fuck. I fight the urge to drag a hand down my face. I don't even remember the girl's name. I never bring women around my family—and Daniel and Hannah are my family, blood or not—but when I tried to leave the woman I'd met the night before in her hotel room by telling her I had to head out to watch my godson play, she told me she loved hockey and would be happy to accompany me.

What was I supposed to say? It's a public place. And she was hot. We spent that night together too. But I have no idea what happened to her after that.

"Oh, uh, Lynne," I say. "She's, uh, she's away this week."

Hannah rolls her eyes. "Oh my god, you have no idea who I'm talking about."

"It was, what, three weeks ago?" Or four? I honestly can't remember.

"Her name was Jasmine," Hannah says.

Daniel cups a hand over his mouth, hiding a smile, but his dark eyes are full of delight.

"Oh." I wave a hand and sit back. "We didn't see each other again after that night, but I met Lynne after that."

Hannah breaks into a devious grin. "Okay, where's Lynne, then?"

I shrug. "Didn't make it past the second date."

She straightens, her chin lifting in challenge. "No one makes it past a second date with you."

"Hannah." Daniel pulls his wife close, his facial expression darkening. "Leave Cam alone."

I shrug and grin at my best friend. "I can take it. But rather than talking about me, let's talk about Mav's game." As my godson's name leaves my mouth, the little shit saunters up wearing a cocky grin. "Speak of the devil."

He's got his dad's thick brown hair and his mother's blue eyes, though he inherited his confidence from them both. He's smart and surprisingly funny, and he's the closest thing to a son I'll probably ever have.

"Hey, Uncle Cam."

I stand and pull him into a hug. "You looked great on the ice tonight."

"You catch my dangle in the third period? Uncle Harry taught me that." He mimics the move he made with the stick. The one that sent the puck between one guy's legs and into the back of the net.

A chuckle rumbles up my chest. "Yeah, those are the plays of the future center of the Boston Bolts." I clap his shoulder, turning him to face his parents.

"Yeah." He juts his chin. "Future since Mom won't let me join the draft next year."

"Mav," Daniel growls in warning.

Maverick slumps, looking properly chastised. "Sorry, Ma."

Hannah only grins. "It's fine. You joining us for dinner, or are you going to hang out with the boys?"

"War ordered pizza for Beck and me," he replies as he rounds the table. He bends at the waist and pecks her cheek.

"Okay," she says. "Go have fun with the team. Good job tonight."

"Thanks, Ma. Love you." He straightens, gives his father a nod, and turns back to me, wearing a smirk. "Good to see you, Uncle Cam. Work on her for me, 'kay?"

I chuckle as he wanders off.

War passes him, patting his shoulder, and heads for us. Even after all these years, I straighten like he's still my captain. He's wearing a long-sleeved black T-shirt with the boys' team's name on it. It's rolled up to the elbows, exposing the tattoos that seem to multiply every time I see him. He's just as strong as he was back when we played too. Unlike the rest of us, he still gets on the ice regularly since he coaches the high school team.

"You're making Beck go to college, right?" Hannah says in greeting.

I glance at War, knowing full well he isn't. Brayden was drafted at eighteen, and he's now the captain of our team, just like his old man was. But I'll let him handle Hannah.

He pulls on the back of his neck, head ducked, and peers over at Daniel.

"Oh my god, you aren't," Hannah hisses.

With a shrug, he drops into the seat opposite her.

"How did you get Ava to agree to that?" She grabs her phone from the table and unlocks the screen. "Ugh, I've got to talk to her."

War chuckles, sitting back, relaxed. "She knows what he wants. You know how it is. These boys live for the sport, just like we did. And they're better than we were back then."

"Cocky as shit too," I say.

Daniel tips his drink in my direction in agreement. He's proud of that, and I don't blame him. They're really good kids, but yeah, they need to get knocked around a bit in the NHL. And when they do, they'll be better for it, just like we were.

Hannah blows out a breath. "Shit. I'm outnumbered, aren't I?"

Daniel grasps her chair and pulls it closer. "I'm always on your side, baby. But yeah, you are outnumbered on this one."

"The Bolts have set up a great college program," I remind her. "He can take classes while training. Get his degree along with chasing his dream."

The Langfields care more about their players than any team owners I've ever encountered. It makes my job incredibly easy. Not only do they offer educational opportunities, but they provide free housing and incredible healthcare and mental health resources. Recruiting is like stealing candy from a baby.

Hannah only sighs, her shoulders slumping.

War takes pity on her and changes the subject, eyeing me. "You ready for your party this weekend?"

I lean back in my chair. "When am I not ready?"

He smirks. "Bringing a date?"

"I'm sure I'll bring someone." I should probably start looking. I hate being the only single one at these get-togethers, especially when it's my own party.

Hannah pulls away from Daniel and rests her elbows on the table, grinning. "Okay, I'll make you a deal."

"A deal?"

She bobs her head, her teeth sunken into her lip like she's thinking. "A bet."

"A bet?"

Daniel frowns. "Dream girl, where you going with this?"

"You date someone for longer than two dates," she says, ignoring her husband, "and I'll consider letting Mav join the draft next year."

Scoffing, I pick up my drink. "Consider?"

She presses her tongue to the inside of her cheek and studies her husband. "Okay," she finally says. "Make it three months with the same woman, and I'll let Mav choose what he wants to do about the draft next year."

"What?" Daniel bolts up, his eyes wide.

I cough out an uncomfortable laugh. "Three months?"

Hannah's smile grows, her blue eyes shining. "Yup. Show me you can change, and maybe I'll let my baby boy join that team of yours."

"Whoa." Whistling, War shakes his head.

I roll my eyes. "That's absurd."

"You're really betting with our son's future?" Daniel asks, his jaw slack.

She frowns at him. "I thought you wanted him to play?"

"I do, but I want you to be okay with it."

Hannah chuckles. "The man hasn't dated a woman in the twenty years I've known him."

"Longer," I mutter. More like twenty-eight, but who's counting?

She throws her hands up. "Point made. There's no way he'll win this. But if you want your godson to play so bad, you know what you need to do."

This is ridiculous. I run my hands through my hair and shake my head. Because what's more ridiculous is that I'm actually considering it.

Chapter 5
Savannah

"THIS PLACE CAN'T BE REAL," I mutter as the limo Addie arranged for us pulls up in front of Camden Snow's house.

Mansion is more like it.

I've been to some nice places with the girls over the years, but this is something else. While the Warrens' house is large, it's cozy, more like an oversized cabin set on a sprawling piece of land overlooking a lake.

This? I blink and take it in again, a smile finding my lips. This is the house of a fucking playboy.

The black gate and stone walls do nothing to hide the large white-washed brick house on the other side. The long driveway is lined with every kind of luxury car imaginable. Men in black and white jog around the vehicles, taking keys and moving cars. The outside of the home is lit up with a cool purplish-gray light. Every tree on the property has its own spotlight as well.

And in the daylight, when the harbor behind it can be seen? Hell, I can't imagine how beautiful it is. Properties like this don't exist. Or at least they rarely come onto the market.

"He lives here alone?" Sutton asks, scanning the place the way I did.

Neither of us has been here before. This may be the first holiday party Addie and Josie have been invited to, but they've known Camden most of their lives.

"Yup. He's a perpetual bachelor," Josie explains. "I don't think I've ever known him to have a girlfriend."

Addie shakes her head. "Not everyone needs to get married. Some people love their careers and are content doing what they want."

I shrug. I don't disagree with Addie's sentiment at all, but I don't for a second believe that's what she wants out of life. She may not have ever had a boyfriend—not that I'm aware of, at least—but I don't think it's because she doesn't want one. It has more to do with her profession, I think. She's a freaking badass professional hockey goalie. Not many men can date a woman so tough and established and not feel threatened by her success. And next season, she'll hang up her skates and step into her new role of coach in the NHL. I doubt that will make it any easier. The only men confident enough are the players themselves, but the rule follower would never.

"You're correct. Not everyone has to date, but Savannah does," Josie points out.

While getting ready this afternoon, we told Addie and Sutton about our idea for the new series of articles. I was a little worried that Sutton would be offended. Instead, she's thrilled at the prospect of proving me wrong. She thinks that the right man won't be scared off by the ridiculous tactics I intend to use. Hell, she's convinced that the wrong ones won't even dump me. Says it's because my boobs are so amazing.

She's out of her mind. No one's boobs are that amazing. Not even these babies.

Tonight, they're barely hidden beneath the scandalous dress Sienna personally picked out for me. It's one of her own designs. A short crushed-velvet dress in a deep emerald green. The sleeves are long, and the neckline plunges so low my belly button is nearly visible. I paired it with golden heels I found in the *Jolie* closet. The outfit is worth more than half a year's salary, so I intend to enjoy the hell out of it.

"Okay," Addie says, her face scrunched up, "but no dating any of my family members."

I roll my eyes. "You just removed half the names from the roster."

She giggles. "No coaching staff either."

"Of course not. They're all married. Happily. I've never seen a group of men so smitten with their wives."

Addie breaks into a warm smile. "They're all obsessed, though I'd say Uncle Aiden is the most unhinged about it."

"Who wouldn't be obsessed with Lennox?" Josie points out.

And yeah, she's right. Lennox is gorgeous and the life of any party.

"And you can't date Bray," Josie says.

I pout. "You're ruining all my fun."

She scowls. "Please. I'm not ruining any fun on that front. Brayden is the least fun guy on the team. All serious and focused. He probably won't even see your boobs tonight, and they're in everyone's face."

I give my chest a little shimmy. "They're even sparkly."

Addie giggles. "You are a shimmering goddess."

"Okay, so no brothers, married uncles, or anyone whose last name is Langfield. Does that leave anyone I can test out my dating prowess on tonight?"

The door to the limo opens, and the driver holds out a hand. He helps Addie out first, and we all follow. As we head toward the house, Addie lists the men who'll be in attendance.

"There's our center, Bobby Dean." She nods at a man in a navy velvet suit that shows off his ridiculously large thighs and is cut at his ankle. He's got dark brown hair, and with cheekbones like that? Damn, he could be a model. When he sees us, his face lights up and he gives one of his signature smirks. The kind that could incinerate a girl's panties. Not this girl, though, since I'm not wearing any.

"He's twenty-seven and single, and honestly, I really like him," she adds.

I scrutinize her for a moment, noting the way she stares at him like she's seeing him for the first time. Her light brown hair is pulled back in a messy updo, curled wisps framing her face. With the gold dress that hugs all her curves and red lipstick, she's a fucking knockout. Tonight, every player is gonna wish she wasn't set to be their newest coach. "Oh, and there's Maksim Loob, our defenseman."

"Magnum," Josie mutters, holding her hands out in front of her and dragging them farther apart. "We all can surmise how he got that nickname."

Sutton snorts. "Oh my god. You're awful."

I lick my lips, studying the Russian as he slaps Bobby's hand and the two of them hug in greeting. His light brown hair is pulled back in a messy bun, low on his head. The scar across his cheek, and even the chipped tooth, make him look ruggedly handsome.

"There's my personal favorite." Sutton points to a man unfolding himself from the driver's seat of a white Corvette. "Royal Bombardier."

"He's a winger," Addie explains. "From Canada."

"Those Canadians sure know how to make a man," Sutton whispers. She's practically drooling as she watches the tall man with dirty blond hair that curls at the ends.

With an easy swagger, he approaches the other guys and greets them. But when he spots Sutton, his eyes go wide and his face lights up. He surveys our group, and when he sees Josie, his captain's little sister, he makes a beeline for her.

"*Jo*sie," he says emphasizing the first two letters of her name for reasons unknown to me. "You look gorgeous." Though he's speaking to her, his attention keeps drifting to Sutton, who can't seem to make eye contact and whose cheeks are flaming red.

Yup. She's half in love already. Damn. I wish I was half as interested in a man after a week as she is after twenty seconds.

"Royal, this is Sutton," Josie says. "And you know Addie."

He slips his hands into his pockets and grins. "Hello, Almost Coach."

"And this is Savannah. She works with me at *Jolie*."

His blue eyes light up with what looks like mischief. "JJ has banned us from reading the magazine, so naturally, we take turns reading it out loud before games to annoy the shit out of him."

Addie coughs out a laugh. "Probably not the best way to get your goalie in the right headspace."

JJ's mom is Catherine Bouvier, my boss, so I can understand why he wouldn't want his teammates reading her magazine, which is often filled with advice on sex. Especially her own editorial articles. She's very open about her adventurous sex life with her husband and some-times others.

Like I said, she's my hero.

"We don't read Cat's articles. We wouldn't do that to him. But Calliope's are a must-read."

Josie eyes me, but I shake my head. No one knows I'm Calliope, and we're going to keep it that way.

"She's my favorite," Sutton says. They're the first words out of her mouth, and already, she's flirting.

Head tilted, he hitches a thumb over his shoulder. "Why don't we get a drink, and you can tell me which articles you like best? See what we have in common."

With her lip caught between her teeth, she nods shyly. "Sure."

He holds out an arm and she takes it easily. Then they're gone.

Josie huffs and stomps toward the house. "She better not start talking baby names before we get inside."

Coughing out a laugh, I follow her. My laughter dies, though, when I step inside. The sound of our heels dull on the black carpet that's been laid out to protect the gorgeous light wood floors.

The back of the house is all windows with a view of the dazzling harbor and the pink and orange sky above it as the sun sets over the water.

"Okay, I could maybe put up with a man for life if this house came with him," I mutter.

Josie snorts. "And you haven't even seen the man yet."

"I've seen pictures."

After we were invited to the party, I looked him up, and yeah, Camden Snow is a hot older man. Forty-six, I think, with a full head of dirty blond hair. Bright blue eyes. A cocky smile and a different woman beside him in every photo.

"Pictures don't do him justice," Josie promises.

Addie rolls her eyes. "Your father would kill you."

Our friend lets out a raspy laugh. "Please, I'm far more into the women he's hired for tonight. Look at them!"

Sienna warned me that these parties were over-the-top, but I defi-nitely didn't picture women walking around in little more than silk bows like they're Christmas presents meant to be unwrapped. They're adorned in red, green, silver, and gold silk. And every one of them is gorgeous. Of course, none of them have large breasts like mine. The thick bands of ribbon would never cover a chest like this, and every woman drifting around with trays of drinks in her hands is no bigger than a size two.

I love my body, but damn do I feel extra curvaceous around them.

Camden Snow obviously has a type, and it is tall, slim, and naked.

"Champagne?" one of them asks as she approaches with a silver tray.

"Thank you." I pluck a champagne flute with a smile. "Love the outfit."

She grins. "Certainly doesn't leave anything to the imagination, does it? Make sure you check out the show downstairs in a bit."

Head tilted, I frown. "Show?"

"It's a surprise," a deep male voice says from behind me.

I huff, annoyed at the interruption. I hate when men think it's their right to hold all the cards. Like they can tell women what they can and can't do. "And who are you to keep secrets?"

"That," Josie says as I turn toward the most gorgeous man I've ever seen, "is Camden Snow."

CHAPTER 6
CAMDEN

THE MOST GORGEOUS woman I've ever laid eyes on brings her drink to her glossy lips and sips the bubbly without bothering to respond to her friend. Instead, she eyes me, like she's memorizing every damn inch of my body. Much like I did with hers as she stepped into my house. One look at her, and I practically swallowed my own tongue.

Wide hips and a narrow waist, but fuck me, those curves have nothing on her damn face. My attention is drawn to the small beauty mark above her mouth as she swipes her tongue over her lip. Creamy skin, long, dark lashes, plump fuck-me lips.

I've never seen her before, I know that for certain. A man doesn't forget a woman like her. Her deep red hair is loose and hangs halfway down her back.

I itch to touch it. To wrap a fist around it. Instead, I clench my hands and let out a breath through my nose.

Her green eyes widen, and I swear to god she smirks like she can read my thoughts.

Holy hell, this one is trouble.

I'm entranced. I can't look away. So when her friend says "Hi, Uncle Cam," I startle, blinking rapidly. Holy shit. This goddess's friend is Josie.

Fuck. Please don't let this woman be as young as my honorary niece. "Hey, Josie. Addie," I add when I clock Adeline Langfield beside her.

This isn't good.

I take a step back, putting distance between myself and the woman I am quickly realizing can't be my date for the night, let alone an integral part of my three-month experiment.

Fuck me. If she could be, the bet would have been a damn cakewalk. I could look at this woman for years and not get tired of studying her curves.

My jaw flexes as I survey them one more time. Then I force a smile and will my eyes to avoid drifting to the gorgeous tits she's not even trying to hide.

"Amazing party," Addie says. "This is our friend Savannah. Thank you for inviting us."

Savannah.

My attention slips back to her. Even her name is beautiful.

She licks her lips and holds out a hand. "Yes, thank you for the invite."

I shouldn't touch her, but I've never been good at rejecting my impulses, so I step closer and take her hand in mine, reveling in the warmth of it. Relishing how small and soft it is. "Pleasure is all mine. Enjoy the party, girls."

I release her hand and step back. While Josie and Addie get the message, my silent signal that it's time for the conversation to end, and wander off, Savannah only turns so she's facing me fully. Like she's determined not to obey.

So she's a brat.

Fuck, this keeps getting worse.

"So what's the surprise?" Her voice is sexy, with a slight rasp.

"You should definitely not go downstairs. None of you should."

I run a hand over my forehead. What was I thinking pulling my usual tricks tonight? I keep forgetting how young the players are now. A few are the actual kids of my teammates. Like Brayden. Though at thirty-three, he can't really be considered a kid.

Maybe the problem is that we—I—keep getting older.

"None of us?" she asks, a slight smile on her lips.

I discreetly scan the people around us, feeling like a dirty old man. It appears that all my guests are lost in conversation or ogling the half-naked women serving drinks. Obviously the players would rather look at them than pay attention to me. Though they're fools if they don't realize the best-looking woman in this room is standing here, busting my balls.

I drag my focus back to her, and when our eyes lock, my chest tightens in a way I haven't felt in god knows how long. I stopped feeling years ago.

She rolls her teeth over her bottom lip, her green eyes searching mine.

Fuck it. "How old are you?"

A surprised laugh spills from her. "Twenty-seven, why?"

Twenty-seven. *That's not too young. Right?*

I tilt my head, sip my whiskey. "How's your relationship with your dad?"

"Nonexistent."

A rumble works up my throat. "I can work with that."

With a single step, I'm by her side, my hand pressed to her lower back. Savannah tilts her head, the move bringing her lips so fucking close that mine tingle at the idea of tasting them. She smells like a rich dessert. Like chocolate mousse. The scent makes my mouth water.

"I'm not sure how I feel about that response," she says softly.

I shrug. "I don't like to start things I can't finish, and let's be honest, baby girl, no father in the world would let a beautiful young thing like you anywhere near the likes of me."

She pulls her shoulders back and hits me with a haughty look. "Maybe I'm the type of girl who doesn't listen to her daddy."

I squeeze her waist, desire already threading through me. "Oh, you definitely will. But I wouldn't mind if you were a bit of a brat either."

"Oh my god." Her lips form an O, her eyes widening. "I'm—"

"Turned on," I say, cutting her off. "Don't even pretend otherwise. And you're too invested in what the surprise might be to walk away."

Her plump lips thin as she presses them together. "You seem to think you know a lot about me, Mr. Snow."

I inhale. Damn, this fucking tease of a woman is going straight to my head. Already I'm hard and dying to get her alone. "I don't know nearly enough, but I'm certainly interested in anything you're willing to share."

She sinks those teeth into her bottom lip again, trying to hide a smile. "This house is gorgeous."

"Would you like a tour?"

That smile breaks through in earnest. "Is this where you offer to show me the view from your bedroom?"

A chuckle rumbles out of me. "No. Only good girls get that tour."

She rolls her pretty green eyes. "I doubt that's true."

I pinch her waist and dip in so my mouth is at her ear. "Brat."

"Lead the way." She flutters her lashes and affects an innocent expression. "Daddy."

Chapter 7
Savannah

CAMDEN HISSES through his teeth and turns away, though I don't miss how he adjusts himself before he turns back and guides me through an open door down the hall. I've heard about the dangers of going into dark spaces with strangers, especially older men, once or twice, but with Camden this close, there's no chance I'll follow the rules.

He is the perfect first mark.

Charming, gorgeous, wealthy. A catch in every sense. And totally unattainable. But I imagine women throw themselves at him all the time. That he's the kind of man who will enjoy them for the night and then spit them out the next day.

He's a lucky man tonight, though, because I swallow, and I intend to enjoy the hell out of him too.

I don't even feel bad about using him as my first guinea pig. I'll show him a good time, and then I'll prove my point.

If you want a man like Camden Snow, you don't play his game. You walk away.

There's a pretty good chance he'll let you, and then you'll save yourself some heartbreak.

I guess that could be a part of this series of articles too. Tips for spotting the kind of men who aren't looking for a real connection and how to avoid being ensnared. If, that is, you're looking for an actual relationship. I'm not, so proving my point won't be a hardship.

Tomorrow I'll walk away from Camden Snow with my heart intact.

But tonight I'll enjoy the hell out of this ride.

At the end of the hall, we're met with another wall of windows, and the view nearly knocks me back. "Holy shit."

Camden chuckles low in his throat. "It's pretty nice, right?"

"Nice?" I scoff. "This might just be the best view in Boston."

On the other side of the glass is Boston Harbor in all its glory. The moon glows low in the deep inky sky, giving the water a magical glistening, shimmering effect.

The house is loud, but as he leads me out through a sliding glass door and closes it behind him, silence descends.

"No, the view from my bedroom is absolutely better," he promises.

Heart tripping, I turn back to him. I keep my expression schooled, only raising a brow.

He shrugs. "Doesn't mean I'm going to show it to you."

"You will," I assure him as I walk to the edge of the stone patio.

To my right is a hot tub. The lid is pulled back and the water is bubbling. I almost laugh at how fucking sexy this place is, and that's not even considering the man who owns it. It's a quintessential bachelor pad, and I'm sure he does very well in that department. A woman would merely need to see this place to drop her panties.

I lean against the stone wall that separates the property from the harbor and breathe in the cold, salty New England air. I'll never get enough of the seasons. Being from Las Vegas, the cold of my first winter here was a shock. But the fall season had already enchanted me, and I was in love with the place, so there was no going back. It took some time to adjust, but now, in my opinion, there's nothing as magical as a wintry night in Boston. This already incredible view would only be enhanced if there was snow falling around us.

Almost makes me wish I was going to be around to see it.

But all we get is tonight. It's all anyone gets with me.

With that reminder, I spin and face Camden. He's already watching me, and the intensity in his expression causes my throat to go dry.

"So what do you do, Savannah?" Camden murmurs.

"I work for *Jolie*."

His eyes light up. "My buddy's wife just took over as creative director."

"Yeah, Sienna. She's actually the one who gave me this dress." I hold one arm out. "She told me to watch out for you too."

He chuckles. "She's right. You should."

"Don't worry about me, Camden Snow. I'm not naïve."

"Oh yeah? So what is it you know about me?"

I step closer. Mostly because I'm starting to get really freaking cold, but also because I've found myself trapped in his gravitational field, and at the moment, I don't even want to fight the pull. "I know you used to play for the Bolts."

He nods.

"Were you any good?"

His brows jump, practically hitting his hairline. "So you really don't know anything about me."

"That good, huh?"

With a low huff of a laugh, he grips my waist and pulls me against him. "I was a fucking god on the ice."

I tip my head back and lick my lips. "Bet you're a god in the bedroom too."

He shakes his head, but there's no hiding his cocky smile. "You seem awfully interested in my bedroom."

"I'm just a girl who knows what she wants."

"And what is it you want, Savannah?" His voice is low, the gravel in his tone making me clench in delight.

"A fantastic orgasm. Something I'm sure you could provide."

His eyes dance. "Maybe. But first I want to know more about you."

I roll my teeth over my bottom lip. "I like to be on top."

He squeezes my waist again, his hands higher than I'd like. "I'm being serious."

"So am I. I have fantastic tits. They'll look incredible when I'm riding you."

His eyes don't even drop to said fantastic tits. They just hold mine. "Tell me something real."

His voice is soft, earnest. It makes me want to spill my every thought. I absolutely despise the urge. Real is depressing. At least my real is. I live in an attic-turned-studio-apartment, yet I still live paycheck to paycheck. And I was never wanted. By either of my parents. I have no family and no savings. And outside of some incredible friends, no one really cares that I exist.

He couldn't handle my truths. They aren't sexy. A man who lives in a place like this, who has had the career he's had and looks like he does, would never understand a girl like me.

I lift my chin. "Real is overrated."

"I disagree."

Sighing, I deflate a little. "Our versions of real are very different. You have a gorgeous home and a wonderful career to look back on. My life isn't nearly as pretty. But if you want me to spill so badly, why don't you go first? What's your deepest secret, Camden Snow?"

He holds my gaze, those sharp blue eyes seemingly looking right into my soul. Seeing all my thoughts, all my insecurities.

Then, with a deep swallow, he replies. "I don't think anyone's ever loved me enough to stay."

My heart stutters, and before I can regain control of myself, I murmur, "I don't think anyone's ever loved me, period."

He cups my cheek. "That's ridiculous."

Swallowing back the self-pity threatening to escape from the cage I've trapped it in, I shrug. "I know."

"I think you'd be incredibly easy to love," he rasps. The heat of his rough hands soaks into my cheeks, soothing me.

I don't know what the fuck is happening, but I blink, and when I open my eyes, I find his mouth a mere centimeter from mine.

"You'd definitely make it easy to want to stay," I say, my lips brushing his.

Eyes fluttering shut, he breathes me in. "Fuck, I want to kiss you, but I also want to take this slow."

I push up on my toes, slanting my mouth against his. "Why?"

"Because," he says, those lips still caressing mine, "I'm the type of guy you need to get to know to love."

Without pulling back, I laugh. "And you want me to love you?"

He nods. "I think I do."

"Smooth, Camden Snow, you are so very smooth."

Then because he hasn't done it yet, I lick at his lips, taking my own taste.

Groaning, he clutches my hip with one hand. He uses the other to angle my jaw, holding my mouth in place. "What else? Tell me something else about you."

"That's not how you date." Since he's forced my mouth from his, I use the momentary reprieve to suck in a breath and get my head on straight. I'm supposed to be proving a point tonight, not falling for an unavailable man.

I don't think anyone's ever loved me enough to stay.

His words play on repeat in my head. Why is it always the broken ones who make me want to try?

I'm broken enough for the both of us. I don't need a man to put back together.

"Like I said, I've never dated, so I guess I'm a bit inexperienced." His blue eyes are full of heat. "You can teach me, though."

"You didn't say you didn't date; you said no one has stayed."

He shrugs. "Same thing, really."

"No. If you don't give people the opportunity to know you—which is the point of dating, by the way—then you can't fault them for leaving."

"You're right. And I have no idea why we're even talking about this. I promised I'd show you the surprise. Let's do that." He steps back, and the loss of his body heat hits me almost as violently as his emotional retreat.

Why does that bother me? Why do I care at all. Before I can regain control of my emotions, I'm hit with a bolt of pain straight in the chest.

Fortunately, Camden has already turned away, obviously determined to get inside, so he doesn't notice my reaction.

In the warm hallway once more, he slides the glass door shut. Then he guides me down the hall toward what I assume is the basement.

As we pass the kitchen, I spot the girls, who are snacking, and wave.

Josie smirks, her chin lifted and her eyes full of glee. Addie's mouth falls open in shock.

"Show's about to start," Camden says to the room full of hockey players and women who are probably here in hopes of bagging one of them, at least for the night.

I still haven't seen Sienna, which is probably good. I don't think I could flirt so openly with my boss in the vicinity.

A group of guys passes us and heads down the stairs. When the area clears, I survey my friends again. They seem far more interested in the cheese platter than the surprise on the floor below.

We are not the same. I love cheese like the next girl, sure, but like they say, curiosity killed the cat, and I am so damn curious. How egregious could a show be for this man to warn a group of grown women off?

He peers down at me. "Still with me?"

I smirk. "All night."

With a hand at my back again, he presses his lips to my neck. "You keep teasing me, I'm going to collect."

I lean back against his chest. "Good."

Groaning, he pushes me forward.

As we descend the steps, the music gets louder, but the lighting dims. When my feet hit the bottom step, I pause and take in the space, working hard not to show my reaction.

The basement has been turned into an apparent speakeasy. Women wearing diamond thongs with their breasts completely exposed spin around on poles set up throughout the room. The poles are bolted to the floor and ceiling. They're permanent. Not props for the night. A half-naked woman sits at the piano in the corner, playing, while another lies on top of it, singing a raspy melody.

"You still good?" Camden says into my ear, his warm breath sending a shudder through me. He steps up close and wraps an arm around my waist. Maybe he can sense how unsteady I suddenly feel and he's worried I'm going down. Even so, I lean into him, appreciating the move.

"This is—" I can't even find the words. Incredible. Hot. Fucking incredibly hot.

"Too much?" He presses his lips to the sensitive spot below my ear.

A deep moan rolls out of me without my permission. "No." I met this man half an hour ago, and already I'm ready for my first orgasm. What the hell is happening?

"Good, let's find a seat so you don't miss the show."

I squeeze my thighs together, unsure of what the hell to expect, and nod.

Camden slips his palm into mine and then squeezes my fingers gently, giving me a thoughtful look. The moment is so surprisingly sweet that I forget for a second that he's basically turned his basement into a sex club.

This isn't romantic, Savannah. He's the definition of a playboy.

With those thoughts cemented in my brain, I ignore the butterflies flapping in my chest and allow Camden to guide me deeper into the room. He stops at an open love seat, and as I turn, ready to ease down onto the cushion, he grasps my arm. He holds me there as he sits, then he pulls me onto his lap and loops an arm around my waist, settling his palm on my bare thigh.

"What do you want to drink?" He holds up a hand to summon one of the servers.

"Um, I'll take a vodka soda." I wiggle forward. "Also, my own seat."

Chuckling, he tightens his hold. "I won't be able to hear you if you aren't right here, and I told you, I intend to learn everything I can about you tonight."

Without waiting for a response, he turns to the server and orders our drinks.

I take the opportunity to study him. He's painfully good-looking, and the command he has over himself, the confidence, like he's used to getting exactly what he wants, is really doing it for me. Every person he encounters smiles at him genuinely. That's another thing I like. He's well liked.

I shake off the thoughts. He's obviously a good time, and since I'm only going to spend the evening with him, that's all that should really matter to me.

I lean in close to his mouth and whisper, "Why talk when we can do other things?"

"You're making this so fucking hard," he breathes, the warmth of his body engulfing me.

"I'm trying to make you hard." I wiggle on top of him. "How am I doing?"

He tilts his head against mine and groans. "I've been a steel rod since I first saw your ass. You just have to exist and I'll be hard."

A thrill zips down my spine. I like that. Probably more than I should. Especially when I realize that though the tits of the woman now delivering our drinks are in our faces, his eyes haven't left mine.

Not wanting to be rude, I take my drink and thank her. Cam only grunts as he accepts his. He sets it on the table beside him, finally looking away. But a heartbeat later, his attention is back on me.

"I'm going to be honest," he says, voice low, hand cupping my cheek. "I like you and I want more."

I ignore the hope that unravels inside me at his words. It's something I've never had, and I won't start believing that can change now. "I intend to give you plenty more too."

He sighs like my avoidance is frustrating. Then he nods. "Okay, baby girl. Show's about to start, relax." He shifts and leans back against the couch, pulling away. The move is subtle, but it's enough to tell me that I've fucked up.

I'm annoyed. With myself. With him. But mostly with the possibilities forming in my mind. The ones trying to tempt me into hoping for more rather than focusing on the here and now.

So I do what he says.

I guess I'm a better listener than I thought. Or maybe he's just a better daddy than mine ever was.

CHAPTER 8
CAMDEN

THE WOMAN on my lap shifts and rests against my chest with a sigh. It's mind-boggling how perfect she is. And I almost screwed it all up by being vulnerable.

I blame Cora for that. She's been complaining for years that I never open up, and here I am, dangerously close to telling my whole sad life story to a woman I just met.

I don't think anyone's ever loved me, period.

I wasn't the only one who opened up. Though it's no consolation. If anything, her truth made my heart ache more painfully. How could someone like Savannah exist and not know love? That gnawing question makes me almost delusional enough to believe that I could be good for her. That I could be worthy.

Almost. Because when I push away the longing and cling to good sense, I realize how ridiculous it is. Loving means being vulnerable, and I don't know the first thing about being vulnerable. Nor do I want to.

Hannah appears at the bottom of the steps, her brows arching when she notices Savannah on my lap. When she smiles like she approves, my hackles rise. It shouldn't bother me. I want her to approve of Savannah. I want to win the bet.

And yet that thought feels all wrong.

I don't think anyone's ever loved me, period.

The words call to something deeper inside me. Tempting me to try to fill a role I never have before. One that isn't selfish.

Daniel appears behind Hannah, and she leans back, whispering in his ear. He scans the room, and when his attention snags on us, I have to hold back a growl.

"You okay?" Savannah murmurs.

I rub the soft skin on the inside of her knee, hoping to soothe her in the same way her soft voice soothes me. "I'm perfect. Do you need anything else?"

She smiles up at me, her expression filled with far more trust than I deserve. "Nope."

Fuck. I want to kiss her. I tuck my chin and brush my nose against hers, but before our lips meet, the music shifts, the beat sultry, the lights dimming further.

The show is about to begin.

I nod toward the pole positioned in front of us as a woman leans up against it, her hip tilted out, both hands above her, one wrist on top of the other.

This isn't meant to be like a strip club. These dancers are here to perform a tastefully seductive show. The moment the woman only a few feet away starts to move, undulating her hips in time with every other dancer in the room in choreographed precision, Savannah gasps.

"They're amazing," she whispers, the green of her irises dark as she watches, rapt.

I don't give the dancers even an ounce of my attention unless Savannah points out a move. They don't hold a candle to her.

Within minutes, she squirms on top of me, like she's turned on.

There's no hiding how hard I am, and I know she can feel it. With every second that passes, she gets a little more daring, rolling her hips and sinking deeper against me.

I'm not the only one who notices, either. The dancer closest to us locks eyes with Savannah and drags her hand down between her bare breasts, showing her just how much she's enjoying the attention.

Maksim Loob and Bobby Dean, two of our best players, are sitting across the room, watching the dancer from the opposite angle, though their eyes drift to Savannah far more often than I like.

Normally I'd have my hand up her skirt. I have a healthy sexual appetite, and I don't mind being watched. Don't mind sharing either. But with Savannah, I'm consumed by this hot, desperate need to protect her. I want to cover her up. Hide her from all the prying eyes. So when the dancer drops to her knees and crawls slowly toward us, I press a kiss to the pulse point below her ear. "Don't do anything you're uncomfortable with."

Her pulse races and I swear she whimpers. "I'm not uncomfortable."

The dancer kneels at our feet, focus fixed on Savannah, her bare chest heaving and lust in her eyes. "May I touch you?"

Savannah's nod is quick and harsh. Maybe a little overeager.

The woman settles her palm on Savannah's bare knee beside mine. "Would you like a lap dance?"

Savannah tilts her head in my direction, like she's seeking permission.

The power that rumbles through me in response makes me feel fucking invincible. "Whatever you want, baby girl."

Green eyes dilating, she hums. Then she settles against my chest and inhales deeply.

The woman stands and straddles our laps. I shift my thighs closer together beneath Savannah, the idea of touching another woman making my stomach roll. I only want to touch the gorgeous girl on top of me. It's the oddest sensation, and for the moment, I don't have the mental capacity to consider the reason behind it.

When the woman splays a hand over my chest, balancing herself, that unease grows. But before I can react, Savannah does.

"Only me." Her tone is sharp, a brow arched as she gently grasps the woman's wrist and positions her hand on her shoulder.

My chest swells, along with my dick. "Good girl," I murmur in her ear.

Fuck me. If this woman is feeling as possessive over me as I am her, I don't know that I'll survive the night.

She glances back at me, warning in her gaze. "And your hands stay on me."

Smirking, I shift and splay my hands on her bare thighs, pulling them a little farther apart, giving the dancer a better seat as well.

I can't even begin to describe the sensation that washes over me when the dancer moves against the woman on my lap. The sounds that rip from Savannah's throat are sexier than anything I've ever heard. I'm entranced. We're in a crowded room, and my guests are no doubt watching, but I can't focus on a single thing other than the way Savannah's lips fall open as the dancer swivels her hips.

Holy fuck. I'm trapped beneath Savannah, getting zero attention myself, and I swear to god I could come like this.

"You're so good at this," the dancer murmurs, making me think she isn't just putting on a show. She arches back and her nipples point toward the ceiling.

The guys in the crowd holler and whistle. Shouting about how lucky I am. But I can't even look up to smirk.

"Have you ever danced?" she asks.

"Yes," Savannah answers in the sultriest of ways.

"Then I need to see you up on that pole." The dancer bends over backward and flips off my girl's lap.

Immediately, I tighten my thighs, pulling Savannah's legs together so no one sees up her dress.

As the dancer holds out a hand, mine tightens on Savannah's hips. I don't want to stop her if it's what she wants, but fuck, I don't think I could handle it if all these assholes watched her moving on the pole.

Savannah shakes her head, then glances back at me, her teeth sunken into her lip again. "Can't tonight. Sorry, Daddy," she teases in that sexy tone. "I didn't wear any panties."

Before the last word has left her lips, I'm lifting her and carrying her out of the room.

"What are you doing?" She squirms in my arms, trying to avoid flashing the crowd of people.

As if I'd let that fucking happen. I'm so fucking angry I can barely see straight, knowing that anyone might have seen her bare pussy while I let her play on my lap.

"What the hell were you thinking not wearing underwear?" I growl as I storm up the steps.

"Oh, I'm sorry," she hisses. "I wasn't aware you were my actual father."

There's the fucking brat again. Fury and need tangle inside me, creating a strange sensation. Fuck, I'm going to enjoy this too much.

"I'm going to turn your ass so red there will be no question about it." I charge through the back hallway to the next set of stairs, then through the doors of my private suite.

My hold on her is bruising by the time I approach the bed.

Savannah glares at me, eyes stormy. "Okay, this has been fun, but seriously, you can't just lock me in your bedroom against my will."

I toss her onto the mattress and step back, sucking in a deep breath and willing my heart rate to slow.

What am I doing?

She's right. I barely know her, yet I'm losing my damn mind over her.

"You're not locked in here. You're welcome to go," I say, turning away, fingers laced and hands on my head. My heart is still racing, my chest burning.

"That's—" Her words stop abruptly, and the room falls silent.

I whip around and find her studying me, her expression curious rather than angry.

"That's not what I want," she says.

"Then what do you want?" I take a step back, making it clear that she's in control.

The door is open and the music and voices from the party float around us. Most of my friends, some of my family, and a ton of my players and colleagues are here for a holiday party. Yet I couldn't give a fuck. All that matters to me in this moment is the woman in front of me, the woman holding all the cards and my full attention.

"I just want to slow down for a second," she says, like she doesn't know what to think either. "And maybe a glass of wine," she adds, a small smile finding her lips.

"How about we start with water? Then, in a little bit, if you're still in the mood for wine, I'll bring a bottle up."

"Okay, Daddy." Her voice is back to that teasing tone, her lips tipped up.

A sense of lightness floods me. Thank fuck.

I stride to the mini fridge and pluck out a bottle of water. When I turn around again, she's settling back against my pillows, her legs tucked beneath the throw blanket that's usually draped at the foot of the bed.

I can't imagine that dress is comfortable, so after handing her the bottle of water, I pad into my closet and dig out a T-shirt and sweats. When I come back out with them, she tilts her head and frowns, her eyes full of confusion.

"Thought these might be more comfortable. They're here if you want. But obviously, you're more than welcome to go back down to the party if you prefer. Or sit here in that dress. You're in charge here."

Savannah shifts up onto her knees, and then without tearing her eyes off mine, she shimmies her dress up her thighs.

"Fuck," I mutter, but I can't tear my attention away from her body. With a heavy swallow, I force myself to say, "Want me to give you some privacy?"

"Please don't," she murmurs as she drags the dress up, exposing her bare pussy, her wide hips and creamy stomach, and fuck, those tits. I knew they'd be incredible.

She's completely naked for mere seconds. I refuse to blink as she snags my white tee from the mattress and pulls it over her head. When she's covered, the shirt falling to her mid-thigh, she sighs and plops back onto my bed, ignoring the sweatpants, and settles beneath the covers.

Her wild red hair fanned out over my shirt like that? I swear to god she's the prettiest thing I've ever seen.

"That's better. Thank you," she says, burrowing into the pillows.

I'm three feet from the bed, paralyzed. Pretty sure her naked body has been tattooed on my retinas.

"Can you sit with me?" she asks, her voice soft.

My legs move accordingly. They know who's calling the shots here, and when I settle beside her, one leg still on the floor, she snuggles against me.

Cheek pressed to my chest, she peers up at me. "Will anyone come up here?"

I survey the wide-open door and shake my head. "No. But I can close the door if you'd be more comfortable."

"Then will you lay with me?"

I smile. "Yeah, baby girl, I'll do whatever you want me to."

She hums, the sound going straight to my dick. "That's a dangerous promise."

Chuckling, I press a kiss to the top of her head. Then I ease her back onto the pillows and head for the door. With a centering breath, I close it, keeping my back turned for an extra second. Tonight has been fucking strange. Ten minutes ago, another woman was grinding on top of Savannah in a way that made me pretty confident an orgy was about to break out in my basement. Now I'm toeing off my shoes and climbing into my bed, fully dressed, my only hope for the night that she lets me keep her in my arms.

The fuck is going on with me?

When I'm settled beside her, my back against the leather headboard, she nuzzles into my chest.

I let out a long exhale, and the heavy weight of anxiety I always carry leaves my body along with my breath.

She clutches my shirt, her own breathing steady. The room is nearly silent. The only sound the faint noises from the party. It should be awkward. I only met her an hour ago. And yet…it's not.

In fact, the longer we sit, the more I relax. When she finally tilts her head up and assesses me, I'm completely at ease, until she utters four simple words: "Do you want kids?"

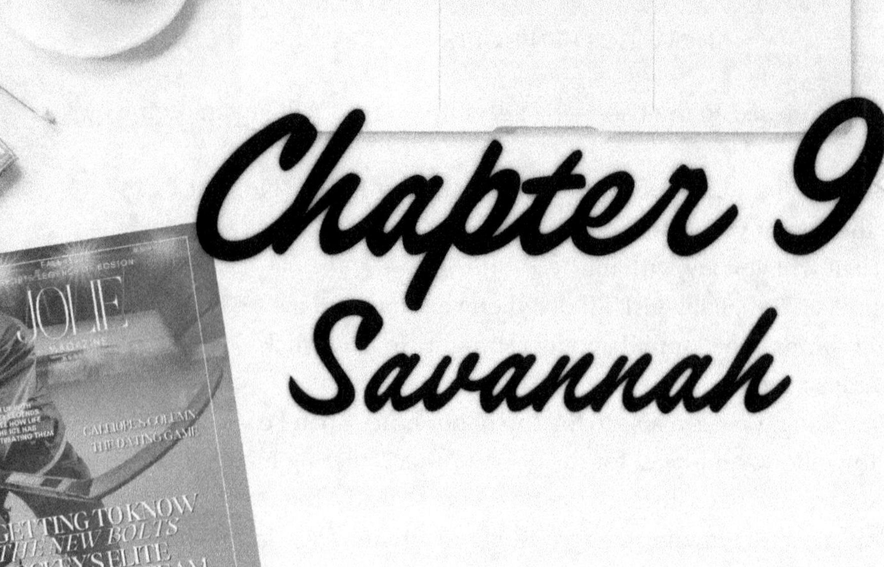

Chapter 9
Savannah

MY HEART POUNDS as I try to maintain a straight face.

How in the fuck does Sutton ask these things and not feel completely exposed?

I shouldn't care what this man thinks. I shouldn't care what his answer is. I'm doing this for the column. It's an experiment. And I'm doing it to help my friend understand what not to do.

But the thing is, when I'm uttering words that are guaranteed to make a man walk away, I wish I wasn't uttering them to a man I think I'd like to stay.

Then again, in this moment, I get how Sutton feels. Vulnerable and hopeful. God, it's awful. Why would anyone willingly put themselves in this position?

Downstairs, dressed up, channeling the sexy vixen who owned the attention of everyone in that room. That is my scene.

Teasing a man by flirting with another woman? Totally my comfort level.

Telling a man I've never been loved? That was my first mistake. The first sign that I should have bolted. Or dragged one of the players into a closet instead.

I should be fucking a guy in some room in this house, preparing to walk away, knowing I have a story for tomorrow. The perfect title too.

First mistake: Don't forget to Play Hard to Get. Or *Don't Fall for the Guy You Fuck on the First Night.*

The story could write itself. We all know that rule.

Asking a guy I actually might like if he wants to have kids while half naked and lying in bed with him? Yeah, no, this is new territory for me.

The strangest thing is that as my stomach flips in anticipation, as I wait for his freaked-out response, I can't help but wonder what my own answer would be. Do I want kids?

Two hours ago, I would have said that I've never considered it. It wasn't an absolutely not. I just never put real thought into it.

Kids need stability. A parent who has their shit together. A partner, maybe; a career, definitely.

A woman who'll lose her job and her apartment if she doesn't do something drastic like ask the hottest guy ever if he wants to have kids is not the kind of person who is ready for that kind of responsibility.

"Do I want kids?" Camden echoes, his expression unreadable.

I nod, barely keeping that straight face in place.

He runs his hand through his short hair, probably trying to figure out how the fuck to get me out of his bed and back down to the party. "Um." He shrugs. "I used to."

"What?" It's the only word my scrambled brain can come up with.

His blue eyes cut to mine and soften as he takes me in. "I always figured I'd play in the NHL, meet a girl like my friends did, and eventually retire and start a family. I'd have a whole other life waiting for me after hockey."

I'd like to say it's the journalist in me that continues to prod, but the curiosity is genuine. "But that didn't happen?"

His eyes fall shut and he rests his head against the headboard. "Nope."

"Why?"

"I was a fuck boy who couldn't get out of my own way." His lashes flutter open and his eyes dart to mine, but his head remains tipped back. "Guess I figured if I stopped trying, it wouldn't hurt so much if no one chose me."

The words speak to me at a cellular level. My constant use of sarcasm to deflect deep emotions. My use of sex to avoid real connection.

When I adjust myself, moving to straddle him, and press a hand to his chest, it's not to distract him, or myself, with sex. "Did it work?"

"Hmm?" His focus drifts to my lips and his palms move to my bare thighs.

"Did losing out on what you wanted hurt less when you stopped trying?" I clarify.

He shakes his head, his attention darting away.

"Does it hurt right now?" I whisper, inching closer.

"Nothing hurts when I look at you." His eyes are on me again, his words strangled, like he doesn't want to believe them yet can't stop himself from saying them.

It's odd, because I feel the same way.

"I bet it would be even better if you kissed me," I prod softly, bringing my face closer to his.

One side of his mouth slants up. "Oh yeah?"

I nod.

He slides those warm, callused palms up my thighs and tilts his head so his mouth is lifted.

Rather than wait for him to make the move, I go for it. The kiss is soft at first. Gentle. Like we're learning one another. Introducing ourselves.

His fingers dig into my thighs. The slight pain only makes the moment hotter. When I roll my hips, his chest rattles with a deep groan. Pulling back, he blows out an unsteady breath and assesses me.

What I see in the depths of those blues can't be explained. Longing, desire, acknowledgment, acceptance.

I'm still processing it all when he brings a hand to my neck and presses a finger to my pulse point. I'm sure the rhythm is scattered and wild. It's how I feel. Desperate.

He watches me, eyes roaming, breathing deeply. "I'm going to devour you, baby girl."

"Please," I whimper, my core fluttering.

Then his mouth is on mine again, his tongue threading between my lips, his taste embedded in me, and I know I'll never be the same.

Chapter 10
Savannah

I SCRAMBLE to undo the buttons of his shirt, fingers trembling. I need to feel his skin. Need to see every inch of him.

Camden smiles against my mouth, a breathy laugh escaping him. "Need something, baby girl?"

Sitting back, I assess the gorgeous man beneath me. And he's exactly that. All man. Older, harder, sexier than anyone I've ever been with.

I'm determined to enjoy every second I have with him. I'm not foolish enough to believe I'll get a repeat of tonight.

"Strip," I order.

"As you wish." He grasps his shirt with both hands and yanks, ripping the buttons clean off, his grin wicked. As the buttons scatter, tapping the hardwood floor, I drink him in, surveying the tan skin covered in dark ink. Dozens of beautiful designs tattooed over defined muscle. Even lying down, without any effort at all, the man has a fucking eight-pack. An eight-pack.

Having never seen one in real life, I drag my nails over every ridge, memorizing detail after detail of the gorgeous man beneath me.

He's quiet, allowing me to take my fill.

"God, is there anywhere that isn't tattooed?" I drag my fingers down his stomach, tugging at his waistband.

"Go ahead, baby girl. Take Daddy's cock out"—he nods at his lap—"and find out."

I practically combust on the spot. Never in my life have I had the urge to call someone Daddy, and if another man called himself that, fuck no. I'd be dressed and out the door in under a minute.

But Camden Snow...Camden Snow could incinerate my nonexistent panties with just a look. When he calls me baby girl, I flush with heat. My core throbs and I'm coated in my own arousal.

"Are you telling me that your dick is decorated?"

"I'm telling you to take my fucking cock out," he says, an edge to his tone.

I whimper at the command, catching my lip between my teeth to hold myself together.

He hums in approval. "Now be a good girl and listen."

Shifting back, I fumble with his belt and zipper, my hands full-on shaking now.

He laces his fingers behind his head and watches me, his ripped shirt hanging open.

When I finally get his pants undone and tug on them, he lifts his hips, helping me fulfill his demand.

And when I peel his tight black boxer briefs down and discover what's hidden beneath, my mouth waters.

"Holy fuck."

Camden's chest rumbles with a pleased hum. "Like what you see?"

I run my finger over the dark, throbbing vein that runs up the underside of his shaft and relish the way it bobs in response, then lean in closer to study the elaborate piercings that are surrounded by the most glorious design.

"What is it?"

"A king's crown, a Jacob's ladder, and, of course, the clit stimulator." He smirks, still resting back, so damn proud of himself.

I eye the ring that runs through the ridge at his crown and the series of barbells along his shaft, as well as the one where the largest cock I've ever seen meets his pubic bone.

"And the tattoo?" I ask, studying the swirling black design snaking up the bottom of his shaft.

He huffs a laugh. "Looked fucking cool."

Heart pounding and excitement coursing through me, I smile up at him. "It does."

"Will look even better inside you, baby girl."

I roll my teeth over my lip again, a bout of nerves fluttering through me. I've never been with a man with one piercing, let alone seven. It's a bit intimidating. And that's before I take his size into account.

He's going to destroy me.

"Don't worry, we'll go slow." He sits up and wraps his arms around me, pulling me close. His warm lips fuse with mine, coaxing me into relaxing.

I push his tattered shirt over his shoulders, and he tugs mine over my head. Then I'm straddling him, both of us completely naked.

"There is not another woman on this planet as perfect as you." He caresses my tits, swirling his fingers around my nipples, plucking and groping.

My breasts are so heavy and so sensitive already. There's no way he won't be the death of me. Head dropped back, I roll my hips, moving seductively atop him just like the dancer did on me.

"Did you like how she felt?" he asks.

My core tightens at the memory. "You know I did."

I'm not shy when it comes to my sexuality. I find both men and women sexy, but this man? Everyone I've ever been with pales in comparison.

"That's it, baby girl. Roll that hot pussy all over me. Get me nice and wet."

Each metal rung of his piercings teases my clit as I gyrate over him. When he flicks my nipple with his tongue, liquid gushes between my thighs.

He hums in approval. "Fuck yes, baby girl. Squirt all over me. I wanna lick up every drop and then fuck you until every person in this house knows whose slut you are."

I whine. I'm a hussy for a dirty mouth, but call me a whore, and I'm on my knees in a second.

I'm sure a psychologist would have a field day with my brain, but I'd rather play with Camden Snow.

"You like that, baby girl? You like being Daddy's little whore?"

He clutches my hips, bringing my clit down on that pubic piercing, and bites down on my nipple and tugs. With a single thrust, he causes spots to dance in my vision. And with two more, along with those deliciously dirty words, I fall apart, coming hard, a scream ripping from my throat.

I'm still pulsing around absolutely nothing when he flips me onto my back and slides down my body until his shoulders are wedged between my thighs.

"Look at you, spasming for me." He peers up at me, blue eyes blazing. "You're aching, aren't you, baby girl? Need Daddy to kiss it better?"

I nod violently. Fuck yes. I need his mouth on me more than I need my next breath.

Holding my gaze, he lowers his face and presses the lightest of kisses against me.

My legs quiver beneath his touch, the heat in my core once again burning hot.

"Don't you dare close those eyes." His words have barely registered when his tongue meets my sex and he licks inside me. "Fuck, you taste so good."

Groaning, he covers me completely with his mouth, sucking and licking like he can't get enough.

I writhe beneath him, entranced by not only the feel of him, but by his sounds and the pure desire bleeding from him. He closes his eyes, wearing a look of pure ecstasy, like he's enjoying every second of this.

With a shaky exhale, I drop my head back. Holy shit. I don't know that I'll survive this.

The first slap takes me by surprise. A sharp, pleasurable pain.

I whip my head up, catching the moment he smacks my clit a second time.

"Did I say you could close your eyes?"

"N-no," I stammer, squirming beneath him. Not because I want to escape the pain, but because I want him to do it again.

"Look at you gushing for me. You love what I'm doing, don't you?"

"Yes," I breathe. "Please don't stop."

The smirk he gives me is almost evil. With a hand hovering above my aching center, he stares me down. "Are you going to keep those eyes open for me?"

I nod.

"Don't make me punish you again. You won't like what I do next time." He spears me with two fingers and thrusts violently. I jolt upward, unprepared for the roughness, but within seconds, I'm moaning and chasing my second orgasm.

"Squirt for me, baby girl. Feed Daddy, and then I'll give you my cock."

I explode. It's not rational. Every time he says that word, though—Daddy—I gush. He clamps down on that bundle of nerves and sucks until the spots in my vision overlap and I nearly black out.

The orgasm flows through me, like fire rolling through my veins. I'm burning alive and in need of more.

"Please," I beg, literal tears streaming down my face.

Camden crawls up my body and kisses my chin, then my cheek. Then he presses his mouth to mine. "Shh, baby girl, I got you. I'm going to give you everything you need."

The softness of his tone makes me gooey and more emotional. I claw at him, grabbing his hips, trying with all my strength to maneuver him so he's exactly where I need him.

"No," he growls.

Head dropped back, I pout.

"Not without a condom." He sits up on his knees. "You need to be safer. You should be asking questions. We should have a conversation first, talk about whether you're on birth control. Whether either of us has been tested. Don't just spread these legs for me like a little slut."

I whimper. Fuck. He's right. And I'm never this reckless. It's wild, what he does to me.

He backs away and digs a condom out of his nightstand. He's already rolling it on when he settles between my thighs again.

"Will it be safe with all those piercings?" I ask, a little of my good sense returning to me.

His lips tick up into a grin. "Good girl. That's a good question." He notches himself at my entrance, nudging in just a fraction. He pulls back out and does it again. And again.

I whimper in earnest.

"Yes, it's safe. It shouldn't rip. But if it does, I'm safe. I can pull up my test results on my phone if you want."

I shake my head, though in the back of my mind, a thought blooms. How much sex does this man have to so readily have that information available? The question should freak me out. Instead, I like that he's a man who knows what he wants.

And what he wants is me.

"Birth control?" He arches a brow.

"I'm on the shot."

He tucks his chin and focuses on where we meet, sliding in a little deeper, then pulling back again. "For now." The words barely register before he's pushing inside for real, pulling a moan from deep in my throat.

CHAPTER 11
CAMDEN

SAVANNAH SQUEEZES me like a fucking vise as I push inside her.

"Breathe, baby girl."

With the smallest of nods, she sucks in one breath, then another. On the third, I bury myself to the hilt, groaning as I find my new home.

I'm a forty-six-year-old man. I've had more than my fair share of sexual encounters, but nothing, and I mean not a goddamn thing, has ever felt this good.

Maybe it's the heat of her. Or how tight she is. Or maybe it's the whimpers that slip from her throat or the way she scratches at my skin, searching for purchase before I even start truly fucking her.

It's definitely her tits and the way they jiggle with the tiniest of thrusts. Those pink pebbled nipples that make my mouth water. They're magnificent. I can't wait for her to ride me so they can hit me in the face.

It's absolutely the color of her hair and how wild it is splayed out on my pillow around her head. And those damn green eyes. The way they watch me, seeking approval.

Though each detail is enough on its own to send my heart rate up another notch, on anyone else, they'd be ordinary. It's her. I don't understand it, but I'm old enough to know there's no point in trying.

Instead, I lean down and press my mouth to hers, moaning and biting and licking and sucking, enjoying the hell out of every second she's in my bed. Working myself in and out of her, ensuring my piercings hit all the right places. I use my hands, stimulating that sensitive clit and lavishing her breasts until she comes over and over again. I flip her over and fuck her from behind. Spank her ass. Lick her hole. Make her scream.

I fuck her in every position. Only when she's exhausted and completely wrung out do I force her to her knees, pull the condom off, and fuck her throat.

She's a dream, a goddamn sexual goddess. She keeps her eyes locked on mine and plays with my balls. She hollows out her cheeks and slips her finger in my asshole. Her teary eyes flash with triumph when I wrap her hair around my fist and come down her throat.

I black out from the pleasure, collapsing on the mattress with a groan.

I'm still trying to formulate words when she stumbles back from the bathroom, naked and fucking perfect.

When she bends over and picks something up off the floor, I sit up. "What are you doing?"

Over her shoulder, she hits me with a saucy wink. "Calling my friends. They've texted a hundred times asking where I am."

She turns back, and then a ringing sound echoes through my bedroom. She drops the device onto the bed and plucks her dress off the floor.

"Hello, hussy. Where the hell did you disappear to?" a woman says in greeting.

Laughing, she peers over at me. "Just finishing up. You gals ready to leave?"

I snatch the phone before her friend can respond. "Hello?"

"Um, hello?" she responds.

"Who is this?"

"Addie." The word is drawn out and full of confusion. "Uncle Cam, is that you?"

Savannah cackles as I slap my hand to my face and groan. "Yup."

"Okay," she says awkwardly.

Accepting that the damage has already been done, I jump in with both feet. "Savannah's not going to need a ride. She'll see you girls tomorrow."

At the foot of the bed, Savannah's mouth falls open.

Addie, on the other hand, giggles. "Okay, Uncle Cam. Take care of our girl."

I pull the phone away from my ear, and as I hit the End button, Savannah lunges for it.

"Wait!" she yells, but it's too late. "What are you doing?" she asks, her tone suddenly irritated as she snatches the phone from me.

I level her with a stern glare and hold out my hand. "Give me your phone."

I've lost all damn sense when it comes to her, but there's no turning back.

With a frown, she obeys. She's still naked, and though her dress is draped over the mattress in front of her, she makes no move to put it on.

I type in my number and save it to her contacts under just one name. Daddy. Then I call myself.

"What are you doing?" she asks again.

Focus fixed on her, drinking in her naked form, I leave myself a message. "Hi, Daddy, it's baby girl. I've just had the best sex of my life and I want to see you again. Tell Daddy hi," I say, holding the phone in her direction.

She snorts and rolls her eyes, but then in the sexiest rasp, she says, "Hi, Daddy."

"Good girl." I end the call and toss the device onto the floor. "Now get back in bed. There's no fucking way I'm done with you yet."

She glances at the door and then at her phone.

"*Savannah*," I warn.

Cheeks pink and eyes bright, she launches herself at me with a squeal.

Yeah, that's what I thought. This girl is mine, and I don't plan on ever letting her fucking go.

Chapter 12
Savannah

"OH, look, Savannah finally made her way home," Addie announces as I slink into her apartment at seven the next morning.

Addie lives a few blocks from Camden's place, so I took the worst walk of shame at six thirty, sneaking out of his room with my heels in my hand. When I opened the front door and the alarm beeped in warning, I rushed down the steps without looking back and ran a full block barefoot. When I could no longer see his house, I stopped and slipped on my shoes. Then, in the scandalous green dress, I walked through Boston, freezing my ass off, wishing I hadn't been such a tragic whore last night.

Tragic because I didn't leave like I should have after our first round. Nope. I went another four rounds. And in between, we talked. For hours.

God, I like him.

Like really like him.

"Need coffee and carbs, not necessarily in that order." I drop my shoes in the corner and rush for the couch where my friends are curled up with blankets and their own mugs.

I knew they'd be awake. Addie rarely sleeps past six, even if she's out late, because of her years of early hockey practices. Sutton could sleep for another seven hours, but she suffers regularly from major

FOMO, so if she hears a peep, she's up. Josie? She looks like she could fall asleep with her eyes open right now. She'll spend the rest of the afternoon napping.

I tug on the edge of Josie's blanket and plop down beside her, but she rolls to her side, taking her blanket and her warmth with her.

"You smell like sex."

Addie holds open her blanket, and I gratefully settle beside her. "You do smell like sex," she agrees, but rather than push me away, she passes her coffee to me. "So how was it?"

I shake my head and close my eyes. Then I take a slow sip and will the caffeine to do its magic.

"That good, huh?" Sutton teases.

"Hey, I'm doing this for you," I snap.

Her giggles ricochet off the walls. "Right, because it was such a chore to fuck Camden Snow all night."

I huff. Not in the slightest. It was incredible and amazing, and I'm going to be sore for at least three weeks. But yeah, definitely not a chore.

"I, for one, didn't sleep with anyone last night," Sutton says proudly. Her blond hair is piled high on her head, and somehow her makeup still looks perfect.

While I'm pretty sure I look like roadkill.

"And before you ask," she goes on, "I also didn't ask Royal what he wanted to name our future children."

With that one sentence, all my stupid comments from last night come rushing back like a fucking freight train. Fuck. Groaning, I drop my head back against the couch.

Josie perks up. "Oh my god, you asked Camden Snow what he wanted to name your kids?"

"No…" I mumble, mortification sweeping through me. I cover my face with my hands. "I asked if he wanted kids."

My friends break into squeals of laughter, kicking their feet and sending the blankets to the floor.

I swipe Addie's blanket and pull it over my head. "I know. It's so embarrassing."

Addie yanks the fleece away, the move causing my hair to cling to my face. "What did he say?"

"He said he used to," I murmur, hastily brushing my wild hair back.

"What?" Josie sits forward, zeroed in on me.

I glare at her. "He said he used to, and then he got all serious for a second."

"Oh my god," she squeals. "Does Camden Snow want you to have his babies? Did he breed you last night?"

I groan and pull the blanket over my head again. "No."

Sutton giggles. "You know what? I want to make a bet."

"No bets."

"Yes bets!" She squeals, and the blanket is ripped away again. "I bet that even when you do everything you say is wrong, you won't end up dumped."

"We'll see," I say, pulling out my phone.

Yeah, I snuck out of Camden's place. But the man has my number. He made sure of it. So if he wants to reach me, he knows how to find me.

Chapter 13
Savannah

Calliope's Column
It's Not Him, It's You (Kind Of)
Rule Number 1: Don't sleep with him on the first date. Or ask him if he wants kids during foreplay.

WITH A GROAN, I finish formatting the title and subtitle of my first article. Then I attach it to an email and send it over to copy for proofing. It's been six days, and I haven't heard a peep from Camden Snow.

I guess I did what I set out to do. Proved that no matter how strong a connection, some actions are just deal-breakers. And it only took a single date to do it.

Even after writing out precisely what I did wrong, I had my doubts. Because with him, it didn't feel like there was a single thing I could do wrong. But here I am. I finally understand how Sutton can feel blindsided. Is this the type of connection she has with every man she falls for? It can't be. Can it?

Then again, who am I to judge? I thought we had a real connection.

Something unique. And he didn't even call me after. Normally Sutton makes it at least a week or two with her guys before she scares them off.

Could his lack of contact have something to do with me sneaking out? Maybe. I suppose he might be angry about it. But he has far too much confidence to give up because of it. Plenty of men sneak out after one-night stands, so why can't women? And he has my number. So if he wanted to call, he would. It's dating 101. The feminine manifesto.

I refuse to be a pathetic cliché and reach out, asking why he didn't call. I'm not the exception, I'm the rule. We all are.

I fling myself back in my chair, making it roll back and hit the wall with a thud.

"What did the wall ever do to you?" Josie teases as she peeks over from her cubicle. Today she's wearing a chic black and white outfit. I'd look like a cow in the loose, flowy fabric, but she pulls it off well.

"Article's done," I say, making my tone light.

Josie arches a brow. "Really? So he seriously didn't call?"

My heart pangs, but I ignore it. "Nope."

"Huh." With a small frown, she shrugs. "Well, onto the next."

I sigh and sit up in my chair. "What are you talking about?"

"Your next date. Who's it going to be?"

Oh shit. I've been too busy licking my wounds—which is absolutely absurd—to even think about it.

It was one night.

I squeeze my hands into fists, and as I relax them again, I release all the negative energy pent up inside me.

She's right. It's time to move on.

"Come on," she says, heading out of her cubicle. "Let's get drinks. Then we'll find you your next victim."

"Addie specifically said no Langfields," I remind Josie as I follow her toward a booth in the back.

She peers over her shoulder and rolls her eyes. "Just walking down the street in Boston, you're bound to run into a Langfield. But yeah, you're definitely not going to date this one."

"What about me?" the shaggy-haired baseball player says as he turns, his face lighting up. When he clocks the two of us, the big brown eyes that are always bright and filled with mischief go wide. With a gasp, he practically hops over the back of the booth and slides in front of us.

"Fucking A, Finn. You're going to get us kicked out." JJ Hanson glowers at his friend, but then he schools his expression and nods a hello.

Ignoring JJ, Finn pulls us into a big hug, squishing us together. That's one of the things I love about Addie's older—and only—brother. He always includes me. He treats me like I grew up alongside him just like the rest of the girls.

It's also why, despite his position as the catcher for the Boston Revs and one of Boston's most eligible bachelors, I have zero interest in dating him. For real or for an experiment. "You don't mind, do ya, Ry?" Finn says to the hostess, who's watching us from a couple of feet away.

The pretty brunette shakes her head and points at JJ "You promised you'd keep him under control."

"I've got a four-year-old to control," he mutters. "I can only do so much."

As Josie pushes me into the booth, I smile at JJ "Where's Tabitha tonight?"

He presses his tongue to the inside of his cheek. Damn, looks like his wife's whereabouts is a touchy subject. "No idea."

"But Grandma Cat is excited about babysitting," Finn reminds him. "So you promised you'd actually relax."

He slides into the booth beside me, and now I'm sandwiched between two unavailable men. It's not exactly how we planned tonight, but I can't complain. I could use a little relaxation too.

"Where's Addie?" JJ asks.

"She's watching the twins for Win," Finn says with a huff.

Easygoing Finn's frustration makes me think this isn't the first or even second time JJ has asked about our best friend. Interesting. Honestly, if he wasn't married, I think he'd be perfect for Addie. But she'd kill me if I told her that. And he is married, and that's another one of our rules. No Langfields and no married men. Tonight I'm surrounded by both.

"Yeah, I think Scar is going over there to relieve her if she gets out of class early enough," Josie says of her younger sister Scarlett, who's in college.

Finn shrugs. "I offered to watch my favorite little guys too, but Win says I only get them more riled up."

I giggle. Finn, get kids more riled up? Can't say I'm shocked. "How old are they now anyway?"

"Four," he says, picking up his drink.

Four already. Damn. She's a badass. Not only is she raising twin boys by herself, but she's the CEO of the local MLB team, the Boston Revs.

"I have no idea how she does it," JJ says, voicing my thoughts. "I have enough trouble with one."

"Yeah, but Ave is the sweetest," Josie says with a genuine smile.

I've only met JJ's daughter a handful of times, but I'd agree with the sentiment.

"She's also obsessed with learning how to skate but doesn't listen to a thing I tell her," JJ grumbles into his drink.

I giggle. "You should ask Addie to help. She's a pretty good coach, I've heard."

JJ runs a hand through his thick brown hair and sighs. He's got these icy blue eyes that always throw me off-kilter. A man shouldn't be as pretty as he is. Especially a married one. "Maybe," he huffs.

Not only is he hot and married, he's grumpy too. But I'd be miserable as well if I was married to a woman who never made time for her family. From what I've heard, his wife Tabby seems more interested in partying with puck bunnies than being a mom. My heart hurts for the little girl. I may not have thought much about having kids, but I know that if I did, I wouldn't want to miss a second with my child. I'd never want a kid to feel the way I did. Unwanted. Unloved.

"You should talk to her," I press.

Avery deserves to have a person like Addie in her life. No matter how Addie feels about JJ, she'd step up and be the role model his daughter needs if asked.

"Yeah," he says, this time nodding like he might actually consider it.

"So what are we drinking?" Josie asks as she picks up a menu. "And who are we doing tonight?"

Finn rubs his hands together. "So it's that kind of night, huh?"

I shake my head and sigh. There's no way I'm having sex tonight. I already did the research for the article. But as I snag my own menu, an idea comes to me, and I straighten in my seat. "Oh, you're both men."

Josie shoots me a glare. "We already established that you can't do them."

JJ pushes back from me, like he really thinks that's what I'm after.

With a groan, I punch him in the arm. "I'm not going to seduce you, goalie. I'm doing research and I think you could help."

He rubs his arm and frowns. "How?"

Finn waggles his brows. "I'm down to be seduced if that's the kind of help you need. I'm a team player."

Josie smacks his chest. "Shut up, Little Langfield."

"I'm the same age as you."

"Doesn't matter," she says with a huff. "That's what my brother calls you, so that's your nickname. And no one is getting into Sav's panties."

True. Because once again, I'm not wearing any.

"And I don't need that kind of help," I say, keeping the panty info to myself. "What you could do to help, though, is give me a list of your turnoffs." I pull out my phone and swipe up on the screen, then navigate to the notes app.

Finn slouches. "I'd really rather discuss what turns me on."

"I haven't dated in a long-ass time," JJ mutters.

Josie breaks into a smirk. "Did you even date Tabby?"

"Ha ha," he deadpans. "But she's got a point. I didn't, so I'm probably not much help."

Sighing, I flop back against the booth. "Fine. Finn, that means you're my only hope. C'mon. I'm sure in all the time you've been chased by ball bunnies, you've met some crazies."

With a chuckle, he scratches his head, making his messy hair even more chaotic. "JJ probably has equally scary stories, but yeah, one time I walked into a hotel room to pick up a girl for a date, but when I got there, she had balloon animals all over the bed."

Humming, I take a minute to conjure the image. "I could actually see you liking that."

Finn's eyes light up. "The tiger was freaking phenomenal," he gushes. But a second later, his expression sours. "The balloon letters on the bed, though…The 'eat my pussy cat…'" He shudders. "Not so much."

A cackle escapes me before I can stop it. "Holy shit."

JJ bursts into laughter too. "I can totally see it."

"She was upset that I didn't appreciate her hard work." Finn shakes his head roughly, like he's trying to shake the memory from his mind.

"Dating in the Pinterest era," Josie mutters. "It's not for the faint of heart."

"Honestly, all I ever wanted was someone who was kind and good and who didn't care about my last name." JJ shrugs, his posture sagging.

Damn. I can't help but feel for the guy. What he's describing really doesn't feel like much, yet he clearly doesn't think that's what he got with Tabitha.

"Yeah, or someone who isn't obsessed with their ex," Finn says. "I've dated quite a few of those. Like I don't need to hear about your last date or your high school boyfriend who you are totally over," he adds, using a high-pitched voice.

"I once had a girl photoshop us on vacations together," Josie says, elbows on the table.

JJ barks out a laugh. "Oh fuck. Bobby dated a chick a few months ago who made an entire video of their future wedding."

I suck in a harsh breath. "No way."

Laughing, he pulls out his phone. "Give me a sec. I'll find it."

The sound of heavy boots tapping against the floor cuts through our laughter, drawing my attention. I turn toward the source and come face to face with a gorgeous man wearing a fuck-me smirk. As he approaches our table, I drink him in. He's got dark hair and a tan skin tone, and his whiskey-colored eyes are zeroed in on me.

"Theo, you made it." Finn waves the guy over.

I glance at Josie, whose jaw is just as slack as mine.

"Yeah, sorry I'm late. I was having drinks with my dad to celebrate the new barrel we're rolling out."

I arch a brow. "Barrel?"

Finn sits forward, nodding. "Yeah, Theo's family owns James Whiskey."

"You're Theo James?" My flabbers are ghasted.

Maybe I should have recognized him. The billionaire son of Cash James—the pretty boy NFL quarterback who wears cowboy boots to every game, the Cowboy Quarterback, as he's often called—is in almost every magazine. Every one but ours, I guess, considering that his aunt Catherine Bouvier, our editor in chief, is married to the owner of James Whiskey's biggest rival.

Yeah, definitely should have recognized him on the spot. Pretty sure he's even on a billboard just outside Lang Field. I think he's holding a bottle of whiskey in the photo. I know he's wearing his signature cowboy boots. I glance down at his feet now, confirming he's got them on. Yep. I almost ask if I can get a closer look at them. They're pretty famous. Maybe more than even him. Especially in the fashion world.

He holds out his hand to me, seemingly not realizing how interested I am in his footwear. "I am, and you are?"

"Your date for the night," Josie tells him.

Eyes flashing with amusement, he grins down at me. "Sounds like it's my lucky night, then."

I bite my lip and survey him, confirming that the interest there is genuine. I guess I'm going on another date.

As this gorgeous man leads me to the bar, though, my traitorous mind wanders to the last man who touched me. It's ridiculous, really. I doubt Camden has thought of me since our night together.

CHAPTER 14
CAMDEN

"THANKS FOR TONIGHT." Gemma waltzes past me, winking as she goes.

One by one, women in thin camisoles or bralettes and the shortest shorts ever created head for my front door.

I did not expect to be greeted by a house full of half-naked women when I got home, but I shouldn't be surprised.

"I thought your class was last night," I say to Cora as another of her friends appears at the top of the basement stairs.

I don't know her name, but there's no forgetting her face. She's the dancer from my party last week.

"Yeah," my sister says, "but it was so good we decided to have one more before I head back to Vegas." She tips her water bottle back and takes a long gulp.

Her friend stops in front of me, her expression curious. "Hey, Cam, your girlfriend here?"

Behind her, my sister nearly spits out a mouthful of water.

Can't blame her, I guess, since I haven't had a girlfriend in close to thirty years.

"Not tonight," I say, though I'm hoping to change that once this parade of women disappears.

The brunette who's wearing little more than she was the other night pouts. "Would you ask her to come to one of your sister's classes? I'd love to see her dance."

The thought is enticing, that's for sure. But while the memory of the other night is one I never want to forget, I'm not sure I want to share Savannah. At least not for a while.

I'm still irritated that she left while I was sleeping, though I guess it was just as well, considering my sister called while I was still blinking my eyes open. I was out of bed and on a plane within the hour, and I haven't stopped since.

"I don't even want to know," Cora mutters as her friend closes the front door behind her.

There's no fighting my smirk. "No, you don't."

Laughing, she drops her head back, her long blond hair swaying.

The sound is like a bolt of joy straight to my heart. Until a few years ago, I thought she'd lost the ability to laugh like that for good. We've come a long way since then, though.

"You have time for dinner?" she asks. "My plane doesn't leave until ten."

This is what I hate most about this arrangement. I fly home and she has to fly back.

My twin and I are finally on speaking terms after years of no communication, yet we can't have a true relationship because one of us always has to be in Vegas.

Fortunately for me, at least, Cora is willing to be there most of the time.

Still, I'm exhausted from my week there. The travel and less than desirable sleeping arrangements are nothing compared to the mental toll these weeks inflict.

"Yeah, but let me hop in the shower first."

An hour later, we step into a restaurant that's right around the corner from the arena.

"Camden," the hostess says when she spots me. "Want your usual table?"

She assesses my sister, probably trying to figure out whether this is a work thing or something a little more personal. I rarely come here without the guys, so her reaction isn't surprising.

"Sure. Thanks, Ry." I rest a hand on Cora's back and guide her toward the hostess stand. "This is my sister Cora."

As Ryanne leads us to our table, we pass person after person dressed in business attire. Most have probably just gotten off work and are starting their weekend off by letting loose a little. I, on the other hand, can't wait to get home to bed.

After some much needed rest, I'll call Savannah and make plans to see her again. Hopefully tomorrow night.

"A bunch of the guys are here, though I haven't seen any of the coaches tonight," Ry says as she guides us past the bar. I'm too tired to put on a smile and talk business anyway, so I keep my focus ahead, hoping like hell no one spots me.

"Oh," Cora whispers, her tone full of mirth. "Any players you can introduce me to? Wouldn't mind having a boy toy lined up for my next visit."

With a sharp exhale, I glare at my sister. Being a sex therapist means she's got zero filter, and she's a huge proponent of an age gap. I can only imagine what she'll have to say when she finally meets Savannah. It'll probably include a diatribe about how I'm working out some of my own daddy issues.

Dammit. I really don't want to have my sister's commentary in my head next time Savannah moans that name.

I've thought about it every night this week, while lying in bed alone. Before her, I'd never asked a woman to call me Daddy, but fuck if the moment she said it, my dick didn't grow a size.

"Cam," a deep voice calls from my left.

Since I've already been spotted, I force a smile and search for the source of the voice. My expression turns genuine when I discover Finn Langfield walking my way. I've known him since he was a kid. Back when he came to Bolts games to support his uncles, Aiden and Brooks. His mom married their brother Beckett, the CEO of the entire Langfield enterprise, when he was little. Kid is huge now, but he's still got the same affable personality.

"Finn, hey."

As he shakes my hand, he eyes my sister just like the hostess did. Yeah, it's rare I show up anywhere with a woman, and very few people know much about my personal life, including my twin's existence, so I understand the confusion.

"This is my sister Cora," I say. "Cora, this is Finn Langfield, catcher for the Boston Revs."

As she slips her hand into his, she smirks. "Large hands," she murmurs with a wink in my direction.

Fucking A.

"It's nice to meet you. I had no idea Cam had a sister," Finn says with a smile. "You want to join us? JJ's here, though I'm sure he'll bounce soon, and Bray just arrived with Bobby and Royal, and Ollie's on the way."

"Don't forget me," a female voice says from behind him.

When Josie peeks around his large frame, my first thought is of Savannah. Is she here too? My heart jumps as I covertly scan our surroundings.

"Hey, Uncle Cam," Josie says, leaning in and giving me a hug.

As I release her, she scrutinizes Cora, and I once again introduce her.

"Just you tonight?" I ask, hoping like hell no one catches on to my eagerness.

"Savvy was with us," Finn grumbles, "but Theo stole her away."

My damn heart drops. "Theo?" I scan the restaurant more thoroughly, searching for the redheaded vixen. What kind of game is she playing?

Josie grins. "Yup." She points to the bar. "Right over there. Aw, they look so cozy together. They'd make beautiful babies, don't you think?"

I whip back around, frowning at the sarcasm, only to find her smiling innocently. She was a lot fucking nicer when she was a kid.

Then, because I can't help myself, I turn back to the bar. And what I see has my blood running cold. Why the fuck does another man have his hands on my girl?

Chapter 15
Savannah

Calliope's Column
It's Not Him, It's You (Kind Of)
Rule Number 2: Talk About Yourself, Not Your Ex…and Definitely
Don't Flirt with him in Front of Your Date.

IT'S TRULY a pity that the men I've met for this project are so damn interesting.

I have a job to do, though, so unfortunately, Theo James and his beautiful smile will have to pay the price.

The key to all of this is to actually have chemistry with the person I chase away. Sutton is a desirable, intelligent woman. There's no way she doesn't recognize true chemistry.

Her issue is that she's too eager.

Tonight, my goal is to hook Theo. I'll flirt with him, get him to ask me on a date. Then the next time we meet, I'll flip the script. I'll cry on his shoulder, weeping about my ex. It'll be perfect.

I've got the title of the article written and everything.

Talk About Yourself, Not Your Ex.

I've mentally added Finn's balloon animal thing to my list of faux

78

pas, but I won't be using that technique on Theo fucking James. Just the thought of the mortification that would come along with it has my cheeks heating.

Fortunately, my goal tonight is to relax and flirt with him, which, it turns out, is not hard at all.

"So Vegas?" He hums, swirling the amber liquid in his glass. "Do you miss it?"

We're in the middle of the whole *where did you grow up?* portion of the get-to-know-you game. It's slightly unfair, I suppose, since everyone knows the Jameses are Boston royalty and that these are his stomping grounds.

"I prefer the seasons," I say honestly. What I don't mention is that the only way I'd return to Vegas is against my will, kicking and screaming the whole way. Every memory I have of that place is tinged with sadness.

He takes a sip of his whiskey, his eyes never leaving me. "Nashville's beautiful this time of year. You should come visit."

He plays for the pro team in Nashville, though he assures me he travels to Boston at least monthly, as if that's a future concern of mine.

"I'm more of a city girl."

He grins. "You ever been to Nashville?" he asks. "It is a city. And it's the perfect place to visit in the winter, when the weather is fucking miserable here."

I shake my head. "I love the winters here. Give me snow and a roaring fire any day of the week."

His eyes, the same shade as his drink, dip to my lips. "That could be arranged."

I swallow back a huff. Only a billionaire would assume he could manipulate the fucking weather to get a woman into bed.

I take a sip of my vodka soda, chastising myself for being so judgmental. He's a nice guy, and he's making an effort to get to know me. I'm supposed to be flirting with him so I can get that much-needed date.

It wasn't this hard with Camden. Not even close. The conversation flowed so easily. It may have turned ridiculous at points, but there were no awkward silences and no grasping for topics to discuss.

Here I go again, thinking of the man who's already forgotten me.

"I'm a big fan of music, though," I say, pushing thoughts of Camden from my mind. "So I'm sure I'd love Nashville."

"So you haven't been, then?"

"Nope. I haven't traveled much. I moved here after college and never left."

"And outside of working for my aunt," he asks, "what do you do for fun?"

"Pole dancing," I say with a smile.

Of course, that answer immediately makes me think of Camden again. This is getting absurd.

Coughing, Theo sets his glass down a little too hard. "What?"

A laugh bubbles out of me. "I take pole dancing classes at a gym down the street from my apartment. It's a really good workout."

He breaks into a smile so pretty it hurts. "I'm sure it is. Maybe I should try it. You think you could show me how to do it?"

Shrugging, I bite down on my lip, turning up the flirtation a notch. "I'm sure that could be arranged."

"The fuck it can," a low voice growls.

Before I can turn, my chair is being yanked back. I'm gripping the seat on either side of me to keep from wobbling when a hard-jawed Camden Snow comes into view.

His tone shouldn't make me wet. The possessive attitude is ridiculous after he failed to call me for six freaking days. Yet I have to squeeze my thighs together so I don't leave a mark on the seat.

"What the fuck?" Theo says from my other side. "Savannah, do you know this guy?"

"This guy," Camden grits out, his expression lethal. "Go on, baby girl, tell him who I am."

The way my mouth almost forms the word should be criminal. I will not say it. He doesn't get that title.

Has he lost his damn mind? Have I?

I flatten my lips. I don't trust my slutty mouth to behave.

"Camden, what the hell?" A blond appears at his side, fingers wrapped around his bicep, and tugs him backward.

It's exactly the glass of water my libido needs to be doused with. Of course he's here with another woman.

The nerve of this man.

With absolute daggers in his direction, I say to Theo, "Yeah, unfortunately, I do know him." Sitting taller, I pull my shoulders back. "This is Camden Snow. As you can see, he's a bit older than us, so maybe he's a little senile. I guess he forgot that our time together came to an end quite a while ago."

Camden's blue eyes go glacial as he shakes off the woman at his side.

Rather than get upset, the blond throws her head back and laughs. "Oh, this one's a keeper." Blue eyes bright, she smiles at me. "Don't mind my brother. He's had a rough week, and he's a terrible flier." She holds out a slim hand. "I'm Cora."

Her brother?

And what does she mean by *terrible week*?

I hate that my attention immediately snaps back to him. Even more, I despise the concern that overtakes me when I note the dark circles under his eyes.

Jaw flexing, he looks away from me.

The disappointment in his expression hurts more than it should. He has no right to be upset with me. He never called, and I'm not doing anything wrong.

The two of us are not in a relationship. We spent one night together, and he hasn't reached out all week. Having a drink with someone of the opposite sex is completely acceptable. Appropriate, even.

"I'm Savannah," I mutter, unsuccessfully trying to force a friendly expression to my face.

"Well, Savannah, I hope this isn't the last time we meet," Cora says.

Beside her, her brother scoffs, avoiding eye contact.

A wave of annoyance rolls through me. What the hell? How is it that I'm the bad guy?

Before I can ask him what his issue is, he grabs his sister's arm and tugs her toward the door without looking back.

Leaving me to wonder, what the hell just happened?

Chapter 16
Savannah

THIS IS the dumbest thing I've ever done.

Glancing over my shoulder, I pull my jacket tighter around my body, fighting the bitter midnight cold.

Yeah. Definitely a stupid idea. I pull out my phone and navigate to the rideshare app. Why didn't I ask the driver to wait until I confirmed Camden was home?

Of course I'd actually have to ring the doorbell to do that. But then he'd know I've made this idiotic gesture. That I'm standing outside his house in the middle of the night because I can't shake the uneasiness swirling in my chest. The fear that I did something wrong.

I've never felt this type of guilt before. Probably because I've never owed anyone an explanation for my whereabouts.

My mother never cared where I went, my father was long gone by the time I was old enough to go anywhere alone, and I've never had a boyfriend who cared enough to be concerned about me.

Not that Camden Snow is my boyfriend.

God. I tip my head up and silently curse at the night sky. Why is dating so confusing?

I've never understood Sutton as well as I do in this moment. With a sigh, I request a ride. Then I click out of the app and text her, figuring she won't see it until morning.

> Me: Current me would like to say sorry to past you for being so judgmental. This dating crap is hard.

My phone lights up with a response immediately.

> Sutton: Apology accepted. And I feel you girl. BUT I took your advice and played the game last weekend, and I have a date with Royal tomorrow night!

I'm smiling down at the screen when a burst of wind hits me, the icy blast burning my cheeks and making me shudder.

When my phone buzzes again, I expect it to be Sutton. Instead, another name pops up, striking me stupid.

> Daddy: Are you going to ring the doorbell, or am I going to have to warm your ass up with my palm to stop you from shivering?

A loud gasp escapes me.

Did he just…?

Also, he seriously put himself in my phone as Daddy? I don't know how I missed that. What an egotistical asshole.

And what the fuck is wrong with me that I'm once again turned on by his attitude?

> Daddy: You have five seconds to make up your mind before I make it for you.

I scoff and glare at the door, searching for the camera. "You wouldn't."

"Wanna bet?" The garbled words come from a speaker on a panel near the door.

Head dropped back, I huff. Asshole.

At the sound of a car turning down the street, I straighten, formulating a plan. He thinks he can order me around? Joke's on him. He's about to watch me leave.

"Savannah." The bark is louder this time. The door swings open, and the man himself appears, lit from behind.

Without a word, I turn on my heel and stomp toward the road, where a dark car is approaching.

"You're not getting in the car with a stranger at midnight," Camden commands from behind me.

I wave my phone over my head. "His name is Ron, and he's not a stranger; he's on the app."

He makes a noise that sounds like a growl. "Can we stop playing these games for a minute? It's not safe."

I whip around and cross my arms, once again fighting the icy wind. Games? He thinks I'm playing games?

I don't play games. I don't even know why the hell I'm here right now. He's the one messing with my head. Telling me he's not done with me, then not calling, then getting pissed when he sees me out with someone else.

"Yeah, I'm all set with whatever this is," I say, motioning between the two of us. "I've gone twenty-seven years without being told what to do, and you're not my father, so cool it with this whole fake concern. I'll be just fine."

I spin and continue toward the car that's pulled up to the curb.

Before I can open the door, I'm lifted off the ground and flipped upside down. I barely have a chance to scream *what the hell?* before Camden's palm makes contact with my ass. "You're damn right I'm not your father. I'm your goddamn Daddy, and you're being a brat."

"Ma'am, are you okay?" the driver calls through the window. "I'm calling the police."

Camden turns his back to the road so that I'm facing the driver. "Tell him you're fine."

I shove myself up, my hands splayed on Camden's back, and sigh, the annoyance flowing through me growing stronger. Yeah, I'm irritated as shit by Camden's ridiculous behavior, but I don't actually want the driver to call the police.

"Just a little argument with my…" I almost say daddy. I seriously want to punch myself repeatedly in the face. "Date," I grind out. "We're fine. Sorry to bother you. I'll put a hundred percent tip on the ride. Thank you!"

The guy stares me down, brows furrowed like he's not sure I'm telling the truth.

With one hand braced on Camden's lower back, I wave. "Seriously, I'm fine." Though the blood rushing to my head is making my brain a little foggy. "Could you put me down?" I hiss to my captor.

"I will when we get inside."

I bounce with every step he takes, my eyes level with his amazing ass. And yes, noticing that right now is strange, but it's seriously incredible. Like a bubble, except he's tall and large, so it's perfectly proportional with the rest of his body.

I actually consider taking a bite out of it before I catch myself and curse under my breath.

I will not bite Camden Snow's ass.

Only when we're in his living room does he flip me back over and ease me onto the couch. Then he takes a good ten steps back, heaving a breath, like he's just realized how absurd he's being.

He should be embarrassed by the behavior. He's a grown-ass man.

Honestly, I'm embarrassed. I don't understand the effect he has on me, and I don't know how to make it stop.

"Can I get you something to drink? Tea?" He runs his hand through his short hair and turns one way, then the other, his movements jerky, like he doesn't know what to do with himself.

While he's freaking out, I search for something to focus on that isn't the gray sweats hanging low on his hips. Or his bare tattoo-covered chest. Or the eight-pack I'd like to lick again.

See? There we go with the absurdity again.

I'm borderline feral for him and I hate myself for it. Because while

I'm eye-fucking every inch of the man, he can barely look me in the eye.

"No, seriously," I say, my cheeks flaming. "I'm sorry I showed up here. I'll see if one of my friends can pick me up." I stand and shuffle to the door, unlocking my phone as I go.

I'm sure Addie will come get me. I feel bad waking her, but she only lives a few blocks away.

Camden groans, the sound loud enough to echo around the enormous room. "Why are you determined to piss me off?"

"What does that even mean?" I spin back to him, hands on my hips. "I apologized and offered to get out of your hair."

He stalks toward me, fists balled at his sides, jaw clenched.

On instinct, I take a step back, then another, stopping only when I bump into the door.

"Does it look like I want you to leave?" he grits out. "I just dragged you inside." He slaps his palm to the wall beside my head and heaves in a rough breath. "Fuck, you make me want to put you over my knee and spank some sense into you."

As heat floods my veins, I jut my chin. "So do it."

His attention drops to my lips, but only for a second before his eyes are locked with mine. "Baby girl, you have to stop with these games." Slowly, he angles in and brushes his stubbled cheek with mine. When he ghosts his mouth over mine, I suck in a breath, trying to steal a taste.

It's irrational how fiercely I need this man.

"What if I don't know how?" I whisper.

His blue eyes flare with heat. "Then I'm going to be forced to teach you a lesson."

I press my chest into his and nip at his lips, tugging on his bottom one until he groans. "Okay, Daddy."

CHAPTER 17
CAMDEN

MY COCK STRAINS against my sweats. Fuck. I'm dying to get inside this infuriatingly beautiful woman.

Instead, I suck in a breath, holding tight to the modicum of control I still possess.

Today has been a complete mindfuck. After my flight home, the encounter at the bar, and putting up with my sister on the drive to the airport, I'm fucking exhausted. But there was no way I was gonna sleep when I got home. Not when this woman consumed my thoughts. Now, I'm running on pure adrenaline and nothing else.

I press my hips to hers so she can feel what she does to me, and with my mouth on hers, I murmur, "The problem is you want the punishment too much. And it wouldn't be right for me to reward your bratty behavior."

Green eyes flaring with anger and heat, she pushes against my chest.

I don't budge. "You're only making it worse for yourself, Savannah."

She lifts her chin defiantly. "Fine. Then tell me how I can make it better."

I push off the wall and pad to the couch. When I'm settled on it, I lean back and spread my legs wide. Then I pat my thigh. "Face down, ass up. Now."

She stares at my lap, the war raging in her head nearly visible. She doesn't want to like this. Doesn't think she should. But we both know that whatever the hell is brewing between us is too damn strong to be snuffed out. And I for one am too fucking tired to fight against it tonight.

Still, I'm surprised when she pulls off her coat and drapes it on the side of the couch, then shuffles over and stands between my knees. "You want me to lay down?"

I swipe a pillow from the end of the couch and set it on the cushion beside my hip. "Head here." I tap my lap next. "Ass here." Then I slap the other side of the couch. "Legs here."

She rolls her eyes.

I tsk, stretching my arms out along the back of the couch. "That's just going to earn you another smack."

"How many are we at now?" she mumbles as she settles into the position I requested.

The moment she's in my lap, her warm weight covering me, her head turned so she can see my face, her eyes on mine in beautiful submission, all the stress from the last week begins to recede.

I set one palm atop her ass and brush her beautiful red hair back from her face with the other.

Her eyes fall shut and her body sags, like she's also feeling a sense of relief despite her position.

"That depends on you."

Her eyes flutter open. "Me?"

"Yes. Tell me how many men you've been out with since I was last inside you."

"You want me to…to…" She stumbles over her words, her eyes searching mine. "To tell you about other men?"

My stomach rolls at the idea that there've been more than the one from tonight, but I nod.

She grits her teeth, like that internal battle has picked up again. Like she wants to tell me to fuck myself, but also, she doesn't. "Just Theo."

Theo. The name alone makes my vision go red.

I tug at her skirt, exposing her bare ass. "No panties again?"

"I'm sorry," she mumbles, true remorse in her tone.

It's too late for that, though. I pull my hand back, and it lands against her ass with a loud thwack. "That's for Theo."

She sucks in a sharp breath, but she doesn't look away from me and she doesn't flinch. With a deep breath in, I wind up and do the same to the other cheek. "And that's for no panties."

The way she holds my gaze only serves to make me harder. Fuck.

Breathing unevenly, she says, "I told him I'd go to dinner with him tomorrow."

Another crack. This one turns her skin a perfect shade of pink. "Did he touch you?"

She shakes her head quickly, but the movement stops abruptly, and she groans. "Well, he kissed my cheek."

Another smack.

She moans this time.

"Did you want him to kiss you anywhere else?"

She bites her lip.

"Savannah."

"No." She shakes her head, the movements jerky.

"Are you lying to me?"

"No. I just…" She squeezes her eyes shut.

I drag in a harsh breath. Fuck, if she tells me she—

"I want you to keep doing that."

My eyes fly open. "What?"

"The spanking." She wiggles her ass, practically humping my lap. "I—" She sighs. "I want to piss you off so you keep spanking me. I don't want you to stop until I come."

A wave of pleasure rolls through me. Confidence too.

I squeeze her cheeks, massaging them roughly. Damn, she feels good. I love that she's got real meat on her. That she's not all muscle or bones. I slip a hand between her thighs, humming. "Are you wet for me, baby girl?" I drag my fingers through her silky perfection, and a groan of satisfaction works its way out of me.

Hell yeah. She's absolutely soaked.

"Yes. More. Please," she whimpers.

As a thought strikes me, I spear her with one finger.

She squeals, her back arching, her breathing turning even more ragged.

"I have an idea," I murmur, stopping all movement but keeping my finger in place.

"Okay," she pants, grinding her hips, trying to fuck herself on my hand.

I pull out before she can get too carried away, then curl over her, bringing my mouth to her ear. "Tell me the name of every man you've fucked, and I'll spank you once for each of them."

Her breath catches and her eyes fly open. "What?"

I press a kiss to her cheek. "Come on, baby girl. I wasn't born yesterday. I know you haven't only been a slut for me."

Eyes wide, she assesses me. That fight is back. She wants to curse me out. Wants to tell me I'm an asshole. She'd be right. But I've fucked plenty of women in my life, so I have no room to judge. And fuck knows why, but I need this information. I want to know everything about her. I want to erase the memory of every other man she's ever been with. Spank her until she can't even think their names without remembering the orgasm I'm going to give her tonight.

After tonight, when she thinks about sex, I'm going to be the only man she ever associates with it.

"Why?" she says, because she's still fighting this connection.

"Because I'm going to fuck their names from your memory, baby girl. After tonight, you're going to know the only man you belong to is me."

She hums, her body quaking. She loves this as much as I do.

"Tim. Sophomore year in the back of his car. He never made me come."

Tim. I want to fucking kill him. I drop my hand to her ass with a loud crack.

She whimpers. "Um, Landon." Her eyes fall shut. "He was a senior in college and my TA my freshman year. He talked me into blowing him a few times after class, and I think we fucked twice in my dorm."

Jaw clenched, I take out my anger on her extremely red ass.

"Senior year, I had a boyfriend. Dean. We fucked a lot—"

I spear her with my finger again, and she grinds against me like she did before. I let her chase her orgasm until her walls flutter, signaling that she's close. Then I pull back and smack her ass again.

"Fuck," she whines.

"Who else?"

"Um, a dozen or so one-night stands since I've moved to Boston. Maybe more." She lifts her ass like she's waiting for the rapid series of smacks she's absolutely going to receive.

"How many of them made you come?" I demand.

"Um, three," she pants. "No, wait. Kacie definitely did, so five, I think."

"Kacie?"

"She's in my pole dancing class. We fucked around a few times."

Jealousy rears its ugly head. "Currently?" I don't like the idea of her with anyone else. I don't give a fuck whether it's a man or a woman.

She shakes her head. "No."

"And whose pussy is this?" I spear her again, not bothering to be gentle.

"Yours," she says like the desperate slut I want her to be.

"Count for me." I smack her once, then again and again. One for every person who's been lucky enough to have her.

When she gets to twelve, she's a crying mess, humping my leg and in need of the orgasm she's more than earned. I drag her along the couch, face down, and maneuver her so that I'm between her legs. Then I swipe my tongue against her sore flesh, kissing away the sting. She's squirming again when I lick her from front to back and panting out curses when I lift her hips and dive back in, eating her from behind.

She wiggles that perfect ass in my face, chasing her orgasm, and when I finally give her two fingers, curling them and pressing down in just the right place, she screams into the couch cushion and soaks my face.

I lick up every drop of her, relishing her taste, her scent, her warmth. Then I tug down my pants, drop to the couch, and pull her onto my aching cock.

She's wrung out already, her body limp, her head on my shoulder with one arm draped lazily up and around my neck.

Groaning, I slip a hand beneath her shirt and pluck at her nipples beneath her bra while I fuck up into her. She feels like heaven, her tight heat squeezing me in response to every thrust. Her little moans spur me on, and when she digs her nails into my thighs, bracing herself on top of me, my vision tunnels and I barrel toward an explosive release.

"See, baby girl?" I say, gritting my teeth to stave off my orgasm. "We were meant for one another. Tell Daddy how much you love his cock."

"I love your cock," she whimpers, head whipping from one side to the other, body thrashing.

"Tell me you're sorry for saying yes to Theo tonight."

"So sorry."

"Yeah, you are." I thrust up into her with force, the base of my spine tingling, my vision darkening. "You're glad that I interrupted you, aren't you?"

She cuffs my neck again and arches into me, riding me backward. "Yes."

"And why is that, baby girl? Why do you need Daddy?"

"Because you can fuck me better!"

With those dirty promises flying from her lips, the two of us fall apart, coming in waves, over and over again.

Chapter 18

Savannah

"WHY DIDN'T YOU CALL?" I can't hold the words back any longer.

I didn't dare attempt to leave after we had sex. If I did, it would only lead to another punishment, and as delicious as being spanked by Camden was, I'm going to be sore for a week.

After, he carried me upstairs and took me into the shower. He gently cleaned me from head to toe and then guided me to lie face down on his bed. He pulled a bottle of oil out of his nightstand, and after rubbing me down with it, climbed in beside me and pulled me to him.

Snuggled up to him like this, I swear I've never been so cozy. The man's chest may be pure muscle, but it makes an excellent pillow.

"I was planning on it. I just had a busy week and didn't expect you'd be out with someone else so quickly."

His scolding tone, while hot downstairs, is really annoying right now.

"How was I supposed to know you were still interested?" I snap. "You had my number. You said you'd call and then you didn't."

Do I sound like Sutton? Maybe. But why does this have to be so hard?

Brow furrowed, he stares down at me. "It's been a week."

"Exactly, it's been a week. What the hell was I supposed to think when I didn't hear a peep from you?"

He presses his lips together, eyes searching mine, like he's really considering the question. Finally, he pulls in a harsh breath, like maybe he finally gets my point. "Fuck, I—" He groans and drops his head back against the pillow. Then he blows out a breath and turns to face me, his blue eyes intense and full of honesty. And maybe a little bit of remorse. "Baby, remember how I said I never date?"

I nod.

"I don't know how to do this."

"Do what?"

"Date. Show you that I'm interested. I thought you knew, but apparently I didn't make that clear enough last week. I'm sorry." He brushes a thumb over the apple of my cheek. "Because since the second I met you, you've been on my mind. I'm just not used to having a person in my life who cares to hear from me."

I nibble on my lip. "I get that."

He presses a kiss to my forehead, sighing. "I hate that you know what I mean. Hate that you've been made to feel unimportant, because I can tell you right now that you are incredibly important to me, and we've only just met."

I roll those words over in my head, considering whether I believe them. I understand not being good at dating, but there are simple golden rules that apply to everyone. If someone cares, they call. It's not hard.

Then again, we just met. He couldn't actually care that much. And why should I want him to?

I swallow that thought back. I don't have enough brain power to deal with that tonight. It's after two, and I'm beyond spent.

Still, I can't help but push back a little bit. "You didn't have five minutes to text me? To let me know you'd been thinking about me?" The moment I ask the question, I wish I could take it back. Or maybe I don't. Maybe I want to push. "Just seems a little convenient that you're upset after catching me with another man after not talking to me for a week. Seems more like possessive shit than actual caring, if I'm honest."

He strums his fingers through my hair gently. "I know this is going to sound like a cop-out, but I had to go home, and when I'm there, it takes every ounce of energy I possess not to slip into a really dark place."

My chest aches at the pain in his voice. "Why?"

Eyes falling shut, he shakes his head. "Can I take a rain check on that for now?"

I offer him a gentle smile. From his tone and the agony etched on his face, the topic is a heavy one. And we're not there yet. We probably never will be, since I'm supposed to be pushing him away. "Of course."

He continues playing with my hair like it's as soothing to him as it is to me. "I thought about you a lot while I was there. You were the one bright spot in my whole week. When I say I don't date, I mean I've never allowed myself to. Not for a really long time, at least. But with you." He shakes his head, studying my face. "I can't help but want everything."

My heart trips over itself. "Why me?"

His blue eyes fill with wonder as he examines me like I'm a treasure. Like he can't get enough. "Because you're the first person who's ever looked at me like you need me too. And the last thing I want is to let you down."

While another woman might be offended by the admission or assume he pities her, my instincts tell me that our connection is different. Unique. He wants to protect me. He's referring to the unexplainable bond between us. One that makes it natural for him to want to be there for me.

And I feel the same way. Like I want to allow him to care for me, like in letting him do so, I'm caring for him as well.

I've never been the girl who wanted a man to save her, but maybe I've always longed for someone who cares. And it's clear that Camden does.

I'm supposed to be pushing men away, but that's the last thing I want to do when it comes to him.

What the hell am I going to do now?

CHAPTER 19
CAMDEN

Cora: I saw Tara…

Me: Fuck. I'm sorry, Cor. Do you want to talk? What happened?

Cora: No. I just thought you should know.

Me: Are you okay?

Cora: Yeah. It's been almost thirty years. I should be over this.

Me: But you aren't. Neither am I. And you're usually the one saying that it's okay not to be.

Cora: Ha ha. The student becomes the teacher.

Me: I had a really good teacher.

Cora: You seem…okay. Is it the girl from last week?

Me: It just might be.

Cora: Wow…I didn't expect you to be so…

Me: Yeah, me neither.

Me: It's so unexpected. Being this happy. I think I'm finally ready to take something for myself.

Cora: Oh shit. Okay, this is real.

Me: Yeah, I think it is.

Cora: I wish Mom would come to Boston with me. I wish we could spend the holidays with you. I'm so happy for you. And you're right. It's okay that this is still hard for me, but I'm happy that you're allowing yourself to have some joy. You deserve it. And if I haven't said it, you aren't to blame. For any of it. Tara, the affair, Dad's death. It happened to all of us. You're not to blame.

I DON'T RESPOND. As much as I appreciate the sentiment and have done the work in therapy to make peace with the past, she's wrong. I was to blame for a lot of it. I was too selfish, too much of an asshole, too young and too stupid to care about anyone but myself.

But I'm not that person anymore.

Or at least I'm trying not to be.

And the last thing I'm going to do is waste any more time thinking about Tara. That woman was a terror on my heart. The last time I really let myself think about her was years ago. The last time I saw her. And it did a number on me. Because she was with the daughter that, if given the chance, she would have passed off as mine.

My stomach twists. Back then I had no interest in being a father, and I thank God that I wasn't tied to that woman for life because of a child.

Though I can't help but feel bad for her daughter. She got stuck with the two most self-destructive and selfish people I've ever met: my ex-best friend and Tara.

When I walked in on my girlfriend with my best friend, it was like my soul left my body and I was watching the scene play out from overhead. Jeremy had been dating my sister for years. I'd always thought he was a good guy.

And I thought Tara was it for me. The four of us were inseparable.

Apparently they were a little too close.

I squeeze my eyes shut, banishing the thoughts from my brain. More than two and a half decades later, it still hurts. And it still makes it hard to trust people. To let them in.

"They're looking good out there," War says, pulling me from my morbid thoughts.

With a look his way, I nod. "Yeah, they're one hell of a team, but they'll be better if we get Mav and Becks out there next year."

I came down to watch the Bolts practice this morning because I'm meeting with Gavin after to discuss the prospects for this year's draft.

War arches a brow. "Does that mean you've found someone to date for the next three months?"

With a shake of my head, I turn back to the ice. I'd like to say I'd forgotten about the damn bet. In fact, I wish I had. But it's been haunting me. The bet has nothing to do with Savannah, and vice versa. But there's no doubt that if I'm gonna date anyone, it's her.

"Oh shit. There's really a girl." He chuckles, the sound deep and loud, drawing the attention of Gavin and Aiden, who are out on the ice with the team.

"What girl?"

I turn to my other side and discover that Daniel has joined us. He's wearing a smirk like he knows precisely what girl. He and his wife were there that night, and ever since, they've been harassing me via text nonstop about how I disappeared from my own party like a caveman.

I did, and I don't regret it for a second.

What I do regret is getting myself into this situation with this damn bet, but here we are.

"Could the two of you at least try to focus? I'm working here," I grumble.

Daniel laughs. "I don't think I've ever seen him with a crush."

Though I refuse to look at him, War's watching me with an intensity I can feel. "Me neither. A different girl a night, sure."

"Sometimes two," Daniel teases.

I close my eyes and grit my teeth. "I'd be happy to talk to your wives about all the one-night stands you fuckers had—"

Daniel laughs, a goofy grin on his face. "Oh, my wife knows I was a playboy."

War folds his arms across his chest, chin lifted. "And I got my wife's name tattooed on my balls. She knows she owns me."

"Okay," I say, drawing the word out. "So you understand that when you meet the girl, the past doesn't matter."

"Holy fuck," Daniel hollers, startling the shit out of me. "Did he just say *the* girl?"

"He fucking did," War crows.

"If the three of you are gonna continue gossiping like teenagers," Gavin shouts from the ice, "then move along. I'm trying to lead practice over here."

I shrink under the glare of our former coach. The other guys do too. Never did like disappointing him.

Only now do I realize that the guys on the bench are all watching us, and Brayden's chewing on his mouthguard with a fucking smirk on his face.

"Sorry, Coach," we say in unison.

With a huff, he shakes his head and turns back to the team. "Okay, show's over. Go get showered and get some rest. These next two weeks are going to be brutal."

The guys start collecting their gear and heading toward the tunnel, but before they get far, Coach whistles.

"And if I hear that any of you break curfew, I'll have your heads."

That's something these guys do regularly. They're young and stupid, and not one of them is married yet.

Back when I joined the team, almost everyone was single. But I swear, once Brooks fell for Sara, the rest toppled like dominoes. All but me, I guess. And fucking around lost its thrill when I was on my own, so hockey became my focus. The rest of the guys were damn dedicated too, and we've got three cups to show for it. We had a pretty fucking great run, though it's been a decade since we've carried the cup around this rink, and Gavin is looking for one more before he hands over the reins to someone else. Likely Aiden, though I'm not sure if he actually wants the title of head coach. Only time will tell, I guess.

If we're gonna get that championship, I need to do my fucking job and get Beckham Warren and Maverick Hall on our team. Wish we could have convinced Addie Langfield to wear the Bolts jersey too, but she'll do a hell of a job as goalie coach.

"When can we meet her?" War asks.

I smirk, knowing my next words will earn me a smack to the back of my head. "You have met her."

He frowns. "I have?"

"She's a friend of Josie's," Daniel says with a shit-eating grin.

"She's what?" War's blue eyes sharpen as he looks from me to Daniel and back again. "Like, she's Josie's age?"

"I'd like to remind you that we're not as old as you," Daniel says.

Fucker may irritate the shit out of me some days, but he's got my back. No one in my life, other than Cora, has been as good to me as he has.

War's muscles tense, his jaw hardening. "Yeah, but you've known my daughter since she was a kid, so—"

Daniel chuckles. "Yeah? And Gavin married his best friend's kid. What's the issue?"

Eyes closed, I pinch the bridge of my nose. Dammit. Yeah, I've known Josie most of her life. I still think of her as a kid. And while Savannah is close to the same age, there's no fucking way—

"Who the fuck is the girl?" War grits out.

I inhale through my nose and straighten. "Savannah."

War's expression contorts into one of pain. "Josie's best friend Savannah? As in the girl who has spent the last handful of Christmases at my house Savannah?"

I shrug. Didn't know any of that, but I don't doubt the truth of it. They're clearly close.

He runs a tattooed hand through his dark hair and shakes his head. "Fuck, I can kind of see it."

I practically stagger back. This time I'm the one in shock. "You can?"

With a shake of his head, he huffs out a dark laugh. "Yeah, she's sarcastic as shit, an old soul for sure, and a really good friend to Josie." He sighs. "Girl's had a tough life. Doesn't have a relationship with her parents. Hence the reason she spends the holidays with us." He eyes the rink, where the last of the players are filtering out, including his son. "I kind of hoped Bray would ask her out, if I'm honest."

The way my hands ball into fists isn't rational. Neither is the urge to growl a *fuck no*. So it's a good thing War drops an arm around my shoulders and laughs. "Don't worry, Bray only has eyes for hockey, which is good. I'm not ready to be a grandpa yet."

Daniel makes a choking sound and stumbles back. I almost do too. Because I'm talking about dating a girl who's his daughter's age, and he's talking about grandkids.

Fuck, life is strange.

Chapter 20
Savannah

Calliope's Column
It's Not Him, It's You (Kind Of)
Rule Number 4: Don't Talk About Your Past Sexual Partners…or Compare Him to Them…(Or do and Pay the Price.)

WHEN JOSIE READS the tagline of this week's article out loud, there's no holding back the fit of giggles that takes over.

"Wait, what price did you pay?" Addie holds up a red sweater dress, eyeing it, then us, in silent question.

"Go sluttier," Josie says from her spot beside me on Addie's bed. "Your body is literally what dreams are made of. Wet ones. Give the guys a little preview of what they're missing." She drops her phone onto the bed, thankfully pausing her reading of my article, and darts up and disappears into Addie's closet.

"I'm not trying to give them a preview of anything. I'll be their coach next year. Professional, remember? That's what we're keeping this." She widens her eyes at me, looking for backup.

All she'll get from me is a shrug. "I've recently discovered that I get off on being spanked, so I'm the wrong person to look to for moral support."

Addie's mouth falls open and a garbled noise escapes her. "Wait—" She shakes her head. "Did you just say he spanks you? As in Camden *I'm Old Enough to be Your Father* Snow spanks you?"

I snort. If I told them he likes it when I call him Daddy, they'd lose their minds. Something is definitely wrong with me, and I can't say I even care.

"Yup," Josie says, her voice muffled from inside the closet. "He told her to tell him the name of every man and woman she's ever slept with, and then he spanked her for every one."

Clearly, the girl has already read the entire article.

It's a good thing Calliope is anonymous, or I might be embarrassed. I'm not even remotely shy about my sex life, but I'd prefer it if my friends' family members—who also happen to be Camden's friends and coworkers—didn't know about my escapades.

And I don't even want to think of how Camden would react if he knew about the articles. Or maybe I would. He'd definitely punish me. But seriously, would he be upset? I hope not. I'm an open book, and my job is to share my life with the world, so if I'm not giving away our identities, then I'm not causing any harm.

Right?

Still, a little crumb of guilt lodges itself in my brain.

Can't do anything about it now, though. That's a problem for future Savannah, and I'm definitely the type of girl who lives in the present.

And presently, I'm too excited to be stressed, because while I haven't seen Camden since last weekend, I plan to surprise him in a matter of hours. Langfield Corp is putting on a holiday party for its employees and players. For decades, the Langfields have hosted a winter festival with rides and ice skating and all sorts of fun activities.

Showing up to a man's work party without being invited is a definite red flag.

I guess we'll see if this is the thing that sends Camden Snow running.

I can't decide whether I want to prove Sutton right or wrong. Can I be a man's exception? Normally, I wouldn't even consider the thought, but yeah, I'd like to be Camden's. Especially after the way he opened up to me this past weekend. I want him to see that I'll keep showing up. And I will. So long as he doesn't push me away.

"What about this?" Josie wanders out of the closet with a pair of distressed skintight jeans in one hand and a red top in the other. "Your boobs will look phenomenal."

Addie glances down at her chest and then back at Josie. "These?"

I giggle. "Your boobs are adorable."

"Oh great," she moans. "Did you hear that, Jose? My boobs are adorable. Should I dress them up with pink bows?"

Josie smirks. "Don't knock a nipple tassel until you try it."

"Okay, but as a reminder, my entire family, including my very overprotective father, will be there tonight. Still think I should go with the slutty shirt?"

Blanching, Josie tosses the red top over her shoulder. "Sorry, Beckett is literally one of my favorite humans. I can't dress his daughter in slutty clothing."

Addie grins. "So the red dress?"

Josie rolls her eyes. "Yeah, yeah, the red dress is fine."

"Back to overprotective men," Addie says as she disappears into the closet with the dress.

I fall back on her extremely comfortable bed and sigh. "What about them?"

She peers out at me from the closet, holding the dress to her chest. "I think Sutton might have been right."

She disappears again without finishing the thought, and when she comes out, she's fully dressed.

"Tada." She spins slowly while we tell her how pretty she looks.

"Sutton was right?" I prod. A complete glutton for punishment.

Addie nods. "Yup. All the 'wrong' things you do with this guy only seem to make him want you more."

I shrug, tamping down on the hope trying to unfurl in my chest. I'm not supposed to like this man. I don't believe in relationships, and my life is far too messy to be conducive to one. "Only time will tell."

Josie nudges me. "Tell Addie the plan for tonight."

Our friend's eyes go wide, and she darts closer. "Wait, you're going to do something tonight?"

"I promised Sutton I'd follow through, and I'm not a quitter. So tonight I'm going to flip the switch. A little brighter and in public. It's one thing for him to ignore the red flags I'm waving when I'm naked, but I highly doubt he'll go with the flow when I push him in public."

Josie's smile goes manic. "Have I told you how much I love this project?"

I pick up a pillow and toss it at her head. "You're evil."

"You're both diabolical," Addie says, plopping down beside me. "But I want to know every detail of your plan, because I'll be taking notes of that man's reaction."

My stomach twists with nerves, but I force a smile to my face. Then I break down my completely batshit plans.

CHAPTER 21
CAMDEN

> Me: Baby girl, are you ready for our date this weekend?

> Savannah: Feels like this weekend is forever away…but yes.

A WAVE of affection washes over me. This weekend is tomorrow, but I agree. Another twenty-four hours without her feels like a lifetime. All week, while I traveled to colleges around the country to scout our prospects, I counted down the hours. Hell, the seconds. A whole week without her was torture, but the trip was necessary, since I have a meeting with the rest of management next week, where we'll discuss our drafting strategy.

As I climb out of my car, I shove my phone into my pocket. Just gotta make it through one more night of work, then I'm all hers. I considered inviting her tonight, but in the end, decided it was probably too forward in such a new relationship. It's a holiday party—though it's more like a carnival because the Langfields only know how to throw over-the-top events—and holiday parties are for families. Not for casual dates.

It'd be weird if I brought her, right? Actually, it feels like it would be perfect. I can vividly imagine draping my arm over her shoulders while we stroll through the winter carnival. The fake snow that Beckett will somehow have magically falling from the sky will land in her pretty red hair. On the tip of her nose.

Fuck, just thinking of how she'd smile has me pulling out my phone and shooting her another text message.

> Me: What are you doing right now?

It's last minute, but I stop and wait for her response, ready to hop in the car if she's free. I could pick her up and be back here within the hour.

Would she really come? Am I ridiculous for asking? Maybe. But I don't give a fuck.

> Savannah: Going out with friends. Why?

Disappointment pummels me like a blow to my chest. With a shake of my head, I fight off the stupid emotion. Inviting her would have been absurd.

I type out another quick message, playing it cool. Or at least I hope it sounds cool and not like I'm a forty-six-year-old man desperate to see her.

I am, so it would be accurate, but still.

> Me: Just like to know where you are. Have a good night with your friends. Make sure you get your rest. You'll need it for tomorrow.

Her response is a winking emoji. What the fuck does that even mean?

I don't have the bandwidth to figure it out, so I shove my phone back into my pocket and lock the car.

The carnival is set up inside Lang Field, and the stadium has been completely transformed into a winter wonderland. It's like a Thomas Kinkade painting come to life. Every surface sparkles. Beneath my feet, fake cobblestones are covered in snow, even though the city has yet to be hit with even an inch of winter precipitation this early in the season.

To my left, kids are throwing snowballs and making snow angels. Of course they are. Beckett Langfield doesn't half-ass anything.

Toward the back, a Ferris wheel is lit up in red and green lights, and in the middle of the ball field is an oversized Christmas tree that rivals the one at Rockefeller Center, along with a small skating rink, where more kids are skating.

A handful of them are showing off, doing spins. Obviously hockey players' kids.

Then there's a row of carnival games, complete with prizes—all of which are high-quality stuffed animals, not the cheap kind typically found at a real carnival. Once again, it screams Langfield.

Food vendors are set up throughout the space, filling the air with the smell of greasy deliciousness and sugary goodness.

There's a chill in the air, because the one thing Beckett couldn't control was the weather. But the crisp temperature only adds to the ambiance. I'm in a black sweater and a pair of dark jeans, but I may have to play a few games and win myself a scarf. The longer I stand with the fake snow falling around me, the colder I get.

"This is sick," Bobby Dean says, popping up from out of nowhere.

"Yeah, the Langfields don't skimp on anything."

JJ wanders over, his daughter Avery riding on his shoulders.

Her curly blond hair is mostly hidden beneath a Bolts toque, but her bright smile is on full display. "Hi, Uncle Cam."

I've been Uncle Cam to almost every kid that's passed through the halls of Bolts Arena, and while I love every freaking one of them, as I look at Avery, note the way she clutches her dad's head like he's a damn horse and she's leading him, an old ache—a stubborn sensation that won't go away no matter how hard I try to rid myself of it—returns with a vengeance. There was a time when all I wanted was to find the right person to settle down and start a family with. When I saw myself as a husband. As a dad. When I thought I could have a family of my own.

The universe had other plans, though. First, my ex's affair destroyed me. Then my sister's disappearance. And then, when I thought I'd finally gotten my life back on track, when I finally had my family back, we lost my father and my mother completely broke.

So I'm forever Uncle Cam. I've got a good life. A great one, even. I love my job, and I'm surrounded by friends who treat me like family, along with all their kids. It's hard not to feel selfish when I allow myself to wish I had more.

But maybe I do have more. Because I've found Savannah. Just the thought of her has a smile tugging at my lips. Fuck, I really do like her.

Is that why I'm thinking of kids? She's young. She has a whole life ahead of her. Marriage. Kids. That could be in the cards for her. For me.

Shit, I'm getting ahead of myself. We haven't even been on a fucking date, and I'm thinking about putting a baby in her. What the hell is wrong with me?

"Cam?" JJ says, reminding me that I've yet to greet him or his daughter.

"Sorry, Ave. How's my favorite little hockey player?"

With a giggle, she shakes her head, the ends of her blond curls bouncing. "That's Daddy. I'm just a girl."

Jaw dropping dramatically, I hold out my arms to her, and when she jumps into them, I pull her in for a hug. "Nah, I heard you're our future winger. Just gotta get you out on the ice for practice, right, JJ?"

He arches a brow, no doubt thinking I'm ridiculous, but when he notices the big smile on his daughter's face, his expression melts into one of pure adoration, and he nods. "Whatever my girl wants."

JJ is an incredible dad. Maybe one of the best I know, and that's saying something, because I was lucky enough to witness both War and Daniel become dads.

But JJ's done it pretty much on his own. His wife couldn't care less about motherhood or her child. It's hard to watch.

"Can we go on the Ferris wheel, Daddy?" Avery asks, her focus turning quickly like any four-year-old's would.

"Course," he says, holding his arms out to her.

I give her one more squeeze and hand her back. "Tabs?" I mouth over her head.

He shakes his head, jaw ticking.

My heart sinks for the little girl, but I plaster on a bright smile. "Find me when you're done, and I'll win you a stuffed animal."

Avery lights up and lets out a squeal, kicking her legs.

Despite bearing the brunt of her excitement, JJ holds her close and smiles. "Thanks."

"Can Uncle Bobby ride the Ferris wheel too?" our star center asks Avery.

That affection is back and only growing. The current team is just as close as the team I was part of. They're a good group of guys. Maybe a little wild sometimes, but they do okay keeping each other in check, and they'd bend over backward to help one another out. It's exactly what JJ needs, considering that Avery travels with the team for now. Can't imagine that won't change next season, though. She'll start school, and if Tabitha doesn't step up and become the mother she needs, I don't know what JJ will do.

Avery eyes Bobby, then her dad. "I don't know. What do you think, Daddy? Can Bobby's ego fit in our cart?"

A roar of laughter bursts out of me. Damn, this kid. This is one of the perks—or maybe it's a downside—that comes with bringing a four-year-old on the road with a hockey team. She's got the one-liners down and she doesn't let the guys get away with anything.

JJ smirks. "Probably not, but we'll let him come anyway."

The three of them disappear, and I'm still smiling after them when a hand lands on my arm and squeezes.

The familiar fruity perfume registers before I even turn around. Wincing, I give myself a little pep talk. I gotta play nice, even though I want to tell the woman to get her hand off me.

"Erica," I say, turning and giving the team photographer an easy smile.

"I didn't know you were going to be here tonight," she says in a flirty tone.

Erica is a very pretty woman. Blond hair, blue eyes, a strong jaw, a button nose, and killer curves. She's photographed on the sidelines as often as she does the photographing. Women are being drafted to the NHL finally, yet the league's commentators are still misogynistic fools who love to talk about how she will make a great wife for one of the players or staff one day rather than about the incredible shots she takes or the awards she's won.

She's never paid the commentators any mind, and I've never seen her look at any of the players unless it's from behind the camera.

But me? She's made it obvious several times that she'd love to share more than just a drink.

I haven't gone there. I try really hard not to mix business with pleasure. Nothing has ever mattered more to me than my job. The Bolts are my family, so a few hours of pleasure have never been worth the risk of awkwardness at work.

She's got a good head on her shoulders, though, and she is excellent at her job, so her advances haven't been overt or out of line. She's got a great sense of humor too, so I have spent a few nights in her company in a hotel bar while traveling. But I've always turned down her offer for more.

"Can't miss a Langfield party."

She grins, her glossy pink lips shiny in the stadium lights. "Ain't that the truth. And this one is spectacular. I wish I'd brought my camera, because seriously, this is a winter wonderland." She scans our surroundings, wearing a look of appreciation.

"I'm sure you'll get some good ones either way. I've seen what you can do with your phone's camera alone," I say honestly.

She steps closer, her cheeks going pink. "Thanks, Cam. I appreciate that. Want to walk with me while I snap a few pictures? Maybe take a ride on the Ferris wheel?" She splays a hand on my chest and peers up at me through dark lashes.

I'm racking my brain for a gentle way to turn her down when a cool hand lands on my neck and I'm tugged backward.

"Hey, baby," a sexy, raspy voice says. "Sorry I'm late."

Chest tightening, I whip around and clutch Savannah's hand to my chest. "Baby?" I whisper, taking her in.

She breaks into a smile so bright it rivals the stadium lights overhead. "Aren't you going to give your girlfriend a kiss hello? I missed you."

Fuck. Girlfriend? My heart somersaults at the word. Never have I wanted a woman to wear that title more than her. And sure, maybe she's only tossing it around because she's jealous, but I like it. Possessive Savannah is hot as fuck.

I may be an asshole, but I plan to take full advantage of this opportunity. I'll show her exactly how I feel about this surprise while making sure Erica knows where my interests lie.

Cuffing her neck, I press my fingers into her pulse point and revel in the way it thrums wildly as I lean close and brush my lips against hers. "Missed you too, baby girl," I murmur. Then I take the kiss deeper. I go all in. Tongue and teeth and so much need that it takes effort not to grind up against her.

Savannah whimpers into my mouth, just as desperate for me, and clings to me, fingers clutching my sweater.

With a low groan, I pull back. If we keep this up, I actually will take this too far. "Thought you had plans with the girls." Unable to resist, I press one last kiss to her mouth.

She licks her bottom lip, her chest rising and falling. For a second she just stares at me, a dreamy look in her eye. But she quickly shakes her head a little and blinks three times in rapid succession. "Uh, yeah. Apparently the plan was to come here."

She shrugs like that was a surprise to her, but the little glint in her eye gives me the feeling that isn't the complete truth. My girl wanted to surprise me. The question is why?

Did she want to test me? Did I pass?

I glance at Erica, who is standing awkwardly a foot away. Shit. Forgot about her. I wrap an arm around Savannah and tuck her into my side. Then I make introductions. "Savannah, this is Erica, the team's photographer. Erica, this is my girlfriend, Savannah." At the word girlfriend, I give the woman under my arm a secret little smirk.

She peers back at me, eyes wide and cheeks flushed.

Yeah, she was testing me. She probably didn't think a world existed in which I would be okay with her being this possessive. Guess I've got my work cut out for me when it comes to showing her just how invested I am. And, more importantly, that not only is she mine, but that I'm so very okay with being hers.

Calliope's Column
It's Not Him, It's You (Kind Of)
Rule Number 5: Don't Be Clingy. Jealousy Is Unattractive. (Or Is It hot?)

I THOUGHT I had the title for my next column. Figured I knew precisely how tonight would go. Showing up at a Christmas party and acting jealous when a man talks to a beautiful coworker is the reddest of flags. A guaranteed way to send a guy running.

So why the fuck is Camden Snow pulling me closer? Why is he smiling when he says the word girlfriend like my claiming of that title when we very obviously are not at that stage yet is the best thing in the world?

"It's nice to meet you," the blond who was just hitting on Cam says to me.

The annoying thing is, she seems to mean it. The woman stepped back the moment I grabbed Cam, aggressively I admit, and gave us space while we played tonsil hockey. And now she's smiling at me sweetly.

"You as well. You must love traveling all over the country and capturing images of all those beautiful men in action." I let a sly smile curve my lips at that last part.

She tips her head back and lets out a loud laugh. "Sometimes I catch the type of action I shouldn't," she agrees, catching my innuendo, "but they're all good guys. So yeah, I do love my job. What do you do?"

"I work for *Jolie*. I'm a junior editor there."

She lights up. "Oh my god. I can't even imagine how incredible it would be to work for Catherine Bouvier." She says Cat's name the way we all do, with complete reverence. Even at nearly sixty, the woman is a fashion icon. And honestly, she doesn't look a day over forty-five. She's timeless.

"It is pretty awesome."

"The Calliope articles are my favorite. The most recent ones are killing me. Did you see how she's dating guys and—"

"Ah, yeah. They're the best," I say, my heart lurching.

"I know the woman who used to write the Calliope articles," Camden says. "The original Calliope."

My breath catches. "Really?"

He nods. "Yup. The whole team used to read them." He laughs, genuine humor dancing in his eyes. "I haven't kept up since she sold the rights years ago. Maybe I'll have to check them out."

I shake my head, going for blasé, hoping like hell I can stop him from even bothering. "They're sex columns. Nothing you don't know about already."

He smirks like he thinks I'm being possessive again. Like I'm pointing out that of course I know about his sex life because I'm his girlfriend and we have sex. But I'm not actually saying this for Erica's benefit. I'm saying it because if he reads the articles, there's a good chance he'll realize that I'm Calliope and he's the man I'm trying to drive crazy enough to dump me.

Erica clears her throat, doing a poor job of hiding a grimace, and changes the subject. "I was just telling Cam how pretty it is tonight and how I wish I'd brought my camera." She pulls out her cell phone. "But I'm going to get some shots with this. It was nice meeting you, Savannah. Hopefully I'll see you again."

Cam nods. "You will." Then he presses a kiss to the side of my head.

Thrown off by his reaction, I can only nod and smile as she wanders off.

Shit, now that we're alone, how am I supposed to act?

"Want to grab a drink?" he asks, his tone totally relaxed.

"You're not mad?" I study him, searching for a reaction beneath his easy façade. Some hidden thought or perhaps an internal freak out that I'm missing.

He smirks. "That you got jealous and claimed me?"

Cringing, I nod a little.

"Wouldn't that be a little hypocritical, considering how I acted when I saw you with Theo James?"

I shrug, a little of the tension easing from my chest. He's got a point. Still, he didn't call me his girlfriend that night.

"Baby girl," he husks, dipping his head so I can't look away. "The title isn't exactly the one I want to give you, but it'll do for now."

Frowning, I roll the words over in my head. What does he mean by that?

He chuckles like he knows I'm lost and presses another kiss to my lips. "Come on, I want to get my girl hot chocolate and then win her a teddy bear."

Off-kilter, I accept his hand and allow him to pull me through the crowd.

Around us snow falls from the "sky." Lang Field is one of very few baseball stadiums with a retractable roof so it can be enclosed in the winter and on rainy days. The designer of the event worked some kind of magic and made the ceiling look like a night sky filled with stars and falling snow. It doesn't even feel like a baseball field.

We walk down the "cobblestone street" toward a stand selling a variety of drinks, and as Cam steps up to order hot chocolate, I dig my buzzing phone out of my pocket.

Addie: Sav, where'd you disappear to?

Josie: I literally turned away for one second,
and you were gone!

Me: Shit, sorry. I saw Cam with another
woman, and I don't know what came over me.

I can't explain the emotion that hit me when I saw the two of them. My stomach twisted into a painful knot, and then my legs were moving. I'd like to say it was because of the article. That I saw an opportunity to push the envelope. But I can't lie to myself. For the first time in my life, I was overtaken by jealousy over a man. It felt like if I didn't do something in that moment, I'd miss out on something wonderful.

A quick glance at Camden only reiterates that sensation.

And when he catches me staring and winks, my stomach flips in a way I'm not sure I've ever experienced either.

Addie: You like him. That's what came
over you.

Me: It's for the article. I told you my plan for
tonight.

Josie: And how's that going for you? Did he
freak out when he saw you? Ask why you
would show up to his work function uninvited?

Um, no. I'm pretty sure he was about to invite me himself fifteen minutes before I spotted him. I'm in over my damn head.

I should probably text Sutton.

No. With a shake of my head, I push that thought out of my mind and refocus.

Me: No. He kissed me and told me he's happy
I'm here. We're getting hot chocolate and then
he's gonna win a teddy bear for me.

Addie: Okay, why is that the cutest thing I've ever heard?

Josie: Sutton is so going to win this bet.

Me: She can't, because that would mean I won't have an article to write, which means I lose my job.

My heart pounds as I type out the words. I'm so fucked. What am I thinking, falling for a bachelor like Camden Snow? This is just a fling for him. Probably his usual MO. I'm hot, sure. That's what he sees in me. He's the type of guy who has stripper poles in his basement and throws erotic holiday parties. He's not the guy a woman throws her career away for.

No man is.

And I'm not stupid enough to put a man ahead of my career.

Internal pep talk completed, I remind myself of the details of the plan that I laid out for the girls earlier. Then I lean into Camden, head tipped back, and smile sweetly. "You're really gonna win me a teddy bear?"

The smile he gives me in return makes the skin around his eyes crinkle. "Yeah, baby. Let's go get you a prize."

It's completely ridiculous how quickly he wins three items. He's good at every game he tries. When he beats the first game, I select a bear as my prize. Then when he spots the Burberry scarves displayed with another grouping of prizes—seriously, what is wrong with the Langfields? Freaking Burberry scarves as carnival prizes?—he wins two.

When I notice the Burberry baby outfit hanging near them, I point it out. The opportunity is too perfect to pass up. "Aw, look how cute that baby outfit is."

Camden presses his tongue to his cheek, eyeing the prize.

I hold my breath and wait for it. Wait for the look of horror. Wait for his muscles to lock up. For the distance between us to grow. For the look that says where are you going with this? The one that confirms that I seem to be way ahead of him in this relationship timeline.

Instead, he breaks into a genuine smile. "Matches our scarves. Should I win it?"

The breath I'm holding escapes in a wheeze. "For our future child?" I ask slowly.

Holy fuck. Camden Snow, where the hell are you going with this?

Chuckling, he pulls me into his chest and presses a kiss to my forehead. "Maybe one day, but for now, let's put it on the bear."

I breathe out and relax against him. I kind of hate myself for the way I don't hate how he said maybe one day. How I now realize I was holding my breath because I was worried he'd say *No, obviously not for a future child. What the fuck, Savannah? What is wrong with you?*

That would have been a reasonable reaction, though, right? Men freak out when women talk about their future shared babies before the official first date, right? That's how this is supposed to go.

And yet…I'm glad he didn't.

I need to get a grip.

As Cam steps up to the counter, I take a step back and survey him. Damn, he looks good. Dark jeans that hug his ass and thighs. A sweater that's just tight enough to show off his biceps.

He throws three balls, getting three strikes in a row. Then he tells the attendant we'll take the Burberry baby outfit.

"Got a baby at home?" the guy asks.

Cam glances at me, his brows arched. "Not yet." Then he hands me the outfit. "You gonna put it on the bear now?"

The attendant watches him with wide eyes, no doubt thinking that Camden Snow has lost his fucking mind.

Okay. So I'm not the only one confused by this. Good, good.

"Uh, sure," I hedge. "We should probably name him, huh? Since he's our first baby?" I don't know how I manage a straight face as I force the words out.

Lips twitching, Camden guides me away from the stand.

"Should we name him after Daddy?" I push, going from slightly deranged to full-on delulu. The second the words are out, I'm back to holding my breath.

Waiting for him to finally snap. To find a polite way to send me on my way.

Then, when he's finally dumped me, I can write this article and move on with my life.

When he opens his mouth and an unintelligible sound comes out, my stomach free-falls and I clutch his shirt, tugging him closer, and force a laugh. "I'm just kidding," I get out quickly, shaking my head. I don't want him to dump me. I'm not ready for this to be over.

Shit. Fuck. I like him for real. Oh, dammit. What the hell, Savannah?

For the first time tonight, Camden looks at me with confusion in his expression. Like now he thinks I'm being ridiculous. He cups my face and brushes a soothing thumb over my cheek. "No, I kinda like it. Snow Bear? Has a nice ring to it."

"Uh, yeah—"

My words are cut off when he presses his lips to mine.

Snow Bear?

What the hell, Camden Snow?

He pulls back and laces his fingers with mine. "Come on, baby girl. Let's take Snow for his first ride on the Ferris wheel."

Chapter 23
Savannah

Calliope's Column
It's Not Him, It's You (Kind Of)
**Rule Number 6: Don't Sync Your Ovulation Calendars Before the
First Date.**

IT'S OFFICIAL. I've developed an impossible crush on Camden Snow.

I suppose it's not really a revelation so much as it is an acknowledgment of feelings that grow stronger by the day.

I can't even blame the texts he's sent over the last thirty-six hours, though I will admit that they're just over the line enough for me to be concerned.

> **Daddy:** I still can't believe you sent me home with Snow by myself.

> **Me:** LOL. You better take good care of our baby. He's our love bear.

> Daddy: Why don't you come over and help me
> take care of him? See what a good daddy
> I am?

He sent pictures of himself and the bear in bed. Followed by another, assuring me he wouldn't roll over on our love bear. This morning he sent me an image of them having breakfast together and watching SportsCenter.

The smile that hits me every time I think about it shows just how far gone I am already. Which is a problem.

But honestly, it hasn't scared me away the way it should. The guy likes me. It's nice. If I was any other person, a woman without enough daddy and mommy issues to fill a library, maybe I'd see where this goes.

Though a late-night phone call from my father followed by an early-morning one from my mother remind me that I still need years of therapy to deal with the trauma they caused before I can actually consider entering a real relationship.

What did my parents say in those calls to send me back to that way of thinking so quickly? Just the run of the mill shit they always spout. My father, in so many words, reiterated his opinion that I'm a spoiled bitch who ruined his life. Every so often, he feels the need to remind me. I should block him, yet I can't. Why is it that I feel this familial obligation to a man who literally tells me I'm the worst thing to ever happen to him? He was drunk, obviously. A month from now, on a night he's sober, he'll call and ask how things are, having no clue the devastation he's wrought, because he'll have no memory of spewing the hateful words that play repeatedly in my head.

My mother's call was far less dramatic but equally disappointing. She wanted me to know that she can't come for Christmas—which is no surprise and actually appreciated, since I didn't invite her—but that she'd be sure to visit for my birthday.

My birthday was a month ago. It came and went without a word from either of my parents. Which is fine, really. I spent it with Josie, Addie, and Sutton. We took our first pole dancing class, and it was a blast.

The point is that my own mother doesn't even remember my birthday, and that type of hit leaves a mark.

With all of that on my mind, it's clear that seeing Camden again is a bad idea. I entertained the arrangement to prove I could push him away, and tonight, that's what I'll do. Then I'll focus on my article. I'll bust my ass to keep my job and my apartment, to remain where I am, surrounded by the people who actually feel like family.

My plan for tonight is diabolical. Heart thumping, I open our text thread and send Camden a link to my ovulation calendar. No man in his right mind wants to be with a woman who links her ovulation calendar before the first date.

"Savannah, sweetheart," Rosalie asks from the stove. "Do you want extra red sauce with that?"

I survey the heaping plate of food I had no intention of eating before I entered this apartment and shake my head. "This is more than enough. Thanks."

She watches me over her shoulder, waiting for me to take a bite, and I indulge her, because that's what good girls do.

I'm supposed to meet Camden for dinner in a half hour, but now that he's received the text, I expect him to come up with an excuse to cancel. It's actually a relief knowing that this is almost over.

Though I can't figure out how to stifle that part of me that wishes I could have a normal relationship with a man as incredible as Camden Snow. It would take years of therapy to get there, so pushing him away now is for the best. And far less scary than showing him the real me, then watching him walk away.

Because no one chooses me.

But I'll choose myself and that's good enough.

"It's Saturday. Why aren't you going out?" Rosalie takes a seat in the chair opposite me, the plastic cover beneath her squeaking.

"She's not dating," Nick calls from the other room. Though his volume is closer to a yell, since he's got the six-o'clock news blaring.

"Turn down the television," Rosalie hollers. "We can't hear you."

He hits mute and repeats himself without lowering his volume. "I said she's not dating."

"Why are you yelling?" she yells back.

He's ten feet away. This is kind of absurd. Even if I have to fight a smile as I watch them.

"Because you said you couldn't hear me."

I focus on my plate as they bicker, and when my phone buzzes, I ignore it. I'm not ready to deal with the repercussions of my most recent antics. If I don't look, then Camden Snow hasn't broken up with me yet.

Broken up with me. Ha. Like because I called myself his girlfriend for a few hours one night, what we're doing suddenly qualifies as a legitimate relationship.

"Are you going to get that?" Nick asks when my phone buzzes again, his voice suddenly right behind me.

Startled, I glance over my shoulder.

He's peering down at my phone, where it's still vibrating on the table.

I shake my head. "No. Rosalie has a rule. No phones at the table."

She snorts. "Like you've ever followed that rule. Five minutes ago you were sitting there texting."

"Pick up the phone," Nick hollers. "It keeps buzzing."

"She's right here," Rosalie snaps. "Stop yelling at her."

"I'm not yelling, I'm talking at a normal volume."

He is in fact yelling, but it's only because he can barely hear.

And now I can barely hear, so I finally snatch the device from the table. If I don't, I worry one of them will.

"Hello?" I say, the single word coming out far too loud after the shouting match I just sat through.

"Savannah?" Camden asks from far away, like he's pulled the phone away from his ear.

"Yeah, sorry." I bring my voice down an octave. "What's up?"

He clears his throat. "I—uh," he stammers. "I got your text."

Wincing, I brace myself for the brush-off. Dammit. I was counting on him doing it via text.

Why can't he be like guys my age who probably wouldn't have even replied to the text, instead choosing to cut ties by ghosting me?

Oh, because he's a grown-ass man. That's why.

"Yeah, um, just thought it was important information for you. And us. And you know…because of our relationship and how invested I am in our future," I ramble.

Fuck, I was not prepared to actually explain the message to him, let alone in front of Rosalie and Nick, who are both staring at me like I've just told Camden I have a venereal disease.

"Are you feeling okay?" he asks.

Finally, he's acting the way I thought he would. He thinks I've lost my mind. He's questioning my sanity.

"Yup. Feeling great," I tell him. Might as well go all in and make him believe that I think this is rational behavior for a brand-new relationship.

Just rip the Band-Aid off, Cam. Break my heart and let's move on. I sent you a damn ovulation calendar, for god's sake.

He clears his throat again. "Well, obviously, we don't have to go out tonight."

I thought I was prepared for the rejection. I thought my mental shields had been built high enough to block the blow. But I swear those words hit me like a frying pan to the chest.

"Yeah," I croak. Fuck, why do I feel like I'm going to cry? What is wrong with me?

"But is there anything you need?"

"Anything I need?" I parrot, confusion washing over me.

Like a parting gift? I almost snort at the thought. That's probably something Camden Snow would do. Send his ex a vibrator to keep her company since she no longer has access to him.

Okay, maybe that's a bit much. But he'd probably send sympathy flowers or a fruit arrangement. Actually…I eye my full plate of food. A fruit arrangement would be nice. Especially if it was dipped in chocolate. "I guess I wouldn't say no to chocolate," I hear myself replying.

What the hell, Savannah?

"Of course," he responds immediately. "Yes. Absolutely. I already picked some up."

"What?" Jaw unhinged, I blink, then blink again. Disbelief hits me first, though it quickly morphs into anger. I texted him less than ten minutes ago, and he's already purchased breakup chocolate for me? Wow. Jeez. "Do you keep chocolate stocked for all the girls you date?"

"What? No." There's some shuffling on the other side of the phone, and when he speaks again, his tone is more even, though still hesitant. "I bought this for you. I also picked up a heating pad, and my sister says she likes salty foods when she's on her period, so I'll stop for fries as well. I'll be at your place in ten. Do you need anything else? And think about what you want for dinner. We can have it delivered."

"Delivered?" I peer down at my plate again. "You're on your way? What are you—" I swallow back the question and shake my head. "Camden, what are you talking about?"

"You sent me the link to your app to tell me you're on your period, right? I totally get that you wouldn't want to go out when you're feeling crappy, so I thought I'd bring dinner to you. Is that not what you want?"

Tears prick the backs of my eyes, my nose tingling. Shit. I shift so I'm facing the wall because both Nick and Rosalie are watching me like I'm the nightly news.

He thought I was telling him I'm on my period. He's not breaking up with me, he's bringing me chocolate.

Without my permission, the tears fall. I'm crying about a man. And I'm not even on my period. Shit. Why is Camden Snow so perfect? And how the hell am I going to break up with him now?

CHAPTER 24
CAMDEN

Me: You're sure salty food and chocolate are the key here?

Cora: Yes, Cam. There's not a woman in existence who doesn't like chocolate when she's on her period.

Me: Okay, it's just…she seemed off.

Cora: Honestly, I'm shocked she told you she was on her period. Women don't typically talk about that stuff early on in a relationship. Either she feels exceptionally crappy, or you've been so great with her that she's already comfortable being vulnerable with you. Either way, chocolate is key.

Me: Thanks. I'm just not good at this stuff, and I really want to get it right. When she first gave me her number, I didn't call her for a week, and she almost ended up on a date with someone else.

> Cora: Hahaha. I'm sorry. I'm not laughing at
> you. I'm just…well, actually, I am laughing at
> you. But also, it's adorable. You're doing the
> right thing. Promise.

I GLANCE over my shoulder at the bags in my back seat, then peer up at the older apartment building. This is the address she gave me. I've checked twice. But this is not a great neighborhood. I don't think I like that she lives here alone.

She should have security and a doorman. Or she should move in with me, where I can handle her security.

I blow out a rough breath. I'm getting ahead of myself. Way ahead. We still haven't gone on a damn date, and I'm talking about moving her into my house.

And yet the idea doesn't freak me out. None of this does. That alone should freak me out. The not freaking out should totally freak me out.

"Get out of the car, man," I mutter.

And now I'm talking to myself. Fuck, I'm a disaster. I check the mirrors before stepping onto the street—because there is no off-street parking—and grab the bags from the back. I hit the lock button on my key fob twice for good measure, a little concerned that my Land Rover might not be here when I come back out.

Though the area isn't the safest, her building and the ones around it are well taken care of. The front door is decorated with a wreath and Christmas lights, and the names on the buzzer panel aren't even faded. Donovan is first. Then Donadio. And finally S.B.

My chest swells with pride when I note that she doesn't have her last name written out on the label next to the buzzer. Smart girl.

Only as I'm looking at her initials do I realize that I don't know her last name. Huh.

I hit the buzzer and take a step back. Half a second later, the door swings open, and I'm practically run down by a little girl.

"Piper!" a man calls as he jogs out of the building behind her. "Sorry," he says as his daughter, I'm guessing, turns and gives him a mischievous grin. "She's a quick one."

My hands are full, so I can't introduce myself properly, but I smile and dip my chin. "No worries. I'm heading up to Savannah's."

The little girl watches me, eyes narrowed with curiosity, and returns to the entryway.

The man nods, assessing me. "She's at the Donadios' place right now."

I frown. How does he—

"I'm not stalking her or anything. Swear it. It's just that they're pretty loud up there. It's impossible not to know when they have visitors."

"And they're on the second floor?" I ask, scanning the names next to the buzzer again.

Nodding, he snags his daughter by the hand. "How do you know Savvy?"

My smile grows. I like that he's a bit suspicious and vetting me. "Camden Snow, Sav's boyfriend."

He staggers back a step. "Really? Wow. I had no idea she was seeing someone. That's great." Head tilted, he studies me thoughtfully. "Camden Snow. Why's that name familiar?"

I smile. "Hockey fan?"

He points at me, his dark eyes going wide. "That's who you are. Man, you were on the dream team. I was still in high school when you played. My friends and I even got tickets to a game our senior year. It was the year you guys won the cup."

"Which one?" There's no sense hiding the cocky smirk that takes over. I'm well-known for it, after all.

Chuckling, he looks down at his daughter. "Pip, this guy is famous."

"And Savvy's boyfriend," she says in the cutest high-pitched voice.

I grin. "Yup. It's still pretty new, though. Think you could put in a good word for me?"

She nods. "I can do that."

"Thanks."

"Want me to walk you up?" the man asks, gesturing for me to enter the building.

"Nah. Thanks. I'll call her and see if she wants me to wait for her at her place or meet the Donadios."

"They're loud," he warns, eyeing the stairway. "But no one makes a better meatball than Mrs. D. I'm John, by the way. I live here"—he points toward the door to the left of us—"Savvy helps us out with the kids sometimes. We've got four of 'em."

"Shit." The word has barely left my mouth when I realize my mistake. Face heating, I cringe. "I mean duck."

He chuckles. "Oh my god. That's a Bolts thing, right?"

"More like a Langfield thing, but yeah, all the Bolts say duck."

He shakes his head, a huge smile on his face. "This is so cool. I can't wait to tell the guys at the station."

"It was nice meeting you, John. Make sure you keep an eye on Sav for me, yeah?"

He nods. "Anytime."

He and his daughter head out into the cool night, and I head up the steps. I consider knocking on the Donadios' door but decide to text her instead, thinking she may need an excuse to leave. I wouldn't mind meeting more people in her world, though. Every day I realize I want to know more about her. I don't think there's a thing I won't like discovering about Savannah.

> Me: Hey, baby. I'm here.

> Baby girl: I'm at the neighbors' place. I'll leave now and meet you upstairs.

A moment later, I hear her voice on the other side of the door on the second floor. I can't make out what she's saying, but her neighbors' loud voices are crystal clear.

"Make sure he's good to you," a woman with a thick Italian accent says.

"Who says she wants him to be good to her?" a man hollers in response. "She's not dating, remember?"

"She wasn't dating, but she obviously is now," the woman replies as the door swings open and Savannah appears on the other side, cheeks flushed, looking flustered.

Her eyes go wide when she sees me.

"Oh, is that him?" The woman pushes into the doorway next to Savannah. "He's cute," she yells over her shoulder, presumably to her husband. When she turns back, she takes me in from head to toe without an ounce of shame. "And old. Savannah, sweetheart, how old is he?"

Savannah's eyes fall shut and her chest and neck turn as bright as her cheeks. "He's not that old."

With a chuckle, I shrug. "I'm forty-six."

"Forty-six," the man hollers. "That's old."

"He's not that old," Savannah says, louder this time.

A full laugh escapes me. "They're not wrong."

She huffs a sigh. "Don't encourage them. I'll never hear the end of it." Pasting on a smile, she turns to the woman. "Good night, Rosalie. I'll stop by tomorrow afternoon."

"You should bring your man friend."

"Boyfriend," I correct with a grin.

She shakes her head. "You're too old to be a boyfriend."

I still can't see the man, but his words ring out loud and clear. "Forty-six is too old to be a boy."

"My Nico is never wrong," Rosalie tells me. "But yes, you should come tomorrow. Sunday dinner. Bring wine."

Savannah huffs. "He might have plans. You don't just tell people to come over and tell them what to bring."

I smile. "No plans, and I'll cover the wine. No problem."

"See? That's a good boy," Rosalie says.

It's tempting to point out that she just told me I'm too old to be a boy, but by the exasperation on Savannah's face, it looks like she's desperate to get out of here. I'm itching to get my hands on her anyway, so I only nod in answer and step back so she can exit.

When she finally does, I angle in and press a kiss to her cheek, then bring my mouth to her ear. "If they don't think you should call me your boyfriend, do you think they'd approve of the name you use when it's just the two of us?"

She whacks me in the stomach. "Stop." The single word is sharp, but when she looks up at me, her eyes dance with amusement.

"Come on, baby girl. Say it for me. Just once."

She purses her lips, trying hard to hide her smile.

"Daddy," I say in a higher-pitched voice, pretending to be her.

She snorts.

"It's fine. I'll get you to say it before the night is over." I press another kiss to her cheek and then motion toward the stairs. "Now lead the way so we can finally get our first date started."

Upstairs, Savannah opens the door to a studio apartment. The walls are red brick, the room small. Rather than a couch, there's a bed pushed up against the wall, its purple comforter a rumpled mess. To the left is a wall of kitchen cabinets and a black fridge, along with a small black two-person table. On the right, beside the doorway, is a television set up to be viewed from the bed. All in all, the entire space is probably four hundred square feet.

"It's not much, I know," she says, like she's taking in the room from my perspective.

The embarrassment in her tone is like a knife to the gut. I rush to set the bags on the table, then turn back to her and cup her upper arms, ducking so we're eye to eye. "You've got great neighbors and a warm bed. Seems like it's exactly what you need."

She nods, her shoulders relaxing a bit. She's in a pair of oversized black sweats rolled at the waist and a soft-looking black ribbed long-sleeved shirt. Her red hair is piled high on her head, and there's very little, if any, makeup on her face. Maybe the remnants of the day's mascara.

As I catalog her, it hits me. She never planned on coming to dinner. Does that mean that when she texted, she was trying to cancel? Did I misread the signals?

Shit.

"How are you feeling?" I hedge.

She shrugs, eyes darting to one side. "Fine."

"I've got a heating pad for your cramps. If you get them, that is—"

"I'm okay for now, but thank you." She nibbles on her lip, eyeing the bags on her table. "And thank you for bringing all of this. You seriously didn't have to."

"If you want me to leave, it's okay."

It's the last thing I want to do, but she's been acting weird since she sent that text, and I can take a hint. I might not like it, but I won't force her to spend time with me.

She grasps my hand and squeezes, her green eyes shining as she looks up at me. "No. Please, stay."

"Are you sure?" Even as I ask the question, I step closer.

She nods, then gives another shoulder shrug. "I'm a bit thrown having you here, but that's a me issue, not you."

My heart sinks a little. "Why is that?"

She nods toward her bed. "Can we sit? I know it's weird that my bed is my couch, but I don't want to sit in a stiff chair right now," she says, eyeing the little kitchen set against the other wall.

I smile. Damn, her awkwardness is adorable.

I've had my tongue in her ass. I've smacked her pussy and I've been buried to the hilt inside her when she comes. She was a goddess in every one of those moments, but right now, standing before me, I swear I'm seeing the real, unfiltered version. And I fucking love it.

So I follow her to her bed, and when she settles beside me, I pull her onto my lap. "Baby girl, you're killing me," I murmur into her neck. "What's going on in that head of yours?"

She pulls back and presses her palm to my cheek, her eyes boring into mine. "I don't have people here. I don't show them this side of me."

Unease swirls in my gut. "But why?"

"You've seen the Warrens' house. And all the Langfields' homes too, I'm sure. And Sutton Jones, another one of my closest friends—her mom is Elizabeth Sweet," she says, her shoulders sagging. "Every one of my friends has a perfect family and their own beautiful apartment. And let's not even talk about your place. I'm sure the women you date—"

"I don't date," I say gruffly.

She rolls her eyes. "You know what I mean. The women you fuck."

That unease curls into a ball in the pit of my stomach. "I can't change who I was before I met you."

She shakes her head, huffing out an annoyed breath. "I'm not saying I want you to. I'm just saying that I'm not like them. Any of them."

Despite my concern, I can't help but smirk. "That's true."

She frowns, those beautiful green irises dulling a little.

"You're not like any other woman I've ever met." I lace my fingers with hers and kiss her knuckles. "So yeah, I've fucked a lot of women in my life, and sure, maybe they came from money, or maybe they hid behind a façade. Honestly I don't ask a woman to show me her bank balance before we fool around. I couldn't give a fuck how much money you have. I'm not judging you. In fact, I'm crazy as fuck about you. So crazy that, yeah, when I pulled up in front of your building, I thought *she deserves a better home*. Because I want you in mine."

Her eyes widen and her lips part, a small breath escaping her.

"I can't explain this feeling I have when I'm with you any more than I can explain how the moment I put on skates, I knew I was meant to be a hockey player." I feel as vulnerable as fuck right now, but I can't stop myself from being honest with her. "I want this, Savannah. You. All of it. So please just let me get to know you."

She's quiet, searching my face for a long moment. So long, in fact, that I worry I've scared her. That she'll jump off my lap and usher me straight out the door.

But when her shy smile returns, the anxiety in my chest dissipates.

"What do you want to know?" she finally asks.

"Everything," I admit, not having a clue where to start. "Anything you'll tell me. Maybe start with your favorite movie?"

She hums, her lips twitching. "Really? That's the first thing that comes to mind when I ask what you want to know about me?"

Amusement floods me, along with relief. "I figure we can watch it after dinner. I'll rub your back. Then, maybe, if you feel more relaxed, we can have a conversation without all the stress."

The light returns to her eyes. "That's—" She runs her tongue over her bottom lip. "That's a really good idea."

I roll to one side, forcing her onto her back, her head on the pillows, eliciting a squeal from her. With a quick peck to her mouth, I stand and shuffle to the table to unpack the supplies I brought. First out is the bear I won for her.

"Oh my god, you brought our love bear!" she squeals.

I chuckle at the ridiculous term she continues to use. "Didn't have a babysitter and I didn't want you to think I couldn't take care of him properly."

She breaks into a face-splitting grin, and when I hand him to her, still dressed in his Burberry sweater, she squeezes him tight to her chest. "I trust that you were an excellent daddy to our first baby."

Halfway to the table, I spin back to her. "First, huh?"

Her eyes widen and her mouth drops open, but no words come out.

Before she can get too worked up about her slip of the tongue, I chuckle and get back to unloading the bags.

"So, um," she says, voice full of nerves, "what else did you bring?"

"French fries and ice cream to start. We'll eat those first, since temperature matters."

She laughs, her expression easing.

"I also have chocolate. Watermelon Sour Patch candies because my sister says she craves them during her period too. I got the kid ones too, because why not? And Twizzlers, peanut butter cups. The big ones. Oh, and I picked up a few magazines. Honestly, I went to the store and picked up everything I thought Aiden Langfield would bring on a normal travel day."

She snorts like she thinks I'm kidding. Clearly she doesn't know my buddy well enough to know that he has one hell of a sweet tooth.

"Okay, I agree," she says. "We should start with the ice cream and French fries. Oh, and the peanut butter cups."

I grab the requested items and go in search of a spoon. It's not hard to find, since she has a whopping three kitchen drawers.

She's a big fan of rom-coms, so we turn on *Wedding Crashers*, and for the next two hours we snack and laugh our asses off. When we've officially overdosed on sugar, I clean up and dig out the heating pad.

I plug it in and spread it out on the bed, then urge her to lie on her stomach so she can watch the movie while I rub her back.

Without hesitating, she pulls her cozy top over her head and then unclasps her bra, revealing her perfect heavy breasts and instantly making my mouth water.

"Hate wearing a bra at home," she tells me as she spins and positions herself on the bed like I asked.

I bite back a groan, willing my dick to stand down. That's not what tonight is about. With a long breath out, I go back for the bottle of massage oil and bring it over to the bed. "You are the sexiest woman I've ever met."

She looks over her shoulder at me. "Right. My belly is bulging from all the junk food, my hair hasn't been washed since yesterday, and I'm in old sweats. Hottie, right here."

I dig my thumbs into her shoulders and lean down, pressing a kiss to her cheek. "If you think a single one of those things turns me off, then you seriously don't have a fucking clue."

Her eyes fall shut and she hums.

I massage her shoulders and upper back, then work my way lower. In minutes, though, she's squirming beneath me, making me wonder if I'm being too aggressive.

"Too much pressure?"

She drops her head and gives it a shake. "No, I'm just—" She groans into the comforter beneath her. "I'm horny. You're making me really fucking horny."

Laughing, I clutch her by the hips and flip her over.

Eyes widening, she tries to adjust her tits, but before she can wrangle them, I duck down and suck a nipple into my mouth.

Her mouth drops open, and she whines. "Fuck, that feels good."

I pull back and drink her in. She looks so goddamn delicious, her nipples pebbled, begging for more.

With a wicked grin, I bite down on the other. Then I lick away the sting. When I tug on her waistband, she squirms and grasps my wrists, stopping the movement. "What are you doing?"

"I'm not afraid of a little blood, baby girl. I'm going to make you come on my tongue, and if that's not enough to satisfy you, I'll fuck you until you come all over me."

I grasp the elastic band of her pants again, but she squeezes my wrists harder, her body tensing. "Wait."

She's breathless, chest heaving and pupils blown out. Yet there's anxiety there too.

"What's wrong?"

She squeezes her eyes shut and blows out a breath. "I'm not on my period."

I pull back, confusion washing over me. "What?"

Eyes open again, she pushes up to sitting and glances at the door before turning back to me but not meeting my eye. "I'm not on my period."

"So when you texted, you were trying to blow me off?" I sit back a little, surprised by the sting that comes with that realization.

She rests a hand on my thigh and squeezes. "No." She swallows thickly, like there's more on her mind, but doesn't say anything else.

"No, what? Please tell me what's going on, because my mind is running with lots of ideas, and none of them are good."

"I wasn't telling you I was on my period. And I wasn't trying to cancel on you." She grunts, focus fixed on the floor. "But I figured you'd cancel on me after getting that text."

I'm so fucking lost, and I'm still spiraling.

"The point of the calendar wasn't to tell you that I was on my period. It was an ovulation calendar." She peers up then, embarrassment shining in her eyes.

"Ovulation," I repeat.

Her lips slant, like maybe she wants to laugh. "You know, like how you figure out when you're ovulating?" She says it like it's a question, her voice going up at the end.

My stomach drops when her meaning registers.

"Wait, you want me to knock you up?"

CHAPTER 25
CAMDEN

"SHE SAID WHAT NOW?" Daniel nearly stabs his face with his fork, the piece of pancake falling to his plate rather than making it into his mouth.

War gawks at me, mouth hanging open, coffee cup hovering in front of him.

Noah bursts out laughing.

I glare at them one at a time. "She said it was an ovulation calendar."

"Because you're getting old," Noah says around a laugh.

Irritation simmers in my veins. "I don't need you to repeat my words back to me."

"He might, considering how old you are," War mutters.

"I'm younger than you, motherfucker."

War narrows his icy blue eyes, channeling the team captain he was so long ago, and on instinct, I shrink back into the booth. We're at breakfast at our usual spot, and yeah, there are kids around. It's a Sunday morning, so the place is packed with families. And this is my family, so once a month we get together for breakfast. Brooks's sons had some football thing this morning—because much to his disappointment, not one of his three boys has any interest in hockey—so he's missing this important update in my life.

Thank fuck.

"How did you respond?" Daniel doesn't take his eyes off me as he successfully shoves a bite of pancake into his mouth.

I shrug. "I said okay."

War, who's finally sipping his coffee, chokes and spits the warm liquid all over his own plate and the table in front of him.

Without a second of hesitation, Noah throws a napkin at him.

Daniel, on the other hand, slumps back and groans. "You spit on my pancakes."

"I'll buy you new pancakes," he grits out. "This idiot told my daughter's twenty-seven-year-old best friend that he'd knock her up." War pats his face with a napkin, the glare he's fixed on me scarier than I think I've ever seen from him.

"No, I said okay to the possibility. Which isn't all that unbelievable. There's a chance we will eventually be ready to discuss ovulation calendars and shit like that."

Noah scowls. "That's the least sexy way to discuss baby-making with a woman."

"Not if you have trouble having kids," Daniel says.

"And what the hell would you know about that?" War points out.

"Mills had trouble, and she used those things," Daniel says with a shrug. Millie is his twin.

"Right, but Savannah hasn't known Camden long enough to find out whether her period is even late, let alone to discuss problems with making a baby," War grumbles.

Noah rests his forearms on the table and studies me from behind black-framed glasses. "Do you think she was serious?"

I shrug. "I don't know. She seems so fucking normal. And she's absolutely incredible in bed."

"Earmuffs," War grumbles.

"What, you can't hear about sex because you're married? That's new."

"No," he growls. "I can't hear about you having sex with my daughter's best friend."

I wipe my mouth with my napkin and toss it to the table. "Get over it. She's hot as fuck and she's dirty as fuck, and honestly, I'm crazy about her."

"But she might be a little crazy," Daniel sings.

With a pointed look at him, I shrug. "Possibly."

Noah barks out a laugh. "She's gotta be fucking with you."

"She's a little quirky, yeah. She brought up kids the first night we were together." I don't mention the love bear or the baby outfit. Honestly, both are a little funny on their own, but added up like this, maybe her actions are a little more on the concerning side.

War sets his napkin down and studies me like he would an opponent. The scrutiny is unnerving. "She had a rough childhood," he says. "Parents who didn't want her, who never bother to visit."

My stomach drops. I kind of assumed that was the case based on some of our conversations, but she hasn't mentioned any of that directly.

"So maybe she's a little overeager to have a family of her own," he adds. "What did you say when she brought up kids that night?"

That's what's so wild. I didn't actually freak out. With anyone else, I'm certain I would have. "I told her that I'd always wished I had them, but that the timing was never right."

Daniel points his fork at me. "You set yourself up for this, then. She's just trying to give you what you want. That's what women do." He stabs another piece of pancake. "Women that aren't Hannah, at least. She takes whatever the fuck she wants, and I just give it all to her."

Noah groans. "Please don't talk about what women do in bed while discussing my sister."

"Knock it off," Daniel taunts. "Your sister and I have been married for almost two decades. You should be used to this by now."

War turns his stern look on Daniel. When he turns back to me, his expression has only softened a little. "He's an idiot, but he's not wrong. You asked for this."

I push back from the table a couple of inches. "How did I ask for an ovulation calendar?"

"You basically told her your clock was ticking. She likes you and she's trying to show you that she's listening to you."

I scowl. "Men don't have clocks."

"I'm telling you, you asked for this," he says.

"And if you want Mav on your team, you've gotta make this relationship last," Daniel reminds me through a mouthful of pancakes.

I close my eyes and pinch the bridge of my nose. Not because I have any interest in ending things with Savannah but because the last thing I need is a reminder of that damn bet.

War points at me. "You better fix this."

Not that I agree with him, but even if I did, what the hell am I supposed to say to her now?

Chapter 26
Savannah

Daddy: What type of wine should I bring?

I STARE at the text like it's come to life, equipped with three heads and dancing before me.

What type of wine should I bring?

He's still coming? After he rushed out of here before I'd fully woken up this morning, I was sure I'd never hear from him again.

Sure, he stuck around last night. And we had sex. But I figured that was goodbye sex. Like, wow, she's hot and I don't know how to reasonably extract myself from this situation, so I'll fuck her one more time before I disappear.

Honestly, I wouldn't have blamed him.

I've known him for a matter of weeks, and I sent a fucking ovulation calendar to his phone and basically told him I wanted him to knock me up. What reasonable man would stick around?

When he dipped out, mumbling about meeting his friends for breakfast while I was still blinking the sleep from my eyes, I will admit a wave of sadness hit me. Okay, more like a tsunami. I was gutted. Because the man behaved like a picture-perfect boyfriend last night.

He showed up with supplies because he thought I had my period. He watched rom-coms with me and binged on junk food right alongside me until our stomachs ached. He was willing—happy, even—to have sex with me while I was bleeding. Even if I wasn't really.

Every single one of those actions told me more about the kind of man Camden Snow is than anything he could have told me on a date. He puts others first. He's caring and sweet and fun as hell to be with. He's the kind of person I would want to date for real.

And then I scared him away by telling him I wanted to have his babies.

It makes sense. Hell, it's what I expected. But still, watching him scurry out, then being left in my silent apartment with nothing but time to come to terms with how I'd chased him away was hard.

Though it isn't nearly as hard as figuring out why the hell he's texting me about wine now.

Does the man have no sense of self-preservation? He's really coming back for more?

Me: Did you mean to text this to me?

The three dots appear right away, and almost instantly, his reply comes through.

Daddy: Obviously. Who else would I bring wine to?

Me: After the way you left this morning, I figured you wouldn't come tonight.

Daddy: I said I was coming.

Me: Yeah, last night before…I said what I said.

Daddy: I have no idea what you're talking about. Did you say something weird?

I roll my eyes, picturing the cocky smirk he's wearing right now.

Me: Don't play coy.

> Daddy: Tell me what kind of wine to bring,
> baby girl. Or would you rather discuss what
> you said last night?

I grunt. He's infuriating. Is this man seriously coming back for more?

I navigate to the girls' group chat, alerting them to the 911 situation on our hands. Then I tell Camden that Rosalie only drinks Chianti and not to spend too much. She's a cheap date.

Two hours later, I've parked myself at a table at a coffee shop close to home, and I'm staring at my computer screen while I wait for Josie.

A blank screen.

Because I don't have a clue what I should write. Every word feels like a lie.

Don't sleep with him on the first date—whoops did that.

Talk about yourself, not your exes—unless he begs you to tell him about everyone you've fucked and makes you come while you do it.

Jealousy is toxic—or he'll find it insanely attractive when you claim him.

Each of those scenarios on their own could be looked past, yeah, but the future baby conversation? That shouldn't be negotiable. I should be able to tell my readers with complete certainty not to do it. But Camden has me questioning everything I've ever known about dating.

"You look pissed."

Startling, I straighten and snap my head up.

Josie is standing over me, an amused expression on her pretty freckled face.

I blow out a breath. "More like confused. Befuddled. Lost."

"Befuddled, huh?" Smirking, she pulls out the chair across from me and picks up the coffee I ordered for her.

"Okay, get this," I say, snapping my laptop closed. "Last night I sent Camden my ovulation tracker—"

"Wait, you're tracking your ovulation schedule?"

I blink slowly, holding back an annoyed sigh. "Obviously not. I just downloaded the app and put in fake information. Then I sent it to him."

She snorts, her fair skin going pink. "Okay, you may continue."

"He showed up with chocolates and a heating pad and all kinds of junk food because he thought I was on my period."

Eyes widening, she gapes. "No, sir."

"Oh yes, sir." I throw my hands out. "He's perfect, Josie. Freaking perfect. And later, when I admitted that it was an ovulation tracker, he still didn't freak out."

"Wait," she says, leaning forward. "How did you explain that with a straight face?"

I shake my head, squeezing my eyes shut. "I have no idea."

She whistles, bringing her coffee to her lips. "Damn, Daddy Snow is obsessed with you."

Forcing my chin up, I roll my shoulders. "I don't know what to do. He won't break up with me. I think Sutton's right."

With a ridiculous smile, she stares at me.

Eventually, I can't take the scrutiny any longer. "What?"

"You don't want him to break up with you. It's written all over your face."

"Yes, I do. I need him to." I stab at my laptop with one finger. "I can't lose this job."

Smile falling, she sets her coffee down. "You're not going to lose your job. The column's numbers are up already. You've hooked your readers. They all want to know what you'll do next to get the poor guy to dump you."

"That's just it." I slump. "I can't do it anymore. You're right. I like him, okay? He's nice and sweet and so fucking good in bed." I lean forward. "Like so fucking good."

She tips her head back and laughs. "Yeah, I can see that. So enjoy it. Your readers are enjoying your antics, and it seems like Camden is too." She shrugs. "If he didn't dump you after the ovulation tracker incident, it sounds like you're in the clear. The man is smitten."

I squirm in my seat, processing her words. "So I just keep doing the crazy shit?"

She shrugs, brows lifted. "Or stop. But then you don't have an article, so yeah, I don't know about that."

I slump back and sink down in my seat. I'm no closer to getting this week's column written than I was ten minutes ago. "What would Sutton do?"

She laughs. "Probably invite him over for the holidays and doodle her first name with his last name on a piece of paper."

Head hung, I bury my face in my hands and sigh.

Josie only laughs harder. "You know she would."

Straightening, I pick up my phone and dial Sutton. The second she answers, I cut her off. "What's the craziest thing you've ever done in a relationship."

She coughs out an affronted laugh. "Excuse you. How about 'hello my dear friend? How are you doing?'"

"Hi, Sutton," Josie singsongs like a goody two-shoes.

"Hi, Jose."

"I'm serious. I need your help," I whine.

"She really does," Josie chimes in. "The man didn't even dump her after she sent him her ovulation calendar."

"Oh my god," Sutton wheezes. "That's amazing. By the way, I'm thoroughly enjoying your article and I've been following all your rules." Her words get faster, her excitement palpable. "Royal and I are going on our third date next week. He's coming to see me when the Bolts get back from their away stretch next weekend."

Warmth blooms in my chest. "Aw, Sutton, that makes me so happy."

"He's really great," she chirps. "And no, I haven't slept with him or doodled our names or even asked him to come to Maine for Christmas. Honestly, your column really is helping me."

Josie beams at me from across the table.

"My column, where I detail the things a woman shouldn't do, even if they're somehow working for me?" I scoff. "Or maybe you're just taking a relationship at a normal pace and not molding your life around that of a man's since he's as busy as you are."

Sutton hums noncommittally. "Maybe. But this call isn't about me. You need help coming up with more what-not-to-do ideas, huh?"

"You should invite him to spend Christmas with you," Josie says.

I lower the phone and pin her with a glare. "No."

She shrugs. "Chances are he's going to be at the Langfields Christmas Eve party anyway, and since Addie has claimed you this year—"

"Yes, like I'm a puppy the three of you pass around," I say with a laugh.

"You know it's not like that," she says, her head tilted and her lips turned down. "We all just want to spend the day with you."

I give her a small smile. My friends make sure I don't feel like the girl without a family by acting like they're fighting over me instead. Last year I spent Christmas with the Warrens, but this year Addie asked me first.

I blow out a breath, my phone back at my ear. "You really think Camden will be there?"

Josie nibbles on her lip. "He's kind of like you in that way. He's always in Boston for the holidays rather than with his family. And since Camden is attached to Daniel at the hip, and Daniel's twin married into the Langfield family, he's always done the holidays with them."

Lips pressed together, I consider it. "I don't think it'll cut it for the article. Doesn't sound like asking him to spend the holiday with me will freak him out."

She scrunches her nose and huffs. "What is something that Camden is super into that we could use to freak him out?"

I snort. "I barely know anything about the guy, other than he loves hockey and he's great in bed."

Josie's eyes light up. "Oh my god, I have the best idea."

CHAPTER 27
CAMDEN

THIS TIME when I pull up in front of Savannah's building, I'm far less nervous. I'm also wondering what the hell I'm doing coming back here.

Without the bet hanging over my head, I don't know that I'd be pursuing Savannah like this. Or would I? If I'd been asked the question a few days ago, I'd have said the bet has nothing to do with my need to see her. I like her. A lot.

But after the ovulation calendar thing…I don't know. It was so bizarre. And so unlike the woman I've been getting to know. Sure, over the years, women have tried to trap me in relationships. Not because of me as a person, but because they wanted the fame. The money. The supposed perks that would come with being the baby mama of a pro hockey player.

I don't get it. Maybe because I've seen what true love looks like and I'd never settle for anything less than that. All my lifelong friends have found it. Aiden and Lennox have the kind of love that's legendary. Brooks and Sara started it all. Brooks fell hard for Sara when she was the head of PR for the Bolts and he was our goalie. Now she's the organization's CEO, and she's one of the coolest chicks I know. Funny as fuck too.

War and Ava have a wild story. Daniel and Hannah too. Even Noah found an epic love. It didn't come easy at all, because his wife was the team's CEO back in our day, as well as Aiden and Brooks's baby sister. Screwing with a teammate's sister is a no. Not even up for discussion. And yet he won her over, and now he's the Bolts' GM and married to the love of his life.

If love like that exists, then why in God's name would anyone want to marry for money and a little magazine time?

My radar for gold diggers is impeccable after all these years. I can tell right away when a woman is only interested in my fame and what I can buy her, and I did not peg Savannah as that kind of woman at all.

But what is she after? Could it really be that she took my comment about how I once thought I wanted kids and got the wrong idea? Maybe this is my fault. After that, I even asked about her damn birth control and said it would be fine for now.

And I can't even fucking say I made the comment in the heat of the moment, because with any other woman, I'd never even consider the threat of knocking her up as a way to turn up the heat in the bedroom.

Never have I imagined a woman pregnant with my child and considered the notion sexy.

But envisioning Savannah, belly slightly rounded and a smile on her face? Imagining her with a newborn with dark red hair in her arms? I can picture the late nights and the early mornings. I can picture the house, the life, and the love. And none of it fucking scares me. In fact, while I sit in my car, parked on the curb, my mind creating a fantasy that involves a family with Savannah, I'm fucking hard as steel.

So maybe it's not so fucking scary that she's thinking about it too.

I adjust myself, take a deep breath, and snag the bottles of wine from the back seat. I'm not any closer to figuring her out, and I'm here, so I'll go inside, act normal, and hope that she doesn't pull out a pregnancy test or a baby bottle tonight.

If she does, then I really will have to leave. Bet or no bet. These feelings be damned.

As I lock the car and head to the door, I consider that this could be the last time I walk toward her place, and the idea makes my chest constrict painfully.

I shake off the sensation. Tonight will go well. I'm sure. Last night was an off night. Everything is going to be fine.

The door swings open as I hit the bottom step outside, and a woman with blond hair pulled up in a messy ponytail appears. Before she can even cross the threshold, a cry sounds from inside. "Mama, please!"

The woman turns around and crouches, talking in soft tones to the crying child. "Mama has to go to work, but Daddy's taking you up to the Donadios' for dinner, and you get to hang out with Savvy."

Ah, this must be John's wife. What did he say she did for a living? A nurse, maybe? If so, the scrubs she's wearing make sense.

John himself appears, scooping the little boy up, then grasping his wife's neck and pulling her in for a kiss.

When she smiles up at him, the warmth already growing in my chest expands, blooming into something stronger. They've got at least two little ones, and with their professions, they probably don't get a ton of time together, yet their love is palpable even from several feet away.

"Night, babe," she says, spinning toward the door again.

I step back so I don't take her by surprise, but when she gets through the door, she spots me.

"Oh!" She pulls up short.

I move the bottles of wine into one arm and hold out a hand. "I'm Camden Snow, Savannah's boyfriend."

Beaming, she adjusts the bag on her shoulder and moves her Thermos from one hand to the other so she can accept the greeting. "I've heard a lot about you."

My heart skips in my damn chest. "From Savannah?"

She laughs. "No. My husband. He hasn't shut up about meeting you, and once he found out you were going to the Donadios' for dinner tonight, he spent all afternoon on the phone with his buddies from work, acting like a gossip girl."

I chuckle. "You heading to work?"

Her smile falls a little. "Yeah, wish I could join you all for dinner but"—she shrugs—"duty calls."

I dip my chin and skirt around her to get out of her way. "I hope you have a good night."

The building is quiet when I step inside, so I head up the stairs and knock on the Donadios' door, assuming Savannah will already be there. Instead, I'm greeted by Rosalie, and Savannah is nowhere in sight.

"Ah, good man. You brought two bottles." She nods at the wine, grinning. "Come in. You can help me set the table."

The scents of fresh baked bread and garlic hit me as I enter the small apartment. The place is bigger than Savannah's studio, with the living room to the right and the kitchen separated from it by a half wall. Nick is seated in a recliner with the television blaring, and past his chair, there's a hallway.

Quickly, I slip off my jacket and hang it on the coat rack by the door. I greet Nick, who gives me a smile and a nod before turning back to the television, then follow Rosalie into the kitchen, where a folding table has been pushed up against the four-person table. Several folding chairs are propped in a stack against it, waiting to be set up.

I put the wine on the counter and turn to Rosalie. "Any particular way you want the table set?"

She's shuffled to the stove and is stirring a pot of sauce. "Nope," she says over her shoulder. "Not much room in here, and it will only get smaller when the Donovans come, so as long as you can get all the chairs around the table, we're good."

I make quick work of positioning them, then bring the stack of plates set out on the counter over and place one in front of each chair. While I work, Rosalie promises to teach me how to make her meatballs and pasta, explaining that they're Savannah's favorite.

When the door swings open, I spin around, a big smile on my face and my heart practically fucking floating.

But rather than Savannah, John appears with the little boy I saw earlier and another little guy who looks almost identical to him. "The girls went up to Savvy's to do their makeup," he says with a laugh.

The little boys—twins, John Junior and Frankie, I'm told—are busy immediately, clambering up on chairs and picking up silverware and napkins.

Rosalie peers over at me, a sweet smile on her face. "Why don't you go tell Savannah that dinner will be ready in a few minutes?"

My stomach flips in response to the idea. Is it nerves, maybe? Yeah, I think I'm nervous about seeing her. Worried, I guess, that things will be awkward after last night. Anxious to find out whether she's back to being normal again.

But more than all of that, I'm excited to see her. I've attended plenty of family dinners like this, where I'm the odd man out. I can make conversation with just about anyone, and considering John is a fan, we'll always have hockey talk to fall back on. But for the first time, I'm attending a dinner with a person I actually want to sit beside. Someone I want to share the meal with. And unlike all the other meals I've had with friends, tonight's includes sitting at the table with the people who belong to the woman I think I'm falling for.

At the bottom of the stairs, I blow out a breath. Then I take them two at a time. When I hit the top, I discover her door is ajar. Panic flares immediately, but it fades quickly when I hear music playing from inside.

Sounds like an old Lake Paige song. I can't help but smile when a wave of nostalgia hits me. Once upon a time, I met Lake at a New Year's party, and she actually married Daniel's dad years ago. It was crazy as fuck back then, but now I see her most holidays.

My smile turns to a full-on grin and my chest pinches strangely when I push the door open farther and find Savannah brushing the hair of a little girl. She stops at the chorus and brings the brush to her mouth, dramatically singing the lyrics along with Lake, much to both girls' delight.

The smaller of the two jumps up on the bed and bounces, hair flying. Rather than stop her or scold her, Savannah holds out a hand to the other girl and helps her up onto the bed. Then she jumps up herself and the three of them flail in what I suspect are supposed to be dance moves and scream-sing the lyrics.

I ease the door shut and lean against it, watching them, and that ache in my chest unfurls. Seeing Savannah like this makes it easy to imagine a future I thought I'd long missed out on.

I feel lighter than I have in years.

When she catches sight of me, she bites down on her lip, trying and failing to suppress the big smile on her face. She's so fucking gorgeous it actually hurts to look at her sometimes. But right now, it's like first aid to my damaged soul. Her smile is contagious.

She bounces off the bed and rushes toward me, the excitement in her expression making me feel more important than I think I ever have.

"You came!"

As she crashes into me, throwing her arms around my neck, I fall back against the door.

"Sorry," she says quickly, pulling back, like she's as surprised as I am by her excitement.

I don't let her get far before I pull her back in and bury my face in the crook of her neck, inhaling the sweet scent of her perfume, or maybe it's her hair products. "Don't apologize for being happy to see me." I press my lips to her soft skin and breathe her in again. "It's nice to be wanted."

The words are meant for myself, but when she pulls back and gives me a soft smile, it's obvious that she heard me.

She pops up on her toes and presses a kiss to my jaw. "I'm really glad you came."

Our quiet moment is cut short when the girls squeal about kissing boys, their voices so high-pitched they make me wince.

Savannah introduces me as her boyfriend. Piper, the older of the two, straightens and informs her that we've already met. The smaller one, Alice, suddenly turns shy and clings to her sister.

Damn. The two boys downstairs and the two girls up here, the oldest of which can't be more than four? The Donovans have their hands full.

We head down for dinner, and the apartment descends into complete chaos. It's tight quarters in the kitchen, and Alice refuses to sit anywhere but on Savannah's lap.

I sit beside her, and while John asks a million questions about my time with the Bolts—and the kids interrupt every five seconds asking for the cheese or another meatball, or to see a video of a play John brings up—Savannah relaxes beside me, squeezing my thigh here and there and shooting me secret smiles. It's not a romantic dinner to say the least, but it's nice, just being with her and observing her as she interacts with the people she cares about.

"Did you know Santa is coming this week?" Piper tells me seriously.

I nod. "Yeah, three more days, right?"

Her eyes shine bright. "He's bringing me a Barbie dream house."

"And me too," Alice says from atop Savannah's lap.

"Maybe," John says. "So long as you're on the nice list."

"Oh, these girls would never be on the naughty list," Rosalie says. "And to make sure, they're going to go sit in the living room quietly while we clean up, aren't you, girls?"

In unison they say, "Yes, Mrs. Donadio."

The girls dart off, and once John has wiped the spaghetti sauce from the boys' faces and hands, John Junior and Frankie toddle after their sisters.

"That was incredible," I tell Rosalie, wiping my face with my napkin one last time. "Thank you for inviting me."

Smiling, she holds up her empty glass. "Thank you for bringing the wine."

I reach for Savannah's plate and stack it on mine, but before I can do any more cleaning, Rosalie waves me off.

"Sit here with Nick. Savannah and I have this covered."

John shakes his head. "Don't even bother arguing with her. She won't listen."

The older woman beams. "I won't."

Savannah squeezes my thigh and stands, collecting our small stack of plates.

"Thank you," I tell her.

She smiles. "Thank you for coming. Truly."

"What do you do for Christmas?" Rosalie asks as she eyes John, who's stacking the kids' plates.

"I'm just going to carry them over for you," he says with a laugh. "I promise I won't wash them."

"Just leave them in the sink. We'll wash them after. I've got dessert ready." She scurries over to the counter, and a moment later, she returns with a tray of cookies.

Once the dinner dishes have all been piled in the sink and on the counter, Savannah settles back beside me. I tug her chair closer and wrap an arm around her.

"So Christmas," Rosalie prods again. "Do you spend it with your family?"

"No," I admit. "My family is actually in Vegas."

Nick perks up. "Oh, so is Savannah's."

I look over at her. "Really? I didn't know you were from Vegas."

She shakes her head. "I don't really…" The words drop off, but I hear the message loud and clear: she doesn't talk about it.

"Her mother is a piece of work and her father never wanted to be one," Rosalie says like she's talking about the weather.

Beside me, Savannah turns crimson.

I reach for her hand beneath the table and squeeze. "Then they're the ones who are missing out."

She offers me a soft smile as Rosalie says, "Of course they are. Our Savannah is wonderful. They don't deserve her."

Savannah shakes her head. "You're just saying that because I'll be here bright and early Christmas morning to cook with you."

"Our best girl always is," she says, her expression one of genuine affection. "Right, Nico? Wish our son had married someone as wonderful as her."

"You love Junior's wife," Savannah shoots back, her smile more vibrant now.

Rosalie stands and collects the half-empty tray of cookies. "Yeah, I do. But that doesn't mean I don't love you."

Savannah settles her head on my shoulder. "Love you too, Rosie," she murmurs.

I smile down at her. She's so pretty like this. So easy to like. She's everything I've ever wanted in a woman. It almost makes me forget what she said last night. Maybe War and Daniel were right. Maybe I did bring that on. I told her what I wanted, and she thought she should give it to me. It's sweet when I think about it like that. And the truth is, the idea of it, of a family with Savannah, doesn't scare me.

"What about you, Camden?" Nick says.

I give my head a little shake, realizing I've been lost in my thoughts. "What about me?"

"What are you doing for Christmas?"

"I, uh, spend Christmas Eve at a friend's place."

In the middle of the kitchen, Rosalie turns around, tray in hand. "What about Christmas Day?"

Savannah shifts and peers up at me, like she's waiting for my answer. I consider lying. I don't want pity, and I don't want to dampen the mood, but I can't lie to her. "I normally just relax on Christmas Day."

"Alone?" Rosalie asks, her free hand clutching nonexistent pearls like I've personally offended her.

I nod.

"Well, not this year," she says, like it's not up for debate.

A discomfort that often hits me with these kinds of subjects surges. "Oh, that's okay."

Green eyes depthless, Savannah studies me, like she's deep in thought.

I give her a little smile, assuring her that I'm good. I'm fine with being alone.

"No, she's right." Savannah straightens, her voice almost scratchy. Then she blinks and breaks into a beaming smile. "You'll spend it with me. Please. We're both going to the Langfields for Christmas Eve, right?"

I nod slowly, unsure that I like where this is going. Is this going to be a pity invite?

"Then you'll come back here with me." She peeks into the living room, where the kids are all settled in front of the television. Then she leans in and whispers, "You can come with me to help the Donovans set up for Santa, and then we'll wake up together on Christmas morning—our first Christmas morning together." She smiles now, even bigger, like the idea sounds as incredible to her as it does to me. "And then we'll have Christmas Day here, with everyone."

I assess her, take in the smile on her face, and allow myself to picture the scenes she's just painted. I consider the memories we'll make, and my heart thrashes wildly in my chest. Because I want it. I want all of that. With her.

"Sounds like the perfect Christmas," I tell her.

She nods, her eyes glittering. "It really does."

Chapter 28
Savannah

"THANK you so much for coming early," Addie says as I walk through the front door to the brownstone where she grew up.

According to her, this place will be a mob scene in a matter of hours, so I'm here to help prep. Josie usually claims me for the holiday, so I've never attended a Langfield Christmas Eve, but I've heard they're epic.

I can only imagine it will be a who's who of the Boston elite kind of night.

Also, this house is incredible. All of the homes on this block are gorgeous, and most of them are inhabited by Langfields. All four Langfield brothers, including Addie's dad, live on the street.

The way Addie tells it, her mom and her bio dad divorced when she was a toddler, and after, her mother, Liv, and her three best friends moved into one house on this street so they could raise their kids together. Then Liv married her boss, Beckett Langfield, in Vegas on a whim, and when they came home, he moved in with all of the women and kids.

The story gets a little fuzzy from there, but eventually Beckett bought every house on this street, and now some are filled with Langfields, and the others are occupied by the friends her mom moved in with all those years ago, along with their families. Sienna is the only one of Addie's dad's siblings who doesn't live on this street.

"I'm happy to help, and I really appreciate the invitation." I hand her a bottle of wine stuffed into a gift bag, fighting the urge to cringe. I spent a good chunk of my Christmas budget on it, but I can't imagine her family drinking grocery-store wine.

"You shouldn't have spent your money on this," she says as she eyes the label on the bottle.

She tugs me into the oversized kitchen. It's all white cabinets and white and gold marble counters. At the island, three kids are perched on stools, each decorating their own gingerbread house. Avery, JJ's daughter, is on one end, and beside her are Winnie's twin boys, Beckett and Declan.

"I didn't ask you to come early to help set up, I texted SOS because —" Brows lifted, she darts a glance at Avery.

Ah. Where Avery goes, JJ goes, and wherever JJ is, Addie tries not to be. Alone, at least. It's going to be awfully difficult to keep this up when she's his goalie coach next season, but pointing that out now won't do me any good.

"Didn't the two of you grow up together?" I mumble when I spot JJ in the back yard with Addie's dad while he talks to what looks like a… raccoon? That can't be right.

With a huff, my friend stomps to the fridge. "Want a water or something? Or should we have wine? Maybe we should have wine now."

I snort. "We definitely shouldn't have wine now. You'll be toasted before the guests arrive, and I am not going to be blamed for ruining Christmas Eve."

She sighs and plucks two bottles of water from the fridge. "No, that'd be him." She nods at the window.

"The raccoon?" I tease.

She glares at me. "That's Junior Jr. She couldn't ruin anything. She's pregnant. My dad is worried she might give birth, but she refuses to let the vet near her. She hisses at anyone who isn't my father."

I turn back to the window, where Beckett is kneeling now, and yeah, he's definitely having a conversation with the raccoon. "I always envisioned your life as a Norman Rockwell painting, picture-perfect family and all. But your dad is weird."

She hums, surveying him. "The weirdest."

"Don't touch my candy!" one of the boys shouts. The outburst is followed by the sound of a sharp smack.

Shoulders slumping, Addie sighs. "Boys."

"He did it first." Declan jabs a finger at Beckett.

"Did not," the other little boy whines.

"Declan took Beck's candy and stuck it in his nose. Then Beck hit him," Avery says without looking up from her project.

My heart melts at the sight of her. She's totally focused on her house, yet she still knows what's going on around her. Such a little woman.

"And Grandpa Beckett isn't weird. He just takes care of everyone he loves." She finally looks up and pins Addie with a look fit for a parent scolding a child.

Addie opens her mouth to respond, but snaps it shut again. She does this a few more times before a look of contrition washes over her and she nods. "You're right, Ave. You are always right."

Damn. It takes effort not to break into laughter.

"I am," the little girl says. "Now could you talk to my dad about signing me up for hockey? He says I have to wait another year."

"Hockey's for boys," Beckett grumbles.

Declan snaps up straight. "Baseball's better."

"Baseball's the worst." Beckett picks up his piping bag of frosting and squirts it at Declan.

"Mom," Declan yells.

"Oh my god," Addie groans, face lifted to the ceiling.

"I now understand why you invited me over," I say with a giggle. "Why don't we separate them?"

She shrugs. "And do what? Winnie is taking a shower, and she said if she doesn't have ten minutes to herself, she'll have a meltdown. And there were tears, Sav, actual tears forming in her eyes. Winnie doesn't cry. And I can't handle crying, period."

A snort finally escapes me, but I rein in control of myself again and just nod. Maybe I should dread the idea of having to entertain a trio of fighting four-year-olds, but honestly, I'm too happy for that kind of negativity. Addie called me over early because she needed me. That alone makes the invite she extended feel a lot less like the pity kind. So I do what I do best. I come up with a game for the boys while leaving Addie and Avery to finish the gingerbread houses.

The party is in full swing a few hours later, but I have yet to spot Camden. I still can't believe we're spending Christmas together. I've got quite the surprise planned for him later. If I don't fall asleep after helping the Donovans set up after the kids are in bed, that is.

Not knowing what to do with myself while I wait for Camden to arrive, I pick up two empty appetizer plates and take them to the kitchen.

"What are you doing?"

I peer over my shoulder, finding Winnie following behind me, plastic stemware in her hands.

"Same as you," I say, lifting the plates a little.

"You're our guest. You should be out there enjoying yourself. Especially after you saved the day with the twins earlier. Thank you."

Warm affection surges through me. "They're sweet. They've just got a lot of energy. Figured a game of freeze tag outside would get some of the zoomies out."

Winnie drops the plastic stemware in the recycling bin and takes the plates from me. "A lot of energy is putting it mildly."

"I only had them for an afternoon, so I wouldn't know. But I can't imagine it's easy raising them on your own."

She blows a strand of her auburn hair out of her face. "I chose this," she says with a smile that doesn't quite reach her eyes.

It sounds like a phrase she uses often. I can imagine she needs the reminder sometimes, that she chose to parent on her own when she chose IVF.

"Doesn't mean you don't get to be tired," I say with a squeeze to her arm.

She sighs, then pastes on another smile. "Addie has been telling me I should read your new column."

I write the column anonymously, though my three best friends know, and since Addie and her older sister are close, I'm not surprised she knows too.

"Oh, her new column is fire." Sienna appears in the doorway, followed quickly by her husband Noah.

I met him when I did a piece introducing our readers to Sienna shortly after she came on as *Jolie's* creative director. The man is insanely hot. Black glasses that make him look just a touch nerdy, yet with the build of a former hockey player and the kindest blue eyes.

He snakes an arm around his wife and pulls her into his side. "Oh yeah? Is it one I should read?"

She pops up on her toes and presses the quickest of kisses to his cheek. "Yes. It's hysterical." Flat-footed again, she beams at me. "Savannah is doing a column on what not to do when dating. She's even going out with guys and testing out these don'ts on them."

Winnie laughs. "No wonder Addie says I need to read it. She's always on me about dating." Her expression sobers a little. "Like I have time for that."

I give her a half smile. "It's not working exactly as I thought it would, to be honest."

"No?" Noah asks.

Sienna giggles. "She's done the most ridiculous things, and still, she can't get this one guy to dump her. She even sent him a link to her ovulation calendar, and he's still sticking around!"

"Shut up!" Winnie wheezes.

Cheeks heating, I wince. "It's not real," I say to Noah. The last thing I want is for anyone to think I'm trying to baby trap a man.

He offers me a tight smile. "So it's just for the story?"

Something about his tone and the way he frames the question makes me uneasy. Or maybe it's because while this thing with Camden may have started that way, it's certainly more than that now. "No, I really like the guy." I shrug. "But the ovulation thing was just for the story, yeah."

Sienna slaps a hand to her husband's chest, still laughing. "And he still didn't dump her."

"Guess Addie was right," Winnie says. "I'll definitely need to read the column."

"Me too," Noah says, still wearing that brittle smile. "Alright, baby," he says to his wife, "I'm going to find the girls. Don't forget, we promised them we'd go see Christmas lights before we head home."

Sienna nods. "Yes, that's my cue. Have a merry Christmas, Savannah. I'll see you next week. Win, I'll see you tomorrow at Aiden's?"

Sienna leans in and gives us both kisses on the cheeks before she and her husband wander away. As they're swallowed up by the crowd, Noah glances back. And I can't help but think that he had more to say about my story.

I exhale a relieved breath. At least he's leaving now. Because while no one but my closest friends knows that Mr. Won't Break Up with me is Camden Snow, our worlds might be too small to keep that secret for long.

CHAPTER 29
CAMDEN

I SCOWL DOWN at the text as I step into Beckett's house. Huh?

Another text appears immediately after, this one a link to *Jolie* magazine's website. I tap it and am redirected to Calliope's blog.

I chuckle. It's been years since I've read one of these, but I really don't have time to check it out right now. I'm far later than I planned to be, and all I want is to find my girl. The holidays are rough for Mom, and today has been an exceptionally bad day. My sister couldn't calm her down and eventually had to call in a nurse to give her a sedative. It's brutal, and we both suffer with a lot of guilt when it has to be done, so I stayed on the phone with Cora for a while after, shooting the shit and trying to take her mind off it all.

After a solid hour, she insisted we end the call, knowing that I have plans with Savannah. In fact, she threatened to fly here and castrate me if I didn't hang up. And then she laughed for five minutes about how sad my girlfriend would be about that since I was stupid enough to tell her about the ovulation calendar.

She also thinks I brought that incident on myself with the baby talk and has teased me relentlessly, telling me I should be happy Savannah is open to having a baby with my old ass. She was still giggling when I ended the call.

She may have been laughing at my expense, but it was good to hear that sound. I imagine the rest of her night will be pretty awful.

After all that, I'm not in the headspace for a Calliope column. My skin is itchy, and if not for my promise to spend Christmas with Savannah, I wouldn't have even come tonight. I'd probably be on a redeye heading to Vegas, actually. But like Cora has told me more than once, my presence wouldn't have been helpful. Actually, seeing me tends to make it worse for Mom.

Which I get, since I'm the reason my dad is dead.

Fuck, my head really isn't in the right space.

The second I see Daniel, head back and laughing, I regret coming. I'm not sure I can fake it tonight.

"Hey, you're here."

At the sound of her voice, my shoulders relax and my heart thumps against my sternum. Those three words are all it takes to lift my mood.

"Hi, baby girl." I pull Savannah into my chest. I've barely gotten a look at her, and I couldn't describe what she's wearing if asked, but with her in my arms, my entire being settles.

Pulling back, she presses her hands to my cheeks. "You okay?"

With a sigh, I lean into her touch and force a smile. "Just an off night. But I'm good now."

Those green eyes of hers dance over my face. I've never wanted to be seen more than I do in this moment.

"You know," she says, "I'm kind of tired. Would you mind if we didn't stick around too long?"

A mixture of relief and a little guilt swirls in my chest. "You sure? I just got here. I'm good to hang for a bit."

She fakes a yawn. The move is so fucking adorable, her gesture so sweet, that I actually feel the moment I fall for her. I thought I knew what she meant to me when I didn't totally freak out over the baby stuff, but it goes deeper than that. No one has ever seen me the way she does. No one has ever been so naturally attuned to me. Hell, no one has ever even tried. Even if they had, it would have been in vain. I realize now that no one but her could have touched this part of me.

"Yeah, I'm sorry for being a downer, but honestly I'd love to just snuggle with you. I think I've over-peopled. Maybe we can watch a rom-com and laugh for a bit before bed?" Her brows lift and she offers me a smile.

"Yeah, baby girl, we can do that." My answer comes out scratchy, heat building behind my eyes. That's exactly what I need. She's exactly what I need.

We leave the Langfields' house without much fanfare. Normally, I'm one of the last to leave, which Gavin is quick to point out when I stop to wish him a Merry Christmas and say goodbye.

"She seems good for you," he says, eyeing her as she slips into her coat in the foyer.

I laugh. "Because she's as young as your wife was when you two got together."

He chuckles. "Some of us just have to wait for our soulmates to grow up."

A bark of a laugh escapes me. "Sick, man."

When his wife walks by and gives him a little wave, he sobers up quickly. "A happy man. And you deserve to be too. Merry Christmas."

"Merry Christmas." With one last pat to his shoulder, I take off toward the woman who really does make me happy.

She lets me take her hand, and then I guide her out into the frigid night.

"Good news," she tells me as we walk to my car.

Under the moonlight, she glimmers, making it impossible to look away.

I stumble over my own feet but catch myself before going down. "What's that, baby girl?"

She bites back a laugh and shakes her head. "The Donovans got the Barbie house put together. They don't need our help."

"So I get you all to myself?" I ask as I open her door.

"Yup." She loops an arm around my neck and presses her lips to mine. What starts as a chaste kiss quickly becomes heated, and when she moans into my mouth, I clutch her ass and pull her tight to my body, deepening the connection.

"Fuck, I needed you tonight," I admit, dragging in a breath of her.

She rests a hand over my pounding heart. "I'm right here."

Forehead pressed to hers, I close my eyes and relish her closeness. "You are."

"Come on, Daddy. Let's get you home."

Her words have their intended effect, making me chuckle. But internally, I'm a mess, my instincts screaming at me to tell her how I really feel in this moment. I rein them in and tuck them away for now, but damn is it tempting to let the words slip. To give her my truths.

I've fallen for you. Don't leave me. I can't lose anyone else.

Chapter 30
Savannah

"NO PEEKING." I spin and peer over my shoulder, checking the straps in the mirror.

"How could I peek?" he asks, his tone still on the grumpy side. "You've got the door closed."

He's been off tonight, so while I'd planned to save this until we were at his place next week so I could incorporate the poles in the basement, I knew I couldn't wait. When he walked into Beckett's looking drained and practically beaten down, it was easy to change plans. I don't really need a pole for this, and I want our first Christmas to be special. And this outfit? It's definitely special.

"Sit down on the bed. Make yourself comfortable," I tell him through the door. "And close your eyes."

He chuckles. "Baby girl, what are you doing?"

"I'm making you smile. And there's a good chance you'll come, so perk up, Daddy. Tonight is just getting started."

I lit a few candles when we arrived, then turned off the lights. Since that kiss outside his car, Camden has been looking at me differently. Like what we have goes deeper than it should, since we haven't known each other long. And I've given up pretending I don't feel that way too. I'm in this. I'm going to put myself out there.

I open the door and peek out, and when I confirm he's got his eyes shut, I dart past him and sit in front of the Christmas tree, my legs tucked beneath me. The tree is small. It had to be in order to fit in my tiny apartment, but I have a feeling the gift he's about to receive will be one he won't ever forget.

"You can open your eyes now," I say sweetly.

He obeys, and when he zeroes in on me, he breaks into a wicked grin.

"Merry Christmas, Daddy."

Without a word, he stalks toward me. The swagger in his step makes my belly warm and tight.

"Are you my present, baby girl?" he asks as he drinks me in, examining the green fabric banded around me the same way the ribbons covered the dancers the night we met. My breasts are far bigger than any of the women that night, so the silk barely covers more than my nipples, but that's fine by me.

Popping up onto my knees, I lean forward so he can see the bow that barely covers my ass. "Depends. Have you been naughty this year?"

"Very." The word is like sandpaper as it leaves him. He bends at the waist and brushes a finger over the ribbon stretched across my back. The gentle touch makes me shiver. "Where'd you get this?" He pulls at the fabric, and when it stretches easily, he hums and stands straight, looming over me.

I brace myself with my hands on my thighs and stare up at him. Like this, kneeling at his feet while he stares down at me like I'm the prettiest thing he's ever seen, I'm awash with a contentment I don't know that I've ever experienced.

"Online. I got two: one red, one green. My original plan looked a little different, but I improvised."

He smirks, his face cast in shadow. "Two?"

I lick my lips. "Yes. That was going to be part of your Christmas present. My friend Kacie was going to join us."

His eyes flare with what could be heat or jealousy. Either way, it makes my pulse pick up.

"You've spoken to her about this?" he asks carefully.

Nodding, I bite down on my lip. "But when I really thought about it, I wasn't sure if I wanted to share you."

The expression that crosses his face this time is easy to decipher. It's delight. Pleasure. Pride. "That's good, because as hot as that sounds, baby girl, I don't want to be shared."

"Don't even want to watch?" I whisper, face tipped up, my hair tickling my bare back.

He arches a brow. "And what would I be watching?"

The desire stirring in my belly ignites as I consider how to paint the erotic scene for him. Sometimes the dirtiest thoughts alone can get me off, and I guarantee the one I'm imagining will work wonders for him too. "Go sit on the bed and I'll show you."

He swallows, the sound audible, a hint of unease in his eyes.

"She's not here," I promise.

He nods once and takes a step back. But rather than walk away, he hovers lower, and with a hand to my jaw, he brings his mouth to mine. "You are the most perfect gift I've ever received."

I smile against his mouth and then lick at his lips. "And I'm just getting started." With that, I push him back.

He groans, staggering a little, his focus firmly fixed on me.

"Go, baby," I murmur.

A flash of pleasure mixed with pain crosses his face, like his heart has cracked wide open.

I ignore it for now. That's not what we're doing tonight. I'm taking his mind off the emotions, keeping him here in the moment with me.

When he finally settles on the edge of the bed, as close to me as he can get while still following my instructions, I tip forward, and on my hands and knees, I prowl toward him. Ass up, back arched, eyes never leaving his.

"Fuck," he drawls, the word low and deep.

My core clenches in response to the heat in his voice.

When I reach him, I set a palm on each of his thighs. "If she were here," I say, "I'd make you watch us first. I'd lay her back beside you and I'd kneel like I am right now, between her thighs. I'd tell her to play with her pretty tits. I'd slide the fabric between her legs over an inch and lick her cunt while you watched."

Camden's throat bobs, his jaw clenching.

"You'd like that, wouldn't you?" I tilt my head. "Watching me fuck her with my tongue?"

Nostrils flaring, he nods.

I flex my fingers over his thighs and lean forward. "Would you take your cock out while you watched us?"

"Yes." The word rushes out of him in a breath.

"Do it. Now," I tell him. "Show me how you'd fist yourself while I played with Kacie."

With a grunt, he squeezes his eyes shut. "Don't say her name."

A thrill courses through me. "Jealous, are we?" I tease.

He's clumsy and gruff as he removes his belt and tugs down his pants. I lean back to give him room to remove them, but he leaves them pooled at his ankles and fists himself. He's fully erect, veins bulging, looking damn near angry. "Impossibly when it comes to you."

I return to my position and caress his thighs, soothing him. "Then it's a good thing I'm just talking you through it."

He heaves a loud breath, his expression clearing a little. "Then what would you do?"

I smile. "I'd tell her to suck your cock. I'd want to see it. See if she could swallow you like I do. See if she could please you like I do."

"She couldn't. No one can," he says gruffly, slowly pumping over the barbells and ring at his crown.

"Then maybe you'd rather watch her please me. Would you prefer it if I took you into my mouth while she made me come?"

He grunts and shakes his head. "I'm the only one who gets to taste you."

"So possessive," I tsk. "But fine. Then I'd ride your face while she sucked you off. Sorry. If she were here, you'd have to choose one."

He laughs, the rough, dark sound making me ache between my thighs. "Suck me, baby girl." He brings his crown to my lips and drags it back and forth.

I lick up the wetness, moaning when the taste of him hits my tongue.

"Fuck my throat," I urge him.

The laugh he lets out this time is lighter. "Always making me do all the work."

I grin and then stick out my tongue, waiting.

Eyes blazing, he fists my hair at the back of my head. Then he stands and slides himself all the way into my mouth, only stopping when he hits the back of my throat.

Tears prick my eyes as I gag around him.

He hums in response to the sound. "There's my perfect whore. I love when you're a slut, baby girl, but only for me."

Gaze locked with his, I swallow around him.

A low moan rumbles out of him. "Fucking perfect. Look at you, dressed like a Christmas present, tits barely covered, pussy drenching the ribbon. You're a complete mess." He sets a rhythm, his every thrust rough.

There's no way my throat won't be raw come morning, but I love every single second of it. I squeeze my thighs together, hoping the damp ribbon running between my legs will give me a little friction.

When he swells in my mouth and lets out a curse, I palm his balls, massaging them, dragging a whole slew of expletives out of him. Words ragged, he pulls me in until my nose hits his stomach. Then he comes down my throat.

Focus fixed on my face, he blows out a long breath. Then he releases my hair and breaks into a blinding smile. "Jesus fuck, Savannah, I think you just sucked my soul out of my body."

I swipe a thumb against my lip and smile. "Merry Christmas."

"Get up here." He slides his arms under mine and hauls me onto the bed. Then he crawls over me and takes my mouth in a rough kiss and spears me with a finger. "You're soaked."

I nod against his mouth, gasping at the intrusion.

"Is this what she would do to you? Would she fuck you with her fingers?" He pushes up on his other elbow and watches the way his fingers disappear inside me.

The heat low in my belly extends outward, moving through my extremities. It feels too good. The dirty images he's painting, the way he's playing with me. It's all too good.

"Yes."

"And you like that. You wanted to do that for me?"

"Yes."

He pulls his fingers out of me and flops onto his back. Then he drags me over his body and positions me so I'm straddling his shoulders. With his teeth, he tugs at the fabric barely covering me. Then he sucks my clit into his mouth.

I throw my head back, a scream ripping from me, my pussy already pulsing. I'm going to come and he's barely touched me.

"I don't think I could handle it unless I was inside you," he grits out.

I grind against his face, desperate for more.

But he clutches my thighs, holding me in place. "I'd need to bury myself between these thighs. Would she like that? My cock wedged tightly into this pussy? Would she eat you while I fucked you?"

Without waiting for an answer, he sucks my clit into his mouth again, and a wave of bliss washes over me. I come with a scream, the sensation only building when he bites down on the sensitive bud, then tongues it while he spears me with two fingers.

My vision is still spotty when he pulls me down his body and enters me in one rough thrust, then fucks me with a fierceness that borders on angry. "Would she, baby girl? Is that what you want? Someone else here to please you? Am I not enough?"

I convulse around him, my whole body shaking, one orgasm bleeding into the next. My vision goes black in earnest now. I don't know how I'll survive this feeling, yet I never want it to end. From this angle, the barbell at his base teases my clit, setting off another orgasm. This one is slower, more like a rolling wave, and I ride it out, grinding my pelvis against him.

"You're everything," I sob, my lungs burning, my breaths choppy.

He swells inside me, and with his big hands gripped tightly around my thighs, holding me tight to him, he releases. This time when he comes, he does it with a quiet groan because our mouths are fused and neither one of us wants to let go.

We breathe each other in. We breathe for each other.

CHAPTER 31
CAMDEN

THIS MAY COME AS A SURPRISE, but I laughed when I read *Calliope's Column*. The one I couldn't dredge up enough energy to look at when Noah sent it to me. I finally scrolled the article while lying in bed, Savannah asleep in my arms, when I couldn't get my mind to quiet.

My thoughts were jumbled after my hellish day and the incredible evening. I was restless despite how exhausted my body was.

When I laughed out loud at the column, Savannah barely moved. She let out the tiniest sigh, her warm breath hitting my neck, and I pressed a kiss to her forehead and kept reading.

It took less than ten seconds to determine that Savannah had written the article. And it was obviously about me.

Calliope's Column
It's Not Him, It's You (Kind Of)
Rule Number 6: Don't Sync Your Ovulation Calendars Before the First Date.

. . .

I thought this would be the deal-breaker. It should have been. Ladies, this is not me telling you to pull a stunt like this. Seriously, you'd have to be off your rocker to even think about allowing a man to knock you up before you've gone on a first date. Sex on the first date, debatably hot; ovulation calendars, not so much.

So when I tell you that the man I'm seeing didn't so much as blink, and he most certainly didn't dump me, this is not me paving the way for you. I know I've told you that I'm not the exception, but here's the thing I'm quickly learning: he is.

He's a man who knows what he wants. Who is there for the people who need him. He's fiercely protective too. My man—and yes, I'm claiming him; he didn't dump me and now I won't let him—always gives the people he cares about what they want. So I guess it shouldn't have surprised me that when I told him I wanted his baby, he shrugged like it was no big deal.

I'm not sure what, if anything, I'm teaching you through these columns anymore, but I'll keep doing them and reminding you to be patient and wait for the exceptional man. When you find him, there's a good chance that the rules won't matter so much. Until then, it's not him, it's you. (Kind of.)

X,

Calliope

When I finished that column, I went back and read every one she's written on this subject. I was worried, at first, that she started this before she met me. And though I don't give a shit about who she was with in the past, I had no interest in reading about her with other men. Being teased about her with another woman: hot. Reading about her real dates with another man: enraging.

Fortunately, I seem to be her only victim. Yes, that's what she called me in her first article.

That's fine. I'll be her victim any day of the week if it means I get to wake up with her in my arms.

From the sound of things, she's looking for more subject matter to write about, and I feel like a little payback might be fun. So with a plan forming in my head, I carefully climb out of bed and rush outside while she's still asleep.

Chapter 32
Savannah

CHRISTMAS MORNING, I wake to the most delicious scene. Camden Snow, bare chested, in a pair of gray sweats, padding across my tiny apartment with a cup of coffee topped with whipped cream.

I smile as I reach for it, deliciously sore from last night and ready for more. "This might be the best Christmas morning ever."

His expression goes from cocky to radiant. It's one of the things I love most about this man. He doesn't hide his emotions. He might not be an open book, and I have a lot to learn about him, but I always know how he feels. If he's upset, the anger or frustration are written on his face. If he's turned on, his facial expression isn't my only hint. But moments like this might be my favorite. When he's happy, he lets the emotion show. It's freeing, seeing him like this. It gives me permission to be happy too. And yeah, I shouldn't need permission, but I grew up in a house where a smile would be snuffed out quickly, so I hid any joyful emotions. If I didn't, the feelings would be bled from me in one way or another.

"This is unequivocally the best Christmas ever, baby girl, because I woke up beside you." He settles on the bed beside me and leans in for a kiss.

Eyes falling shut, I smile against his mouth. "Merry Christmas."

He pulls back, and with his blue eyes burning with passion, he pushes my hair behind my shoulder and drops a kiss to my neck. "Merry Christmas, beautiful."

My stomach tightens in response to his attention. "Why are you looking at me like that?" I take my first sip of coffee, and when the flavor registers, I moan. "Oh, you found the cinnamon creamer."

With a nod, he brushes another kiss to my shoulder.

"God," I sigh. "You make it hard to think, let alone drink coffee."

He pulls back. "We can't have that."

I huff into my mug, disappointment rising and dampening my joy a little.

A quiet laugh escapes him. "What?"

"Nothing, I just like it when you kiss me."

"There'll be plenty more of that when you've finished your coffee." He tips his head toward my mug. "I've got to grab your present anyway."

My heart stutters. "Present?"

"Don't be coy, baby girl. You don't play it well. You know damn well I got you a gift."

When he stands, happiness pours out of me in an embarrassing squeal.

Face lit up, he drops to his knees in front of me.

The move is so startling I almost drop the coffee cup. "What are you doing?" I scramble around, setting the mug on the side table, ignoring the liquid that sloshes out of it.

He pulls a jewelry-size box out of his pocket and sets it on the bed in front of me.

I scramble back. "What is that?"

If the man proposes right now, I don't know what I'll do. I really like him. Might even love him a little. Not that I'm ready to dive into that emotion. But no matter how strong our connection, we can't get *engaged* after only a month.

He chuckles. "Don't you want your present?"

I inspect it, still keeping my distance. "That depends."

Eyes dancing, he says, "Depends on what?"

"On what it is. It's not like a forever type of thing, right?"

He frowns, dark blond brows furrowing. "A forever type of thing?"

I huff, my heart pounding. "Don't be coy, Camden Snow," I say, mimicking his earlier words. "You don't play it well."

He coughs out a laugh loud enough to wake the Donadios. Then he grasps me by the thighs and tugs me to the edge of the bed. I'm naked and wrapped in the sheets, but my breasts hang heavy between us. My pulse races as I stare into his eyes.

"Just open the box, Savannah," he says, voice gruff, smile gone, and holds it up between us.

Head bent, I study it. My heart is in my throat, my hands trembling. I hate myself for my next thought. Literally despise my very being, because in this moment, all I think is *please let it be what I think it is*. Please let him be my forever. Looking into his blue eyes, so beautiful, waking up to him in my kitchen, loving him, would all be so easy. It could be everything I've ever wanted.

Holding my breath, I take the small square box from his hand and search his face, looking for answers. "I really like you," I muster.

His expression immediately softens and his lips spread into the softest of smiles. I think he'll always be gentle with me. I think we'd be good to one another. And suddenly, it doesn't feel so scary. Forever with him wouldn't be so bad. It might just be perfect.

He cuffs my neck and hauls me against him. With his lips brushing mine, he whispers, "I really like you too, baby girl." His kiss is warm, his touch soothing. "Now open your present."

Butterflies fluttering in my stomach, I flip open the box. When I'm met with a small bronze object, I choke on a laugh. "A key." There's disappointment in my tone, but relief too. Because yeah, now I know that I want him forever, but my initial reservation was appropriate. Not yet. There's no rush. He's not going anywhere.

"To my house," he says, eyes holding mine. "*Our* house."

"Our house?" I repeat.

"Move in with me, baby girl." He presses his forehead to mine. "I hate waking up without you. If I had my way, you'd be at my side at all times, while at work, while traveling. But that's not realistic. This, though, could be. Move in with me." The confidence in his tone, along with the hint of desperation, like he doesn't even know where the words came from, like they just spilled from his lips, has me nodding along and agreeing.

"Okay," I say, breathless.

"Okay?" His eyes widen in surprise.

"Yeah, I'll move in with you. Okay."

He hauls himself up in one quick move and tackles me in the bed. We're a mess of limbs and kisses, scrambling to get rid of his clothes and free my legs from the sheets. In a matter of seconds, he's pushing into me with a rough thrust. "Fuck, baby girl, what are you doing to me?"

I shake my head, tears stinging my nose. His expression is filled with awe. With what I can only hope is the beginnings of love.

"Whatever it is," I say, "it's happening to me too."

"Good. Stay with me," he says as he buries himself deep inside me.

"I'm right here," I promise, my hand going to his heart as my walls clench around him.

He fucks me slowly, his fingers entwined with mine between us, our eyes never leaving one another.

It might not have been a ring, but this feels a hell of a lot more like forever.

CHAPTER 33
CAMDEN

"YES, RIGHT IN THE FUCKING NET!" I punch the air as Maverick takes a victory lap. "He looks good, man. Really fucking good."

Beside me, Daniel's wearing a matching celebratory smile. "Yeah, he does. Kid doesn't rest. Even sleeps with the damn stick at night."

Affection for my godson overflows from me. "I remember those days."

"Please, my husband still has those days," Hannah says as she walks away. "I'm on raffle duty. Have to go make the money."

She sways her hips suggestively, without a doubt knowing that he's still looking, and Daniel hums in appreciation.

When she's out of sight, he shakes himself from his stupor. "Okay, now that she's gone."

I whip my head in his direction. My best friend does *not* keep secrets from his wife. Where is he going with this?

"When the fuck were you going to tell me that Savannah is Calliope?"

The air escapes from my lungs, and for a second, all I can do is stare at him. Then I burst into laughter. Definitely didn't expect him to say that.

He grabs my arm, expression serious. "Did you not look at the article Noah sent you?"

I roll my eyes, unable to wipe the smile from my face. "Of course I did."

"And? Aren't you freaking the fuck out? She was pulling one over on you the whole time."

I breathe in through my nose to keep from laughing again. "Yeah, she definitely was."

"Why are you still smiling?"

Amusement rolls through me, along with affection for my best friend. "Because she's cool as shit and I'm happy."

He grimaces. "And you aren't worried she's taking advantage of you?"

Head tilted, I pin him with a look. "She's not Tara. Hell, she's not like any woman I've ever met. And if you read the articles, then you know her feelings for me are real. She didn't want to like me, but she does." I grin. "I'm just that charming."

He smacks my chest. "No, you're just that full of yourself." He blows out a breath and shakes his head. "Jesus, here I was worried you'd be spiraling. Instead you're fucking laughing your ass off. What did she say when you told her you knew?"

I press my lips together. "I didn't, exactly."

His dark eyes go wide. "What?"

"I asked her to move in with me instead."

And his jaw practically unhinges. "*What*?"

To be fair, I only intended to give her a key. Figured it would freak her out a little. Lighthearted payback and all that. Because it's way too soon to give a woman unfettered access to my place. My end goal, really, was to give her content for her articles. But I don't know what the fuck came over me when I was down on my knees and looking into her eyes, but I told her to move in with me, and then she said yes, and nothing has ever felt so right.

I'm getting anxious, though, that it might not really happen. I've been traveling so much for work that we haven't had time.

"I don't know what came over me," I admit to him. "I was thinking I could give her a taste of her own medicine. Do the opposite of what she expects, then laugh about it later."

"But instead you went all in?"

I scrub a hand over my face. "Yeah, I guess."

"So now what?"

My lips twitch as I think about the plan I concocted. It'll give her another good story to write about.

"Oh no," Daniel mutters. "What's that face for? You're up to something."

I shrug. "Just thinking I could make her articles even better now that I know what's happening."

"Oh fuck."

Another laugh. I think I've laughed more today than I have in years. Yeah, *oh fuck* is right. Baby girl played some games, and now Daddy's gonna teach her a lesson. And it's going to be enjoyable as fuck.

"But I'm going to need your help."

Chapter 34
Savannah

"THIS IS REALLY what your friends do on couples' nights?" I ask as we approach the entrance to the studio.

Camden smirks. "Getting cold feet?"

I glance down at the sneakers he insisted I wear. "Nope. They're perfectly warm. Just didn't expect your friends to use group workouts as an excuse to socialize. What's wrong with grabbing dinner and drinks at a bar?"

He drapes an arm over my shoulders and pulls me into his side. "I appreciate you coming. They do different things once a month, and I never come because, well, it's more of a couple activity, and I've never been part of a couple until now."

The vulnerability bleeding from his tone makes my heart squeeze. Dammit. Why am I being so judgmental? The girls and I plan random activities too. Like pole dancing and ice skating. Last week we even went to an improv comedy class, Sutton's choice, of course, and it was a blast. So if this is what his friends like to do, who am I to judge?

"I'm excited." I pop up on my toes and press a kiss to his cheek. "Thanks for including me."

He pulls the door open and with a hand at the small of my back guides me inside.

The studio is empty except for a lone woman, and when she turns, I suck in a breath and smile.

"Angel." That may not be her real name, but it's the name she used when I met her.

She beams at me. "Savvy? I didn't know you'd be here."

Camden steps up beside me, brows furrowed as he looks from me to Angel and back again.

She's got more fabric covering her body than she did the last time I saw her, in a pole dancing class, but not much more. She's in a pair of red spandex shorts with a matching crop top, and her dark hair is pulled back in a sleek ponytail.

"My boyfriend's friends planned it," I explain to her.

"Oh, cool! I'm teaching the class."

"The class," I repeat. Huh. I didn't know she was a fitness instructor as well as a stripper, though with flexibility like she has, I guess it makes sense. Could this be a Pilates class?

And if so, isn't that a strange couples' night activity?

I curse myself and shake my head. There I go, being judgmental again.

Angel claps, practically bouncing on her toes. "Yes. This is going to be so fun. I have to get the playlist sorted before the rest of the class arrives, but I'm so glad you're here." With a squeeze to my arm, she scurries to the wall of mirrors at the front of the studio and digs a phone out of a bag.

While she scrolls, head down and back turned, Camden turns so he's facing me directly. "How do you know Angel?"

"She's a friend of Kacie's."

His eyes narrow. "And where did you say you met Kacie again?"

I frown. "Pole dancing class."

He raises his brow. "So she's a dancer?"

"Not everyone who takes pole dancing classes strips for a living," I point out.

He cocks a brow but he doesn't respond.

Finally I sigh. "But yeah, she's a dancer. Do you have a problem with that?"

"I'd be a fucking hypocrite if I did, wouldn't I?"

I shrug.

"So you've danced before?" he asks, his tone uncertain, his gaze hot on my face.

"Not professionally." I snort. "But she's tried to talk me into it plenty of times. She makes a killing."

"I'm sure she does," he grumbles.

"*Camden.*"

"I'm sorry." He squeezes the back of his neck. "I just don't like the idea of you dancing for anyone else. Especially like that."

"Well, I don't plan on it." I plaster on a smile. It's time to lighten the mood. "Not sure if you heard, but I have a hot boyfriend, and he's more than enough for me."

"And money-wise, you're—"

My stomach lurches. "Oh my god, Camden. Don't you dare offer me money."

His eyes fall shut. "I'm sorry. I didn't mean for it to come out like that. I just…" He shakes his head. "When you move in, you should get rid of your place. Save that money."

I grit my teeth. It's been two weeks since Christmas, and we haven't talked about moving in together again. We spent the week after Christmas in a sex haze, choosing to ring in the New Year alone, in his house, naked, much to my friends' disappointment. I don't regret a second of it, but he didn't once bring up the potential move. I don't want to rush things, but it's unnerving that he hasn't mentioned it again. I'm starting to think he's realized how outrageous the idea is.

Regardless of whether we live together, I won't mooch off him. "I figured I could help with the mortgage."

He gapes at me, as if the suggestion is ludicrous. "I don't have a mortgage."

"Okay." I wince. "So I'll pay you rent."

"Not happening." He brushes an imaginary hair from my face and swipes his thumb along my cheek. "I like taking care of you, baby girl. You know that's my thing."

I roll my eyes, but I can't fight the smile creeping up my face. "As much as I love that in the bedroom, outside of it, I need to feel like I'm contributing. I don't want to be like my mom."

He rears back a little, searching my face.

Chest tightening, I curse my stupid mouth. Why did I mention my mother? "I don't really want to talk about it," I say before he can ask questions.

He nods, eyes locked on mine. "Okay."

"Just know that I want to contribute."

He presses his lips to mine in a sweet, comforting kiss. "We'll figure it out."

"Are we ready to get this party started?"

At the boisterous voice, I peer over Camden's shoulder.

Daniel has stepped inside, and he's wearing an outfit that literally leaves me blinking in disbelief.

Camden drops his forehead to mine. "I apologize in advance."

I giggle, because he hasn't even seen what I'm seeing, and he's going to *die*.

When he turns, he staggers back a step. "Holy fuck."

"I tried to tell him that he looked absurd," Hannah calls as she appears beside him. Like me, she's in a pair of tights and a T-shirt.

"I don't even get it," Camden says.

Daniel tugs on the fabric of his *tight* tank top. "I've been working out."

Hannah snorts. "Oh, Baby Hall, don't ever change."

His shorts are bright orange and so tight that the outline of his package is on full display. It's…something, to say the least.

I think I can see a piercing. I squeeze my eyes shut and try to erase the image from my memory.

Camden steps in front of me, his back to my front, and I grasp his sides, laughing silently. "Please tell me you have actual clothes to put on."

Daniel rolls his hips suggestively. "But why? We're having sex lessons."

"We're having *what*?" I screech.

"You didn't tell her?" a blond woman says. She's just stepped in behind them, wearing a big smile.

Ah, Sara Langfield. I saw her at the Christmas party a few weeks ago with her husband. I've met her a few times, and the woman is loud. I might have a girl crush on her. She's got an incredible career as the CEO of the Boston Bolts, and her husband is absolutely obsessed with her. They've got four kids, I think. The oldest is a girl, and I think they have three sons. Even as a mom of four, she's full of inappropriate jokes. She told at least a handful during the five minutes I spent with her on Christmas Eve, and by the time our conversation was over, my cheeks hurt from laughing.

"Cam probably figured she wouldn't come if she knew," Brooks, her husband, says as he strolls in behind her, his long hair pulled back in a loose bun.

I poke Cam in the side. "Is this true?"

He glances over his shoulder and winks. "I told you it was a couples' activity."

"Not sex class with your friends."

"Us old people have to put in the work to keep up with people your age," he teases.

"Speak for yourself." Lennox Langfield steps in next, her husband Aiden at her side, his hand wrapped around hers. Lennox is probably the most recognizable Langfield because her hair is a beautiful faded pink color. "She'll have to figure out how to keep up with us."

I step around Camden and point at her. "I can get on board with that."

"Don't worry, we'll go slow for your first time. I'll talk you through it." She gives me a salacious wink, and a shiver works its way down my spine. Shit. Do I have a crush on her too? I think I might.

Hannah cackles and Sara squeals. "Ah, I love this."

"All right, everyone, thank you for coming to my tantric sex class."

All the air leaves my lungs when Angel's words register.

Beside me, Camden is covering his mouth, shoulders shaking, trying but failing to hide his quiet laughter.

"Tantric sex," I mouth.

He grins. "Have I told you that Hannah used to write a sex

column? Have you heard of Calliope? She's the original. She always loved teaching her readers about the wide variety of sexual positions."

My throat goes dry. Calliope?

Thankfully Camden is looking at Hannah, so he doesn't notice my reaction.

"Yup." She holds a finger to her lips. "But don't tell anyone. Calliope's identity is a well-kept secret. Don't want people to discover that those old articles were about Daniel and me."

Daniel shrugs, a cocky smile in place. "I wouldn't mind if the entire population knew how I rocked your world back then and now."

Sara throws her head back and laughs. "You mean the article about the bad sex you had on night one?"

I look from one person to another, unable to keep up with the banter. I'm too in my head. What are the fucking chances that Camden's best friend's wife is the original author of my column? The column where I write about all my dates *with Camden.*

Shit.

"Let's get into position." Angel lies on her mat, demonstrating the correct position. She spreads her legs and tilts her pelvis up. "We're going to start with pelvic thrusts."

Daniel drops to an empty mat. "Oh, I've got this down, baby."

Brooks glares at him, then his wife. "Why the fuck are we here?"

Sara pushes him toward a mat. "Be a good boy for me, okay?"

When he gives her a look that's both heated and annoyed, like he's obsessed and he wishes he could hide it, I have to look away.

"We all know you've still got those goalie thighs," she teases, plopping down in front of him. Even after four kids, the woman has an incredible body. And she flaunts it, sticking her ass up and thrusting her pelvis down like Angel is.

"You really want me to do this?" I mumble to Camden.

He's already in position, grinning up at me. "You heard her, baby girl. Ass up. Give me a show."

"Okay, Daddy," I breathe out so only he can hear me. "You've been warned."

For the next forty-five minutes, Angel walks us through each movement. The girls tease their men relentlessly. Aiden and Daniel are all about it too, their movements pure sex.

Brooks is bright red the majority of the time. Mostly because every few seconds, Sara yells out obscenities like "Yeah, Brookie, just like that. Make Mama proud!" *and* "Shit, girls, can we get them to take it off?"

Hannah laughs so hard she has tears rolling down her face while she does every move with precision.

Angel wanders the room, encouraging the class and correcting posture. When she comes up behind me, she presses her hand to my back. "Right there. Push down with your pelvis and up with your ass. Yes, you're doing so well."

"I'm going to come. This is so hot!" Sara yells.

I hang my head, cackling.

Beside me, Camden groans. "Remind me why I thought it would be a good idea to bring you around my friends."

I'm eyeing him, grinning, when Angel presses her hips against mine, demonstrating how she wants me to move. She's basically humping my back. If I had any fucks left to give, I might be embarrassed by the show I'm suddenly part of in front of his friends, but I don't, and Camden asked for this.

Angel smacks my ass and backs away. "Your girlfriend is hot," she says to Camden as she saunters to the front of the room. "All right, let's put on some slower music and practice our thrusts."

The music cuts out, and the room is filled with a buzzing sound. Huh. One that sounds very much like—

"What the fuck is that buzzing noise?" Brooks hisses.

From the front of the room, Daniel groans.

Hannah is still crying, but her laughter has turned to cackling.

"Oh my god," Aiden giggles, collapsing to the ground.

"Again!" Lennox squeals, ass still in the air.

"Again what?" I ask. This is the hard part about being the newcomer. Not getting the inside jokes.

Sara collapses too, wheezing and clutching her stomach. "He's wearing a cock ring."

"Jesus Christ." Camden falls to the floor with a thump.

Wide-eyed, I turn to him. "Okay, I take it back. Old people are weird."

Chapter 35
Savannah

Calliope's Column
It's Not Him, It's You (Kind Of)
Rule Number 7: Don't Bring a Cock Ring to a Sex Class with His
Friends (They've Got it Covered!).

JOSIE SNORTS from just over my shoulder. My column goes to copy this afternoon, but I like to get her feedback before I submit, so here we are.

"Thank god my parents didn't go," she mumbles as she scans the article. "If not for Scar's dance competition, I'd be reading about my parents gyrating to tantric music, huh?"

I drop my head into my hands, torn between laughing and groaning. "It was so fucking awkward."

When I straighten and brush the hair from my face, Josie is grinning. "You're happy."

I roll my eyes, cursing the way my cheeks heat at her observation.

Obviously, I am. And not just because of Camden. It's hard not to feel good when so much is going well for me. The articles are getting good traction, and with Sienna at the helm, work is better than ever. I've been added to the group chat with Sara, Lennox, Hannah, Ava, Millie, and Sienna. It's a little weird, considering Ava is Josie's mom and Sienna is my boss, but I absolutely won't complain about the way Camden's friends have included me so easily.

On top of all that, I haven't heard from either of my parents in weeks. That always makes my life feel more stable.

And yeah, Camden. Things are good. I'm moving into his house this weekend, and though he's been traveling a lot, he texts all day long and calls as often as he can.

"I am happy," I tell her. "And also a little nervous because I haven't seen Camden in a week, and he just texted, asking me to join him and his friends in the owner's suite for tonight's Bolts game."

"Oh!" Josie's eyes dance. "That's fun."

"I guess. But the girls texted, insisting that I wear Camden's jersey. They mentioned something about a 'jersey effect.'"

Eyes narrowed, my friend steps closer. "Wait, I'm your girl. What do you mean 'the girls'"—she uses air quotes—"texted you?"

Snorting, I pick up my phone. "So possessive." I unlock the screen and show her the group chat I've been added to.

> Sara: Oh my god, I just found out the studio has cameras. We can relive the glorious moment when Hannah made Daniel come in his short shorts.
>
> Millie: I've done a lot of shitty things in my life, I know, but I DON'T DESERVE THIS.
>
> Hannah: Sorry, Mills. To be fair, you weren't there or I wouldn't have done it.
>
> Lennox: LOL. That is SUCH A LIE.
>
> Ava: Agreed. Pretty sure we've all seen Daniel's dick at this point, and it's your fault, since you can't keep your hands off him.

Josie gasps. *"Mom."*

I shake my head. "Their chat is more unhinged than ours. It's"—I shudder—"disturbing."

> Millie: Sienna, I'll pay you fifty bucks if you tell us a story about Noah.
>
> Hannah: Noah's an angel who doesn't have sex.

Ha. One look at Hannah's brother in those slutty glasses when he's with his wife makes it clear that he's game for all sorts of dirty things. I'm still certain that on the day I showed up at her office door to interview her, he'd just serviced her. He was leaving, and she was flushed. Not to mention the buttons on her shirt were done up wrong.

> Sienna: Three of you are married to my brothers. I'm saying nothing because I don't want to know a thing about your sex lives.
>
> Lennox: My sex life is incredible. The things your brother can do.
>
> Sienna: LENNOX!
>
> Sara: 10/10 recommend Brookie's blinged-out dick.
>
> Hannah: Speaking of blinged-out dicks... Savannah, you've been awfully quiet since we added you. Tell us, does Camden have jewels like our guys?

Josie shakes her head. "I shouldn't be reading this. Please tell me they don't talk about my dad."

I snag the phone and scroll past the confirmation that almost all the guys, including her dad, have blinged-out dicks. From what I gather, it started with a truth or dare game between Aiden, Brooks, and Josie's dad. But yeah, she doesn't need to know that.

"Okay, you're safe to start here." I hand the phone back.

"Wait." She swallows audibly, her face paling. "Does that mean you now know what my dad's…thing looks like?"

Huffing, I hop up on the edge of my desk. "Almost the entire OG Bolts team has blinged-out dicks. Get over it."

She gags, her whole body convulsing. "I hate my life."

"You love it. Now read." I point at the screen. "I need your help with the jersey thing."

She's quiet for a moment, then looks up at me and shrugs. "They want you to wear a Camden Snow jersey. That makes sense." She taps the screen a few times, then passes my phone back.

Nerves swirl in my stomach. "What did you just do?"

Before she can answer, my phone buzzes. This time it's a message in the group chat with *my* girls.

Me: This is Josie. Today I learned things about your uncles and my dad that I never needed to know. I'll spare you the pain, Addie, but long story short, your aunts suggested that Sav wear a Camden Snow jersey to the Bolts game tonight. Thoughts?

Me: Yeah, they swear there's something about a woman wearing a man's name.

Addie: Definitely not just a man thing.

Across from me, Josie snorts and pulls out her own phone.

Josie: Oh my god, did we just unlock an Adeline Langfield kink?!

Addie: Lol. Like any man would ever wear my name on his back. But yeah, that's hot. You should totally do it.

> Me: Where would I even find one? I can't imagine they're still being sold. He retired years ago.

> Addie: wear HIS jersey. All these guys are the same. He definitely has a few hanging in his closet.

Humming, Josie peers up at me, her phone screen lighting up her face. "You do have a key to his place."

I shake my head. "I can't just break into his house and steal a jersey."

Brow creased, she gives me an exasperated look. "Thought you were *moving in*. So it's not exactly breaking in, is it? Come on, let's go to his place. We can find a jersey, and I'll help you get ready to hang out with my mom and her ridiculous friends."

"You seem very bothered by the fact that I'm hanging with them."

She darts into her cubicle and pulls her purse from a drawer. "It's just weird. But I'm serious. I'll help you get ready."

Nerves flutter in my belly again. Yes, I have a key, but it doesn't feel right to just walk into his house with a friend in tow and rifle around in his closet. "I don't know."

"Come on." She snags my bag from my desk and holds it out to me. "We're doing this."

Knowing there is no point in arguing with Josie, I type out a quick message to Camden.

> Me: Hey, I was thinking about stopping by the house with Josie before the game. Is that okay?

The fluttering turns into full-on flapping in my stomach as I wait for him to respond.

I should have known better than to be nervous, though, because of course the man comes back with the perfect response.

Daddy: It's your house, baby girl. Have friends over. Make yourself comfortable. I can't wait to see you tonight.

CHAPTER 36
CAMDEN

Cora: Try not to worry. I promise she'll calm down. She's taking a shower now. Then she'll go to bed early. Tomorrow will be a better day.

I FROWN at my sister's text, my head pounding. A better day? That's laughable.

My mother hasn't had a truly good day in years. And it's my fucking fault.

Cora's wrong. I should worry. I shouldn't have even left, but I'm selfish enough to let my need to see Savannah win out this time. I spent five days in Vegas so my sister could take a break, and though I usually stay through Sunday when I visit, Cora agreed to come back early when she discovered that Savannah is set to move in this weekend.

I told her we could postpone it a week, but my sister wasn't having it.

This truly proves that I'm a selfish asshole. She takes care of our mother at least three weeks out of the month. More if I can't make my travel schedule work. She rarely has time for herself, and when she did this month, she came home early for me. I should have stayed.

Me: I'll stay for two weekends next month, promise.

Cora: Go have fun. Please. You deserve this.

I don't, but I don't want to argue with her, so I let it go and slip my phone into my pocket. Then I make my way to the private elevator that leads to the owner's suite where Savannah should be waiting.

My hope was that I'd land early enough to spend a little time with her at home first, but the plane got delayed and then there was an obscene amount of traffic leaving the airport. There wasn't a chance I'd make it home. Hell, I barely made it here before the puck drop.

I force a smile as I pass one employee after another at Bolts Arena. This place feels more like my home than anywhere else. It's the place where I got my ass kicked, where I discovered that I wasn't, in fact, the best of the fucking best like I'd grown up believing, where I found friends who became family, and where I eventually became one of the greats on the ice alongside them. It's where I became a man and learned what truly matters in life. Not the actual Stanley Cup, but the team of people who won it along with me. The friendships that grew from the countless hours we spent together chasing that dream.

Outside the owner's suite is a team picture from Noah's last season. It was the last time my core group of friends was on the ice together, when we raised the cup above our heads and brought their kids out onto the rink and celebrated.

I smile. That was the season I realized I had something really special here. And I've built upon that year after year. I may not put on that jersey or the pads anymore, but I still bleed Bolts blue.

My smile only grows when a loud cackle sounds from inside the owner's suite. I'd recognize Sara's laugh anywhere. And when it's followed by my girlfriend's raspy laugh? Damn if my heart doesn't skip a beat. I peek inside, and when I spot her, my chest expands, flooding with affection.

Her smile is huge, her head tipped back, eyes closed, her wild red hair practically hitting her ass.

Like she can sense my attention, her lashes flutter open and she zeroes in on me. That's when her outfit registers. Holy shit. She's wearing a Boston Bolts jersey. And not just any jersey.

Her eyes glitter with excitement. The feeling is fucking contagious. And just as strong as my need for her. My pants are suddenly a little too tight, because I know without a doubt my girl is wearing *my* jersey.

No woman has ever worn my jersey. I've waited decades for this.

I stalk toward her, and like the good girl she is, she spins and pulls her hair over one shoulder, giving me the perfect view of my name and number on her back.

My heart beats wildly, and my world falls into place.

My name. My woman. My jersey.

Fuck, I love her. And I'm so fucking tired of hiding it.

I survey every inch of her, then I lean in and press a kiss to her cheek. "Hmm," I say in her ear. "What's the title of the next column going to be? Don't wear your boyfriend's jersey unless you're ready to get fucked in front of thousands?"

She whips around, her green eyes going wide. "*Camden Snow.* How long have you known?"

Head tipped back, I bark out a laugh. "Since Christmas."

Laughter sounds nearby, reminding me that we're not alone. Damn. I was so focused on her I forgot our friends were here too.

"Oh my god," she says, turning to the group of women gathered near us. "You all knew too?"

Sara holds up a hand. "Guilty."

"*Assholes,*" she bellows, but she's smiling.

Chuckling, I pull her against me. "To be fair, they really do weird couple things, and the sex class was Sara's suggestion."

"I've been dying to do one for years," she says without an ounce of shame. "It was the perfect excuse."

"Assholes," Savannah mutters again.

"Maybe, but we're also your new besties. That's official now that your man is looking like he wants to ravish you in that jersey, so you're welcome." Sara winks at her.

"Come on, girls," Hannah says. "Let's give them some privacy." They all filter out, laughing as they go, and Hannah squeezes my shoulder as she passes. "Happy for you."

I'm still grinning when Savannah turns to me, her lip between her teeth, and the room falls silent. "You're not mad about the articles?"

I cup her jaw and drag my thumb over her smooth skin. "No, baby girl, it explained why you were off your fucking rocker those first few weeks."

Her mouth is wide open again, so I take advantage and drag my tongue along her bottom lip, then go in for a kiss.

She sighs. "So the moving in thing?" She lowers her gaze, her expression turning to one of uncertainty.

"Was all me," I tell her honestly. "I want this. I want you. Jesus, when I first saw you in my damn jersey, I nearly came in my pants."

She giggles, her cheeks going pink.

"I'm serious. I've never felt this way about another person in my life."

She hums, a soft smile on her face, and pushes up on her toes. Before her lips can meet mine, though, my phone blares in my pocket.

My heart sinks. The ringtone is the one I set specifically for my mother. "I'm sorry," I mutter. "I have to get this."

I consider walking away so she doesn't hear the conversation, but hell, I asked this woman to move in with me. I'm in love with her. And yet she doesn't know anything about this huge part of my life. It's ugly, and it paints me as the selfish person I used to be and often still am. But if I want her in my life for good, this is part of it, and I can't continue to hide it. So with a deep breath, I stay by her side and slide my thumb over the screen. "Hi, Mom."

"Camden," she breathes as I bring the phone to my ear. "I can't find your father. He's not answering his phone."

I press my fingers into my forehead. I can't tell her the truth. The doctors have told us it's best to just redirect her and calm her down. Telling her my father is dead and isn't coming home repeatedly is cruel. "Mom. Where's Cora?"

My mother sobs. "Cora ran away. You know that."

A groove forms between Savannah's brows as she studies me, but she doesn't leave.

"Mom, take a deep breath. It's going to be okay." I bring the phone down and tap out a quick message to my sister but before I can even hit send I hear her voice.

"Sorry, Cam," my sister says, her voice far away. There's a rustling, and when she speaks again, her words are clear. "I got her. *Mom*," she says in a soothing tone, "it's okay."

The line goes dead, but I don't drop my phone. I'm too drained to move.

"Camden," Savannah says, voice soft.

My heart hammers in my chest. How is it possible to go from such a high to such a low in a matter of seconds? Why is this always my life? Every time something good happens, I'm reminded of how quickly life can shift. I'm reminded that nothing lasts. That I don't deserve happiness.

When I don't respond, because my throat is too tight to get a word out, Savannah gently pries my phone from my hand.

Eyes closing, I take a deep breath, trying to find words.

"We don't have to talk about it," she says.

"We do." I lock eyes with the beautiful woman in front of me. She's an anchor, keeping me from drowning in the storm that is my life. Life may be unfair, and I may have lost a lot, but she's here, and she cares. I've been around long enough to know how rare that is. To find a person who will stand with me through the storm.

"We lost my father in a plane crash. It was fucking awful." I wince. "Obviously." I shake my head. "My mother blamed me afterward. Rightfully so. The two of them were supposed to be at my game. It was a small plane. I'd chartered it so they could see me play." I look out toward the ice. It's easier than seeing the heartbreak reflected in Savannah's eyes. "My sister had run away years earlier. That was also my fault." My shoulders tighten and my stomach roils, the familiar shame and regret descending. As the emotions thicken, making it hard to breathe, I shake out my shoulders and look back toward Savannah.

She's still quietly waiting for me to tell my story. No trace of judgment on her face.

"My sister had come back a month or so earlier, so my mom stayed home, too afraid that Cora would disappear again if she turned her back for more than a second. My dad came on his own. And then the plane went down."

Heat stings the backs of my eyes, but I refuse to let the tears come.

"Anyway, she hated me after that. Our relationship was nearly nonexistent for almost a decade. But then she was diagnosed with Alzheimer's, and this is a sick thing to say, but I got my mom back. Because she doesn't remember that my dad is gone because of me. She doesn't blame me anymore. But now I have to go through *this*."

I blow out a breath and squeeze my fists, tamping down the emotions threatening to break through. "Most of the time, she's content with having my sister around. But I hate leaving Cora to do all the work, so I help as often as I can. The only problem is that after I visit, shit like this always happens. Either way, I'm a selfish fuck. If I stay away, which would be better for her mental state, that means all the responsibility falls on my sister—"

Savannah squeezes my hand. "Camden, I'm so sorry."

I shake my head. "Please don't apologize. I don't deserve it."

"Yes you do. And you're not selfish for wanting a relationship with your mother. Or for wanting to give your sister a break. You're not selfish for wanting a family and you're not to blame for the plane crash." She steps in closer, and her scent hits me, a soothing balm to my aching heart. "Shit happens. Life is unfair. You're not a bad person for feeling that."

Chest tight, I reach for her. I don't deserve her, but I need her. The moment she's in my arms, a fraction of the weight lifts from my shoulders. It's not a lot, but at least I can breathe.

"He was my biggest fan. Even after I broke my sister's heart, he still showed up. He was so damn proud of me. He was everything anybody could want in a dad," I say, a sob escaping me on the last word.

This is the first time I've allowed myself to cry in front of another person. And there's been a lot to cry over in my life.

Savannah squeezes me tight. "I'm sure he's still proud of you. I wish I could have met him."

The tears come faster, my chest burning with emotion. "I wish he could have met you. Because you're it for me. I'm sure of it. And he would have loved you."

She gives me a wobbly smile, her own eyes filling with tears. "You're it for me too. I've never had this kind of connection with anyone. I'm glad you had a wonderful dad." She sighs. "Mine pretty much hates me."

I wrap my arms around her waist and bury my face in her hair. How could anyone hate her? How could anyone—especially her parents—take her for granted?

I deserve my mother's anger. I'm to blame for Cora's pain too. And I've come to terms with that burden. I shoulder the blame of my father's death as well. But Savannah? I can't imagine anything she could have done to deserve hatred from a parent.

Frustration mounts inside me, slowing my tears. Because as those thoughts run through my mind, I see the irony of not believing I deserved the same unwavering support from my mother.

"You'll always have me, baby girl. We'll have each other." I grasp her face and tilt her head back, taking in the tears that track down her cheeks. "No more tears." I press a kiss to each one.

She laughs awkwardly and sucks in a shaky breath. "God, I didn't see tonight going like this."

I give her a wry smirk. "No, I imagine you figured wearing my jersey would result in something very different."

She studies me, her eyes depthless and full of uncertainty. "You aren't freaked out seeing me with your name on my back? Concerned I'm trying to wife you up?"

I raise a brow, hiding the way my chest tightens at the thought. This woman as my wife? I can't think of a damn thing I'd like more. "You been doodling our names together lately?"

She gives me a small smile, and that ache that was oh-so-tender only moments ago eases. "Maybe."

I smirk. "Can I see?"

"What?" She laughs, her eyes darting away.

I scan the room, and when I spot a piece of paper on the bar, I dart for it, then go in search of a pen.

"What are you doing?" Savannah asks as I return with the tools I need.

I hit her with one of our looks, the one that tells her to be a good girl and be quiet for a moment, then I hold out the pen. "Show me."

"This is such a weird kink," she teases. She gives me the kind of eye roll I seem to earn from her often, but her smile is bright as she takes the paper from me too. In her pretty, dramatic handwriting, she scrawls her first name. Then, after a second of hesitation, she adds my last name after it.

"Savannah Snow," I say aloud. That pinch in my chest releases. Or maybe it bursts. I think I could probably fly right now. I know I could score a fuck ton of goals.

Savannah Snow. Fuck, those words look good together. Sound even better.

I snatch the paper *and her* from her chair.

"What are you doing?" she squeals.

"We're going to the tattoo shop," I tell her as I collect my phone and her bag.

"Are you out of your mind?" she asks, pushing back against me.

I set her on her feet, gazing into her eyes. "Yup. I'm going to tattoo your name right here, baby." I snag her by the wrist and press her hand to my heart.

"Camden," she whispers, looking at me in what can only be described as awe.

"I love you, and I want your name on my chest."

She freezes, blinks twice, then exhales.

"This is…" she whispers.

Her voice dies there. Like she's speechless. Like she can't believe I said those words. But I can. The article she wrote was right. When it comes to her, I act as the exception. But only because *she's* my exception. The one I want to spend the rest of my life with. The one I'll spend my dying breath loving.

"Meant to be," I finish for her. "You're mine, baby girl. I love you and you're mine."

Tears fill her eyes again as she stares up at me. "I love you too."

Those words from her lips are the sweetest surprise. No one's voiced that sentiment to me in decades. For most of my life, I've felt undeserving of love because of what I did to my sister. Cora would hate it if she knew. She'd want me to be happy, and she'd tell me to stop living in the past. So I don't hesitate to accept the admission as truth from Savannah. She loves me.

I sweep my mouth against hers. "Say it again."

"I love you," she rasps, her lip quivering.

I take her in a desperate kiss. I can't get enough of her. "Again."

"I love you," she says louder. Then she laughs, tears running down her cheeks. "I didn't see tonight going this way either."

I smile. "I like to keep you on your toes. But tell me, how did you see tonight going?"

She bites her lip, heat suddenly igniting in her eyes. "Figured you'd have me bent over, jersey bunched up, fucking me in a closet because you couldn't wait."

I groan as the image materializes in my head. "We can definitely make that happen." I grab her ass and pull her against me. "After the tattoo."

She peers up at me, eyes misty. "You're really doing this?"

"Yeah, baby, I'm really doing this."

Two hours later, she sits by my side while I get her name inked on my chest, and when the artist shows us the finished product, she turns to him and says, "Do me now."

Chapter 37
Savannah

Addie: Happy move-in day! Wish I could help.

Me: Thanks, babe, but there isn't much to move. It's a perk of being non-sentimental and cheap.

Josie: Good luck at your game, Addie! And don't worry, she turned my help down too. She's all about my mom and your aunts now. We're old news.

Me: Oh my god. Shut up, you jealous whore!

Josie: Oh, a new nickname. I like it.

Sutton: So MY way of doing things apparently wasn't so bad after all, huh? You got a boyfriend and a new roommate out of it.

Me: Haha. Yes, thank you, Sutton. I forgot to tell you girls—he FREAKING KNEW about the articles.

Josie: Wait! Why haven't you called me to explain this already? I'm actually Jealous Whore Barbie now. WTF?

Me: Sorry, the last 24 hours have been a whirlwind. I even got a tattoo!

Sutton: Holy crap! Send pics!

CAMDEN BENDS down to pick up a box, and with that perfect bubble butt on display like that, I can't resist giving it a good smack. "C'mere, babe."

Over his shoulder, he smirks. "Don't hate the nickname, but if you want my attention, you know how to get it."

I roll my eyes. "Fine. *Daddy*." I can't even hide the stupid smile that graces my lips. "Could you please come here and take a picture of your new branding with me so I can show the girls how I own you?"

Eyes dancing, he slowly drags his shirt over his head. Everything is a show with him. And it's all for me. I love every second of it.

And when he removes the bandage covering his tattoo, my heart skips a beat. I still can't believe he got my name—followed by fucking *Snow*—tattooed over his heart. It's so permanent.

"Fuck." I pant, unable to catch a breath as it all hits me again.

Camden's cocky smirk goes soft. "I know, baby girl."

I shake my head, my eyes going to his. "I have to keep reminding myself that this is real. That you're really here, with my name inked on your skin and—" I roll my lips, my emotions building, making it hard to speak.

"Loving you," he finishes for me, stepping close. He gently grasps my chin and tilts my head up. "I know, baby girl. People like us, we don't trust it. But trust *this*: I love you. And I'm so damn proud to be branded with your name."

I tug my lip between my teeth. "Well, it's really your name."

His expression turns stern. It's the kind of look that gets me wet.

"Don't make me take you over my lap and remind you that it will be yours as soon as you're ready."

As soon as I'm ready? I exhale sharply.

He dives in, his mouth on mine. I sink into him. Sink into this feeling. Never in my life has another person read me so well. This man knows precisely what to do to quiet my racing thoughts.

With his hands on my ass, he lifts me up and sets me on the bed. Then he tears my leggings down, wedges himself between my thighs, and drags his tongue against me in the most deliciously dirty way, making my toes curl.

"Why the fuck do you always taste so good?" He curses against my thigh. "I could stay between these legs for days, baby girl. I'm never going to get enough."

Head falling back, I thrust my hips, pushing myself against his mouth. "Good, because I'll never get enough of this."

With a hum that only drives me higher, he gets back to work, teasing me with long strokes.

My phone buzzes over and over. The sound makes me grin. The girls—mainly Josie—are probably teasing me about getting distracted.

They wouldn't be wrong. Camden Snow and his wicked tongue are completely distracting. And I wouldn't have it any other way.

We get carried away twice more, fucking on my kitchen counter and then in the shower. Once we're finally cleaned up, we gather a few more boxes. It's not quite everything, but my lease doesn't end until April, so I can come back for the rest when I have time.

"What about these?" Camden points to the three boxes sitting on the kitchen table.

They're full of memories. Items from when I was a kid. Photos from college and high school. The only picture I have of my mom and me together is in there too.

I shake my head. I don't want the past to touch what we have. I can't avoid my mother, and I really haven't been trying. She's the one who hasn't returned my calls lately. But for now, I'd rather not think about her.

The box on the end, though, snags my attention. Some of my fall decorations are inside, I think. Along with a few toys I loved as a kid and couldn't bring myself to part with. Stepping up to the table, I pick it up. "Just this one."

He presses a kiss to my lips and takes it from me. "Okay, baby girl. Let's go home."

My breath catches, and a goofy smile spreads across my face. "Home."

That word and the big smile he's directing at me make my heart flutter. The excitement dancing in his eyes makes me believe this means as much to him as it does to me.

"Yeah," he says. "Home."

I flick off the lights to my studio apartment and lock up. Then I follow Camden down the steps. When we pass the Donadios' door, I hesitate. I'm going to miss them.

Camden stops at the top of the steps leading to the first floor, then backs up and nods. "We have a few minutes."

Despite my sadness over leaving them, I still can't stop smiling. I probably look ridiculous as I knock.

"Did Junior say he was coming over?" Rosalie hollers inside.

"Do you want to rev my motor?" Nick shouts in response.

"What?" she yells as the door flies open. "Oh, Savannah. Camden. Never mind, Nico," she hollers over her shoulder. "It's the other kids."

"What kids?" The motor of his recliner whirs. "And what do you mean rev my motor?"

I glance back at Camden and find him biting back a laugh.

"I said—"

"Why are you yelling? I'm right here," he says, joining us in the doorway.

With a sigh, she turns back to us. "Never mind. Are you all packed?" she asks, her face suddenly a mask of worry.

I nod. "I'm going to miss you both so much."

She gives Camden a serious look. "You better take care of her."

He shifts the box onto one hip and wraps an arm around my waist. "I will. And we'll still come by for Sunday dinners when I'm not traveling."

Rosalie's stern expression brightens dramatically. "Such a good boy."

I hold in a laugh, my mind going straight to the gutter, but when Rosalie focuses on me, her eyes filled with emotion, tears suddenly threaten to escape.

"I'm so happy for you, Savannah. No one deserves this more. Remember, you're family." She opens her arms wide.

I throw myself into her embrace, relishing the softness of the woman who has become more of a mother to me these last few years than my own.

Family doesn't have to be blood. Hell, sometimes the people meant to love us are the ones who hurt us the most. So it's hard to believe that a person who has no obligation to me whatsoever could ever show me this kind of love. But Rosalie broke down those walls with her loud voice and her pushy attitude and the sweet moments sprinkled in here and there.

She pulls back and squeezes my shoulders. Then she pushes me toward Nick, who gives me a big hug as well.

The first floor is quiet, meaning the Donovans must be out. It's a relief, really. I'm not sure I could handle saying goodbye to the kids. Last night, when Piper and Alice sat on my bed, crying about how we can't have random playdates, was hard enough. I promised to visit often. As excited as I am for this next phase, there are parts of this transition that are hard.

When I get in the car, I finally look at my phone and am bombarded with texts from the girls. They're so ridiculous that they instantly lighten my mood.

Josie: Um, hello? Where are the pics for proof?

Addie: I'm a little nervous to see this tattoo after hearing where SOME people put their tattoos.

Josie: I swear to god if this is about my FATHER, I'll unalive you.

Sutton: Definitely avoid reading Sav's chat with your mom's friends, then, Jose.

Josie: I hate you all.

Josie: Savannah?

Addie: Sounds like she got distracted

Sutton: She got Di-something

Addie: Bahaha. SUTTON, did you make a DICK joke?

Josie: She's been DICKMATIZED, let's be honest.

Sutton: Bet his is tatted too.

Josie: I will need 7-10 business days before I speak to you again.

"What are you giggling about over there?" Camden asks as he pulls out into traffic and heads toward his—*no, our*—place.

Giddy, I smile at him. "Josie's trying to come to terms with the fact that her father is also the infamous War that I now know far too much about, thanks to Hannah."

Camden barks out a laugh. "Fuck."

"Is it true he has Ava tattooed on his balls?"

He laces his fingers with mine and rests our joined hands in my lap. "Not exactly. But close."

"Like it's on his perineum?" I tease.

Camden's loud laugh fills the car, the sound making me feel lighter. "Fuck, I love you."

"That's not an answer."

He chuckles. "Her nickname. And it's right above his balls, yeah."

I shake my head. "Jesus, you actually know the precise location?"

"Listen, I've seen more of those guys than I have of anyone else in my life, you included."

Shifting his way, I scrutinize him. "You trying to tell me you got *that* close with them."

"No, baby girl, I never fucked around with my teammates. Other than a threesome a long fucking time ago, I guess," he says. "*Not* with War."

"Let me guess—Daniel."

His laugh is so beautiful, and I hear it more each day. "I think some things are better left in the past."

I lean against the window and sigh. "What a smart observation, Mr. Snow."

Eyes heated, he gives me a once-over. "Baby girl, you say my name like that, you're going to get fucked."

A thrill shoots up my spine. "Well, we wouldn't want that, now, would we?"

Chapter 38
Savannah

I PAD AROUND UPSTAIRS, going from room to room, a big smile on my face. How is this really my home? I've never had a home before. Not a real one. Not one where I was loved and wanted. Where I didn't have to be quiet or hide my things.

Camden already cleared out half his closet, and it's now filled with my stuff. We ate pizza in the closet while I unpacked, the cardboard box open between us. A bottle of wine and two glasses now sit empty on the shelf. I'm properly tipsy and excited for our first night in our home together.

Our home.

Giddy, I tighten my robe and head down the stairs.

Camden disappeared a few minutes ago to open the hot tub, so I head out back. The view is just as gorgeous as it was that first night. It's wild to think about how much has changed since then. It's only been two months, but already the man I thought was nothing more than a playboy—my future one-night stand—is now the love of my life.

The sky is an inky black lit by a smattering of stars and the moon hangs low over the city. The sound of the hot tub bubbling doesn't quite drown out the sounds of the ocean thrashing against the retaining wall. And it's snowing. Big, fat glistening flakes fall from the sky. God, this place is gorgeous. And it's only made better when I find Camden seated in the hot tub, a cocky smirk on his face, eyes alight with promises of all sorts of dirty, naughty things.

"It's official. This is my favorite spot in the house," I tell him as I saunter closer.

"It'll be mine too once you take off that robe and let me see what's mine."

My stomach tightens, delicious heat rushing through me. Still, I brace myself for the cold as I kick off my slippers and step onto the stairs leading to the hot tub. When I'm at the edge, I finally slip the robe off and place it on the side table. A table, I notice, with a heater on top of it to keep our towels, and now my robe, warm.

The man thinks of everything.

I've barely sunken beneath the surface when Camden is gripping my foot and tugging me through the water and into his lap. "New rule."

I raise a brow.

"When we're at home, I need to be touching you at all times."

"Only when we're at home?" I tease.

He wraps a hand around my neck, rubbing a thumb against the center of my throat. "You're right, I shouldn't restrict us like that. I want my cock buried right here at all times." He presses against my windpipe.

My pussy flutters with delicious excitement. "Promises, promises," I taunt.

Camden slams his mouth to mine, licking at my lips and then sucking on my tongue, holding me hostage as he grinds up into me. He tugs my top off one of my breasts and squeezes my nipple tight.

I yelp, yet the sound doesn't leave my throat because he still has my tongue.

With the restricted breath, my vision blurs and I sway. Camden catches me immediately, releasing my neck and my tongue and pulling me to his chest, cradling me.

"My pretty brat," he murmurs as he strokes my back.

With desperate movements, I reach for the waistline of his trunks. Fuck. I want his cock buried deep inside me right this very minute.

Rather than lift his hips and help me, he tuts, like he's disappointed.

At the sound, I clench around absolutely nothing. I love when he treats me like a naughty girl who needs to be set straight.

"You know what I've always wanted?" he asks as he arches back and picks up an open bottle of champagne from an ice bucket just outside the tub.

Unsurprisingly, it's Dom. The bottle he bought on the way home to celebrate.

"What?" I ask, distracted by my need for him.

"To drink champagne from your pussy."

I snort. "Really?"

With a nod, he flicks a finger toward the edge of the tub. "Up."

"What?"

"Up." The word is firmer this time, and like the slut I am, I heat at the commanding tone, my body warming all over.

I scramble to the ledge of the tub, and as I settle, the cool air causes pinpricks against every droplet clinging to my skin. One breast is still exposed, though I don't know whether covering it with the suit will make it better or worse.

"You are the hottest woman in existence," he murmurs, his gaze roving over my body.

I settle my hands on the ledge on either side of me, pushing my tits out, preening at the compliment.

From here, the house next door is visible, and when I note the light flickering on in the bedroom upstairs, a thrill rushes through me. Yup. The neighbors could definitely see us if they wanted to.

Why does that only make me hotter?

Like he knows exactly what I'm thinking, Camden's attention drifts to the side and he smirks. "You going to put on a show for Daddy?"

"What kind of show?" As I ask the question, I spread my thighs, already knowing exactly what he wants.

He slicks his tongue over his bottom lip and lets out a cocky chuckle. "You're made for this, aren't you, baby girl? You crave it just as much as I do."

"Crave what?" I ask, my voice raspy.

"Being my whore. Being my salvation. Being my fucking everything."

Heart thumping, I nod. I really do. It's what I love the most about us. There's no pretense between us. We're at our most basic with one another. Our wants and needs are nothing to be ashamed of. I thrive when he calls me his slut, when he treats me like I'm his undoing, because he's mine. "Please," I say, unable to stop from rolling my hips.

"Please what, baby girl? What's the magic word?" His voice is a soft caress, coaxing me to give him exactly what he wants.

"Please, Daddy. Please make me come. Please let me make you come."

"Shh." He presses a kiss to one thigh, then the other. "I've got you, and I'm going to make you feel good."

Camden

Savannah sits on the edge of the hot tub, one tit out, her other nipple, still restrained, practically stabbing through the red fabric of her bikini top. Her red hair is up in a beautiful mess and ringlets frame her face.

She's a fucking vision.

I take a swig from the champagne bottle and stand between her thighs. Towering over her, I pinch her chin, pull at her bottom lip, and lean in close. Pausing there, I meet her beautiful green eyes. Then, with a smirk, I spit the expensive drink onto her tongue.

Because my girl knows me so well, she doesn't swallow. She doesn't even try to close her mouth. Instead, she patiently peers up at me, probably freezing, waiting for me to make my next move. "You're such a perfect little slut." I lick her lips and push up her chin gently, giving her a nod to swallow.

She moans, though as I pour champagne between her tits, the sound turns into a hiss.

I follow the trail the liquid left behind with my fingers, tracing it between her breasts. "I can't wait to fuck this right here." With the bottle still in one hand, I push her breasts together, creating the perfect space for my cock to fit. I squeeze and release her flesh, then roll my thumb over her hard nipples. Fuck, they feel phenomenal.

If her whimpers are anything to go by, she's enjoying it too.

"Gonna make you come first, and then you're going to take Daddy's cock. Aren't you, baby girl?"

She nods violently.

I lean in and lick the champagne from her chest, tugging the fabric completely to the side so I can lavish them both with attention.

Head dropped back, she cries out, and I swear to god my dick leaks. Pretty sure we could both come like this. Her sounds send bolts of need through me, obliterating any sense of self-preservation. My hips move of their own accord, like I'm a fucking dog humping the air, my every cell desperate for her sweet, perfect cunt.

Roughly, I tug her bottoms to the side. Then I douse her puffy pink pussy in the fizzing liquid. As I dip between her thighs and lick up her center, she whimpers, though I barely register the sound, too busy relishing the taste.

"Hold on," I warn.

Listening perfectly like I knew she would, she digs her fingers into the side of the tub. When she's steady, I pull her closer and fuck her thoroughly with my tongue. I need her to come. Need her to scream. Need to release all this pent-up tension inside me. I'm wound tight for no other reason than because I can't get close enough to her. I want to live inside this woman. I want to breed her. Want her stuffed so full of my cock and my cum that it leaks out around us.

But not until she's had at least one orgasm. So I spear her with two fingers and suction my mouth over her clit until she's riding my face, chasing her release, screaming my name.

She doesn't have time to catch her breath before I drag her back into the water and kiss her senseless.

"Oh my god," she mutters, over and over.

I chuckle against her mouth. "*Daddy*, baby girl. That's the only name you should be muttering."

She angles back and presses her tits together with her hands. "Okay, Daddy. Why don't you make a mess of me?"

I stand and tug down my shorts, a deep rumble running through me, and once she's situated, I kneel on a higher step, then fist my cock and straddle her.

Like this, her body isn't completely submerged. She's chosen the perfect spot. She's mostly under water, keeping her body warm, yet her tits hover just above the surface, creating the perfect slot for my dick. And holy fuck does she look beautiful between my thighs, her gorgeous red hair falling over the edge of the hot tub, her skin pink from the heat, her face glistening. As snow falls around us, I smile down at her. "Should I give you a pearl necklace tonight, pretty girl? Or are you going to suck me down and make sure we don't make a mess in the tub?"

"I'm going to do whatever you want," she breathes. With a lick of her lips, she adds, "*Daddy.*"

Fuck. Spine already tingling, I roll my piercings between her tits so she feels every barbell.

"Tits tighter," I demand.

She obeys, and when the friction increases, I grunt. "Perfect, baby girl. You are so *fucking* perfect." I stroke her cheek.

The way she looks up at me, with so much love in her expression, is unreal.

I can't help but tell her how perfect she is. "You are the love of my life, my perfect whore."

With every thrust, my control frays. As I tease her nipples, she lets loose the sweetest little sounds. I grunt and she whines. And when I can't take it anymore, I give her the choice. "Where do you want it?"

She shakes her head. "Where do you want it?" she pants.

Roughly, I stuff myself between her lips and explode.

She's perfect.

Tonight was perfect.

I'm the luckiest fucking man alive.

CHAPTER 39
CAMDEN

MOVING in with Savannah is like having a sleepover every night with my best friend. The best friend I fuck. It's fantastic.

Every day for the last two weeks, I've made a point to get my ass home as quickly as I can. It didn't matter where I was. Work? It can fucking wait. The guys? I've been hanging out with their old asses for years. I can handle a little time apart. Even hockey games don't hold the same appeal. If I didn't have to scout so many damn high school and college games, I think I could be perfectly content not watching another hockey game for the rest of the season. I need at least that long to get fully acquainted with every one of Savannah's curves. Her every sound and smile.

I'm happy. In a way I never knew was possible. Sure, I witnessed my friends fall in love, one after another. I watched them trip all over themselves when their women were close by. I didn't get it then. I'm a sucker now.

"Baby girl," I call as I throw the door open. Damn, I'm already aching for her.

"In the kitchen."

I toss my jacket on the couch, knowing she'll tease me about not hanging it up later. I've discovered how fun it is to reprimand her for the mess she makes in the bathroom each morning, so it'll be well deserved. I love the sight of every open lipstick and spilled eyeshadow because my once barren bathroom is now full of life. But I love spanking her for being messy even more.

As I enter the kitchen, tugging on my tie, I find Savannah bent over the open oven, wearing nothing but a tiny little tease of an apron. With her folded in half like this, ass in the air, her pink pussy taunts me, making my mouth water. Making me swell with need.

"Hungry?" she coos, swaying from side to side, giving me a show.

"Savannah," I warn as I stomp up behind her and caress one cheek. "What if I'd asked one of the guys to come over for dinner, and we walked in and found you looking like a little slut?"

She stands, closing the oven, and turns around, a sexy smile on her face. "Guess you'd have to punish me."

"Problem is you like the punishments."

She breaks into a sexy little pout. "Seems like a you problem, then, huh?"

Chuckling, I dip low and kiss her. It's messy and rough, one hand buried in her long red hair and the other squeezing her bare ass.

"Dinner almost ready?" I ask. "Or do we have some time?"

She smiles against my mouth. "We have some time."

"Good." I scoop her up and carry her into the living room. Settled on the couch, with her legs straddling me, she's the most gorgeous sight.

"Missed you today," she says, her hands on my chest.

Distracted by the way her nipples poke against the fabric of her apron and the way her tits spill from the top and the sides, I reach around her neck and untie the strings there. Then I lift her tits so I can see my name inked on her bra line on the left side. My name on her skin like this makes me feral. It's taking everything in me not to demand we go down to city hall and make it official.

I pull her nipple into my mouth and suck hard, and in response, she grinds against my lap, moaning.

"I always miss you. And I love coming home to you like this." I swipe a thumb over her other nipple, then tug on it. "But make sure I don't on Wednesday."

Savannah pulls back, her muscles tensing. "Why?"

I grin. "Because my sister is coming to visit."

Eyes widening, she tries to scurry off my lap.

I grip her hips, keeping her where she is. "She's not coming now," I promise with a huff of a laugh. "She's fucking seven hundred miles away. You've got time to get dressed first."

She smacks my chest with an annoyed sigh.

I grasp her wrist and kiss the inside of it. "What?"

"When were you going to tell me she was coming?"

My lips twitch, even as I try to hold back a smirk. "Now. She called when I was driving home."

Her eyes bounce back and forth between mine, the emerald color dulling. "Do you want me to go back to my place? I don't mind if you want alone time with her."

Growling, I clutch her to my chest and lean back. "Baby girl, this is your place. *Our place.* And she's coming because she wants to spend time with you."

A shy smile spreads across her face. "Really?"

"Yes. That, and she has a few classes to teach."

"Classes?"

"Yeah, the poles in the basement. She instructs pole dancing classes down there."

A laugh sputters past her lips. "What?"

"My sister is a sex therapist. She helps women take back their sexuality after abuse or heartbreak. She's very passionate about it."

She splays her hands over my bare chest. "And here I thought you were the ultimate playboy with a bunch of stripper poles in your basement. But really, you're just a caring brother."

I stroke her hair. "You are painting me as entirely too good of a guy."

A smirk plays at her lips. "Let me guess; you've fucked a few of her clients."

I snort. "You barely sound jealous."

"Like you were jealous when I told you about my past." She cocks a brow.

I cup her ass and squeeze. "Just because I gave you orgasms, baby girl, doesn't mean I wasn't jealous. I hate thinking of you with anyone else. I know you're open to sharing, but I don't know if I could now that I have you."

Just the idea makes my chest tighten. I've had friends who were into that, and in theory, it's hot, but now I can't imagine someone else touching her.

"That's the beauty of this, baby," she says, her tone soft. "It's your decision whether or not we share. Because I'm *yours*."

I study her, memorizing each freckle, still amazed that she really is mine. "I love you."

Her face softens, the sexy, taunting seductress fading away. I love that side of her so much, but I love this expression even more. Because like this, she isn't putting on a show. There's no artifice. She's just this beautiful girl who feels safe opening up for only me. "I love you." She nibbles on her lip, her focus lowering. "Can I ask you something?"

I hum. "You want to know why my sister took off, don't you?"

And awkward laugh escapes her. "How'd you know?"

"Figured it was only a matter of time before you asked." I twirl a strand of her hair, watching the way the many beautiful shades of red blend together.

I hate telling this story. But if anyone needs to hear it, it's Savannah. I want to spend my life with her, so there can't be any secrets between us. At least not big ones like this.

She shifts off my lap and pulls a white chenille blanket off the back of the couch. It's one she brought from her place, a simple, cozy piece. She settles under my arm, putting herself in a position where I won't be forced to look at her as I speak.

My heart pangs. I appreciate her thoughtfulness, but it's completely unnecessary. I can barely go a few seconds without glancing her way. She's too pretty, and as much as it hurts to talk about this, opening up to her doesn't feel so awful.

"My sister and I were extremely close growing up," I start. "We shared a lot of the same friends. We're twins. I'm not sure I've mentioned that before."

Savannah shakes her head, giving me an encouraging smile.

"I played hockey. She was a figure skater." I shrug. "We basically lived at the arena, and since hockey is nonstop, she spent a lot of time watching me play, and our family traveled for games pretty often. In high school, she dated one of my best friends. He and I played hockey together."

I smile, though the expression isn't a happy one. More ironic.

"My teammates always gave me shit about it because I didn't mind. I loved that my sister was dating my best friend. He was a good guy, you know? Or at least I thought he was. So why wouldn't I want my sister to date him?"

She peers up at me, her teeth sunken into her lip. "I'm guessing he wasn't as great as you thought?"

I curl a piece of her hair around my finger, focusing on the movement. "No. Turns out he just liked attention, and when he got it from *my* girlfriend, he was all too happy to forget that Cora was *his*."

Savannah's jaw drops open.

"It gets worse," I warn her. "She wasn't just my girlfriend. She was my sister's best friend. His girlfriend's *best friend*. The four of us were as close as people can get."

"*Camden*." Savannah shakes her head, frowning, like she doesn't know what to say.

Of course she doesn't. She would never do something like that. It was the definition of fucked up, and she's good and kind. She'd never do that to a friend.

"I caught them at his house. We made plans to hang out after practice, but he must have forgotten. When I got there, I walked in on the two of them butt-ass naked, fucking in his bed."

Sav drops her head back against the cushion and squeezes her eyes shut.

"Yeah." I huff out an irritated breath. "I was fucking hurt and angry. I didn't know what the fuck to do, and in the end, I did the wrong thing."

To this day I don't know why I didn't tell my sister. When I found out, I went silent. I didn't talk to anyone about it. I didn't want to hurt Cora. And it was easier to ignore it all. We were in the middle of hockey finals, and while I couldn't look at Jeremy, I couldn't *not* play.

"What did you do?" Savannah asks softly, bringing me back to the present.

"I didn't tell my sister. I—" I squeeze her hair in my fist but relax it when I realize I'm tugging a little too hard. "I broke up with my girlfriend, and at practice, I couldn't look at my best friend. Couldn't talk to him. But otherwise, I acted like everything was okay. I just…" I shrug. "Pretended it didn't happen. I focused on hockey and ignored everyone. Started drinking a lot, fucking around with other girls. Anything to bury the hurt of their betrayal."

Savannah presses her hand to my cheek. "You were just a kid."

"She got pregnant," I breathe. "My ex-girlfriend." I frown. "So yeah, I'm not the kid in this mess. The baby was. And my sister was the victim of it all too. Because when rumors of her pregnancy got out, my ex swore the baby was mine. She didn't want to ruin her friendship with Cora, and I guess Jeremy had no interest in being a father. I don't know. So she told her the baby was mine and that I wasn't stepping up to help."

"That bitch," Savannah mutters.

I chuff out a bitter laugh. "Yeah. My sister was so angry. We'd never fought before, but she called me every name under the sun. She caught me when I was drunk. It wasn't hard to do. I was always drunk back then. I lashed out and told her the truth. And right there in front of me, the fight left her and her heart shattered. *I* did that to her."

"No," Savannah says fiercely, grabbing my face again. "They did it to her."

"Yeah." I huff. "Well, I was no hero in this story. My sister took off." I close my eyes, finding the image of my parents that day waiting for me.

We searched everywhere, with no luck. They were devastated. It took a couple of days before the letter came. She wrote that she was safe but that she needed to get away.

"We lived in Vegas, so you can imagine the kind of people she got caught up with. The life she led for years after that." My gut twists into a painful knot. "The things she was forced to do."

Cora hasn't opened up about much that happened during that time, but I've sat in on some of her pole dancing sessions. The way she speaks makes it clear she's experienced the kind of abuse she treats.

"Anyway, that's why she ran away. She couldn't face the pregnancy and the lies and betrayal. But she put herself back together. She put herself through school and got her damn master's degree, and now she's dedicated her life to helping people."

Savannah sighs. "That's incredible."

I nod.

Her hand is on my cheek again, her skin warm, her touch gentle. "I'm so sorry that happened to you."

"I'm not," I say honestly. "I probably would have married that girl. And I'd probably still be friends with that asshole. Had I not caught them, she would have passed the baby off as mine, and I probably would have married her and been stuck with her for life."

I squeeze my eyes shut again. Just thinking about Tara makes my blood pressure rise. I despise the woman for everything she was and everything I imagine she still is.

"I played one season in Vegas. Long time ago. And I saw her and her daughter one night. The little girl couldn't have been more than ten or eleven. And they were in a *bar*." Frustration and pity—for the girl, not Tara—swirl in my gut. "I should have done something. I could see her daughter didn't want to be there. Her expression was so sad. She looked so lonely. She was parked at a table, playing with this doll with pink hair. I can still picture it."

Savannah tenses in my arms.

Shit. We haven't talked much about her childhood, but from the bits and pieces I've discovered, it probably wasn't a whole lot different. Her mom probably wasn't much better than Tara.

"Anyway." I sigh. "Instead of stepping in, I walked away. Left her there in the bar while her mom flirted with a man nearby, ignoring her completely. I went straight to another bar and got drunk. Called Daniel that night and said some awful shit to him. I'm lucky he still talks to me after that."

I blow out a breath and stroke her hair, comforting myself.

She's gone still. *Fuck.*

I cup her cheek and force her to look at me. I was an asshole back then. What I did wasn't right. But I'm not that person anymore, and I fucking hope she can see that.

"It's better for the girl that I wasn't her father. I was a disaster. Took me a long time to get my shit together. But I'm okay now—*finally*—because I have you."

Chapter 40
Savannah

WHERE IS THAT GODDAMN BOX?

Heart thumping against my sternum, I stumble through the guest bedroom where we stuffed the belongings I didn't need immediately. It's got to be in here somewhere.

My skin itches and my stomach rolls. I don't need to see the damn doll to know it has pink hair, but I can't fight the urge to dig it out, praying I'm wrong. I'm grasping at straws here because the stories are too coincidental. Or maybe they're not. Maybe Camden's almost child is a female roughly my age, who grew up in Las Vegas, was raised by selfish parents, and isn't actually me. It's possible. My story isn't unique.

I vividly remember the nights in the bars. When my mom would hand me a toy and tell me to be quiet. The nights where she'd tell me to sit in a booth while she went outside with yet another strange man.

A time or two, she even left without me. I would find my way home, terrified and in the dark, because I was more scared of being taken *from* her than I should have been.

She'd stumble through the door, surprised to find me home.

Looking back now, it almost seemed like she was waiting for someone to take me away. Maybe she would have been relieved. Then she wouldn't have had to be responsible for me. She tried to pawn me off on my father countless times, but he was just as uninterested.

I squeeze my eyes shut. No, I will not cry over them. They don't deserve it. But Camden. *Fuck.* If I'm really his ex's daughter…

I swallow down the rest of the sentence. No. It can't fucking be true. I can't lose him. I won't let her take anything else from me.

Even as I make that vow, I can't help but remind myself that life has never been that kind to me. I've always lost the things that matter to me most. I don't ever get to keep them. But over the last month or so, I let my guard down. I got cocky and deluded myself into believing I was free of her. But I'll never be.

As if the universe is taunting me, my phone rings and her name appears on the screen.

Heart in my throat, I answer. "Hi, Mom."

"You know better than to call me that. *Mom* makes me sound old. I'm too young to have a twenty-seven-year-old child."

"And yet you do." I slump onto the guest bed, willing the dread building in my chest to subside. This has to be a coincidence. It's my brain playing tricks on me. Telling me I don't deserve good things. But I do.

I grab a pillow and squeeze it to my chest. The scent alone brings tears to my eyes. It smells like Camden. It's not *his* pillow, but in general, the house smells like home, which is what he smells like.

God, I'm emotional.

"You know what I mean," she says, ignoring my sarcasm.

"Fine, Tara," I say with a sigh. "How was your Christmas?"

"Oh," she says, her tone suddenly bright. "It was good. I spent it with the pilot I've been seeing for a bit. He was supposed to be home with his family, but he got stuck here because of weather. It worked out nicely for us."

I blanch. She's awful. And yet pointing that out won't do me any good. So I swallow down my commentary and say one thing I do truly mean. "I'm glad you weren't alone."

"Never am."

A shocked laugh tries to escape me, but I do a brilliant job of choking it back.

"Anyway, I'm calling because I ran into an old friend a few weeks ago. My ex-boyfriend's sister, actually."

The uneasiness in my stomach returns. "Huh?"

Clearly not sensing my panic, she babbles on. "Anyway, I looked her up online after seeing her. Her brother has always been the one who got away."

More like the one who ran away, and for good reason.

"He lives in Boston."

My stomach drops. Fuck. Shit. Fuck. *No.* I gulp down oxygen, trying to get my bearings. It could still be a coincidence.

My mother barrels on, totally unaware of the pain she's leaving in her wake. "Isn't it a small world? I knew he played hockey there for a while, but I never knew what happened to him after that." With every word, her pitch gets a little higher. "Now that I know he still lives there, I decided I'd surprise him."

The hope and delusional belief that this wouldn't blow up in my face is gone in a flash. "What?" I ask, panicked. "Why?"

She laughs. "Because I want to see him, Savannah. And I can see you while I'm here too."

Of course. I don't have enough energy to be bothered by the fact that my mother is finally making a trip out here because of a man, not to see her own daughter.

I shake my head. No way. I'll talk her out of it. Then I need to figure out if Camden is really her ex.

"Mom—*Tara,*" I correct. "It's been decades. He's probably married with kids by now."

"He's not." The devious laugh she lets out chills my blood. "Even if he was, I guarantee I'd be hotter than his wife. I look far better than most women my age. That was the one good thing that came of having you at nineteen. My body bounced back right away."

"I'm so glad you found one positive aspect of my existence," I mutter, standing up.

She sighs. "Stop making everything about you. This would benefit you too. He's got loads of money, I'm sure. I always told you he'd have made a better dad than your lowlife father."

I pull my phone away from my ear and gape at it. How in the hell am I related to this woman? It's mortifying.

"And maybe Camden can set you up with someone on the team. Pro hockey players make a ton of money, and from what I found online, he still works for the Bolts."

My abdomen spasms and my breakfast threatens to make a reappearance. "Mom, I've got to go."

"Wait—"

I end the call without a second of hesitation. I can't talk to her right now. God, I wish I never had to talk to her again. But I'm not that lucky. I'll have to deal with all of this eventually. First, I need to throw up.

When the doorbell rings while I'm brushing my teeth, I say a prayer that it's not my mother. That would be my fucking luck.

My phone has been blowing up since I ended our call, but I can't look at it. I can't talk to her. Honestly I can't talk to anyone. But I can't ignore the door either. If Camden checks the camera, he'll see her standing there, and I don't know how the fuck to deal with any of this right now.

I can't imagine Camden will take the news well. But maybe if I explain that I had no idea who he was and that I have virtually no relationship with her, he can get past the shitty details.

With a steadying breath, I head downstairs, taking the steps two at a time. "I'm coming," I call as the doorbell chimes again.

I swing the door open, and when I find a teenage boy on the doorstep rather than my backstabbing mother, I let out a relieved groan.

"Whoa. Who are you?" the kid says as I slap my hands to my knees and bend in two, sucking in lungfuls of air.

I peer up at him, heart still racing. "Savannah, Cam's girlfriend. And you are?"

"Oh." He straightens and grins. "I'm Maverick, his godson."

I point at him, a memory surfacing. "Right, Daniel and Hannah's kid."

He chuckles. "I guess we can go with that. Is Cam here?"

Standing, I shake my head, feeling only slightly better. At least this kid is a distraction.

"No, he's at work, I think." Maybe. I was too preoccupied this morning to pay attention when he told me his plans. I barely got through the night without breaking down and confessing my suspicions to him.

"Damn." He sighs. "I just wanted to drop off these forms." He holds out a large manilla envelope. "I appreciate what you're doing, by the way."

Frowning, I take it from him. "What I'm doing?"

He nods, his thankful expression genuine. "Yeah, I don't know what he's paying you or anything like that, but thanks. You have no idea how much this means to me."

Discomfort builds in my chest, making it feel tight. "Paying me for what?"

He looks at me like I've got two heads. "The bet."

"What bet?"

"The one Cam made with my mom. That he could make a relationship last three months." His expression falls. "Ya know, so that I can enter the draft…" His words die and his eyes go wide, like he's realizing that I have no fucking clue what he's talking about. "I, uh. Forget it," he says, taking a step back. "Just tell Camden I dropped off the—" He shakes his head. "Actually, ya know what? Don't tell him anything. In fact, forget everything I said."

With that, he's gone, rushing down the steps, and I'm left nodding at the empty porch, my thoughts scrambled.

I'm pretty sure this kid just told me that my boyfriend, who used to date my mother, is only dating me to win a bet.

Wow. When shit goes wrong, I'm not usually surprised. I've come to expect that everything inevitably goes south. But I *really* didn't see this coming.

Turns out it really was him and not me. I officially lost the guy. Then again, I guess Camden was never really mine to lose.

You can't lose something you never had.

CHAPTER 41
CAMDEN

Aiden: Who's ready for another wager?

Brooks: I'm out. I'm not playing games with you. I either end up with a pierced dick or watching Playboy hump the ground.

Daniel: My wife was controlling my dick. How many times do I have to say this?

War: I'd really like to know nothing about your dick, Playboy. Lep, what's the wager?

Aiden: How long until the Iceman puts a ring on Sav's hand.

Brooks: Lennox totally stole your phone

Aiden: Did not!

War: Hahahaha. One thousand percent.

Daniel: Okay, new rule! Wives can't be in the group chat. We need a modicum of privacy, girls.

Aiden: Still me.

> Me: Don't worry, you'll all know the minute I pop the question.

> Aiden: Hear that, fellas??

> Brooks: Sara! Aiden just walked into practice, and he said you said you needed to borrow his phone.

> Aiden: Oops. New number, who dis?

I CHUCKLE as I click out of the chat and send a quick text to Sav.

> Me: Baby girl, better check your messages. It seems the girls are taking bets about when I'm going to propose. If you want to win, I can give you the inside scoop.

I add a wink emoji and shove my phone into my pocket. In the other is the ring I just picked up. I want to ask her before my sister comes to town. For so long, I haven't been able to celebrate the big moments in my life with my family. Cora was gone when I was drafted into the NHL. She missed the Stanley Cups and the celebrations.

But now that we've rebuilt our relationship, I want to celebrate with my sister after I pop the question to Savannah.

And since Savannah has made it clear that she isn't close to her parents, I'm doing something a little unconventional. I'm headed to her old apartment building to ask Rosalie and Nick for their blessing and to convince them to help me with the proposal. And the Donovans. The people in that building are her chosen family. Along with Josie, Addie, and Sutton. They'll be my next call.

I want to show Savannah that the people she cares about care about her in return. And that we'll always choose her. That she's our family. And what better way than by throwing a big engagement party? And tonight is the night. I'm going to ask while I make Rosalie's meatballs for her. I've planned a simple night with my girl. One of thousands of nights together we'll have if she agrees to forever.

Not that I'm worried she'll say no. For the first time in my life, I'm confident that someone will choose me.

I feel like I'm floating as I navigate through Savannah's old neighborhood.

I've even started looking at facilities in Boston that could handle my mother's care. My sister deserves to choose where she wants to live, but she loves Boston, so I have an inkling that if we can get Mom here, Cora will be ecstatic. And I want them both here. I hope that one day I'll have a child of my own, and I don't want my family to miss out on any time with them. My relationship with my mother will always be complicated, but Cora and I are in a good place, and I'll do anything to continue to foster our relationship.

As I jog up the steps to the building, I smile at the snowman that's fallen over. I've just reached the door when it swings open, so I step back, making room for the person heading out, bracing myself for a conversation with one of the Donovan kids. They're adorable, but Piper is the only one who speaks clearly enough for me to understand.

Rather than Rosalie or Nick or one of the Donovans, an unfamiliar woman with platinum blond hair steps out, gripping her chest in surprise. "Oh. You scared me."

"Sorry about that." I take another step back, hands in my pockets—one cupped around the ring box—and give her a cordial smile. "After you."

She narrows her brown eyes, the lines on her forehead creasing severely. "*Camden?*"

I frown. I don't recognize her. Yeah, fans still spot me sometimes, but the way she said my first name only, as if she knows me, makes me hesitate. With another quick scan of her face, I confirm that I don't recognize her. A fan, then. So I offer the kind of easy smile I save for situations like this. "Yes, that'd be me. Hockey fan?"

She coughs out a laugh. "Oh my god. What are the chances? I was just telling my daughter about you, and here you are." She throws herself into my arms, squealing. "I can't believe how long it's been."

I cup her upper arms and push her back. "I'm sorry, I, uh—" I study her again. I guess maybe she looks a little familiar. But she honestly looks like dozens of blondes I've met over the years.

Shit. My stomach drops. Because the longer she looks at me, her eyes full of excitement, the more obvious it is that we probably fucked at some point, and she apparently thought it meant more than I did.

"You seriously don't recognize me?" Her shoulders sag, her tone chiding.

I shake my head and give her an apologetic frown. "I'm sorry."

"Tara *Brewer*," she says with a tight smile.

My already uneasy stomach pitches. *Fuck.* It's been years. Probably fifteen since I saw her that last time in that bar. What the fuck is she doing outside Savannah's old apartment? Unease slithers through my veins and anger sets in. "Are you stalking me?"

She jolts back, her eyes going wide. "What? No. I was just visiting my daughter."

I glance over her shoulder at the building. Erin is her daughter?

"What are you doing here?" She squints at me, like she's considering that I'm the one following her. Fuck no. I'd be happy if I never saw this woman again.

"My girlfriend lives here," I grumble. I guess that's not true anymore. And thank fuck. I don't want Savannah anywhere near here. Poor Erin. I can't believe she was raised by this sorry excuse for a woman.

She peers back, surveying the building. "Really?" Then, wearing a flirty smile that causes bile to climb up my throat, she says, "I was hoping I'd run into you while I was here. Do you have some time? I'd love to grab a drink and catch up."

I scowl. "You are the last person I'd ever want to catch up with."

"Camden, don't be like that." She takes a step closer to me, her lashes fluttering.

My skin crawls. I hate this woman. It fucking guts me that I've allowed her to control so much of my life. That her betrayal kept me from trusting anyone—until Savannah.

Though I can't help but see the silver lining and focus on that instead. Had she not betrayed me, I might have married her. And even if I saw sense and didn't, then without her betrayal, I wouldn't have been so broken and I probably would have met another woman and settled down, and that means I wouldn't have Savannah. I wouldn't have found the true definition of happiness, and I wouldn't be ready to propose. If the only way to get here was to live life as a shell of a man for almost three decades, then so be it. I'd do it all over again.

"Take care of yourself, Tara." I turn on my heel and head back to my car. I can talk to Rosalie and Nick another time. Right now I want to get home to my girl. We don't need perfect to be happy. I just need her.

"If you change your mind," Tara calls, "I'll be staying here with Savannah for the next week or so."

A bark of a laugh rips its way out of me. Like I'd ever change my mind. I'm halfway to my car when the rest of her comment registers, and I whip around. "Did you say Savannah?"

She gives me another one of those fake flirty smiles and saunters toward me. "Yeah, my daughter Savannah. She lives here."

It's like a punch to the gut. Like being hit by a train. And as the pieces fall into place, my world crumbles around me.

How's your relationship with your dad?
  Nonexistent.
  I can work with that.

I didn't know you were from Vegas.
  I don't really…

Her mother is a piece of work and her father never wanted to be one.

• • •

Memory after memory pummels me, stealing my breath and all my strength. I bend at the waist and suck in air, my chest burning. No fucking way.

"Camden." Tara sounds like she's in a tunnel. I can't make out a word she's saying. None of them matter anyway.

Because Savannah, my Savannah, is Tara's daughter. The woman I was about to propose to is the daughter of my ex-girlfriend. The daughter, that for a moment in time, she tried to play off as mine.

The nausea wins out when reality sinks in, and my stomach lurches violently, and then I lose my breakfast all over the goddamn street.

How the fuck did she do it to me again? She ruined everything.

Chapter 42
Savannah

EVERY SINGLE PHONE call to Camden goes unanswered. It's been three hours, and I haven't heard a fucking word. My heart is in my throat and my stomach is in knots.

I've tried to convince myself that I overreacted. There's got to be an explanation. Even if the bet was in place when we started dating, he cares about me. He couldn't have made it all up. Couldn't have lied that well. And why? He could have just dated me, or anyone for that matter. He didn't need to tell me he loves me and move me into his home. He isn't that cruel.

I text him again.

> Me: We need to talk. Please call me back as soon as you can.

I set the phone on the bathroom counter and stare into the mirror. My eyes are red rimmed, my skin pale. I'll wash my face, do my makeup, and get dressed. Cam will be home soon, and we'll figure this out.

There has to be an explanation.

The stress weighing on me over the bet situation is heavy, but the whole ex-girlfriend being my mother thing is almost enough to make my knees buckle.

My stomach rolls again. This fucking day can go get fucked.

I blow out a breath. Time to be a big girl. I should call my mother and talk to her. Convince her not to come. Maybe if I cut her from my life for good, Camden never has to know.

Do you hear yourself? I glare at my reflection.

Yeah, there's no hiding this. With my mind a mess, I call my mother. I need more information. It rings once and then goes to voicemail. Ugh. This woman. She can't drop a bomb on me like she did today and then just ignore me.

After the beep, I sigh. "Mom, we need to talk. Call me back."

When I end the call, I find I already have a text message from her.

Mom: Hi honey. Sorry I missed your call. I stopped by your apartment, but you weren't there. My pilot friend is going to be in Boston tonight, so I'm headed back to the airport. Hope you don't mind, but I saw the cash in the envelope on the counter. I'll pay you back. Promise!

I squeeze my eyes shut and ball my fists. That fucking money was for my landlord. *Shit.*

But then I breathe out. Because she's gone. And she can't blow up my life if she's not here.

I don't even let myself feel the sting that should come with finding out she's running off with a man rather than sticking around to see me. It's nothing new. At least she's not trying to seduce my boyfriend like she originally planned.

The second I finish that thought, I close my eyes and shake my head. My life is such a damn circus. I don't know how I'll pay my rent if she doesn't pay me back, and I don't actually believe she will, but right now I'm more concerned about why I haven't heard from Camden.

Pulse pounding, I call him again. I just need to hear his voice. I need to know I still have him. I'll feel so much better if I can just talk to him.

But it rings several times, and then his voicemail picks up. A minute after I end the call, a text finally comes through.

Daddy: I can't do this. I'm sorry. You should go back home.

A manic laugh breaks free as tears blur my vision. "Home?" Where the fuck is home? Is he serious? I call him again, but this time it goes straight to voicemail. When the robotic voice tells me to leave a message, I throw the phone against the wall. *"Fuck."*

He wants me to go home. Do I even have one? Have I ever? *This* was supposed to be my home. My safe space.

And thanks to my mother, I can no longer even afford the small space on the third floor of my apartment building. The only other place that ever came close to feeling like home.

Camden felt like home too. And now I don't have him either.

CHAPTER 43
CAMDEN

MY HEART HAS SHATTERED into a million pieces. Jagged little things that will never find their way back together.

This is it. This is the point of no return. Over the years, it's been sliced and bruised, but the damage could be patched up. Now, after this, it's irreparable.

I really thought I'd found it. Happiness. Fuck, I even silently thanked Tara for breaking me, because if she hadn't, I wouldn't have found the love of my life.

Only the love of my life is Tara's daughter.

Her fucking *daughter.*

I hold up a hand, getting the bartender's attention.

He saunters over, a brow cocked. "You sure you should have more?"

I toss a handful of hundreds on the bar. "Leave the bottle and keep your opinions to yourself."

With a shake of his head, he drops the bottle of brown liquid next to my tumbler. Then he slides the money his way and wanders off.

I don't even bother pouring the whiskey into the glass. I just tip it back, take a swig, and drop it onto the mahogany. Then I pick up my phone.

Chest aching, I reread the last message I sent.

> Me: I can't do this. I'm sorry. You should go back home.

That was hours ago.

Maybe yesterday. I have no fucking idea what time it is. I considered getting on a jet. Flying away. But where the hell would I go?

Instead, I parked myself on a stool at the airport bar. It never closes. Just goes from lunch to dinner to late night...to breakfast, I think? Is that next? Yup, the sun is coming up. Fuck.

And not a peep from Savannah. So it's done. She knows. I'm sure she fucking knows. She's probably seen Tara by now. They've put together the truth.

That's why she texted that we needed to talk. Why she called so many damn times.

But I can't see her. If I do, I'll fold. I'll sweep her back into my arms and do whatever I can to make peace with the idea that Tara's daughter is the woman I want to be my wife.

Wife.

I take another swig of whiskey. Then I tap on her contact and hit Delete. There. It's done. It's over.

Fuck, it's hard to breathe.

But it's better this way. There's a chance I could have worked past the truth, but how the fuck could I ever ask my sister to accept it? What Tara and Jeremy did destroyed our family. It cost us years. Forced my sister to leave. Led her to a situation where she had to sell her goddamn body for a living.

With anger burning in my chest, I down the last of the bottle's contents. It does nothing to dull the ache, though.

"All right, you've had enough," the bartender says. "Is there someone I can call?"

A sharp, short laugh bursts out of me. "Nah, I've got no one."

I clutch the stupid empty bottle, heft it in one hand, then reel back and throw it against the wall.

"Camden Fucking Snow, I cannot believe you."

My head pounds, the familiar high-pitched voice too loud. I smell like death and piss, and I just want to go back into the damn cell.

"Why are you here?"

My sister fists her hands on her hips and huffs. "Good question, since you're not the one who called me after you got arrested."

I can't open my eyes without being hit with piercing pain. That's good. I don't think I could look at her right now anyway.

"You can thank this nice officer. You're lucky he was a fan of yours when he was a kid. When you refused to use your one phone call, he called your emergency contact—*me*."

"That's a total violation of privacy," I mutter, head bowed.

"Oh, you want to file a complaint against the cop who got you bailed out of *jail*?" She smacks me on the back of the head, then stomps to the door.

I force myself to straighten and survey the group of officers milling nearby, witnessing our interaction. By some miracle, I manage to summon some common sense and decency. "Thanks for getting me out," I say to the group, not knowing which one helped. "I'll drop off some signed merch from the team next week."

One of the guys lights up. "Could you get me a puck signed by JJ Hanson? And a jersey from Hawke?"

I nod, the movement sending another bolt of agony through my head, and close my eyes. "Yeah, no problem."

"What time is it?" I ask my sister as we step out into the brutally cold February day.

"One," she says, dropping my phone and wallet into her purse.

"And what day is it?" I ask, keeping my gaze on the sidewalk in front of me.

She glares at me. I still can't look at her, but I can feel her ire. "Tuesday."

"Fuck."

"Yeah, fuck. What the fuck were you thinking?"

She pulls up short and digs through her purse. "Why are we stopping here?"

"Because I need to order a fucking Uber. I didn't have a car, and your car is MIA."

"It's at the airport," I tell her.

She huffs. "One more thing to deal with."

"I'll have one of the guys drop me off there later."

She ignores me, tapping away at her phone screen.

"I know we need to talk," I say, "but can I shower and eat something before you tell me what a complete disappointment I am?"

"Yup."

It takes several minutes for the rideshare to arrive. We spend the time standing side by side in silence.

No matter how hard I try, I can't stop thinking about Savannah. I haven't seen her in three days. She probably hates me. I don't blame her. I hate myself.

She's better off without me. They'd all be better off without me. My sister included.

Cora doesn't even sit in the back of the car with me when it pulls up. I settle behind the passenger seat, my head against the window, and she gets in the front and keeps up a friendly conversation with the driver the whole way.

When we pull up to my house, I take in the façade of the place that, only a few days ago, I thought we'd raise a family in. I thought we'd be engaged this week. That when my sister arrived, we'd celebrate. That we'd be planning a wedding.

Maybe she's here. Maybe she didn't leave when I told her to go home.

With a burst of hope, I stagger out of the car and take the steps two at a time. I type in the code for the front door and throw it open.

"Savannah? Baby girl?" I rush past the kitchen. "Savannah?" Upstairs, I dart down the hall toward my bedroom. When I pass the open door to the guest room, I pull up short, and the pieces of my shattered heart disintegrate further. Because the room that was filled with all her boxes is completely empty.

She's really gone.

"She's not here," Cora says when she finds me still standing in the empty bedroom.

I nod.

"What happened?" Her voice is soft. Too kind. I don't deserve it.

Head hanging, I squeeze my eyes shut, fighting back the tears.

She cups my shoulder and squeezes. "Go shower. I'll order lunch, and then you can fill me in. We'll figure this out."

"There's no figuring this out." I cough out a painful laugh. "Tara ruined everything. And then I pissed all over it and lit it on fire."

"I can't believe she's Tara's daughter," Cora says for probably the fifth time since I finished telling her the whole sordid story.

"So you've said." I take a bite of the burger my sister had delivered and bite back a moan. Fuck, that's good.

"So how are you going to fix this?"

I freeze mid-chew and snap my head up. "Fix what?"

"Your relationship with Savannah. You went off the deep end when you found out, right? And now she's pissed at you? So how are you going to fix it?"

"She's Tara's daughter. There is no fixing it."

Cora's lips turn down as she studies me. "But you love her."

The place in my chest where my heart used to be pangs. "Yeah, and? I can't be with her. She's Tara's fucking child."

"You really need to stop saying that. It's not like she's *your* daughter."

I drop my burger and pound a fist against the table. "But she could have been."

My sister's head snaps back and her eyes go wide. "Whoa. Calm down before you have a heart attack."

Maybe I should listen to her. My chest feels like someone is sitting on it. I can barely get a breath in.

"How am I supposed to calm down? For the first time in my life, I had it all. I was in love. And I found a woman who truly loved me back. I've never felt like this before, Cor. Savannah was"—I suck in a deep breath, ignoring the pain that comes with it—"*is* everything to me. I thought I'd finally found her. I finally understand what all my friends have been talking about for years. And now to find out that she's *her* daughter? That she's part of the reason you ran away—"

Cora throws a hand up. "No." She shakes her head. "We aren't doing this. We aren't going to blame an innocent woman. She had nothing to do with her parents' decisions. Or *ours*. Jeremy was an asshole." She sucks in a long, angry breath and closes her eyes. "And Tara is the worst. But they don't get to control any more of our story. Or hers." Her shoulders lower a bit, her usual calm, confident demeanor returning. "Because it sounds like they were even worse than we thought they were, and she is stuck with them for parents. Doesn't she deserve to be happy?" She tilts her head, her brow furrowed. "Take you and me out of the equation. Does Savannah deserve to have another person disappoint her? Another person to let her down?"

The thought of Savannah having to deal with all of this bullshit alone kills me. It's like being tossed into the ocean during a storm. She doesn't have family to rely on. No mother or father to pick up the pieces.

My mother may hate me when she's lucid and be confused when she's not, but at least I have Cora. Savannah has no one. No sibling to help her shoulder the burden of being brought into this world by hateful parents. No reprieve from that sadness.

And I just turned my back on her.

I push back from the table. "Fuck."

"Exactly," Cora says. "So how are you going to fix this? Maybe you're right. Maybe you don't deserve her after the way you've acted, but doesn't she deserve you? Doesn't she deserve to be loved?"

Chapter 44
Savannah

I GROAN AT MY PHONE. Shit. I can't ignore them any longer.

Dammit, Camden. Not only have you destroyed me, but now you're destroying my peace.

I just want to wallow in self-pity for one or two more days. Then I'll make a plan. Get my act together.

And what do they mean he's been arrested? Fucking idiot.

I refuse to look it up on the internet. I won't give that man even another second of my time. I fell apart when he told me to go home on Saturday. But I only allowed myself five minutes to break down. Then I reminded myself that I've been in this position before. Unwanted, unloved, and without a home. I picked myself up at eighteen when I had no money and no job. I got loans, worked in restaurants, and got my freaking degree without the help of another soul. Now, at twenty-seven, I have people. And a job. Yeah, I'm dead broke right now, but it's nothing compared to those days. I can figure this out.

Once I dried my tears, I called John Donovan, and he helped me move my stuff back to the studio. Then Rosalie fed me, and not a single one of them asked me to explain.

They're the family I've chosen, and they show me far more love than I've ever had before. I won't spend another second thinking about the man who didn't even care enough to break up with me in person.

With a sigh, I respond to my friends.

Me: Fine. We broke up and I'm wallowing. Let me have this. I promise I'll be back at work next week.

Addie: I'm so sorry, babe. I'm here if you need me.

Me: I just need time. And to be left alone. Josie, I'm serious. Don't come storming over here. I'll be okay, and I love you all for caring, but I just need time.

Sutton: I'm sorry too. You know where to find me if you need to get away for a few days. You can even hide out at the island house.

Me: I think I'll pass on a ferry ride in February in Maine, but thanks.

Josie: It's taking everything in me to remain at my desk. I love you. And for the record, I'm going to castrate Camden when I see him.

Me: Don't. He's not worth it.

A man who could walk away without even a glance back after promising the world truly isn't worth the energy it takes to even hate him. Or at least that's what I'll keep telling myself.

I drop my phone and groan. Rent is due in two days, and I don't have near enough to cover it after my mom disappeared with that envelope of cash.

Stupidly, I spent too much on Christmas gifts and decorations for Camden's house. I wanted to make it homey. Add my own little touch to the place. He said I should make myself at home. He also gave me his credit card. Not that I used it. That's not who I am.

Maybe it's who I should have been.

Then maybe I'd have the fifteen hundred dollars I owe my landlord on Friday. I asked if I could pay by credit card. That was a no. Not that mine have enough credit left on them anyway.

The next few months are gonna be tight. But I'll find a way. I always do. I just need a quick influx of cash now. Then I'll pinch pennies until things level out.

When my phone buzzes again, I drop my head back and whine. "Why can't they just leave me alone?"

With a huff, I pick it up. But the message on the screen isn't from the girls. Or at least not from *my* girls.

> Kacie: Hey, babe. We still need that rain check.
> What are you up to this weekend?

Kacie. Nerves swirl in my belly, but a little bit of hope blossoms in my chest. This is exactly what I need. The perfect way to make some quick cash.

Without letting myself overthink it, I tap out a reply.

> Me: Hi! I'm free, but I could actually use your
> help. Is your boss still hiring new dancers?

CHAPTER 45
CAMDEN

I TAKE in the old brownstone with weary eyes. My arraignment was this morning, but my lawyer says with a well-intentioned donation to the airport and an in-person apology to the bartender, along with the merch the team is getting together for me, we can get this ordeal cleaned up quickly.

The legal aspect of it, that is. None of those things can help me put out the blaze I created when I set fire to my life. I know well enough that no amount of money will fix the biggest issues.

No, it'll take some damn good groveling and a whole lot of promises to show Savannah how sorry I am. I fucked up. Badly. I haven't tried to call her because I don't know what to say.

But it's Friday. It's been almost a week since I destroyed everything.

And I can't go any longer without seeing her.

I'm halfway up the porch steps when a little voice stops me.

"Go away, you meanie!"

The angry expression plastered on Piper's face as she hangs out the first-floor window is more adorable than fearsome, but I can appreciate the effort.

"Can't do that, Pip. I need to apologize."

The front door opens and John steps out, immediately giving his daughter a stern look. "It's freezing. Close the window and go help your mother set the table."

"But dad, he—"

He sighs. "I know what he did. But this is grown-up stuff. Go do what you're told."

Huffing, she pushes the window down, but before it touches the sill, she yells, "Make it hurt, Dad!"

I wince. *Jeez.*

John turns back to me. Arms crossed. Pissed off.

I hold my hands up in surrender. "Go easy on me."

He shakes his head, the disappointment in his expression hurting more than it should. "What are you doing here?"

"Just want to talk to Sav."

"She's not here." His response comes without any hesitation, making me think he's lying.

I take a step forward, shoulders hunched against the cold. "Are you—"

He jabs me with a finger, the disappointment turning into anger. "You were supposed to take care of her. You were supposed to be different. She was happier than I've ever seen her. Told Rosalie and Pip that for the first time, she'd found someone who genuinely loved her." He shakes his head. "But then you broke her."

A wave of shame washes over me. "I know."

"No. You have no fucking idea. You weren't there when we packed up her things. You didn't hear the way she sobbed in the bathroom when it was time to go."

I may not have heard that, but because of the camera above the door, I saw the devastation in her expression every time she went up and down those front steps, loading up the belongings she'd only just moved in.

He's right. She was broken. I did that. I watched it on repeat, welcoming the pain that came with it, wishing I could take hers. Wishing I could go back in time and fix it.

But I can't. I can be here now, though. "I just want to talk to her. Explain." I shake my head and inhale deeply. "Apologize."

He stares at me for a long time. So long that I squirm under his scrutiny. "Well," he finally says, "like I told you, she's not here."

"Then I'll wait here until she gets home." I don't for a second think they'd let me wait inside, so I shuffle to my car instead.

"You'll be waiting all night, then," he calls.

I whip around, frowning. "What? Why?"

He shrugs and tips his head back, sighing. "I don't even know why I'm telling you this. You really fucking hurt her."

I hustle back to the porch. "I know. And I want to fix it, John. She's it for me."

He huffs, his breath a white cloud in front of him. "You didn't hear it from me, but I overheard her telling the landlord that she just needed a few more days to come up with her rent."

The pain in my chest is back. Why wouldn't she have enough money to cover her rent? "Okay?"

"And then she told Erin she couldn't watch the kids last night because she had to work."

"At *Jolie*? They let her work after hours?"

He shakes his head. "No idea, but when I heard a car door slam at four this morning, I looked out the window. Saw her coming in."

"That makes no sense."

He shrugs. "She left a little while ago. No idea where she's going, but she said she'd be back late again."

Unease threads its way through me as I consider the details. "I don't like it."

"Me neither. You have any idea where she'd be working?"

"No, but I can find out." Quickly, I head for my car.

"Don't make me regret telling you this," he calls after me.

I hold up a hand, but I don't slow. "You won't. I promise."

Car running and heat blasting, I pull away from the curb, headed for War's house. Pretty sure I'm going to need his help convincing his daughter to talk to me.

CHAPTER 46
CAMDEN

"WHY DO you have to live so far from Boston?" I grumble when War opens the door. "The drive is a pain in the ass."

With a nonplussed look, he waves me in. "It's thirty minutes, tops. And if you really need my help, let me tell you: complaining isn't the way to get it."

"Is she here?" When I called, he told me I was in luck because Josie and Ava had made plans to watch a movie tonight. It's their thing. Once a month or so, they hang out in the game room in the basement, just the two of them. They watch rom-coms and play board games like they did when Josie was young and going through cancer treatments. Damn, life has changed so much since then. Josie was a long-term resident at the hospital the first time I met her. She couldn't have been more than eight.

It's crazy to think how much life has changed since that time. It's even weirder to think I'm now dating her friend.

Okay, not dating. Pretty sure I was broken up with when Savannah moved out. Or maybe I broke up with her when I texted her. Fuck, this is a mess.

"Yeah, she's in the kitchen." He leads me to the massive open kitchen and living area. There's a fire roaring in the fireplace, and the view out the floor-to-ceiling windows at the back of the house is as breathtaking as always. Nothing but trees and quiet out there. And the little pond they turn into a skating rink every winter. Right now it's lit up with Christmas lights like it was years and years ago when War taught Ava, Josie, and Scarlett how to skate.

It's the picture-perfect home for a family.

Maybe, if I'm lucky enough to get a second chance with Savannah, I'll look at houses in this neighborhood. The thirty-minute drive would be well worth it for this view alone.

Ava and Josie are standing together in front of the oven. When Ava spins around, her red hair sways, instantly making me think of Savannah. Damn, I physically ache for her. I'm such a sorry fuck.

With a plate of cookies in her hands, Ava grins at me. "You look like you could use a chocolate chip cookie."

A step behind her, Josie glowers. "He doesn't deserve one."

I wince. This family has been such a big part of my life, but if I can't fix this, I'm not sure Josie will want much to do with me. "She's right." I cuff the back of my neck and squeeze. "I don't."

Ava hip-checks her daughter. "He'll make it right. Camden always does." With a smile at me, she pads around the island. "Come on, Ty. Let's let these two talk. You can help me set up Monopoly." She stops in front of me, presses a kiss to my cheek, and hands me a cookie. Then she disappears with her husband.

"Get on with it," Josie says when they've gone. "You're already ruining my favorite night of the month."

With a sigh, I rough a hand down my face. "Do you know where Sav is working?"

Josie frowns. "Um, at *Jolie*?"

I shake my head. "No. I went to her place to talk to her, but she wasn't there. I was told she's working somewhere at night."

Eyes narrowing, she cocks a hip and leans against the counter. "Who told you that?"

I set my hands on the cool surface of the island. "Listen, I don't want to get anyone in trouble."

"Why are you even here?" she demands. "You broke her heart, Cam."

The name slashes at my skin like a sharp knife. Not Uncle Cam; just Cam. I guess I deserve it.

"I'm trying to fix it," I promise. "I just want to make this right, but I'm worried that she's in some sort of trouble. John overheard her say that she couldn't make rent on time. Did she say anything to you?"

Josie shakes her head, her shoulders falling. "She asked me to give her some space. Do you really think she's in trouble?"

"I don't know, but I'm concerned. Could you call her and make sure she's okay?"

Josie hums out a groan. "I don't know," she whines. "She'd kill me if she knew I was helping you."

"I'm not asking you to help me." I hold up a hand. "I'm asking you to check on her. That's all. I swear it."

Whether Savannah can forgive me is up to her, but I won't stop caring either way. If she needs money for rent, I'll make sure she has it. I hate thinking of her all alone, feeling as if she has no one.

And knowing I'm the reason she feels that way is gut-wrenching.

Finally Josie blows out a breath and picks up her phone. "Fine, but I'm not doing this for you."

I nod. "I know."

She taps the screen a few times, then the ring tone echoes loudly through the kitchen. With the device on speaker, she sets it on the counter between us.

After two rings, Savannah picks up. "Hey, Jose. I can't really talk right now."

"Well, you're going to need to because your boy toy just showed up at my house and demanded I tell him where you work," Josie grouses. "And since I was under the impression that your only job was at *Jolie*, I was a little thrown."

"Fuck, sorry about that," Savannah says.

Just hearing her voice kills me. I want to reach through the phone and hold her.

"It's not a big deal," she rushes out. "I just needed a quick influx of cash because my bitch of a mother stole my rent money."

It takes everything in me not to growl and take the phone. Tara is such a fucking cunt.

"What? Why? When? Why didn't you tell me your mother was in town?" Josie narrows her eyes at me, throwing figurative daggers, then picks up the phone and starts pacing with it.

"Because she's a bitch? I don't know. I don't want to waste any more time thinking about it, honestly. This week has been hell, but I'm finally starting to feel like I can breathe again. I made enough over the last two nights for this month's rent. Hopefully I'll make enough tonight to cover next month's. Then I should be good."

"But what are you doing?" Josie says, her tone full of suspicion and concern.

I feel the same way. Hands fisted, I focus on breathing evenly, even as I want to dart out of here and hunt her down.

"Don't worry about it. I'm fine."

"You don't sound fine," Josie says. "And why did you and Cam break up? What's going on, Sav? You're making me nervous."

"Honestly," she says, her tone resigned, "I think he found out that he used to date my mother and he freaked."

Josie spins around, her eyes wide.

My own fall shut. So she does know. I assumed she did, but fuck.

"He what?"

Savannah groans. "It's gross, I know. My slut of a mother cheated on Cam when she was a senior in high school. She got pregnant. The story is far too long to tell now." Her tone gets a little watery when she continues. "I don't know how he figured it out, but a few days ago, he told me this story about seeing his ex and her daughter in a bar. He mentioned that she was carrying around a doll with pink hair. That's when I realized the connection. I remember being at a bar with my mom, playing with that doll while I waited for her. I put two and two together, and my suspicions were confirmed when my mother said she was in town to seduce him." She gags.

Face screwed up in fury, Josie stabs the mute button. "So help me god," she whispers, "if you fucked her mother—"

"*I didn't,*" I hiss.

Her expression doesn't soften as she unmutes the phone. "So did she? Seduce him, I mean?"

Savannah makes another gagging noise. "I really fucking hope not. But I don't think so. She sent me a text later that day saying she got a call from some married pilot she's been having an affair with and that he was in Boston." She sighs, the sound making the crumbled pieces of my heart hurt. "Yeah, my mother is that kind of winner. So she took my money—borrowed, is how she put it—and took off to meet him."

"Your mother sucks," Josie grumbles.

"Tell me about it," Savannah mutters. "That same day, Cam sent me a text telling me he couldn't do this anymore. And he asked me to leave his house."

Josie hurls a cookie at me, but I've still got good reflexes, and I dart out of the way.

"Camden Snow sucks too," she says, glaring at me.

I do. I so fucking do.

"Yeah," Savannah says, her tone full of sadness, not anger. "I don't know, Jose. I really thought he was it."

The pain that's been torturing me for days only compounds. I have to see her. I have to find her. I take a step toward Josie, ready to grab the phone to tell her I am it, that I'll fix what I broke, but before I can, a woman on the other end of the call says, "Come on, Sav. It's your turn for the glitter."

"Oh shoot, I gotta go," Savannah says. "Kacie's waiting for me."

"*Wait*," Josie urges, just like I want to. "Whatever you're doing, you don't have to." Her eyes are locked on mine now. We're like-minded when it comes to this. Allies, even if she's ready to dig my grave.

"I do, though," Savannah says. "I need to fix this for myself. But I love you for caring."

"I'll always care, Sav." Josie sniffs. "Be safe please."

"Of course." And then Savannah is gone.

The room falls silent, the two of us staring at one another.

"You know where she is, right?" she finally asks.

I nod, heart in my throat. "Yeah, I think so."

"You're going to fix this."

Either that, or I'll end up behind bars again. Because yeah, I know exactly where Savannah is. And I know what she's doing to earn the money she needs to cover her rent.

And I don't fucking like it one bit.

Chapter 47
Savannah

I'VE NEVER ENVISIONED DOING something like this for money. For fun? Sure. I have a blast on the pole when the only people watching are the other women in the class. And the idea of dancing in front of a group of hot men? Well, that never sounded terrible.

But this isn't that. The men in the audience are strangers. Some are decent-looking guys in business suits—*out with the boys*, they probably tell their wives—but a larger portion are creepy older men. Then there is the handful of belligerent assholes.

This is night three, and belligerent assholes aside, it hasn't been bad. And even where they're concerned, the club has great security. They keep the patrons in check.

And this is temporary anyway. I'll get through tonight and be done with it. I can see how tempting it is to do this night after night, though. I made two thousand dollars over two nights, and that's without doing private dances. I told the owner I wasn't interested in that. I'll earn enough dancing on stage alone, and I'm not in the mood to be any closer to these men than I need to be.

I feel a little better after talking to Josie. It was a relief to get so much off my chest. I didn't intend to word vomit like that before going on stage, but I couldn't stop once the explanation started flowing.

Josie has no idea how much it means to me that she's on my side. That she thinks my mom is as terrible as I do. That she's pissed at Cam too.

Being disappointed by my mom is nothing new. She did exactly what she always does, so while it's upsetting that she could so easily take my money like that, it's not shocking. But with Cam? I feel like I've been flayed open. He hasn't reached out. I really thought I was important to him. But with every day that passes, I'm more convinced that he really did jump into the relationship because of the bet. That it was all fake.

"You okay?" Kacie catches my eye in the mirror. Only then do I realize there's a tear trailing down my face.

God, how embarrassing. I swipe it away quickly and then turn around to face her. Kacie is thirty, and she's got the most beautiful thick black hair. She's wearing a robe over her costume, which is red and sexy as fuck. We're all wearing red tonight, since it's February and the club is really embracing the month of love.

Gag me. Not a single person in this place cares about love. It reeks of baby oil, hair spray, and desperation, tinged with alcohol and cigar smoke.

"Just having a moment," I say.

"If tonight's really your last night—"

"It is," I say, lifting my chin. "After tonight, I'll have enough to cover this month's rent and next."

"Fine." She sighs. "But I'm taking you out for a drink this week, okay?"

Smiling, I squeeze her arm. "I appreciate all your help the last few days."

I didn't go into many details with her. Just that I'd broken up with my boyfriend and didn't want to talk about it. And she didn't push. She's the kind of friend that's always up for a good time, but she's not the kind of person who makes me feel safe enough to really open up to. That'd be Sutton. And sometimes Josie. Addie would rather have a root canal than talk about her feelings, so she's probably the one I'll call this week if I need company.

"Kacie, you're up. Sav, you're on deck," a woman calls from the dressing room door.

"If you change your mind about the private room, we could do it together." With a wink, Kacie turns around and struts away.

While the money is tempting, there is no way in hell I'm going into a private room with anyone tonight.

CHAPTER 48
CAMDEN

THANKS to my sister and her friends, it didn't take long to find the club where Kacie works.

"Do not get yourself arrested again," Cora says as we pull up to the club.

She refused to let me come alone, and after what I've put her through this week, I knew better than to argue.

"I promise. I just want to talk to her."

My sister arches a brow. "And if she refuses to speak with you?"

"Fine. You can come in. But stay at the bar. If I throw hands, you can step in, but I need to do this myself."

With a roll of her eyes, she opens the car door.

"And don't talk to anyone," I add.

Over the roof of the car, she gives me an *are you fucking out of your mind?* look. "Cam, I used to dance for a living. I can handle any person in this bar. Promise."

Of course she can. That doesn't mean I like it. I hate that she worked in a place like this. Just as much as I hate that Savannah currently is inside, maybe on that stage now. Just the thought has me hustling to the door.

By the time the bouncers let us in, my heart is pounding so loud I can barely hear the music. It's dark in here. The walkways are lit, as is the bar and the stage, but the main area has very few overhead lights on.

The smell of booze and cheap perfume hits hard, making my stomach roll. Savannah does not belong in a place like this.

Fortunately, the woman on the stage is unfamiliar. Maybe Savannah is just bartending.

"I'll grab drinks and keep a look out for her," Cora says, grasping my arm. "And remember, don't get arrested."

"I won't," I promise. My head is on straight now. For the first time, it's crystal clear just how much my fuck-up has cost Savannah. She's working here because of me. I can't hurt her again. I need to get this right.

The woman wearing nothing but a G-string crawls across the stage and kneels on the edge. Men lean forward and push dollar bills into the string she holds open. The nausea in my gut builds. Not Savannah. But I need to find her.

The music cuts out, and the woman on stage stands and collects the money the men in the audience have thrown at her. It's demeaning, the way she's forced to collect it all in front of them while almost naked. Fuck. I hate that I've been to places like this dozens of times and never considered the perspective of the women here to make a living. Hell, I hired strippers for my Christmas party. The same party where I met Savannah. I have no room to judge, and yet here I am, a huge fucking hypocrite, ready to rip out the eyes of every man in this room if they've gotten so much as a peek of Savannah.

The next woman saunters out, a new song beginning. At the sight of dark hair, I breathe a sigh of relief. Not Savannah. Though I do recognize her. This is Kacie. Savannah showed me pictures one night last week. I was curious, and Savannah had fun with it.

She stands in front of the pole, and when the light hits her, she flips upside down.

The crowd of men goes wild. Since I'm guaranteed a few more minutes before the next act, I need to fucking look for Savannah in earnest.

I catch a server's eye, and when she smiles, I crook a finger, gesturing her over.

"Hey, sugar," she says. "What can I get you?"

"The manager, please."

Her smile falls. "Everything okay?"

Nodding, I pull my wallet out. With a fifty held between us, I say, "Just get me the manager. Everything is fine."

She slips the money into her bra and smiles again. "Will do."

I search for Cora, on high alert. Fuck. How is it that the two most important women in my life are in a dark room filled with horny men?

When I find my sister seated at the bar like she said she'd be, with a soda in front of her, watching the show, I breathe a sigh of relief.

"Heard you were asking for me." The man approaching me is dressed in a suit and has slicked-back hair. Stereotypical seedy club manager.

"I'm looking for Savannah."

The man's eyes flash in recognition, but he covers it up quickly with a cough. "We don't give out dancer's real names."

"I don't need you to give me her real name, I know it. I just need you to find her for me."

He chuckles. "Listen, man, if you're her boyfriend and you just found out about this, I understand it can be a shock, but the girls are safe here. You can talk to her when her shift is over."

My anger flares to life, my vision darkening. "She's not doing a shift," I growl. I yank out my wallet again and count out ten one-hundred-dollar bills. "This is yours if you go back to that little room and tell her that she can go home."

He scoffs, his slicked hair reflecting the colored lights from the stage. "She's not going to just leave. She needs the money."

I close my eyes and breathe, ignoring the way the place smells.

Fuck. *Get it together, man.*

When my anger has dissipated a little, I pin him with a look and flash him my wallet. "Fine. There's another ten in it for you if you make sure she's not on stage and send her to a private room."

"Private rooms are fifteen hundred."

"Ten *grand*. You and Savannah can split it. I'm sure she'll agree to that. Tell her she's got a private client and then disappear. Understood?"

He swallows thickly, surveying me. "You're not gonna hurt her, right?"

I reel back. "What? No. I just want to talk to her."

"You're going to pay ten grand to talk to her?"

"Yeah." I'd pay a hell of a lot more than that, but I know this ass is gonna want to keep at least half of it for himself, and I'm not feeling that generous. This way, at least Savannah will have enough to pay her rent and then some. More than anything, I want her to come home with me tonight and never leave again, but knowing my girl, this isn't gonna be that easy.

"Damn, you must really love her."

I run a hand through my hair. "You have no idea."

Chapter 49
Savannah

"*SAVANNAH*," Max barks from the back of the dressing room.

"I'm about to go on," I tell him as he stalks toward me.

"Carrie, you're up. Sav, you're coming with me."

The blond next to me scurries to the door leading to the stage. The rest of the girls watch me, brows lifted in curiosity.

"Is something wrong?" I stand and adjust my robe.

Rather than focus on my face, his attention drops to my chest. Gross. "Yeah, you're not going on tonight."

"But—" I scan the room, then lean in closer and lower my voice. "Did I do something wrong?"

"Special request came in for you. Got a customer who wants some private time."

I don't even have to consider it before I shake my head. "No."

He shrugs. "I've been paid to keep you off that stage. And we'll both get paid more if you go in and give this guy his private show."

I narrow my eyes. "Who?"

He digs his hands into his pockets and rolls back on his heels. "We'll call him Mr. Ten Grand."

"Ten *Grand*?" I shout. My heart rate shoots up. And I'd get what, five of that? *But what does a man willing to pay ten grand expect?*

I shake my head again. I can't, no matter how tempting. It's bad enough dancing on a stage. In a private room, I'd have to give a lap dance at a minimum. And if this man is willing to pay ten grand, I can't imagine he'll be satisfied with the minimum. "Sorry, I can't."

Eyes narrowed, he straightens. "I'll go forty-sixty with you."

Heart rate picking up, I shake my head.

"Thirty-seventy. It's my best offer. You'll walk out of here with seven thousand dollars under the table. You understand what you could do with that money? All the guy wants to do is talk."

My stomach bottoms out. "What?"

He sways on his toes again. "Yup. Just wants to talk. And then you and I will be ten thousand dollars richer."

All I have to do is talk? Seriously? This place has cameras in the private rooms, and they're well-monitored. So just talking? I could do that. And that amount of money would ensure I don't ever have to come into a place like this again. So long as I keep my head on straight and don't get wooed by any more older men. And so long as I keep my distance from my evil mother.

I lean in close. "No, I'll be seven thousand dollars richer. You'll only be three."

Eyes lighting up, he coughs out a laugh. "You sure you want to quit after tonight? You've got the balls to make it here."

Smiling, I pat his shoulder and skirt around him. "And after my little talk, I'll never have to set foot in here again."

As Steele, one of the club's bouncers, leads me toward the back where the private rooms are located, I breathe through my nose, willing my nerves to settle. Men have the weirdest fetishes. What the hell kind of conversation is worth ten grand?

"Don't go far," I tell Steele.

When he nods, I turn toward the door, reminding myself that I'm safe. That he and the other guys will ensure it. But then he pushes the door open for me, and I come face to face with Camden, and I realize no one can protect me from this.

"What the hell are you doing here?" I mutter.

He looks disgustingly good in a pair of dark jeans and a black T-shirt, his muscles and the tattoos on his arms on full display. At the sound of my voice, he snaps up straight and zeroes in on me.

"*Savannah,*" he breathes, his entire being shuddering.

The sound of his voice, the not so quiet desperation and relief stitched into every syllable, causes my heart to flip. Without my permission, my body angles his way. I nearly stumble forward, the baser parts of me wanting the comfort that felt so familiar and real only a week ago.

He takes a step in my direction.

"Don't." I hold up a hand, that single word coming out like a sob.

He flinches, his eyes flashing in the dim lights. "I'm not going to hurt you, baby girl."

Pain lances my chest, making it hard to breathe. "You don't get to do that. You don't get to walk in here and buy me and then call me *baby girl.*"

Panic and horror flit across his face. "What? Buy you? *No.* I just want to talk."

Anger and devastation flood me, goading me to tug at the silky tie holding my black robe closed and pull the fabric to the side, exposing what's underneath.

Camden hisses in a breath, and with a muttered *fuck*, he looks away.

Bile rises in my throat. He can't even *look* at me now that he knows where I came from.

I wrap the robe around myself, holding it to my chest, and swallow back a sob.

This is pure torture. Seeing him here. But it hurts so much more knowing he doesn't want to see me.

"Wow, you really did just want to talk," I huff, spinning toward the door. "Keep your money."

"Savannah. Please."

I peek back over my shoulder, a mess of pain and confusion and maybe even a little hope.

He doesn't look up. His focus is fixed on his feet. Even as he begs me to stay, he can't look at me.

"The last thing I'd ask you to do is fucking strip for me," he growls at the ground.

That pain in my chest spreads, and tears prick my eyes. Could this man really be this disgusted by me? "Is it because I'm a stripper now, or is it because you fucked my mom? Which one disgusts you more?" I say through tears.

Camden snaps his head up, his blue eyes blazing. "You have it all fucking wrong."

"Oh yeah? You can't even look at me." I swipe the tears from my face, hating how weak I am.

"Savannah, *no*." He stalks toward me.

I back up until I bump into the door. Even then, he doesn't touch me. He only searches my face, shaking his head.

I hold my breath, refusing to inhale his familiar scent, and I try like hell not to look into the eyes I once believed were my forever. It's nearly impossible, though. I want to sink into those depths. I want to throw myself into his arms and never let go.

"That's not what's happening," he grits out. "But I'm not taking advantage of you right now. Just come home with me, baby girl."

My heart cracks in two. "Home? I have no fucking home. And I never have. Not with my mom or the joke of a father who never wanted me. Then you told me to leave. You sent a fucking *text message*. Not sure my mom was right when she told me I would have been better off if you'd been my father. Doesn't matter, though. You're not, so if you don't want to touch me, then get out so someone else can take their turn putting their hands on—"

He cups a hand over my mouth, his irises so dark they blend in with his pupils in the terrible lighting, looking like black holes of anger.

"*Fuck. That*," he forces out through gritted teeth. "No one is putting a finger on you unless they want it broken. And we both know I'm nothing like either of your parents. Maybe I woulda been a better father than that asshole, but baby girl, I'm *not*. So no, I'm not disgusted that you're Tara's daughter. She ruined enough of my life already. I won't let her ruin this too. You are mine, Savannah. *Mine*. And you do have a home." His voice cracks on the last word. *"With me.* Please, baby girl, just come home with me."

"Stop calling me that." Tears stream down my face. I want to believe him. So badly. But when I needed him the most, he turned his back on me. He disappeared. "How did you even know I was here?"

"Everyone's worried about you. Everyone loves—"

This time I'm the one who holds up a hand to stop him from speaking. I can't hear him tell me he loves me. That anyone does.

And he didn't answer my question. How did he…

It hits me then, and my heart sinks. *Josie.* I didn't tell her what I was doing, but during our conversation tonight, I think she figured it out. "Wow, she really stabbed me in the back, huh? Were you there when she called me?"

"Savannah, please," he rasps, his eyes filling with tears. "Please let me explain. Please give me a chance to make this right."

I shake my head, not trusting myself to speak. Not trusting my stupid brain or my traitorous heart. Both want to give in. Both long for him. But I feel so betrayed. By him. By Josie. By my parents. By every single person who was supposed to be on my side.

"Please go," I whisper, dragging my gaze to the floor.

He drops his forehead to mine, but I close my eyes to shut him out.

"I will get you back, baby girl." He ducks, forcing me to look at him, his blue eyes haunted and desperate. "I will make this up to you. We belong together. I won't lose you."

Lose me. That thought gives me the strength to steel my resolve. He only dated me because of a bet. He doesn't love me. No one does.

So I swipe the tears from my face and push away from him. "Oh yeah? Maybe we should *bet* on it."

CHAPTER 50
CAMDEN

MAYBE WE SHOULD BET *on it.*

Savannah's words play on repeat in my head long after she's left the room.

Fuck. I squeeze my fists and breathe through the pain and rage eating me alive. I want to punch a hole through the wall. I want to bang my head against it. Because that's what I deserve. I need the fucking sense knocked into me. I deserve to hurt like she is.

She was so frail. So sad.

I've never seen Savannah look anywhere near this tortured. My heart aches for her. My soul. My body feels like I'm moving through sludge. Like I'm in a haze. This can't be real. I couldn't have destroyed her so thoroughly.

Yes, I could. I've always been selfish, so of course I forced her friend to tell me where she is. Of course I damaged the trust Savannah had in Josie. I'm a fucking monster.

My phone buzzes in my pocket, and I yank it out quickly. There's no way it's Savannah, but I can't help but check just in case.

Cora: Savannah just came out of the dressing
room and walked out the front door. What
happened?

I exhale a long breath. Thank fuck she's out of here, at least.

Me: It didn't go well. You should go home.

Cora: I'm not leaving without you.

Me: I just need to go hit some hockey pucks or
something. Maybe hit the gym.

Cora: It's almost midnight.

Me: Please, Cor. I appreciate you, but I need to
breathe. Just take the car and head home.

Cora: I love you. You're going to get through
this.

I'm not so sure, but I don't want her to worry.

Me: I know. Love you too.

A knock sounds on the door, startling me. "Time's up."

Wow. Apparently ten K only gets a guy twenty minutes.

I straighten my shoulders and walk out of the room. As I pass the oversized bouncer who's meant to intimidate me, I stop and pat him on the chest. "Let your boss know that if I find out he allows Savannah back here again, the place will be shut down within a week."

With that, I stalk out of the bar and order a car. My next text is to Daniel.

Me: Any idea how the hell Savannah would
know about the bet?

My phone rings immediately.

"Hello," I grumble.

Daniel is gonna have a million questions. I've been avoiding him since my arrest. Don't really want to talk to anyone about any of it, but I need to figure out what Savannah thinks she knows.

"What the fuck? I've been calling you for days, and you text me that shit at midnight?" Before I can answer his questions, he yammers on. "If you got arrested again, so help me god—"

"I didn't get arrested. I'm going to the arena."

He's quiet for a second. "What? Why?"

"Because I'm spiraling," I admit, kicking at the asphalt. "Because I lost Savannah and I deserve it. Because for the last couple of months, everything's been good, and now it's all gone to shit. And I almost wish I never knew what good felt like because before Savannah, at least I was naïve enough to believe I was happy. Now I can't breathe, and my skin feels too tight. Because I love her and I broke her and I hate myself for it."

The words bleed out of me, pulsing with a vile need to force this negative energy out of my body.

"I'll meet you there."

"What?" I scan the road, brow furrowed.

"Go to the arena. I'll meet you there," he says. "And Cam, it's going to be all right."

The rink is illuminated when I walk down the tunnel. Guess Daniel is already here. During the ride over, I replayed my conversation with Savannah over and over. Dissected her expressions, her body language.

Every single cell in my body tells me I fucked up. By not looking at her—because I was trying to be respectful—I made her believe I was disgusted by her. That I could ever feel anything but a bone-deep need for her is absurd. She's the most attractive woman I've ever met. Yes, she's gorgeous on the outside, but her heart is where her true beauty resides. And her personality. With her, my heart feels like it's beating outside my chest. Because it belongs to her. No one has ever come close to making me feel so important.

So if she hurts, I hurt.

The familiar sound of skates scraping over ice hits me as I push into the arena.

A laugh echoes around the huge empty space, and a puck goes flying into an open net.

"You're getting slow in your old age," Daniel taunts.

I step in farther and discover Brooks, who is shaking his head as he skates toward the net. What the fuck is he doing here?

"I told you I wasn't ready." He crouches and picks up the puck, then spins around. "And I'm not playing goalie without gear, asshole."

"You're grumpy tonight." Across the ice, Aiden does a fucking pirouette.

"It's after midnight," our former goalie mumbles.

"I'm here."

I spin around at the sound of the voice.

War steps through the door I just entered, wearing a pair of sweats and a long-sleeve black shirt. It's the same outfit he was in when I left his place hours ago, though he's added a backward Bolts hat.

He nods at me when he spots me. "Hey, how'd it go?"

I pull on my neck, fighting the stinging behind my eyes. "Obviously not great since you're all here at fucking midnight."

He slaps my shoulder and guides me toward the ice. "We'll figure it out."

It's about as cold in here as it was outside, but once I'm moving, my blood heats. There's nowhere in the world that I'm more comfortable than in this rink. It's home in a way no other place ever has been.

Other than in my bed with Savannah in my arms. Or in my kitchen with her. Or my couch. Basically with Savannah in my arms, I always feel at home.

Right now, she's right: neither of us has a home.

"We playing a game or just hitting?" Brooks asks as we gather at center ice.

"We can't talk while playing. Let's do slapshots at the net," Daniel declares.

It's a relief, letting him make the decision. I've got no plan and no energy to put one in place. Though just being here with my closest friends has taken the edge off the stabbing pain in my chest.

Immediately I feel bad about that. Because I took away Savannah's only safe space tonight when I revealed that I'd talked to Josie. I don't deserve friends if she doesn't feel like she has anyone.

"I..." I scan my friends faces, words failing me.

War slaps my shoulder. "Shoot first, then talk. We got time."

I nod, grateful that these guys know me.

For a good twenty minutes, we hit puck after puck. Aiden, hotshot that he is, plays it like a game of pool. We tell him which part of the net to hit, and he aces it every time. He learned that from Noah. Beauty was one of the best snipers to ever play. We were all fortunate when he took over as GM after he retired, not only because he always does right by his players, but because he'd spend hours out here, teaching us how he did it.

Aiden, naturally, was the only one of us to master it.

My shoulders have relaxed and my chest has loosened, and the bantering is in full swing when Aiden breaks out in song.

And for the first time in a fucking week, I actually laugh. It's loud and sharp and filled with emotion. It takes a second to get a hold of myself. When I do, I slap a hand over my mouth. What the fuck am I doing laughing?

"Hey," Daniel says, getting in my face. "It's okay."

With more force than I should, I push him away. "It's not okay. I fucking broke her." I smack my chest. "Just like I break everyone. First it was my fucking sister. She ran away because I kept a huge secret from her. Then my father. He's only dead because he got on that fucking plane to see me. My mother hates me, and to make it worse, I'm an asshole who's grateful that she doesn't remember most days. That though she might not know twenty years has passed or that my father's dead, at least she doesn't look at me with contempt. That when she sees me, she hugs me, and for a little while, I have my mom back. How fucked is that?"

My voice echoes around the arena for a solid couple of seconds after I snap my mouth shut.

"It's not fucked at all," War says softly. "I'd give anything to have that with my mom."

I drop my head and lace my fingers at my nape. "And I hurt Savannah. Somehow she found out about the stupid bet. The one I couldn't give two fucks about and haven't cared about since the beginning."

"Hannah will explain. I'll explain," Daniel says. "We see the way you look at her. Those feelings have nothing to do with the bet."

I shake my head. "It won't matter. I broke her." I force my head up, meeting Daniel's eyes, and blow out a long breath. "She's Tara's daughter."

His mouth drops open and his stick clatters to the ice.

"Who's Tara?" Aiden asks.

"His high school girlfriend," War explains. "She cheated on him with his best friend. Ended up pregnant with the asshole's baby."

"Fuck," Brooks mutters.

I blow out a breath. "Yeah, fuck." I pull on my hair. "How the hell am I going to fix this? I pushed her away when I found out. I lost it. I—"

"You felt like you were drowning," Aiden finishes. "Like you couldn't catch your breath. And pushing her away felt kinder than dragging her down with you."

My head snaps up. "Yes." I frown. "How did you know?"

Aiden's expression is filled with sympathy. "Because I've been there. Remember my panic attack on the ice? My life hasn't been half as traumatic as yours, but my mind was fucked up and I couldn't see past my own pain."

"Have you talked to anyone?" War asks, brows furrowing. "Like a professional? About what happened back in high school?"

The chest tightening is slowly creeping back in. "Like a therapist?"

He nods.

"We all had to go to therapy when we played," I say.

"That's not what he asked." Brooks swallows audibly. "After Seb's betrayal…finding out that the person I looked up to, my mentor and uncle and our coach, had cheated on my aunt, had lied for years about who he was, had taken advantage of Sara, I was totally consumed by anger."

"He almost killed that asshole," War agrees.

"I probably would have too," Brooks admits. "If he"—he nods at War—"hadn't stopped me." Green eyes downcast, he lets out a heavy breath. "I would have sliced his throat with the blade of my skate."

I reel back. Brooks has always been the steady one. He's huge, but he's relatively quiet. Gentle. Except when he's on the ice.

Aiden's been open about his depression for a long time. After his panic attack during a game, he made it his mission to talk about mental health with players in the NHL and in youth hockey, to destigmatize therapy and asking for help.

But I had no idea Brooks struggled too.

"I had to work through my animosity toward my father," War says. "After my mom died, I hated everyone." He lifts his chin. "But if I wanted a shot at a healthy marriage and to be a good father, I knew I had to do the work. I had to accept the loss of my mother and how fucked-up my childhood was. We don't always get the apologies we deserve," he murmurs, though his tone is even. "People disappoint us regularly, but we can't control that. We can only control how we process it. And Camden, you haven't processed any of it."

I grip my stick harder, my knuckles turning white. "I'll never forgive them for what they did. Not after what it did to my sister. But I don't hold that against Savannah."

"Put Savannah and your sister out of your mind for a second," Aiden says softly. "Ever think that maybe you need to forgive them for you?"

My heart thumps against my ribcage as I survey him.

"And forgive yourself," Daniel says.

A scoff escapes me. "I don't deserve forgiveness."

Aiden shakes his head. "Until you realize how wrong you are, you're right; you won't be able to fix things with Savannah."

I blow out a breath and glare at the ice. "I need to be better for her."

My friends are silent, standing close by, more supportive than I deserve.

I swallow and let out a heavy breath. "And I guess the only way I can do that is to be better for me too."

War nods.

"But how?" Where do I even start? It's overwhelming to even think about. "I want to fix this, so tell me, what the fuck do I do? How can I make this better?"

Aiden takes the stick from my hands. I only now realize I've been twisting so hard that I'll have blisters in the morning. "First step is acknowledging that you need help," he says. "And that's exactly what you just did. It's a big hurdle, and you've already cleared it. And we're here to help you. Every step of the way."

"I have an idea that just might help you win Savannah back," Daniel adds. "But it won't be quick, and you've got to be willing to put in the work."

Hope has me nodding quickly. "I'll do anything."

Chapter 51
Savannah

Calliope's Column
It's Not Him, It's Me. And I Lost Him.

I'VE BUILT this column by being honest with you. I told you from day one that there are rules when it comes to dating. That if you want a man you've just met to keep calling, there are certain things you shouldn't do.

I did this because my dear friend, a woman who is lovely and deserving of a real true love, kept getting her heart broken when she put it on the line.

My point to her, and I suppose to all of you, was that she should stop putting her heart on the line so early. That she should hold back a bit.

And to prove this, I did all the things she said she normally did, and more, before she was ghosted.

The idea was genius, right? Witty. My articles were clever because I did all the wrong things, and yet I kept the man.

I thought I was the exception because he was exceptional. That's what I sold you on, right? Because that's what he sold me on.

I thought that if he's the right one for you, the rules don't apply. And I almost had myself fooled into believing that my sweet, romantic friend might have been right all along.

But I was wrong. Because the only reason he stuck around was for a bet.

I'm not the exception.

Any reasonable man would have left after all the things I did, and now that he's gotten what he wanted, that's exactly what he's done. So yeah, I guess I lost the guy. It's not surprising, really, since in my experience, no one ever stays. And maybe that's the real lesson here. Be enough on your own so that when they leave, you can stand on your own two feet. You can look at yourself in the mirror and know you're enough.

I'm working on that as we speak. I'll keep you posted if I have any suggestions on how to heal a broken heart and how to start loving yourself again.

It's after three a.m. when I finish the column. For a minute, I stare at the screen. The cursor blinks, taunting me.

You won't.

But I've got zero fucks left to give and nothing left to lose, so I roll my finger over the mouse and hit Submit.

Monday morning, I walk into *Jolie* with my emotions under lock and key.

I gave myself the weekend to cry. To replay all the shit that went down. And I avoided Josie's many calls and texts.

So when I arrive at my cubicle, I'm not the least bit surprised to see her sitting in my chair waiting for me.

"I brought you coffee," she says brightly, holding up the to-go cup from my favorite spot. "And your favorite crumb cake." With a waggle of her brows, she points to the little brown bag on my desk.

"Thank you."

She pushes up from my chair and stands. "I'm so sorry, Savannah."

I eye her. "But?"

"No buts. I was worried about you, but that's no excuse. I shouldn't have called you while I was with Camden. It was wrong."

I blow out a surprised breath. "Yeah, it was."

When she doesn't try to downplay the hurt she caused or justify her actions, I'm thrown for a loop. Out of sorts, I ramble on. "But I understand that you've known him for a lot longer than you've known me. And I get that you were worried about my radio silence."

"Nope." She shakes her head. "Still not an excuse. I shouldn't have done it. It's truly that simple. I was worried about you, but that didn't give me the right to betray your trust." She sighs. "I read your article." She zeroes in on me, her eyes welling with tears. "You aren't alone. And I hate that I made you think for even a second that you were. No matter what you do or who you do or don't date, we're family, and I should have chosen you."

I take the coffee she's still holding, set it on my desk, and then fling my arms around her neck as tears rain down my cheeks. "Thank you," I say through a sob.

She squeezes me back tightly. "Please call me next time. I don't want you to ever have to put yourself in a bad position for money again."

I huff a sardonic laugh. "I was flipped upside down, but I'm pretty sure I looked good doing it."

With a swat to my arm, she giggles through her tears. "Bitch, of course you looked good. You always do."

I swipe the tears from my own eyes. "Thanks."

Josie bites the side of her cheek, her voice lowering. "So what happened with Camden?"

Heart clenching, I pick up the coffee and take a long sip, wishing I could avoid the question completely. When the rich flavor of the dark roast hits, a low hum escapes me. "This is so good."

Her response is an arch of one brow.

I sigh. "I don't know. It wasn't good."

"He was really worried." She tilts her head. "And sorry. Swore he was going there to fix things and apologize."

I huff out a sarcastic noise. "Yeah, well he paid ten grand to chat, so hope he thinks it was worth it."

Eyes bulging, she leans forward. "What?"

"Yup," I say, making the *P* sound at the end of the word pop. "Picked up my money from the club yesterday. And I swear, that is the last time I'll ever go there."

"Good." She shuffles over and hugs me again. "Want to grab lunch later?"

I squeeze her back. "Please."

My computer has just come online when Sienna's voice crackles over the intercom. "Hey, do you have a minute?"

I pick up the phone and wedge it between my ear and my shoulder as I type in my computer password. "Sure, want me to come to your office?"

"If you don't mind," she says, her tone subdued.

My stomach flips with nerves. It's rare that any of my bosses requests a meeting like this. Considering I went off script with this week's column, I have a feeling that's the reason behind the impromptu meeting.

"Of course. I'll be right in."

I take another big swig of my coffee, push back from the desk, and stride to her office.

Her door is open when I approach, and when she sees me, she motions for me to come in.

"Hey, how are you?" Her tone is laced with genuine concern. Like she actually knows just how bad I am.

I shrug, swallowing back a wave of emotion. "I'm guessing you read the article."

She nods. "I did. And I'm not the only one. Have you checked the comments? There are thousands of them."

My breath wheezes from my lungs. "What?"

She nods. "Your article was honest and beautiful. The entire segment has been. The readers are really connecting with it. They're leaving comments about their own experiences. How they thought they'd found the one, only to later realize how many red flags they missed."

I scrub a hand over my face, my heart pounding. "I really didn't see them." My shoulders slump and a sigh escapes me. "Honestly, I think that should probably be my last Calliope column. I think I need a break from writing about my own life."

Sienna pushes back and stands, her heels clacking against the hardwood floor as she rounds her desk. With a gentle smile, she perches on the edge, much closer to me. "I don't want to overstep…"

She pauses there, the silence making a nervous energy race through me.

"But before you do that, I think you should see this." She pushes her phone into my hand.

My stomach drops. I don't even want to look down. If this is what I think it is, I'll be livid. If Camden has used his connection with my boss to send me a message…

When all I do is stare at her, she points to the phone. "Don't kill the messenger. The advertiser paid a lot of money for this."

Confusion shrouding me, I finally tuck my chin and focus on the screen.

How You Get the Girl:
It Wasn't Her. It Was Definitely Me. And I'm Working on It. I Promise.

My stomach flips.

"I'm going to give you some privacy."

Blinking, I look up at her, and a tear breaks free, trailing down my cheek. Swiping it away quickly, I shake my head. "No. I'll go back to my desk."

She snags a tissue from her desk and hands it to me. "Take it from someone who pushed away the man who loved me for a good long while and made him work for it," she says. "Let him put in the work. But make sure you do too. You deserve to be happy. Your job is safe. Take the time you need away from the column. Calliope will be here when you're ready."

Nodding, I mutter a thank-you. Then I rush out of her office. Instead of going back to my desk, I head to the bathroom, and when I'm safely locked in a stall, I slip my phone from my pocket and search for the article. Then, through blurry, tear-filled eyes, I read every heart-breaking word.

How You Get the Girl:
It Wasn't Her. It Was Definitely Me. And I'm Working on It. I Promise.

*I'd like to think that with or without Calliope's Column or the bet, I'd have called *Calliope* after I met her and asked her out on a first date. But I'm not sure that's completely true, and since I'm determined to get this right, I'm going to be as honest as I can.*

Without the bet, maybe I'd have run for the hills the first time she mentioned kids, but I don't think so. To be honest, the bet was the last thing on my mind the night I met her. When we stood together, just the two of us, that first time, the world stood still for a few minutes.

But regardless of what might have happened, there was a bet. My friend's wife pointed out that I rarely go on more than a date or two with a woman before moving on. She said if I made it three months with one woman, she'd give me something that meant a lot to me, so I agreed.

I didn't date Calliope, pursue her, or fall in love with her to win that bet. My reasons were far more selfish. I did it because Calliope made me happy. Because for the first time in my life, I really was thinking about kids and marriage and settling down.

But I should have told her about the bet. The funny part is, if I had, she would have laughed. She would have gone along with it too. Because we both knew we'd make it to that three-month mark. We both knew that what we had was forever.

So, Calliope, from the bottom of my heart, I'm sorry that I let you think, even for a moment, that it was about anything but you.

I asked her to come back home, but she said no. And you know what? I'm glad. I need to earn her, and I can't do that until I fix me.

But here's my promise to you, baby girl: I'm going to do that. And don't go easy on me. Make me work for it. Because you deserve it. But know this: you will always have a home with me. And I love you. Every day. Whether

I'm with you or not. And I'm so proud of you. I just need to learn how to be proud of myself too.

Until then, know that I'm here, and I'm always yours.

How You Get the Girl:
It Wasn't Her. It Was Definitely Me. And I'm Working on It. I Promise.

Today is an important day for a few reasons. Some good, some depressing as hell. I'll start with the good first.

Today, I went to my first therapy session. Though almost every second of it was awful, I got to talk about her. I allowed myself to remember the good moments. To relive the night we met and think back on how we fell in love. I felt validated because speaking it out loud, memorializing our story, proved, beyond a doubt, that it was real. It wasn't lust. It wasn't too soon. And it was beautiful.

Then my therapist reminded me that if I had any shot of getting that back, I had to talk about the hard stuff. So that's what we'll do during our next session.

As of today, it's been two weeks since I blew up our lives. It kills me to think that it's gone on this long already. That it's been over a week since I saw you. I miss you, baby girl. I know it seems like I'm not coming for you. No, I haven't called. And I won't. But it's not because I don't want to. It's not because I don't love you. It's because I need to change and I don't deserve to make that call until I've done it.

So please remember that I love you and I'm doing everything I can to come back to you.

Until then, know that I'm here, and I'm always yours.

How You Get the Girl:
It Wasn't Her. It Was Definitely Me. And I'm Working on It. I Promise.

*Maybe this admission isn't the most romantic, but not everything in a relationship is, I suppose. The first night I met *Calliope*, she asked me about kids. For those who have been with us since the beginning, you probably remember it was her first attempt at pushing me away.*

It backfired tremendously, because it stopped me in my tracks. For so long I thought that part of my life had passed me by. I'm older, as she'll happily tell you with a teasing smile.

God, I miss your smiles, baby girl.

Because I haven't been in a long-term relationship in my adult life, I'd never considered that I might not be able to have children. Never worried. In fact, I think most men just assume we can knock a woman up anytime we want.

But my brilliant sister recently pointed out that might not be the case. And since I want that—I want it with you so bad my chest aches, baby girl—I went to the doctor to make sure that's a possibility for us.

So here's a friendly reminder in case you have a man in your life who doesn't have an awesome sister like me: tell your man to make an effort when it comes to family planning. It's not just on you. If a man loves you, he'll be thrilled to do this for you. Or not exactly thrilled, but he'll go.

I'd go anywhere for you, baby girl. Do anything to be with you again.

Until then, know that I'm here, and I'm always yours.

How You Get the Girl:

It Wasn't Her. It Was Definitely Me. And I'm Working on It. I Promise.

Today, my therapist asked me to make a list of five things I'm grateful for. I'll admit that I was in a lousy mood. I don't know how to do this anymore. With each day that passes, it feels less likely that I'll get her back. Her smell no longer lingers in the house and I'm beginning to forget the sound of her laugh. It's been months. I still have work to do. I'm not who I need to be for her yet. And today I was drowning in that.

So here are my five good things:
1. That I know what true happiness is because I met her.
2. That my sister is finally back on the East Coast and we celebrated the opening of her practice here in Boston.
3. That my mother is finally settled here as well, and we've had quite a few good days.
4. That my team is heading into the finals.
5. I have some of the best friends a guy could ask for, who show up weekly to make sure I still know how to laugh.

My therapist was right. After the exercise, I realized I have a lot to be grateful for. So I suggest making your own lists. It helps even in some of the darkest moments to remember what you do have.

And baby girl, you still have me. I miss you like crazy. And I'm doing everything I can to come back to you.

Until then, know that I'm here, and I'm always yours.

Chapter 52
Savannah

I GLANCE down at the address on my phone's screen and then back up at the building, my stomach in knots.

What am I doing here? This is a terrible idea. It's been two months, and I haven't picked up the phone, let alone showed up at his home. Still, even though we haven't said a word to one another in that time, I feel like he talks to me weekly.

Because of the columns.

So often, I'm tempted to reply in the comments, or maybe through a Calliope column, but I've never worked up the courage.

Still, Camden keeps writing. At least once a week, often more frequently. According to the columns, he's been in therapy for seven weeks, and he's been to a doctor to check on the viability of his swimmers. That alone is mind-boggling. And because of the columns, I know that his mother and sister have moved to Boston, and that his sister has opened a practice here.

Cora Snow, LPC.

There's her name. On the sign beside the door.

I blow out a breath, nerves skittering through me. Am I really doing this?

Camden isn't the only one who's been working through past trauma. After reading his first column, I cried for hours. I wanted to run back to him. I wanted to forgive him and tell him he was already good enough for me and always has been.

But I knew, deep down, that neither of us was truly ready. And if we didn't do the work separately, we'd end up here again. And I can't lose him a second time. Once was hard enough.

But the truth is, I've barely scratched the surface in therapy. I'm not sure how I'll ever unpack the hurts that come with having two parents who truly never wanted me.

The best I've come up with is that it's not something I can understand. I definitely can't control their feelings or behavior. And I'm not sure if I'll ever get over the trauma they've caused.

But what I do understand and what I know I can control is how I allow it to affect my other relationships. I can't assume that because my parents don't care about me, no one else does either. I can't put what my parents did on other people. It's unfair. Especially when I have people like Rosalie and Josie and the Donovans, who show up every day to let me know they care. When I have friends like Addie, who texts me no matter where she is during her last hockey season to let me know she loves me. Or Sutton, who will randomly show up after rehearsal with snacks and tell me it's a rom-com night.

They've proven to me that I deserve to be happy.

And I've realized I can be happy on my own. I don't need Camden for that. But I really want him. Though I'm not sure we can ever truly move past who I am, who my parents are, to his family.

Which is why I'm here.

Camden's relationship with his sister is incredibly important to him. As it should be. And I can't stop thinking about the haunted look in his eye when he told me what my parents put Cora through. While they'd never apologize for what they did, I feel like I should.

So though I lack the courage to walk in there confidently, I force myself inside anyway.

Josie called and scheduled an appointment for me under a fake name. I'm an asshole for being deceitful, yes, but I was worried that if she knew I was the one coming in, she'd refuse to see me, and I didn't want to come by unannounced and disrupt her time with other clients.

Inside, when I realize that there is no receptionist or waiting room, I stop in my tracks. It's a tiny vestibule, nothing more, and on the second door is a sign directing patients to knock when they arrive.

Before I can back out, I rap my knuckles against the solid wood door, and when it swings open a moment later, I try my damndest not to squeeze my eyes shut and run.

"Hi, come on in—" Cora's words die, and her eyes widen in shock. "Savannah?"

Oh goody, she recognizes me. I'm not sure if that makes this easier or harder.

Knees wobbling, I swallow past the lump in my throat. "Yes, hi. I'm not sure this was a good idea." I hitch a thumb over my shoulder. "I'll just go."

"No, wait," she says, reaching for me but dropping her hand before making contact. "I'm meeting with a client, but if you give me your information, I can call you after."

Heart in my throat, I wince. "I'm actually the client."

She frowns. "You are?"

"Yeah, I made it under another name because I was afraid you wouldn't want to see me. But I really wanted to talk to you."

She studies me for a moment, her blue eyes full of curiosity. It's odd, how familiar the look is. It's like Camden is standing in front of me, studying me. The two of them share so many features. Same eyes, same cheekbones, same lips.

Hers turn up into a friendly smile after a heartbeat. "Come in. We can chat in here."

On one side of the office is a tidy desk, but on the other side are two cozy-looking chairs with a small table between them.

"Take a seat," she says. "Can I get you something to drink? Coffee? Water?"

I shake my head. "I'm okay, thank you."

With a nod, she settles in the opposite chair and laces her fingers in her lap, her expression far more relaxed than I expected.

I was so eager to speak to her, but now that I'm here, my thoughts are jumbled, the things I need to say twisted with the words I'm trying to hold back.

More than anything I want to ask how Camden is. Does he really miss me? Has he gone out with anyone else? Will you ever be able to look at me and not think of my mother?

I twist my hands together, sweat breaking out at the back of my neck. "I want to apologize for"—my chest tightens painfully—"well, my existence, I guess. I never would have come to Camden's party had I known who he was."

Brows knitted, she tilts her head.

"It's just—that's something my mother would do. In fact, she considered trying something similar when she found out Camden lived here." I suck in a shaky breath. "But I'd never do that. He talked to me first…I had no idea who he was. I swear it."

Cora nods. "I believe you."

"Okay, good." I glance at the door, my heart thumping in my ears. "I don't want to take up any more of your time. I just—"

"Savannah, relax. I apparently don't have a client," she says with a smile. "So I have the hour to spare. There's no rush."

"I feel like an idiot," I admit, the words rushing out of me. "You must hate me. First, because, well, I'm me and I totally caused your life to spiral." I slap a hand over my mouth and shake my head. "Not that I think your life is bad or anything."

"Savannah," she laughs. Then, with a sincere smile, she adds, "Seriously, I'm not offended. You can truly say anything, and I won't be upset. I learned a long time ago that I can't control what other people think, so I try not to let it affect me. And in your case, I assure you, I don't hate you."

"But how could you not? It's because of me that—"

"No. It's because of Jeremy and Tara. You did not cause them to do *anything*. In fact, Cam and I hold more responsibility than you do. We were there. We were involved with them. We should have seen who they really were. We were close friends. Your mother was always selfish. I knew it back then." She shrugs. "Even if the betrayal was a shock. We were teenagers. We all made bad decisions. You are not responsible for any of it." She gives me a pointed look, the blue of her irises piercing. "And you are not a mistake. You were a child who was dealt a really shitty hand. I'm so sorry that they never got their crap together for you."

Disbelief washes over me. "You do not owe me an apology."

"Just like you don't owe me one. But I'll accept yours. And I hope you accept mine."

She's right. An innocent child is not to blame for the sins of her parents. Even so, I still feel guilty. I'm disgusted by what my parents did to her and Camden. And I'm not sure how to reconcile that with my other feelings for her brother.

"How is he?" The moment the words leave my lips, I want to pull them back in. That's not why I came, and I don't want her to think I'm digging.

She smiles. "He's okay. Therapy is really tough after the things we've been through. So it's a journey, and we'll always have scars. Therapy isn't about being cured of our demons. We put in the work so we can learn how to handle them. Because let's be honest, the demons will always be there."

I nod. I've discovered that myself.

"But he misses you," she adds.

The constant ache in my chest intensifies. As much as I wanted to hear that, needed to, even, this conversation has dug up the very real problems that I'm not sure we can ever get past. Because our demons will never go away completely. He's better off finding a woman who isn't a permanent reminder of all he lost.

"He does," she urges, like she can see the war raging in my head. "But it's okay if the situation is too much to move past. He's accepted that it might be."

My stomach flips at her words. So he realizes it too.

"Have you talked to anyone?" she asks gently.

I nod. "I'm seeing a therapist, if that's what you mean."

"Good." She nods once. "I truly hope that you find healing and happiness, even if that's without my brother. And Camden feels the same."

My nose stings with tears that have been nearly impossible to hold back lately. So I force a smile and stand. "I appreciate that. And I appreciate your willingness to talk to me. I'm glad you moved back. And I'm glad your mother is doing well."

She stands and tilts her head in a type of shrug. "She is, I suppose. I'm not sure things will improve on that front, but I'm glad that she's here too. This way I can be here for Camden while still taking care of her."

I swallow. "Thank you for talking to me. And thank you for supporting Camden."

Before the tears can fall, I turn and head for the door.

Just as I reach for the knob, she calls my name, stopping me.

I spin around. "Yeah?"

"For the record, I've never seen my brother happier than when he was with you. So I'm rooting for you both."

My heart lifts in a way it hasn't in months. "Really?"

She steps in close. "Yes."

"But…" I shake my head, searching for the right words. But again, my thoughts are jumbled, so when I speak, there's no eloquence to the questions I'm dying to ask. "Could you really handle seeing your brother with someone whose existence caused you so much pain? Wouldn't seeing me all the time be a problem? Because I can't go back to him if it means he'll lose you." I lift my chin. "I won't."

Cora squeezes my arm. "I'm a big girl, and you're right on one front. Those are issues that I will have to work through. But with or without you, those demons exist. I have the skills to work through them, and when I don't, I have people to turn to so that I don't ever fall back into the destructive behaviors that exacerbated so many of my problems. It's not a person's trauma but how they react to it that does the most damage. And I'm not interested in doing more damage to myself or anyone else."

I nod, though I'm not completely convinced.

"But Savannah?"

I inhale, steadying myself.

"I'd be thrilled to see my brother happy. So if you are what brings him joy, then I assure you, seeing you will never be painful."

As tears well in my eyes, I take a single step closer. "Can I hug you?"

Cora holds out her arms and we embrace. And for a moment, I allow myself to hope.

Chapter 53
Savannah

How You Get the Girl:
It Wasn't Her. It Was Definitely Me. But I Lost Her Anyway.

I REALLY DIDN'T WANT to write this article. It'd be easier just to stop. To mourn this loss on my own, without so many strangers out there witnessing my failure. But that seems unfair. And it's also not completely true.

Because while I have come to the conclusion that the thing that tore us apart might be too big to overcome, I know that the work I put in to heal was worth it for me. Now I can look at my reflection and not hate what I find. Now I know that I'm not to blame for all the tragedy that's befallen my family. And now my family is here, in the same city. So I'm not alone. And honestly, I never was.

This may not be the happy ending you were all hoping for—nor was it what I hoped for—but it is still a happy ending.

I think maybe some people come into our lives for a short time but still make an impact that will forever affect us. And that's what you were for me, baby girl. You changed me. You helped me see that there's more to life than how I was living. You pushed me to be a better man, and for that, I'll always be grateful.

Above all, you taught me what true love is.

So while this may be goodbye, it's also a thank-you. You are the love of my life, and it was the privilege of my lifetime to love you. I only want you to be happy. And I want you to know that if you ever need support, I'm here. No questions asked, no expectations needed.

But as for everything else, I'm letting you go.

As Josie bounces up to my side, I quickly click out of the article. "It's freaking freezing in here."

"It is an ice rink," I grumble. My mood has tanked over the last couple of days. I've probably read Camden's column a dozen times, and no matter what I do, the words don't change. The outcome remains the same. It's over. Officially.

And tonight isn't about me. This is Addie's last PWHL game.

"I know I should be used to it," she says. "But I don't think it's possible. I'm always freezing. I think it's because of all the meds they pumped into me as a kid."

I wrap an arm around her and squeeze her tight. "Well, then let's get you out of here and into the warm bar."

She grins as I release her. "Now *that* sounds like a plan. I'm sure Beckett went all out for the party, so I'm getting top-shelf booze."

A hint of joy weaves through the full-body ache I've had for days. The Langfields are throwing a surprise retirement celebration for Addie at Ground Zero, and we've all been sworn to secrecy. Addie thinks they're going to dinner, just the family, afterward. She should know better. Her dad would never allow such a low-key celebration. Josie and I even packed a sexy black dress in case Addie shows up in jeans and a T-shirt, thinking it really is just family dinner.

"Sutton already leave?" I ask, looking around for our friend.

Josie nods. "She's riding over to the party with Royal."

Affection blooms in my chest. Sutton is still seeing the guy she met at Camden's party in December, and she's yet to tell him she loves him. After five months, he still follows her around like he's an adorable little puppy. She's taking things slow, wanting to see what will happen after hockey season and the two of them spend some real time together. Josie and I have already decided that there's no way they won't spend the entire summer together in Monhegan, and we're taking bets on whether they'll be engaged when September rolls around.

But who knows?

She says she learned a lot from my articles, so I suppose I accomplished what I set out to do in the beginning. I helped her slow down and enjoy each day as she started a new relationship, and she does seem genuinely happy.

By the time we get to Ground Zero, the place is packed, though Addie hasn't arrived yet.

When we spot Sutton and Royal chatting with a few other Bolts players, we head that way.

"Addie just texted," she tells us when we greet her. "She says she'll meet us after dinner."

"So she still has no idea," JJ muses.

Behind him, Avery is seated at a booth with a coloring book, along with three other kids and a woman with long reddish-brown hair.

I eye JJ "Who's that?"

"That's Hope, Theo's sister," Josie says before JJ can.

At the sound of her name, Finn steps closer. "She just moved back from Nashville. Her dickhead of a husband left her."

Beside me, Josie snorts. "And Finn here is very protective of her."

He rolls his eyes, his dark, messy hair hanging over his forehead. "How could anyone do what that jackass did and then walk away from his own kids?" He clenches his jaw.

Wow. This is a first. I've never seen Finn anything but jovial.

He shakes his head. "Just reminds me of my childhood, I guess."

"And you care about her," Josie says, squeezing his arm.

He peers over at Hope, his expression softening. "Of course I do. She's Hopie. She's my best friend."

I survey the woman who obviously means a lot to Finn. She's got that girl-next-door look down pat. Her hair is pin straight, her makeup minimal, and she's wearing that tired expression that so many moms have. With three children, none of whom could be older than six, it makes sense.

Finn turns back to me. "Anyway, she was close with Addie growing up and wanted to be here to celebrate."

"Avery loves having her cousins around," JJ says with a smile. "And we got her, Finn. Don't worry. Between James, Theo, and me," he says, mentioning his younger brother and his cousin, Hope's brother, "we'll make sure she is fine."

With a nod, Finn takes a sip of his drink. As he swallows, he takes in the space, suddenly breaking into a huge grin. "Man, my sister is gonna hate this."

I burst out laughing. "Don't act so happy about it."

"He can't help it," Theo says, suddenly standing at my side. He presses a hand to my back and angles in, pecking my cheek. "He's acting like a typical little brother."

My cheeks heat, my mind immediately going to Camden and how he reacted when he found me with Theo so many months ago.

What would he think if he saw us together?

I remember the article, and my whole being deflates.

I'm letting you go.

"I'm older than her," Finn argues.

Theo doesn't take his eyes off me as he replies. "And yet you sound like a little brother."

Josie snorts. "You really do."

Turning, Theo greets Josie. It's a relief, honestly, when his attention is no longer on me. The reprieve is short-lived, though, because a moment later, he turns back, his hand brushing mine. "Can I get you something to drink?"

"Um—" I glance at Josie, who is wearing a wicked grin. "I'll take a vodka soda. Thanks."

He nods, holding my eyes the whole time. "Don't disappear on me again."

As he heads toward the bar, Josie pushes closer to me. "Damn, I always forget how hot Theo James is."

I sigh. "How could you possibly forget? He's on at least five billboards in this city."

"The man does wear a pair of cowboy boots and jeans really well. Especially for a billionaire."

Head tipped back, I cackle.

"What are the two of you laughing about over there?" Sutton asks.

I shake my head. No way do I want to get into a conversation about how hot Theo is. "What's her ETA?"

Perking up, she glances at her phone. "Winnie just texted. They're walking in now."

Finn sticks two fingers in his mouth and makes a loud whistling noise. "They're almost here!"

JJ smacks him on the back of his head. "They could probably hear you from the arena, numb nuts."

Finn rubs the back of his curly head. "Duck, that hurt."

JJ scoffs. "I'm not raising my kid to say duck. Use proper words like a man."

The girls laugh, and I can't help but join them, the ache in my chest loosening. I really needed this night.

I'm letting you go.

As the words hit me, I squeeze my eyes shut. *Stop thinking about him. Just make it through one freaking night without being sad.*

"Okay, everyone be quiet," Lennox says, standing beside the light switch.

The room falls silent, and then we're shrouded in darkness.

"Don't be scared," Theo whispers in my ear as he rests a hand on my low back again. "It's just me."

"Thanks for the warning," I mutter.

He hums against my ear, the sound sending a shiver down my spine. He smells good, like a cologne ad. With a sigh, I lean back against his chest. "What happened to my drink?"

He chuckles, low and smooth. "Left it on the bar so I wouldn't spill it."

"Smart move."

"I'm a smart guy."

"Oh yeah?"

"Shh," Sutton hisses. "Stop flirting. I'm trying to record the surprise."

I snap my mouth shut, stifling a laugh. Theo, on the other hand, leans in and chuckles against my neck and presses a kiss to my skin.

Immediately I tense. It feels wrong being kissed by someone else. And yet I know Theo will probably be the first of many. The first is going to hurt regardless. I really never thought there would be another. Not after Camden told me he loved me. I thought he was it.

I'm letting you go.

The door opens, and shadows appear in the hallway. "Why are the lights off?" Addie mutters.

The room brightens, and we all shout "Surprise!"

Eyes widening, Addie brings a hand to her mouth and spins to face her sister. "I can't—you—Guys!" She covers her face and shakes her head.

"Congrats, Addie!" Avery screams from atop her father's shoulders.

JJ sets her down, and the little girl takes off.

Addie doesn't hesitate to open her arms and catch Avery as she barrels for her. She's always been a natural with kids. Probably because the Langfields have so many of them.

Addie stumbles back, though she catches herself quickly. "It's officially official," Avery cheers. "You're my daddy's coach. Now he has to listen to you."

Addie giggles, eyeing JJ, who is already walking their way. "Hear that, Hanson? Now I'm in charge."

With a smirk, he slips his hands into his pockets. "Yeah, Coach," he murmurs. "I'm aware."

Addie's mouth drops open, her eyes once again wide.

Maybe it's the way he called her Coach, or maybe it's the way he's looking at her, but I could swear the air between them crackles with tension.

The moment is broken, though, when Winnie's twins launch themselves at her, knocking her over, and the room erupts in laughter.

Warmth bubbles up inside me as her family members take turns pulling her into hugs and congratulating her. This family really is special.

As I watch them, I do my best to focus on how welcoming they've always been to me rather than on how I'll never have that type of connection myself.

Family isn't who a person is born into—not always—family can be chosen.

Josie squeezes my hand, likely knowing exactly what I'm thinking. But when her grip goes from easy to a little too tight, I glance at her. "What's up?"

She searches my face. "The flirting with Theo thing. Does that mean you're really over Camden?"

My heart trips at the sound of his name. It feels like I'm drowning as I say, "It's over. You saw the article."

For several seconds, she studies me, like she's trying to read my mind, to access my real thoughts. She's better off not knowing. They wouldn't comfort her at all. I'm a mess, and moving on is going to be incredibly hard, but I don't have much of a choice. So I force my lips to turn up. "Theo will be a fun distraction."

She lets out an unsteady breath. "So seeing Camden with another woman isn't going to be an issue?" She peers over my shoulder, concern etched in the lines of her face.

The air shifts, my every cell going on high alert. Without my permission, my body angles itself toward the door.

Then my heart constricts painfully. It's been months since I last saw him. I'd forgotten just how good he looks. How thick and strong and broad his body is. The guys around us are all good-looking, but they have nothing on Camden. He is all man.

Maybe it's the age, or maybe he's always been that way. All I know is that no one has ever made my blood heat the way he does.

And no one has ever broken my heart so completely. Because to his left is a gorgeous woman who's probably close to his age. The two of them stand in the doorway, talking to Beckett and Gavin, all four of them at ease with the conversation.

I'm sick.

I'm letting you go.

Because of her? Because he met someone else?

"I cannot believe you guys didn't tell me."

I whip around and face Addie, silently admonishing myself. Tonight isn't about Camden. Or me.

"Dad would have killed us," Finn tells her.

Josie nods. "You know Beckett is my guy."

"He trumps your best friend?" Addie huffs.

Josie shrugs. "Yup."

The whole group breaks into laughter. Except me. I'm just trying to breathe. This continues for the next twenty or so minutes.

Josie nearly bores a hole in my head watching me so closely, but I try to keep a smile on my face. Try not to search the room for Camden and his mystery woman. Try to ignore the pain radiating through my every limb.

Just a few more minutes. Then I can sneak out. Feign a headache. Get out of here before I have to watch Camden leave with another woman.

Bile rises in my throat as I imagine it. Imagine him touching her. Imagine him *kissing* her.

I'm actually going to be sick.

"You haven't touched your drink," Theo says, sidling up beside me again.

I peer down at the glass in my hand. He's right. The ice is melted and my hand is numb around it.

"I'm not feeling great," I admit.

His whiskey eyes trace over my face. "Want to get some fresh air?"

I shake my head. I can't lead him on. I'm not ready to move on. I don't know if I ever will be.

"Uncle Cam," Addie cheers.

Heart stopping, I dart a look at my friend.

There, beside her, Camden stands. He leans in and gives her a hug.

"Congrats. You were amazing tonight, as always. You've had one hell of a career. You should be very proud."

Addie's eyes slide to me, though she quickly focuses back on Camden.

Dammit. I'm a train wreck, and they're all watching the disaster unfold.

"I appreciate you coming."

Camden surveys me. It's the first time I've felt those blue eyes roll over me in far too long. They dip down to the large hand grasping my hip. Theo's hand. Without so much as a flinch, he drags his focus back up to my face, his expression empty. Not an ounce of possessiveness or anger to be found.

My broken heart cracks into pieces and scatters around me on the hardwood floor. I guess that settles that.

"Hi, Savannah," he says, like we barely know one another.

I nod. Forming words is impossible in this state.

Camden turns back to Addie, his lips tipping up. "We're excited to have you next year. You're gonna do great things for the Bolts. Proud of you." His gaze flits to mine again, and for a second, the mask slips, and he offers me a small smile. But just as quickly, he swallows and turns back to Addie. "I'll let you celebrate with your friends."

The air around us is charged with electricity, everyone looking from one person to another like they're waiting for someone to speak.

Finally Addie does. "Thanks for coming."

Camden nods, and then without another look my way, he turns and strides off. He passes Daniel, War, Beckett, and Noah. Not one of them stops him. Then he passes the woman he arrived with, but he doesn't spare her a glance. He just keeps walking.

And I run.

I rush out of the bar, knowing the whole crowd is probably watching me chase him into the hall. My heels clack loudly against the concrete floor of the underground hallway, but he doesn't stop his steady pace to the door to the player and employee lot. Like he's determined to make it out of here without another word.

"Camden, wait!"

He whips around instantly. So quickly, in fact, that I run straight into his chest.

He clutches my arms to steady me, his eyes scouring me. "Are you okay? Are you hurt?"

"Did you mean it?" I rush out, ignoring the pulsing beat of my heart in my ears.

"Mean what?"

"What you said in the article."

Head tilted, he assesses me. "That you're the love of my life?"

I nod, my throat tight.

His eyes soften. "Of course I did, baby girl."

"Who was she?" I squeak.

He frowns. "Who?"

"The woman back there." I hook a thumb over my shoulder. "The one you came with."

My lungs burn, making it hard to breathe, but I need to know.

"I didn't come with anyone." The frown is back, confusion swimming in his eyes. After a couple of heartbeats, he inhales and straightens. "Oh, Janelle? She's one of Addie's coaches. We didn't come in together. We just showed up at the same time." He shakes his head, and his voice goes low. "Savannah, you have to know the last thing I'm thinking about is another woman."

I sniff, tears flooding my eyes.

His shoulders sag, his lips turning down. "Baby girl, please don't cry. It kills me to see you sad."

He reaches for me, but I step back and swipe my cheeks, tipping my chin up.

His eyes fall shut and he balls his fists at his sides. "I fucked up. I own that," he grits out. "And you may be better off without me. I acknowledge that too. But I'll *never* be better off without you. You brought me back to life." His tone is laced with passion, with pain. "You gave me a purpose. Loving you will forever be the reason I was put on this earth. So if you know only one thing, please know that you are loved. *Always.*"

The tears are back. This time I don't try to stop them. I'm frozen in place, wanting so desperately to launch myself into his arms but knowing I can't.

I'm letting you go. I can't reconcile that statement with what he's saying now. Can't decide if he should let me go or if I should fight to hold on.

Eyes falling shut, Camden takes a deep breath. When he looks at me again, he smiles. "Go inside and celebrate with your friends. Tonight isn't about us. Tonight's a good night."

Without waiting for a response, he takes two steps back. Then he turns and strides out the door.

CHAPTER 54
CAMDEN

Aiden: How do we feel about cheeseburgers?

Brooks : In general, or is this something you want to eat right now?

War: Fuck, a burger sounds incredible.

Daniel: I could go for a burger.

Noah: Burger sounds good. Gavin and Beckett are with me. They agree. Want to meet at Dubliner?

Aiden: Sorry. Autocorrect. I meant Chinese food.

Brooks: I'd rather have a cheeseburger.

War: Same.

Daniel: Dubliner it is. What time?

Aiden: Sorry. Autocorrect. I meant Camden.

War: You're asking what we think of Camden? Pretty sure he's in this chat. Cam? You there?

Daniel: He's def in the chat, but if he wasn't, I'd tell you I think he's awesome.

Me: What the hell would you say if I was in the chat?

Aiden: FINALLY. Shoulda known food wouldn't get you but talking about you would. Vain much?

WITH A CHUCKLE, I type a quick response and hit Send.

Me: Heading in to see your sister, but if you're nice, I'll meet you guys after for a drink. Can't deny it feels good to know you're all dying for my attention.

Daniel: Noah, what's Sienna want?

Noah: No idea. I don't track my wife's every move.

Aiden: You should. It's hot. But, like, don't because she's my sister and that'd be gross.

Brooks: 1000%

Me: Okay, guys, seriously signing off now.

I close out of the text thread and silence my phone, the device buzzing with responses from the guys the whole time.

My hands are sweaty, my shoulders tense. It's been a few days since I saw Savannah, but my stomach still aches every time I think about the way she looked at me in that hallway. I want to stop hurting her, but it's all I seem to do. I want her to be happy, and I think it's clear that won't ever happen if she's with me.

Will I see her here? There's a good chance. Shit. If I upset her, I don't know what I'll do. But I promised Sienna I'd do this photo shoot, and I don't go back on my promises.

The receptionist leads me toward the studio, and as we step inside, she asks if I'd like a water. I shake my head, ready to reject the offer, but when I get a look at the one person already in the room, every thought leaves my brain.

Savannah.

The room is set up for the photo shoot, the camera, a black back drop, and lots of lights pointing in one direction.

And Savannah is standing in the middle of the open space, her wavy red hair flowing over her shoulders, a tight black cotton dress hugging her gorgeous curves, and the most beautiful smile on her glossy lips.

She's not sad like she was at the arena the other day. No, she's radiant.

"Let me know when you want the photographer," the woman beside me says.

Savannah nods and then turns her full attention to me. "You can come in, you know. I promise I won't bite." Her lips curl up just a little, a hint of tease in her tone.

All I can do is blink. What the hell is happening? I'm too stunned to come up with a quip in response.

But my body knows where I belong, so my feet take over, moving me toward her quickly.

"Thanks for coming," she says when I stop in front of her.

My hands itch to reach for her, to pull her against my chest. My arms ache to hold her, but if I do, I don't know that I can let her go again, so I settle my hands in my pockets and nod. "The photo shoot is for you?"

She glances back at the setup, nodding. "Yeah. It's for my new job."

I frown. "New job?"

"I've been promoted. And given my own column. With my name on the byline, not Calliope's. I'm calling it The New Romantics." She worries at her lip, but that smile remains. "Turns out readers like my voice and my honesty when it comes to talking about falling in love."

"Savannah," I breathe, my chest expanding, "that's incredible."

She ducks, eyeing me from beneath her lashes. "I thought maybe I could write about our love story in my first article."

I stumble back a step, the air suddenly sucked out of my lungs. "Huh?"

"You know." Her lips twitch. "The story of how the *Ms. It's Not Him, It's You* finally got her happy ending with the *Mr. It Was Definitely Me.*"

"Baby girl," I whisper, my heart racing, my knees wobbling so violently I worry I'll lose my footing.

"It's the story of us," she murmurs. "You and me. Always."

"I'm trying not to get my hopes up here. So"—I blow out a breath and rough a hand through my hair—"so I'm going to ask you a question, and I need you to be really clear when you answer." I lick my lips, swallow past the lump in my throat. "Is this for the article, for some PR thing, or—"

"*Or*," she practically shouts. Inhaling deeply, she takes my hand and squeezes. "It's the Or."

And then she does the most obscene thing. Makes the most ridiculously perfect gesture. She drops to her knees, head tipped back, eyes locked on mine. "Marry me, Camden Snow." Her voice wobbles as she squeezes my hand again. "Marry me and make me whole. Not because I can't be whole on my own. Because I can. I did the work. I saw a therapist, and I know my worth. I know I'm worthy of love. I know now that not everyone will disappoint me. Some will"—a lift of one shoulder, a rueful smile—"and that's okay. Marry me because I love you and I want to spend the rest of my life with you. Because I choose you. Marry me because you love me," she says, her eyes filling with tears. "Marry me because you and I share the kind of epic love that everyone roots for. Our story is written in the stars and fought for on the pages. I promise I'll fight for you every day. I'll fight for us."

I drop her hand, and as her hopeful smile turns to confusion, I shove my hand into my pocket and pull out the ring I've been carrying around for the last six months. Then I drop to my knees in front of her and cup her face. "Marry me, baby girl. Be my wife. Be my family."

She sobs, the tears falling now, and with a whispered *yes*, she presses her mouth to mine. "Yes, yes, yes." She says it over and over until I sweep my tongue into her mouth, silencing her.

Then, with shaky hands, I slide the diamond ring onto her finger.

Sniffling, she peers down at it. "Where did you get this?"

I grasp her jaw and pull her in, taking her mouth with mine. "Had it made a few months ago," I murmur. I truly never thought I'd get to give her the ring, yet I couldn't bear the idea of taking it out of my wallet.

She gasps against my mouth. "Really?"

"Yes. I've spent a lot of time thinking about our life. About what it could look like."

"And how do you think it will look?" she asks through yet another wave of tears.

Collapsing to the floor completely, I pull her onto my lap. Finally, when she's cradled against me, her heart beating against mine, I feel whole again.

When she blinks up at me through wet lashes, I know that this is exactly where I was always meant to be. Loving this woman.

"There will be lots of kissing," I say.

Smiling, she pecks my lips once, then again.

I stroke her cheek. "And lots of laughter."

"And sex," she teases.

A chuckle works its way out of me. "Yeah, baby girl. I've got months to make up for when it comes to that."

Her lips tremble, but they're tipped up in a smile. "What else?"

"I was thinking maybe we could find a house. A home we can make ours."

Green eyes shining, she perks up. "Really?"

"Yeah. Maybe look out in the 'burbs. Near War. Schools are supposed to be good out that way."

"Schools?"

"Yeah, for all the kids the two of us are going to have."

"You want to have babies with me?" she says, voice choked.

"You know I do. So badly that I'm tempted to flip you over and fill you right now."

She bites her lip, her cheeks flushing. "I want that too."

"And maybe we'll host a holiday. Your pick. We'll have friends over for game nights."

"Sounds perfect," she whispers, wonder bleeding from every word.

I nod. "It'll be perfect because we have each other. No matter what."

"I really like the story you're weaving." She snuggles against my chest, her head tucked beneath my chin, her body relaxing.

I press a kiss to her forehead. "It's our story, baby girl, so we'll write it together."

EPILOGUE

Savannah

"WHAT ARE YOU DOING?" I squeal as Camden yanks me out of
the car and cradles me to his chest.

We finished our photoshoot with a bottle of champagne, compli-
ments of Sienna and *Jolie*. Then Josie and our entire department
swooned over my ring and the surprise engagement.

I can't stop looking at it. I can't believe he's had it for all these
months.

"Carrying you over the threshold, baby girl," he says, his face lit up
in a huge smile.

He's been grinning since I said yes. Despite the many good memories we share, I don't think I've ever seen him so happy.

"You're not supposed to do that until after the wedding," I tease
him. Though I love the gesture. I love him. So damn much.

And I'm so glad I got out of my own damn way and went for it. We
have a complicated history, and we both have complicated pasts, but
the love I have for this man comes easy. It's as natural as breathing. I

love him and he loves me and we'll make it work. It'll take a lot of communicating and maybe some uncomfortable conversations, but it will be worth it.

Camden takes the steps easily, but he stops before opening the door and smirks down at me. "I don't know what other people do when they get married, and I don't care. I'm carrying you into our home because you deserve it. I know you've never had a place that really felt like home. And it kills me that when I asked you to leave, I destroyed the semblance of peace you found here. I need to make it right. So baby girl, I'm promising you that from here on out, you will always have a home because you will always have me."

I place my hand on his cheek, so filled with love I feel like I could float away. Luckily I won't, because this man grounds me.

"You are my home, Camden. I love you. Now carry me into our home. No more worrying about the past. We are all that matters from here on out."

With a relieved sigh, he presses his lips to mine. It's a quick kiss. Not nearly enough for either of us.

"I love you." He punches in the code, and I turn the knob. Once it unlatches, he kicks it wide open. "Welcome home, baby girl."

Breathing in, I settle my head against his chest, memorizing every detail of this moment. The smells, the way his heart pounds, the warmth of him wrapped around me. The peace that rolls through me because, finally, I'm home.

He carries me straight upstairs, and I don't have to ask where we're going. Since the moment we said yes, I think we've both been waiting for this. When he tosses me onto his bed, a memory flits through my brain, making me giggle.

"What?" he asks as he pulls his shirt over his head.

My laughter falters at the sight of my name inked on his chest. For months, I haven't allowed myself to think about it, even as I saw his name on my own flesh day in and day out, a cruel reminder of all I'd lost.

I shake my head. No more sad memories. "Just thinking about the first time you threw me onto this bed."

Smirking, he yanks his belt through the loops. When he bends at the waist, dropping his pants, his abs ripple.

"You'd been a very bad girl that night."

Mouth watering, I drink in every inch of him. "You loved it."

Clad in nothing but boxers, he crawls onto the bed and prowls toward me.

With a squeal, I scoot back, falling against the pillows.

He covers me, his body warm and strong, his hands in my hair, his mouth hovering over mine. "My beautiful girl, I love everything about you. When you're bad and when you're good. You're mine and that's all that matters."

My heart swells, and the tears are back, threatening to flood my eyes. "I really am."

He presses a soft kiss to my lips. "Now let me get reacquainted with all my favorite parts of you. I've got a lot of apology orgasms to give you."

My breath catches. "You going to give me an orgasm for every one I had without you?"

Expression suddenly sobering, he squeezes his eyes shut. "I don't think—" He swallows. "I don't think I can handle hearing about that."

I press my hands to his cheeks, my chest pinching with sympathy for him. "Open your eyes, baby."

When he does, pain radiates from him.

"There's been no one since you, and there will be no one after you. Hear me? I didn't mean to say it that way. And I don't expect that it was the same for you, but—"

"Baby girl, the idea of touching another woman makes me physically ill," he rasps. "I promise you, the only reason I didn't come for you was because you deserve better than me. I worried it would be too hard for you to have me in your life."

"I stayed away for the same reason." I let out a sardonic laugh. "We love each other too much, I guess. So much that we got in our own way."

"No more."

I smile, chest expanding. "Yes, no more."

Camden sits back, easing me up and pulling my top over my head. Then he works my pants down my hips while I undo my bra.

Within seconds, the only thing between us is the thin fabric of our underwear.

On his knees, he stares down at me like he's refamiliarizing himself with every inch of my body.

I'm too focused on him to appreciate the feral look in his eye. The man is so beautiful. So achingly perfect. And so mine.

"I don't even know where to start," he tells me.

"I do." Winking, I lean up and tug on his boxers.

When his hard cock bobs free, a moan slips from my lips.

Chuckling, he takes himself in his hand and tugs softly. "Missed this, baby girl?"

"You know I did." I lick my lips. "Can I suck your cock...*Daddy*?" I peer up at him, hoping the nickname is still okay.

When he lets out a feral growl, I relax.

"Yes, baby girl," he groans. "Make me feel good."

I keep my eyes on him as he guides himself to my lips. Then I press a kiss to the tip. "Like this?"

"Fuck," he tips his head back, then tucks his chin, focus pinned on me. "You know I need more than that."

I smile. "Maybe like this?" I lick up his shaft, relishing the warmth of him.

Growling, he clutches my throat, just tight enough to hold me in place.

"No more games. Open your mouth and let Daddy fuck your throat."

Obediently, I relax my jaw and look up at him, silently giving him permission.

In one rough thrust, he slides between my lips. When his piercing hits the back of my throat, I gag, and he breaks into a wicked grin. "That's my good girl. You know I love it when you make those sounds."

He rolls his hips at a quick pace, and I focus on breathing through my nose, taking as much of him as I can.

Before long, his grip on my neck loosens and he caresses my jaw. "My beautiful little whore loves this, doesn't she?"

I nod, tears dripping down my face and lungs heaving for air.

I do. I love how we are together. Love being this way with him. Love that nothing could steal this from us. Our pasts don't matter any longer. Neither do my parents or the bet or Calliope's Column. Even the interaction at the strip club holds no weight. Nothing we have has been ruined because this is special. We're special.

He picks up the pace again, for just a moment, and when I whimper around him, he pulls back.

"Fuck," he groans. "You can't make those sounds."

I pant. "Why?"

"Because you'll make me come, and I refuse to do that until I'm buried deep inside you."

"By all means." I fall back against the pillows with a grin.

"Oh no, baby girl," he chides. "You're going to sit on my face first."

I feign a long sigh. "Ah, what a hardship."

Chuckling, he rolls onto his back. Then he helps me out of my panties and guides me to straddle his head.

The moment I settle against his mouth, he hums, the vibration of the sound ratcheting up my need. "Fuck, baby girl, I missed this." With that incredible tongue, he tastes me, dips inside me, teases me, winding me higher and higher, all without coming up for air.

Within minutes, I'm writhing, riding his face, babbling, "Oh my god. Right there. Yes. Fuck." I grab the headboard and grind against him.

It only spurs him on further. He wraps his hands around my thighs and pulls me closer, if that's possible.

When he does that little twist against my clit, my vision goes spotty and all rational thought flees.

"That's it, baby girl," he growls against me. "Give me what I want."

He curls his fingers inside me, and I detonate, cresting a wave I can't possibly ride.

I fall forward, hands splayed on the headboard, panting for breath.

All the while, he continues working me over, his fingers digging into my thighs as he holds me down on top of him, forcing me to enjoy every delicious second of pleasure.

I'm still panting, my vision still blurry, when he drags me down his body and swipes his tongue into my mouth.

Tasting myself on his lips is intoxicating. Mind-altering.

"I love you," I whisper.

"I love you so damn much, Savannah. So fucking much. Don't ever leave me, please."

"I'm not going anywhere." Desperate for more of him, I sit up, take him in hand, and line him up with my entrance.

"Wait," he says into my mouth.

At the hesitation in his voice, I pull back.

His eyes bounce back and forth between mine, a crease between his brows. "Are you still on the shot?"

I shake my head. "I stopped a few months ago. When you wrote the article about going to the doctor."

He lunges up and kisses me again. It's a thank-you. An acknowledgment that all along, we've both been working toward the same thing. "I can put a condom on if you want."

My heart flutters at his thoughtfulness. "No."

"Really?"

"I mean, I would rather not have a *huge* belly on our wedding day," I cringe, though the expression is a teasing one. "But I want a baby with you. So much. And ya know, you're not getting any younger."

He pinches the skin at my hip. "Brat."

With a sigh. I bend down and kiss him.

"We'll do it this summer," he says against my mouth.

I pull back a few inches. "Do what?"

"Get married. Where do you want to do it?"

My heart trips over itself as I take in the serious look on his face. "This summer is like two months away."

He tips his head back and groans. "Ugh. I don't think I can wait that long. What about next month?"

I giggle. "You're ridiculous."

"No, I'm dying to be your husband, baby girl."

"Husband," I whisper. The ache in my chest when I say the word is nothing like the pain that's plagued me for months. This ache is sweet, addicting. "God, you were barely my boyfriend."

He smiles. "So what do you say?"

"About?"

He drops his head and sucks a nipple into his mouth.

"Camden," I whimper, head tipped back.

"Shh, I'm busy." He swirls his tongue and tilts his hips, grinding against my core.

After the orgasm he's already given me, my nerve-endings are ready to fire off again, the sensation of his piercings rolling over my sensitive flesh making my eyes roll back.

"Camden, *please.*"

"Please what?"

"Fuck me. Put a baby in me. Make me yours forever."

He thrusts inside me in one long stroke, stealing my breath and healing my heart at last, his eyes locked with mine.

"You are mine," he says as he slides out slowly, only stopping when the ridge at his crown rubs at my entrance. Then he slams back into me.

"Yes." Gasping, heart pounding, I brace myself, eager for more of him.

The pleasure builds quickly, and when the sensation is nearly too much to bear, I squeeze my eyes shut.

He tuts, landing a swift smack to my ass. "Open those eyes. Give me what I want."

With a groan, I force myself to focus on his face. "I love you."

"I love you too."

And for the rest of the night we show one another just how much. We fuck, we laugh, we make love, and we remind one another that this is it. This is the love we've always deserved.

I'm finally home.

August

"Don't we normally turn here?" I ask as Camden passes War's street.

We're headed to the Warrens' for dinner. It's weird, heading to Josie's childhood home to hang out with her parents while she isn't even there. Though it feels more natural every day. Since our engagement, we've balanced our time with both Camden's friends and mine. Separately and together.

I still do girls' nights with Josie, Sutton, and Addie. Hope and Winnie have even been coming lately, since Addie and Winnie's younger twin sisters have been home from college for the summer and they're more than happy to babysit. Their presence has only made our girls' nights more fun. I really like Hope James, and I've always loved Winnie.

They're both incredible moms, and they're both doing it on their own. They're the only people I know with young kids, aside from JJ, and since Camden and I are doing everything we can to make a baby, I pay attention to all their advice and watch the way they interact with their children. I've even watched Hope's kids a time or two. Her four-year-old and two-year-old have the most adorable southern accents, and her eight-month-old may be the cutest baby I've ever seen.

Hope herself has a bit of a southern drawl too, and I swear she's wearing cowboy boots every time I see her. I think I may need my own pair. I swear they go with everything.

"I know where I'm going." Without looking away from the road, Camden squeezes my thigh.

I sigh. "Can't tell a man anything."

He chuckles. "Trust me, baby girl."

Head tipped back against the seat, I take in the houses as we pass. "Always. God, I love it out here." The road is flanked by tall trees with branches so long they reach toward one another over the road, blocking out the sunny day. We made an offer on a house out here not that long ago. I absolutely fell in love with it the moment we stepped inside. It was on the opposite side of War's pond, on three acres, with an amazing maple tree in the back, complete with a wooden swing hanging from a thick branch.

The place felt more like home than anywhere I've ever been.

I cried when our agent called and said we'd been outbid.

We haven't looked at anything else. I can't bring myself to. For now, I'm okay staying where we are. Cora has been staying with us, and I like having her around. It's been fun getting to know her, and watching her and Camden always melts my heart. She means so much to him. So honestly, staying put wouldn't be terrible. At least for now.

When Camden makes another turn and a flash of familiarity hits me, I frown. "Wait, isn't this—" The words die on my tongue when we pull up to the house we previously bid on. The one I fell in love with.

There are dozens of cars lining the street, and the lights inside the oversized navy colonial are blazing.

I shift in my seat and study Camden, butterflies fluttering in my belly. "What did you do?"

He smiles. "This is where you and I are going to build a life. Where I'm gonna finally knock you up. Where we'll watch our children grow up. We're going to mark up one of those walls with little lines to commemorate their heights every year, and I'm gonna teach them how to skate out on that pond. You and me, we're going to grow old here, baby girl."

I laugh through my tears. "You already are old."

He leans across the car and cups my cheek, swiping at my tears with a thumb. "Brat."

"We really got it?"

He nods. "I had the realtor call. Told them that we'd pay a hundred grand over the other offer."

My heart lurches. "Camden."

"Tell me you're happy, baby girl. Tell me you love this. Tell me this is where we'll raise our family."

"Yes." Grinning like a fool, I leap across the car and kiss him. "Of course." I clutch his shirt. "This is really our house?"

He laughs against my mouth as I pepper him with kisses. "Yes, it's all ours."

"Who's inside?"

His eyes dance. "Guess we'll have to go in and find out."

"God." I throw my head back. "You're the best."

"I really am." Laughing, he pushes open the car door and hauls himself out with me still in his arms. As he carries me toward the house, I don't argue. I'm too damn excited. Too shocked to ask him to put me down. Halfway to the front door, it swings open, and Josie and Addie appear, wearing huge smiles. "Surprise!"

As Camden carries me past them, I press my hand to his chest. "I love you. Thank you."

"Welcome, baby girl." With one last kiss, he eases me to my feet. "Now go enjoy our welcome home party. Your girls are dying for a tour."

"Yeah we are!" Josie squeals. "I cannot believe you share a pond with my parents." Her eyes shine, her smile wide. "I'm trying not to be Jealous Whore Barbie, but I really feel like my mom is stealing my best friend."

Laughing, I scoop her up in a hug. "No one could ever replace you."

It's true. Josie was my first real friend. The person who brought me into this world. It's because of her that I even met Camden. She took this stray in and gave her a family, and I'll never forget that.

When we break apart, the other girls are eagerly waiting for their own hugs. One by one, they congratulate us. Their extended families file by too. Everyone we love is here.

Even Addie's parents are here. Beckett gives Camden some type of man hug, with a lot of grunting and slapping on the backs, and then he pulls me in for a good one too. "You know," I say to Camden, "it's because of a scholarship from Langfield Corp that I was even able to come to Boston in the first place."

"Really?" Camden looks between me and his friend.

Beckett smirks. "I remember your submission."

I jolt backward. "You actually read the submissions?"

Beckett nods. "Every single one. Even shared it with Livy. Remember, babe?" he asks, grabbing her attention.

Liv gives me a kind smile.

"Savannah wrote an essay for the Langfield scholarship several years ago." He eyes me. "You wrote about your hope for a fresh start. You were all on your own at eighteen and you were determined to create a life greater than what you had in Vegas. Talked about how your father had abandoned you at a young age. Liv had a similar experience. You had us both in tears."

Camden shakes his head in wonder. "Wow, so you wouldn't have moved here if not for Beckett. Guess I should thank you for introducing me to my future wife."

"Oh god, don't get him started," Liv moans.

Beckett chuckles. "I've been known to make a match or two."

"*Dad,*" Addie groans. She loops her arm through mine and drags me away from her parents.

"Sorry. I'll be right back," I call. "Addie," I hiss, "that was rude."

She rolls her eyes. "Please, my dad will be talking about his latest match—a.k.a. you and Camden—for the next twenty minutes. I just saved you. And as a thank-you, you can give us the tour."

As I take my friends from room to room, I fall even deeper in love with the place.

Josie calls dibs on one of the guest bedrooms, and Addie argues that if she's this close to her parents' house, she should just stay there. Then Addie claims it for herself. I laugh at them both. The house has seven bedrooms. They can each have one, and we'll still have plenty of rooms for kids.

When we finish the tour, we return to the kitchen to find everyone around the island, snacking. I sneak in beside Camden and pluck a cracker from a tray on the island. "I really can't believe this is our house."

Camden presses a kiss to my forehead and picks up a cracker for himself.

"Speaking of homes," Addie says, biting her lip.

"Oh, right." I perk up and swivel toward her. "Are you moving into the Bolts building now that you're on staff?"

She groans. "Ha. No. Though the hockey boys would probably be easier to keep in line than my new roommates."

I frown. "Who are your new roommates?"

"That'd be me," Winnie says as she sidles up next to her sister, grinning.

"Yup, and me," Hope says, bouncing her daughter on her hip.

I look between the three of them. "What?"

Liv joins us and drapes an arm around her daughters' shoulders. "Yup. My girls are going to do what my friends and I did."

"Huh?" I'm so confused.

"My parents are moving out of their house," Addie explains.

Cam nearly chokes on his cracker. "You're giving up the brownstone?" he asks Beckett.

"It's too much space for us," Liv explains. "The twins have already left for college again, and Winnie doesn't want to live with her lame ole parents anymore."

Winnie sighs, her shoulders drooping. "That's not what I said, Mom."

"No," Liv says. "You told me you were going to start looking for a place, but it doesn't make sense for you and the boys to move out. They're comfortable in the brownstone. Why disrupt that?"

"It's settled," Beckett says, eyeing Addie.

"It's going to be great," Liv tells her. "Just you wait and see. And it'll be good for Vivi."

"Vivi?" I ask. I've met Gavin Langfield's daughter at a few family events, but I'm not sure what she has to do with Addie's new living arrangements.

Liv leans in close. "Gavin is losing his mind. Says Vivi is acting out. But between you and me, I think she's just acting like a typical twenty-one-year-old. Anyway, she refuses to go back to school for her senior year, and he told her if she isn't going to finish school, she has to find a job and a place to live."

"And I needed someone to help with the kids," Hope says. "My dad's launching another whiskey campaign, so it's all hands on deck at work, and Vivi has agreed to be our live-in nanny."

Beckett frowns at Gavin, who's standing across the room with Millie. "It'll all work out."

"You're all moving into the brownstone?" It'll be interesting to say the least. And I suddenly understand why Addie was so eager to claim a guest room here. It'll be a zoo over there, between Addie, Winnie, Hope, Vivi, and the five kids.

"Yup," Addie says with the fakest of smiles.

Hope looks a bit uneasy, and Winnie's expression when she nods isn't much more positive.

"I, for one, think it will be great," I say, keeping my tone light. "Think of all the memories you'll make."

Josie snorts. "She didn't tell you the best part."

Before my friend can elaborate, JJ steps into the kitchen and strides over to us. "Cam, the house is beautiful. Congrats." They share a man hug, and then he gives me a side hug. "Savannah, I'm so happy for you both."

"You heading out?" Camden asks.

With his lips pressed together, he dips his chin. "Have to finish packing."

"Packing?" I ask.

He looks at Addie, a hint of uncertainty flashing in his eyes, then turns back to us. "Yeah, Ave and I are moving."

"Oh." That's news to me.

And what about Tabitha? Rather than put him on the spot, I give him a smile.

"It's good to see you. Thanks for coming."

He nods, then spins to Addie again. "See you at home, Coach."

My heart leaps into my throat as I watch the two of them eye one another warily. "What?"

Addie's expression darkens into a glare as JJ disappears. "Oh, did I forget to mention that my father invited JJ and Avery to live with us too?"

Wondering how Addie and JJ will fare in the Brownstone among all of the chaos? Make sure you preorder
Paper Rings now.

EXTENDED EPILOGUE

YEARS LATER

Camden

"Honey, I'm home!"

I stomp the snow from my boots and sit on the bench in the little alcove my wife has instructed I use before setting foot on the hardwoods and get to work on the laces.

"Daddy!" a voice echoes through the house.

A smile creeps over my face. I can only imagine what she's gotten into today. My afternoon was spent at the rink watching practice. I don't get there nearly enough, but I'll never get over watching the magic Maverick Hall and Beckham Warren create on the ice. I can feel it deep in my bones. This is their year.

Still, like I do every time I pull down this street, I got antsy because all I want is to get into this house and back to my family.

"Daddy." The voice gets closer, and then there's a little giggle. "Shh, let's surprise him."

Rolling my lips to keep from laughing, I lean back against the wall, hiding in the alcove.

"But I want to go ice skating."

"Shh."

I hold perfectly still, listening as their steps get closer. They stop, and just as I'm about to lose patience, eager to get on with it, my little redheaded girl pops around the corner, the biggest of smiles on her face. "Got ya!" she squeals, launching her little body at me.

Behind her, my son reaches for her hair. "No fair. I want to hug him first."

I grab his hand before he can connect and groan at the stickiness I'm met with. I never knew kids could be so sticky until I had my own, and there's no telling what it is. "Don't pull your sister's hair."

"But I want a hug," he whines.

The little princess in my lap turns around and sticks her tongue out at him. She can be a brat just like her mom.

Speaking of. "Where's Mom?"

Before Logan can whine that I still haven't given him a hug, I grab him with my other arm, making sure to hold him face out so I don't end up a sticky as well, and head for the kitchen.

"Are we skating tonight?" Leanie asks.

We weren't planning to use L names for both kids. We named our daughter Coraline after my sister, but when she was a baby, we started calling her Leanie, and it stuck.

Logan arches his back, chin pointed at the ceiling, his blue eyes meeting mine. "Yeah, I got my stick by the door."

I smile at my two monsters. I fucking love them more than seems possible. More than seems reasonable, really. Every time I look at them, my chest gets tight. Like my heart is literally expanding so it can soak in more of them. Accept every ounce of their perfection. Maybe it's because I was love-starved before I met Savannah. Maybe it's just parenthood. Either way, I can't help the smile that spreads across my face when they look my way.

"Let's see what your mother thinks about that."

As we approach the kitchen, the scents of garlic and tomato sauce leave my stomach growling in delight. I didn't go to lunch with the boys today, knowing my wife was making Rosalie's meatballs, and I intend to devour at least five of them. With no Savannah in sight, I set my three-year-old next to the sink and put my five-year-old girl on the floor. "Go find Momma. I'm starving."

Leanie nods, her messy red hair swaying. Then she runs off in the direction of our bedroom.

"You think Momma will care if we sneak a meatball?" I ask Logan as I wet a paper towel and get to work cleaning off the mess this kid got into.

He's my spitting image. My dad's spitting image. And he bears my dad's name as well. He's a bruiser too. He's rough on his sister, and he's constantly shooting pucks in the house and leaving scuffs on the walls. And he's always standing by the glass door, staring out at the pond in the backyard where War and I have now set up a full hockey rink. One he and I use almost as much as the kids do.

In other words, Logan is me as a little boy. I can't help but think my father would be happy about that. It took time, but I know now that if he ends up like me, then that's okay. In fact, my wife and my sister tell me often that they'd be thrilled if he does.

Yeah, I'm the luckiest motherfucker to ever walk this planet. And it's a damn miracle after spending so much of my life feeling cursed.

It may sound strange to say my life began at forty-six, but that is truly how I feel. Hockey was a great distraction, though, until Savannah arrived and I really started living.

Yes, I met my best friends and made plenty of good memories before that point. I remind myself of that often.

But the life that matters, the one that leaves me constantly smiling, constantly happy, constantly fucking whole? That life revolves around one woman and the family she gave me.

"Hey, *Daddy*," she says now, appearing like the dream she is.

The way she says that word, always with a glint in her eye, a seduction in her tone, makes me want to drag her back to the bedroom to make another one of these monsters. I threaten her daily. Promise to fill her up again and again.

She takes it every time.

"Hi, baby girl."

I set Logan down on the hardwood, and he rushes toward the door, eyes already on the lit-up rink. Then I walk toward my wife. In a green wrap sweater and a pair of leggings, Savannah somehow manages to appear relaxed and also like the sexiest woman I've ever seen. My attention drifts to her tits, and she smacks me before I even reach her.

"Not until after dinner."

I pull her in for a long hug, then tip her chin up and take her mouth, licking at her tongue until she's squirming in my arms. She whimpers as I pull back, cupping her chin so she's forced to look at me.

"You'll take me when I want you, wherever I want you."

She whines. She still fucking loves my dominant side.

I nip at her bottom lip, then kiss away the sting—

"Daddy, Logan's breathing on me!"

Savannah laughs against my mouth.

Groaning, I pull away from her. "Why are you close enough for him to even be able to breathe on you?" I ask without looking away from my wife.

Her green eyes glitter, only making me want to hold her like this longer.

"Come on," she says. "I'll get dinner on the table so you have time to take them skating before bed."

This is how we parent. We each tackle a job. Sometimes it's even and sometimes it's not. More often than not, my wife does more than me, teasing me about being old and needing more rest than her.

That kind of comment is usually followed up by a spanking after the kids go to bed, then a whole night of fucking. That way she knows just how fucking old I am.

Before I let her go, I tug her a little closer. "I love you."

Savannah breaks into a wide smile. "I love you too, Daddy."

ACKNOWLEDGMENTS

Camden Snow. I think that's probably sufficient for the acknowledgments. And maybe a *you're welcome* for finally giving you his story. Seriously, thank you to each and every one of you for hanging in there over these last two years while I figured out his story after we first met him in Revenge Era. Truth is Camden wasn't getting a story until I wrote that line in Playboy about Camden's ex trying to pass off her daughter as his. And then I knew. I knew the only woman who could ever truly meet Camden exactly where he was would be someone who was just as strong willed, and just as broken, as the man himself. I also knew he wasn't ready for her in his twenties. So thank you for giving me the time to find his story, and for always showing such support for all of these characters and me.

We are going back to the Brownstone in 2026 and I am SO excited for this new chapter. Before we go there, we'll be making a stop in Hope Harbor in February/March and you'll get another glimpse at our Boston boys in that book. I've never been so excited for a small town like I am for this one so I hope you join me on that journey as well.

As always, I couldn't have done any of this without Sara. 2026 is going to be another ride and I wouldn't want to do it without you. Nor could I, so yay for job security.

A huge thanks to my editor Beth for always making my words beautiful and my beta readers Sarah, Andi and the wonderful Jill who also helped with the sensitivity read on this one. My books are always better because of all of you! Thank you to my street teams and content creators, I truly appreciate each and every one of you. I love our conversations and all of our beautiful edits.

And to the lovely Elen for the gorgeous illustrated cover and all the beautiful artwork she made to go with it.

If you want to follow along on my writing journey and have sneak peeks into all the characters in my world, follow me on Instagram, join my awesome Facebook group Britt's Boozy Book Babes, sign-up for my newsletter and follow me on TikTok.

ALSO BY BRITTANÉE NICOLE

Bristol Bay Romance

She Likes Piña Coladas

Kisses Sweet Like Wine

Over the Rainbow

Love and Tequila Make Her Crazy

A Very Merry Margarita Mix-Up

Boston Billionaires

Whiskey Lies

Loving Whiskey

Wishing for Champagne Kisses

Dirty Truths

Extra Dirty

Mother Faker

(Mother Faker is Book 1 of the Mom Com Series, but is also a lead in to the Revenge Games alongside Revenge Era. This book can be read as a Standalone, or after Revenge Era and before Pucking Revenge)

Revenge Games

Revenge Era

Pucking Revenge

A Major Puck Up

Boston Bolts Hockey

Hockey Boy

Trouble

War

Playboy

Beauty

Standalone Romantic Suspense

Deadly Gossip

Irish

Monhegan Summers (Co-Written with Jenni Bara)

Summer People

Dad Coms (Co-Written with Jenni Bara)

Who's Your Daddy

Better Daddy